OUTRAGE!

Etrem shot his claws and stretched his tail. The investigator sat very still. "Someone kills our cousins and friends, sir, and we cannot even mourn them or burn their bodies. My cousin Bren's brother and sister disappear. We tell what we know and that is not enough for you, but far too much for us. Can you let us alone now?"

Haynes looked grim and said, "Believe me, I meant no harm. I don't want to add to your troubles."

"I acknowledge that," said Bren.

"Because there are still bootmarks in the snow, and Ungrukh don't wear boots. Or fire rifles at themselves."

"Or skin themselves," said Bren.

"Yes. I won't bother you anymore now."

But for the fierce red cats on Solthree the bother was only just beginning . . .

Ace Science Fiction Books by Phyllis Gotlieb

A JUDGMENT OF DRAGONS
EMPEROR, SWORDS, PENTACLES
THE KINGDOM OF THE CATS

THE KINGDOM OF THE CATS

by

PHYLLIS GOTLIEB

ACE SCIENCE FICTION BOOKS
NEW YORK

THE KINGDOM OF THE CATS

An Ace Science Fiction Book / published by arrangement with the author

PRINTING HISTORY
Ace Original / July 1985

Cover art by Sonya & Enad

For information address: The Berkley Publishing Group, 200 Madison Avenue, New York, New York 10016.

ISBN: 0-441-44453-9

Ace Science Fiction Books are published by
The Berkley Publishing Group,
200 Madison Avenue, New York, New York 10016.
PRINTED IN THE UNITED STATES OF AMERICA

1

The big cat ran in the snow along the Mesa's rim. The moon was at his shoulder: body and shadow formed his quick black shape. Moonlight glanced burning off his red eyes. He did not like the moon and its brightness: it was too close, and though he could not recognize what Solthrees called "The Man" in it, he knew that the men on the moon could not help him. Even if it had been under the earth there was too much light: white snow, blazing stars, the swath of the Galaxy.

Wind blew off the Mesa and swept snow over his tracks. That did not matter any more because no one was following now and he smelled nothing but pinesap. He was not lost, but everyone else was, and he was afraid to find them.

He descended a cleft; smelled blood and ran upward and faster.

He was swift but rather ungainly: his shoulder and hip joints had been a long time maturing, and sometimes his muscles did not seem to fit his bones. No matter; the usual Ungrukh averaging a hundred kilos did not pick fights with one a good quarter heavier, though he was mild-tempered and often fearful. But neither did red Cat People trust one who was very black, when they knew or remembered none like him.

The terrain shifted downward and the wind rose with its smell of blood, cats' blood, and brought voices that were not those of cats.

:Bren! Bren!: No voice rose in his mind to answer, except that one from the past:

Run, Etrem, run! Any fool can see you're growing very fast and that's why it's taking so long for your joints to set!

There aren't many fools around here, then.

She had whacked his nose with her tail for that and dashed circles around him in a fury. *Pick up your lazy fat backside and run!*

He ran.

Below the cliff the scree sloped to the plain, and he saw: the blood on the snow, the bodies, the Solthrees with masks and helmets, snorting laughter and triumph, bent over his friends, cousins, tribe, knives raised and slashing red skin from red flesh, beams of light from their heads sweeping the bloody snow.

He stopped short. *Bren!* He raised his head and howled.

The lights swung.

"My God, there's the black devil! Christ, look at his eyes! Gimme the rifle, I'll turn them off for him!"

She knew the dark figures meant death and there was no way Bren could control the younger ones milling about her. The lights blinded them, the white-hot wave of panic swept them, and they swarmed helplessly in the thin snow until the gas canisters fell. She had time for one glance at the dark line, the hard minds she could not shield from when she had all this terror surrounding her. The faces beneath the helmets were covered with the knitted things they called balaclavas, but there was no time, no clear mind-space to identify the beings inside. The gas spread, held in a mist cloud over the walled flatland. She heard the whisper of the first poison darts just as her eyes began to sting and she dropped, broadcasting the warning that could not penetrate the fear. Her snout pushed into a hollow where the snow was slightly deeper. She closed her eyes, turned her head to burrow into the white depth, let her limbs and tail splay in deadshow. She breathed very lightly through the snow beneath the gas.

The first dart had been a mistake, nerves. Most were not nervous. They aimed through the eye for the brain, to keep the pelts whole. They slid down ropes and shot and kept shooting, and Bren sensed lives darkening around her like fallen stars and could do nothing. There was an ESP of some alien kind, a neutral they had hired. She tightened her shield and dared not even reach for Etrem, who had gone to search for the twins, or the Ranger, who had been lured away.

They were quick with knives, these. She lay shamming dead while they flayed her dead friends and family. Until the dark figure bent over her.

Then her head rose with eyes burning, fangs clamped the arm below the shoulder so that the knife dropped before that one had time to yelp, and one clawed hand knocked off the helmet and pulled the balaclava to stuff it into the open mouth. She rose on fours and with one twist flung the whole body on her back, bound it with her long snaking tail and ran, a burning fury, toward the redwall. She was built, after all, to climb a tree while hauling twice her weight in meat.

"That one's got Charley! Fire there!"

"You'll hit him!"

Bren climbed without pausing to look up. Though fear and rage burned, her strength was draining at seventy percent incline on limestone. She was halfway up; the men, unburdened, were gaining. She dropped the burden and the Solthree called, but not named, Charlie, rolled down, bruised, perhaps broken-armed. Certainly claw-marked. There were five scratches on that face, one from each claw: temple, forehead, nose, cheek, chin. She would know that one. The scars would heal, or be mended, from the skin, but not from the mind. She would know.

One last dart landed a few centimeters from her head.

Etrem had not come near enough to the ledge to see her, and by the time she scrambled over the crest he was gone. The rifle cracked once and stone fragments sprayed below the edge. She jumped into the mesquite, pulled her shield down against the ESP and over Etrem, and followed.

Etrem ran. He felt nothing, saw little, would not believe what he had seen.

:Etrem! Etrem!: The voice of memory—stop it!

Bren had been clever, sharp, swift. Bren had despised him. She was dead and he had no one else.

:Damn you, Etrem, I never do that, and I am alive!:

He could not even save the twins, her brother and sister. He could not outwit one of those armed men.

:They are not dead, Etrem! The twins are only hiding themselves!:

Etrem seeks where to hide. But they will catch and kill him. When better ones are dead, why should he live?

• • •

There is a man ahead of him—no, half a man, risen magically out of the snow. His long straight hair is black, his bare brown skin shines with oil; there are fur bands on his arms, and a slant-stroke of white on each cheek. Both hands are raised: one holds a rifle aimed at the sky; the other is empty. He lowers it and beckons.

Etrem's first thought was: I am crazy. Then: Why rifles and not flamers? And: Because flamers set the trees on fire.

Finally: I am frightened out of my wits but not crazy.

"By Firemaster, about time you realize it!" Bren roared. "Go with the man!"

Etrem did not look back. Bren *was* there. The man disappeared into the snow, but there was an opening where he had gone, and a ladder leading down it. Etrem skittered down; Bren followed, pulling a lid of woven twigs and grasses after her.

The stone walls of the big circular room were skinned with crumbling mortar. There were some burning embers in one of the floor pits, but most of the heat came sensibly from a potbellied stove whose pipes were vented some place outside where presumably their vapors could not be easily seen. Etrem recognized that the people crowding the walls were Indians of the kind called Pueblo, but he had never seen so many at once, nor dressed so strangely. The room was orange-lit from battery lamps hung on the walls, and the people were staring as if they were one great magnified person. The man who had beckoned said something in his own language.

Bren said, "Take that empty place on the ledge." Her voice was oddly flat; she had experienced death in nineteen minds. He crouched on the warm stones, she below him on the floor. The place was uncomfortably warm for him—but he was alive.

He stared back at the people: many were elderly, a few of the men painted like the one who had beckoned, some wearing scurfy buffalo scalps with still-proud horns, others in coarse woven trousers and tunics or full buckskins, yet more in little except multicolored woollen sashes. Some young women in blankets cradled babies, and a few little girls had hair curled at the sides in squash-blossoms almost bigger than their heads.

Bren said, "They are having a sacred dance, but it is only medium-sacred, so we are not disturbing them too much."

But Etrem was still frightened. Why were the Pueblos willing to let two Ungrukh into their—?

:Kiva.:

—when they seemed to be hiding it from others?

:Oh, I always know it is here, and shield it from all others,: said Bren. *:They are glad of that.:* Then she jumped as if she had backed into a thornbush and raced up the ladder. Etrem followed.

A young man was pulling up his moped in a spray of snow. Etrem knew him: Thomson Green Corn, the Ranger's assistant, was the only one of the Pueblos who spoke *lingua*, and the only one tonight dressed in ordinary clothing. "They're picking up the *bodies* and—"

"Intend to dump them down some shaft where no one goes and we have no evidence but some bloody snow!"

"Bill tried to stop them, but they broke his arm with a couple of bullets."

Above, there was a whine that shivered snow off the pines. "Too late," said Bren.

Etrem growled, "You tell me which direction and I follow."

"At that speed? They are past my esp range already. There are no tracks, and no matter how near the area you can reach, the bodies are frozen by then and the wind blows away scent. Also remember we are witnesses and they like very much to kill *us*."

Green Corn said, "I'm sorry, but for your evidence the bloody snow will have to do—and Bill's arm. I've got to ask a favor. There's a lot of police and Security about, and my people will have to clear out and get home. They won't like it, but—"

Bren had skittered down the ladder again, and Etrem followed, as he always followed. He felt depressed and helpless. He felt like somebody's dog.

2

He watched Bren and Chief Sun Rising High glaring at each other, the Chief's eyes habitually slit against weather, Bren's against the light smokiness of the air. She spoke his language in a voice as soft as a big cat can manage.

Etrem, crouched out of the way on the ledge, was thinking that the situation of these People was comparatively simple, at least from the viewpoint Bren had given him. They belonged to many clans, tribes and societies, branches of one ancestral group, and they had gathered to form a secret society in its most innocent sense: Its purpose was to perform their sacred dances and ceremonies in, as nearly as could be managed, the same manner and location as had been done by the Old People from whom they had descended. Unfortunately the place they had chosen was Government Park area which did not belong to any reservation, and if it were discovered there would be a great deal of trouble even for people who knew and disapproved but kept their mouths shut.

"Why is the woman cat speaking for the Cat People?"

Sun Rising High was the savior who had beckoned the Ungrukh into the kiva. Bren pulled herself together.

"My name is Bren. I have no other, and no office. My people are called Ungrukh, and the rest of them are dead. I am the one reader-of-thoughts here and that is why I can speak to you in a language I do not know. Ungrukh men cannot do this. I am very sorry to interrupt you in worship, but I hope your gods and spirits forgive us for trying to keep you safe, as you do us."

Etrem said, "Tell them we follow them halfway home so that if the police bring tracking dogs they go wild smelling big cat. Then we come back and call this our hiding-place from the killers."

"Halfway home is where Tom picks them up in the skimmer he is not supposed to borrow, but if they are quick that is no worry. I am afraid they spoil this place for themselves if our being here makes it no longer sacred."

"I don't know about that, but they certainly do invite us in, woman!"

"If they do not hurry we lose time looking for the twins!"

"We owe them," said Etrem.

Sun Rising High picked out a thought behind the strange words. "Twins! Are they cats—Ungrukh, like yourselves? You said everyone else was dead!"

Bren coughed; the sound was the nearest she could come to a sob. She stammered. "My brother and sister, they run away and we lose them—but they are cats."

The shaman stood. He was younger and more muscular than his Chief, but he was wearing the white buckskin dress and boots of a woman, and his hair was twined in squash-blossoms. "Can you help me to speak *your* language and be understood by my people?"

"I can try."

"Then let me say we've heard you come from a sun far away from ours, like our kachinas, and you know about many other suns and worlds. There may even be some of our people living there, and even though we didn't need to be shown, this does show that what we believe in is true. Twins are sacred to us—and kachinas can take any form they choose. I am sure they are alive, and if you don't find them they will find us and learn what has happened."

Bren would have liked to take this statement in faith, but was still too far in spirit from a Pueblo shaman.

:What are kachinas?: Etrem asked.

:What he says. Spirits who come from far away and can take any shape.:

:Like some of our old friends—and enemies? I doubt they *take the shape of Ungrukh.:*

:It is better not to mention that.: She said in the old language, "Thank you for strengthening *our* belief. Now please hurry and leave this place before more trouble comes!"

Sun Rising High glanced from her to the shaman, Moon's Woman, with a mixture of respect and exasperation. "Where else do we find this winter's moon in a secret place?"

Bren's snarl pulled all eyes. "You forget!" and filled the space with a vision of the plain of writhing red bodies growing still and reddening again in wet blood under the knives. And was ashamed, because the hunkering man, the leader of his people, seemed to shrink without moving a muscle.

"We have also been massacred," said Moon's Woman quietly, and knelt to pull his everyday clothes from under the ledge. He said to Sun Rising High, "There are dances for us on the Mesas tomorrow, with all of the people. I think there will be too many strangers about here for a long time." Men were already dousing the fire in the stove and pulling on heavy mittens to disassemble the hot pipes. No one else spoke.

Bren pulled her thoughts away. She muttered, "You must take everything away from here. Everything that leaves a sign. We close our minds so we do not see whatever you wish us not."

Sun Rising High said dryly, "If you are kachinas, as Moon's Woman wants to believe, it does not matter if you see the masks, and if you are not we can make new ones."

But the Ungrukh climbed the ladder once again and waited in the snow under the moon to avoid watching the men gathering their sacred objects. The etiquette for dealings between Ungrukh and Solthree tribes had not yet been developed.

Ungrukh helped Pueblos load and carry; Bren's choice was three of the children, who giggled and clutched the fur of her back like cubs. Etrem bore several sections of stovepipe which had been rolled in the snow to cool, and then bound together.

Halfway along the trail they let down their burdens and parted without good-bye; on the way back they made tracks in odd configurations, to leave confusion and aggravation in their wake, and waited in the kiva, now lit only by embers, for Tom Green Corn to return.

Willard Gonzales sat on the edge of the hospital bed with his right arm steel-pinned and foam-casted and an unlit pipe in his teeth. He was a big heavy man in his fifties with gray hair and eyes and a stolid jowled face, and looked as if his ancestors had come over on the *Mayflower*. Perhaps one or two had, a near-millennium ago, and the look was useful in his capacity as Ranger. Most of his forebears were Scots, Irish, Paiute, Sioux, Spanish, Portuguese and other odds and ends.

"I gotta stay here a couple days in case my arm rots and falls off. I guess I didn't get out of the way fast enough."

Dawn was breaking, but he had refused to sleep before he saw Green Corn and the Ungrukh.

"They are—what is the word?"

"Sharpshooters?"

"Yes. But you *are* lucky," Bren said. "A few of the guns have those wet bullets that make fire when they strike."

"She means Karnoshkys," said Green Corn.

"And then you lose your arm and your shoulder and likely one half of your head."

"Unh. I wonder why they didn't use them, then."

Etrem said, "If they set some trees on fire they find unwelcome attention fast."

"And fancy darts are too expensive to waste on old Bill, hah? Scuse me, Bren. You know I don't mean any harm. There's no use even trying to say I'm sorry about a rotten thing like that."

"You have enough trouble of your own."

"I'm also responsible." He gnawed his pipestem. "But darts, Karnoshkys *and* old-time rifles? That's weird."

"Means they know a lot about weapons," said Security, who was guarding the door with some heavy weaponry of his own. "Darts and burners aren't allowed to hunters. But on the culling grounds you can still knock down a tonne of meat with one shot from a Winchester, if you've taken good care of it."

Gonzales sighed. "Maybe we better not start the inquiry right now."

Bren slammed the floor with her tail. "*I* think the more we talk the more we discover!"

"Bren," Green Corn said, "Bill really needs his sleep, and we can use it too. Security's out there sweeping the place. There's nothing more to do here now." It should have been clear to Bren that he was worried about the kiva and the unauthorized use of a skimmer meant for transporting overstocks.

Etrem caught the tone that she, in her fear and fury, did not recognize. "That's true. Even we must admit we can get in the way sometimes. Come along, love."

Bren finally picked up the implications and trotted out with head and tail hanging in a great display of sulkiness.

The sun was rising primeval yellow, and the snow's shadows were purple. A Security man moved away from the gate to trail them.

:It seems two Ungrukh can expect to have three tails for a while.: "Where are we to stay now?" she asked.

:I'd keep you at the station but Security might not like it,: Tom said. "The hotel's been cleared out. The guests have been shunted off to see the last three tigers in Siberia whether they like it or not. There's plenty of room."

:Are there ESPs about?:

:You can tell better than I. I don't think there are class-ones in this area so if you can't find them there aren't any.: "Bill and I really did try to save them, you know."

"She knows," said Etrem. "It is like what you call pulling hens' teeth to get a thank-you from Bren."

"I don't want a thank-you. We don't have enough staff, we have two ancient helicopters, the skimmer, three landcars and a bunch of old mopeds. Bill says he's responsible. He isn't. And the area governments are almost as badly off as our people. Even *they* have to be funded by GalFed." The old story. Sol Three, a Mother-of-Worlds, had fed her daughter colonies and got little in return.

: . . . Like to get out, sometimes, can't leave Bill and the People, even when a few of them get foolish ideas . . . you realize they found a body. Part of one. Ungrukh.:

Bren had esped Gonzales and Green Corn when she met them for the first time, but never again below communication level. Once she found them trustworthy she wanted their trust. *:I am not shy about esping Security. One haunch, and the rest burned away. They use one of those Karnoshkys after all.:*

"The hotel's got plenty of food in the freezer, so you won't go hungry." *:Can you identify?:*

He had become Security.

But she applied herself to the question. *:Right forelimb, fifth claw broken off, scarred stub—Magundir!:*

:What was going on? Why would he be burned?:

:I am not sure.: She was not lying, but she was sure that no one would like what might be discovered. She esped him. He was not certain of her, but he wanted to know whatever harmful thing might come out only to protect the Ungrukh he had learned to care for.

Etrem said to Bren, *:That Magundir is the son of—:*

:Don't think it! By and by they put their paws together and find the digits match.: She stopped before the hotel entrance. "We can take care of ourselves from here, and I am not afraid to thank you, Thomson Green Corn, and your Ranger and your People who do more for us than anyone else on this world—in spite of what this rascal says." But Etrem had called her *love*, so she did not sharpen a claw on him.

The hotel knew quite a lot about the Ungrukh, because their guests came to see big cats as much as to look at the Canyon. Bren and Etrem had few demands. They realized that the staff were struggling with mixed feelings about multiple murder and the loss of their customers, and had no idea when they would be open for business again.

There was extreme civility on both sides. Bren made it clear that a person who lived in a cave could also eat from dishes without spilling or breaking, knew how to use a toilet, and was willing to sleep on an old carpet, or a bed with an old carpet on it to avoid clawing the linens. The cooks offered to thaw and serve as much meat (raw) as was needed, and the maids offered extra rugs if required. Some Government would pay. Some day. Bren thanked them and made it clear that none of their staff or guests was a killer. Those who had been shunted off to Siberia were the whole guest list and they and the staff had all been accounted for while the Ungrukh were being slaughtered.

:That does not mean that one of them is not a lookout,: Etrem said.

:Let us pretend otherwise right now.:

Civilities concluded, Bren curled up on a bed and nibbled the end of her tail, a habit she had picked up from her mother. She could see, through the huge window, beyond mesquite and piñon, the lip of the South Rim emerging from purple haze as if it were being born at world's morning. She was not thinking of Magundir. Security was standing guard outside the door and she pushed aside his muttering boredom to scan for Moon's Woman or any other of his people who might be gathering for their dances. She picked up two or three, but they knew nothing about the twins, and she did not speak to them. She had eaten and was a little sleepy, but her spirit was still more raw and bloody than the meat.

"I cannot find them," she muttered. "They may be dead."

Etrem, half-asleep, opened one eye and twitched his tail in annoyance. "They run off long before the killing. You say yourself you lose track afterwards. *I* think they are in some ravine where there is a stream for good water and plenty of small animals. They do not want to be found—by us or anyone else."

This did not please Bren. Unlike Etrem, who seldom pleased anyone, the twins pleased only themselves. Her mind sank to the problem of the deaths, their senselessness. . . . Presently she said, "Etrem—why leopards? Why Ungrukh?"

He realized this question was addressed to the Universe and snorted. "Why black Etrem?"

"Oh, that is what they call a throwback. Black leopard. Do you believe the story of the Qumedon?"

"What matter? Why in all the Pits of Hell do you ask questions you cannot get answers for and never like any answers you get?"

She subsided. Etrem was all she had in this world now that she knew of: his fearful, frightened appearance had probably saved her life. Both of them sulked in as much harmony as they usually reached, and slept.

4

THOSE WHO SAY A QUMEDON CREATED THE UNGRUKH ARE RIGHT

I CREATED THEM

SOME BELIEVE THAT QUMEDNI WERE BORN WITH THE UNIVERSE OR A MOMENT LATER BUT THOSE WHO BELIEVE WE CREATED IT ARE FOOLS BECAUSE KWEMEDN ITSELF DOES NOT KNOW THE BEGINNING

EVERYTHING ELSE SAID OF OUR POWERS IS TRUE

WE CAN ESP EVERYONE EXCEPT EACH OTHER BECAUSE WE COMMUNICATE BY INDIVIDUAL WAVE PATTERNS

AND CHANGE TO ANY SHAPE WE CHOOSE BUT IN OUR OWN FORM WE ARE GLOBES OF ENERGY THE COLOR OF CHAOS BEFORE LIGHT WAS SUMMONED AND SWARM WITH DARTS OF FIRE SEE?

DID I BURN YOU LITTLE ONE?

AND THOUGH WE CAN SHIFT TIME AND REACH OTHER UNIVERSES SOME TIMES AND UNIVERSES ARE DANGEROUS AND UNPLEASANT

OUR LITTLE CONTINUUM IS HOME ENOUGH

WE LOVE TO EXPLORE IT AND EXPERIMENT

AND WHERE THERE IS A NOVA WE ARE NEARBY FEEDING ON ITS ENERGY AND WHERE THERE IS A BLACK HOLE WE ARE BOUND HOMEWARD SATIATED

ONCE UPON AN AEON WHEN I WAS A VERY YOUNG QUMEDON SCARCELY A MILLENNIUM WHIRLED FROM THE FLANK OF MY MOTHER I SET OUT IN MY IRON SHIP

SO YOUNG I HAD SURVEYED MANY WORLDS BUT NEVER LANDED

SKIMMING THE SUNS THAT FED ME AND SHUNNING EMPTY PITS OF GRAVITY AND LITTLE WORLDS THAT CALLED OUT IN VOICES STILL TOO THIN TO BE HEARD BY EACH OTHER

I FOUND THAT MOTHER-OF-WORLDS I LOVED BECAUSE I KNEW NONE SO FULL OF LIFE AND KWEMEDN HAD NEVER EXAMINED THAT MYSTERIOUS ESSENCE

A PRETTY TOY FOR A YOUNG QUMEDON

TAKE ME TO YOUR LEADER?

I KNEW WHERE LEADERS WERE ON A PRIMITIVE WORLD WITH ONE FOR SOME TENS OF THOUSANDS

ONE IN RICH CLOTHES AND JEWELS WHO PACED TO AND FRO IN A SMALL ROOM LIT BY FLAMING LAMPS TO CONSIDER WHICH OF THE ELDEST SONS OF HIS MATES WOULD BE HIS SUCCESSOR

QUMEDON WOULD HELP HIM CHOOSE

I PRESENTED MYSELF TWICE HIS HEIGHT AND SPAN IN MY SPLENDOR FIT FOR ONE WHO CALLED HIMSELF OF HIS PEOPLE HUMAN MAN
AND EMPEROR

MORTAL BEING I COME TO BRING YOU SIGNS AND WONDERS!

HE LOOKED AT ME AND SCREAMED

THE VESSELS OF HIS BRAIN BURST AND HE FELL DEAD

I WAS AN INNOCENT THEN

I THOUGHT THAT ONE WHO BELIEVED IN SIGNS AND WONDERS AND CONSIDERED HIMSELF NEAR DIVINE SHOULD WELCOME ME

EVEN A QUMEDON DOES NOT HAVE PRECOGNITION

I CONCEALED MYSELF WHILE HIS WIVES SONS WARRIORS AND SLAVES SWARMED ABOUT HIM

UNTIL HIS ELDEST SONS WENT TO WAR AND KILLED EACH OTHER

THEN I WITHDREW TO SECTOR THE WORLD AND LEARN

I APPEARED TO MANLIKE ANIMALS THAT SHOULD HAVE HAD LESS FEAR BECAUSE THEY WERE NOT SENTIENT

THEY GIBBERED AND FLED HOWLING

THE HORNED BEASTS STAMPEDED

THE STRIPED AND CLAWED ROARED AND TURNED TAIL

WHEN I EXAMINED THEIR SAMPLES I FOUND THEM INTRICATELY FORMED BUT STUPIDER THAN THE MACHINES OF MY SHUTTLE

AND I DID NOT KNOW HOW ANY OF THEM WORKED

I ADMIT TO STIFLED VANITY AND ONE LAST TIME IN MY ANGER

SHOWED MYSELF MY TRUE AND BURNING SELF TO A CLUSTER OF SAVAGE SPOTTED CREATURES THAT HUNT ALONE BUT FOR ONE TIME HAD GATHERED TO ATTACK A HERD OF HORNED BEASTS COME TO WATER IN A TIDE POOL

AND DID I BURST UPON THEM!

SOME FEW RAISED SNOUTS TO FACE ME SNARLING WHILE THE REST STILL SAVAGED THE FLESH

WHO EAT WHAT PREY THEY FIND OF MAN BEAST OR FISH AND LEAVE *NOTHING*

THOSE LEOPARDS

THEY ROARED THEIR EYES BLAZED IN MY LIGHT

I CAST SPARKS AT THEM AND THEY RAGED MORE FURIOUS AND TRIED TO CLAW AT ME TILL THEY CAME NEAR BURNING

A SPLENDID TOY

THEY TURNED THEIR BACKS ON ME AND WHEN I KILLED ONE ANOTHER SHOVED IT ASIDE FOR ITS SHARE OF A TWITCHING BODY

NONE FEARED QUMEDON

YET

I GATHERED THEM WITH PREY SOIL AIR WATER

WRAPPED THEM IN A TIME BUBBLE

STORED THEM IN MY SHIP AND REMAINED WATCHING TO LEARN WHAT WAS NECESSARY IN HIDING NOT TO FRIGHTEN EVERYONE LIKE A FOOL

A HUNDRED TURNS AROUND THE SUN? I NEVER COUNTED

THEN TOWED THEM ACROSS THE DEPTHS WHERE I KNEW A STAR LIKE THEIR OWN WITH A WORLD MORE COOL AND COMFORTLESS

THEY WOULD MAKE THEIR OWN COMFORT

5

A world somewhat smaller than beast-home, it had similar magnetic poles and atmosphere layers. Its many shallow seas wandered through twisting archipelagoes and it had few extreme features. Three small moons that traveled in a nuclear rock family pulled the equatorial waters into savage riptides; there was no wide disturbance because the water was not deep enough.

Twenty degrees above the equator across the largest continent a fault line had pushed the surface into a latitudinal chain of low volcanoes that spit a gob of fire every few days. Once they had been fierce enough; a third of the continent was covered by their dark red lava, and heaps of tektites and crushed firebombs were scattered about. Much of the world's land was based on reddish quartzite and sandstone. Around the quiet estuaries where the reeds and thornbushes grew the paler sediments had gathered, carried down in streams from the deep strata worn down by polar ice. The soil was not quite acidic enough to grow food for big herbivores.

A quiet place, this world. No roaring winds, a few thunderstorms over the northern hills, no gross features in the southern hemisphere. Inland the air was dry and dusty like that of the strange fourth planet of the other system, with the same pinkish sky. The years were a little shorter, the days slightly longer, than those of the primal home.

I TOOK ALL THE TIME I NEEDED

AND LET THE BUBBLE REST ON THE NEW WORLD WHILE I LEARNED THE LIFE THERE

I FORMED ENGINES AND INSTRUMENTS FROM MY OWN BODY AND TESTED SOIL AIR AND WATER FROM BUBBLE AND PLANET

THEY WERE ENOUGH FOR SUCH WORLDS AS THESE ARE ONLY SPHERES OF ROCK WITH ICE OUTSIDE AND FIRE WITHIN

I LEARNED

BACTERIUM PROTOZOAN PLANKTON

WATER CREATURES FORMING OVER THEIR GENERATIONS

FISH REPTILES PRIMITIVE MAMMALS OF LITTLE MORE THAN ONE BITE FOR MY SPOTTEDS

TESTED PARASITES ON FLESH SAMPLES BOTH WAYS AND WHAT WAS NOT COMPATIBLE DIED AND THE REST LIVED

I MADE INFINITELY SMALLER INSTRUMENTS AND PLUNGED THROUGH LIFE INTO ITS MOLECULAR PARTS TO DECIPHER THEIR UNCOUNTABLE CODES

AND CHANGE THEM

EASILY? I FAILED UNTIL I SUCCEEDED

ENRICHED THE SOIL AND SEDIMENT TO GROW LARGER FISH AND MAMMALS

MAINTAINED THE PARASITES IN SYMBIOTIC RELATIONSHIP
MULTIPLIED THE PLANT FORMS IN THE WATER AND THE SOIL AROUND THEM
UNTIL THE WORLD WAS NEARLY READY FOR ITS PEOPLE BUT MY DEAR CATS
WERE NOT NEARLY READY FOR THE WORLD

I CREATED A GREAT SANCTUARY BOUND BY A FORCEFIELD AND SAID
WAKEN
ALLOWED THEM TO COMPLETE THEIR FEAST FOR WHO KNEW WHEN THEY WOULD HAVE ANOTHER LIKE IT?
AND BRED THEM
NOT BY CLONING BECAUSE I WANTED MORE MIXTURES OF GENES AND HAD ONLY SEVEN MALES AND NINE OF ELEVEN FEMALES FERTILE SO I DECREED ALL BEAR FRATERNAL TWINS

THEY DID NOT LOOK RIGHT FOR THE WORLD

I AM EYELESS BUT DO NOT BELIEVE I CANNOT SEE THAT TAWNY SKINS AND BLACK SPOTS DO NOT SUIT THIS UGLY RED-ROCK
WORLD I MADE ONE RED CUB
ITS MOTHER KILLED AND ATE AT BIRTH

DEAR MOTHER AMHIBFA! DID I EVER COUNT THE YEARS? I SAID
I HAVE CREATED NOTHING
I MULTIPLIED THAT PACK BY TEN DESTROYED ITS SCOURGES OF PNEUMONITIS PANLEUCOPENIA TOXOPLASMOSIS HEREDITARY CANCERS AND DIABETES AND WHAT YOU MAY NAME AND CREATED *NOTHING*
I BEGAN AGAIN

COLORED BY FAINT SHADINGS IN SKIN FUR AND EYES AND IN SEVENTY-FIVE GENERATIONS I HAD

RED SPOTLESS LEOPARDS

I LET KEEP ONE TOUCH OF BLACK THE CHEVRON RUNNING FROM FOREHEAD PEAK DOWN FLANKS WITH A WHITE SNOWDRIFT LINE IN ITS CENTER

THEY WERE BEAUTIFUL

DAMNED FIERCE RED CATS

VICIOUS LONELY HUNTERS FORCED TO EXIST TOGETHER THEY FOUGHT OVER EVERY MORSEL AND SAVAGED EACH OTHER IN EVERY SPACE AND EVERY THICKET I GREW FOR THEM

I KEPT TWO OF THREE ASLEEP ALL TIMES AND LET SOME FEW RUN FREE

AND WOULD HAVE LOST THEM IF I HAD NOT HELD THEM

WOULD YOU DESTROY THE QUALITIES YOU CHOSE THEM FOR?

I BEGAN AGAIN

BODY AND BRAIN

GAVE THEM NOT THE HERD INSTINCTS OF HORN-BEASTS BUT THE LOOSE PACK HABITS OF THE MANED AND STRIPED

DEEPENED BRAIN FISSURES AND INCREASED HEAD SIZE TO LET THE BRAIN FILL IT AND BODY SIZE TO SUPPORT THE HEAD

GENERATION BY GENERATION I LENGTHENED THE DIGITS AND SPLAYED THE HIND FEET FOR GRIP

WIDENED THE ARC OF HIP MOVEMENT TO ALLOW SQUATTING AND FREE FORELIMBS

TO BALANCE HEAD I ADDED BONES TO TAIL AND REFINED THE MUSCULATURE TO MAKE IT PREHENSILE

REARRANGED NEURONS AND REWIRED AXONS FOR SPEECH CENTERS

INCREASED CONTROL OF MUSCLES AND LIGAMENTS ATTACHING THE HYOID BONE TO ALLOW RANGE OF VOICE

AND AS AN AFTERTHOUGHT GAVE TELEPATHY

MAINLY TO FEMALES SO NURSING MOTHER COULD FIND HUNTING MALE IN HIS DISTANCE AND CALL HELP WHILE BIG MALE HAD HIS SHARP EYES AND NOSE AND WOULD NOT BE MUCH OVERBORNE

AND WATCHED THE GENERATIONS BREED TRUE

EIGHT HUNDRED AND FIFTY-FIVE SURVIVORS
THREE HUNDRED AND EIGHTY-FIVE MALE
FOUR HUNDRED AND SEVENTY FEMALE
ONE HUNDRED AND EIGHTY-NINE GRAVID

DID I COUNT THE YEARS? NO
BUT I WAS NO LONGER A YOUNG QUMEDON

I FREED THEM FROM THEIR CLOSET OF STALE AIR AND TRAMPLED BONES
AND SAW THEM RUN

ONE I CALLED BACK
SHE TURNED PUZZLING TO FIND WORDS IN HER MIND FOR THE FIRST TIME
WHAT ARE YOU? I SAID *TELL ME WHAT YOU ARE*
SHE REARED BACK SQUATTING SO HER EYESHINE BLAZED IN THE LAST OF THE SUN
AND ROARED
UNGRUKH
WAS THAT SOUND
YES UNGRUKH FOR EVERY SENTIENT CALLS ITSELF THE PEOPLE AND THAT IS YOUR OWN WORD YOU ARE A PEOPLE NOW

SO THEY ARE

THEY STILL DO NOT LIKE EACH OTHER MUCH BUT NEITHER DO QUMEDNI

7

Qumedon took off for a good feast at a neighboring star.

His report was noted and filed by his peers. It made no great stir. He had created all of the life and psychological sciences for Kwemedn but they did that kind of thing all the time. Someone else would have gotten round to it eventually.

Every few hundred years Qumedon visited his world in the shape of a male Ungrukh, with extra digits for greater handiness, and was considered a bit stupid by the inhabitants, perhaps because he was an Impervious and could not be esped. He called himself Kriku and they called him Seven-toes, or sometimes Feet.

The Ungrukh formed tribes, and though they warred they were fiercely loyal and grew strong leaders. They created gods, some a Water God of equatorial tides, some a Firemaster of volcanoes. They used instruments beaten from stone and glass, discovered what could be done with fire, dug ore and forged rude knives and spears to kill silently and to gut fish.

Qumedon noticed how they twisted reeds and bound pieces of woody shrub for fishing rafts from which they speared and netted; later how they created finger-prostheses to fit their clumsy digits for finer work. He did not notice that the mammals had been hunted almost to extinction by a population grown to a million and that the fish had developed less neutral parasites that killed many Ungrukh until they discovered cooking. Over thousands of years he had outgrown his toy.

When he learned that Galactic Federation had discovered Ungruwarkh and found it good, he gave up.

But one day in a fit of boredom he visited the original planet, Mother-of-Worlds, in a time-warp, to make mischief, and found that he had pulled in two of his own creatures, the ones called Khreng and Prandra. Trapped in his warp by his own carelessness and viciousness—he was afraid to call for help; even Qumedni do not care for too extreme a mischief-maker. Because freedom at last depended on both parties he was forced to defer to the Ungrukh and make peace with bargains that humbled him. He developed a positive distaste for Ungruwarkh.

But he was lured there and trapped this time by one of his own people, as great a mischief-maker as he had been in his recently unreformed days; again he was forced to save Ungrukh and be saved by them.

And astonishingly was left with a certain notoriety, though he was not in great favor with either his people or the Ungrukh. He did not care: there are plenty of places to tell his story.

Not everyone believes it—but the Qumedni do. They know their Kriku.

He taught them how himself.

Bren woke at noon from a whirling dream in which Qumedon was turning caged leopards red by degrees mixed with savage hunters flaying the red people of Ungruwarkh to bare the bloody flesh. She watched Etrem asleep on the other bed, his black glossy cheek flattened against the heave of the pillow. He had no stripe; its only vestige was a scribble of red and white on his forehead. If not symmetrical, it was balanced enough not to make him look ugly or foolish; he had no other color except in his eyes and a trace of pink near the roots of his whiskers. His nose was very wet, like those of all Ungrukh. Qumedon—if his story was true—had not allowed for the dusty air of Ungruwarkh, and sinuses worked overtime.

Etrem opened his eyes, and their red grew as his pupils contracted. "Qumedon is a fool," he said. "We do not breed true."

Her dream had seeped into his mind. "Even he cannot stop us from mutating. Think of the Spotted Pinks."

He frowned. One more thing she should not have said. His father had been a Spotted Pink and he did not care to think of them. "There is something else about Magundir."

"I think something too. Tell me."

"You say it is stupid." He rolled over with his back to her.

"Etrem I am giving you a nasty scratch if you call yourself stupid once more! Only you think that. No one else does."

He rolled off the bed and sniffed for breakfast. "Someone at the hotel may be a lookout but he is *the* lookout."

She took care not to esp him except in emergencies. "I agree but let us see if we have the same reasons."

"They do not skin him as an animal but get rid of him in the horrible way they dispose of *persons*. He is one they do not need and cannot afford to keep."

"That is going further than I dare but I believe it."

He grunted. Bren was not buttering his nose. She always told the truth—sometimes far too much of it. *:Can Security hear us?:*

:No. The doors are solid here because of the weather.:

:Then let us keep this to ourselves.:

"Would you tell me, please, what happened last night?"

The hotel was an old building whose stone and timber had been reinforced from within by concrete composition, and walled in laminated wood. Its appearance was comfortable even in the accountant's office, which had been taken for temporary headquarters by Continental Security, but its District Head was never comfortable. His mind was well protected from esp by blocks and reflectors; it revealed nothing but a name: Wallingford Haynes. He had a concrete wall of a face with a straw thatch roofing it and close-set eyes peering from the eaves.

Bren was sitting with her head up, looking alert; she was. Etrem was lolling every which way looking asleep; he was not.

:Get your big fat head into the air. The man cannot see you and it makes him uneasy.:

:Be damned to him. When is Security not uneasy? I get up when I have something to say.:

Security sighed. "Will you please . . ."

Bren did not say: *We tell all that to the Ranger,* because the answer would have been: *You haven't told me.* She hissed at Etrem and said, "I am sorry, but I am trying to make this one sit up, because you must think him rude. He has no sleep all the night."

Haynes picked himself up to peer over the edge of the desk, and relaxed a little. "He has a square of sunlight to himself. Let him enjoy it. Now . . ."

She told the story, the horrible story, again, without tremor.

Her voice was like cast iron. Once she told an uncharacteristic lie, saying that she had stumbled into the abandoned kiva and stayed there with Etrem, keeping the Pueblos out of the story. The wattled trap door had been removed with all the other articles and the snow had drifted to confuse trackers.

Haynes interlocked his fingers and looked at the ceiling. "I think you know what we've found. It was a place where the wind couldn't disturb it too much. Bloody snow, lots of bootprints—common type—and the burned remains of one of your people. Your brother and sister are still missing. So are the bodies. Thomson Green Corn believed the skimmer headed eastward; we don't think dog teams would help in this weather, but we've been scanning by helicopter with infrared —that is, for heat—and found nothing."

I do not want dogs pawing my people, thank you! "The bodies are likely frozen or under snow by now. When they thaw the eaters come, and in summer you find the bones, maybe. My brother and sister are perhaps alive but when *I* cannot find them they are more than five kilometers away or else deep in some cave."

"We also found five dart shafts, an inexpensive hunting knife, two bullets misshapen from being crushed against rock, and one empty shell. Those last come from the kind of rifle used around here and with the knife could have been bought at the nearest store in the district. If a Karnoshky was used on that fellow Magundir, as seems probable, it would leave no trace." He touched a spot on the desk terminal; not the hotel's, but one he had had installed. "When I was here last spring"—he peered at the screen for a moment and switched off—"it was concerning the poisoning of three Ungrukh by curare and slivered glass—"

"Yes! Your man tells me at that time it is very clever to put tiny pieces of glass just large enough to cut the membranes and let the drug into the bloodstream because we bolt our food and hardly notice."

The cement had turned pink. "That was unfeeling of him, Madam. If you had told me I would have said a thing or two to *him*. But those three were found near death from paralysis when they went out to cull their allotment of mule deer. And since they were far afield the food they took along must have been tampered with while they were resting. It's a pity there was no woman among them; her esp might have forestalled the murderers." Hastily, "I'm not suggesting you were in any way responsible—"

No sir. Only that we are irresponsible.

"—and that's beside the point, which is: we don't have the analysis from the darts, but I don't think the same poison was used."

"No. This is much faster, especially with the gas."

"And they were careful to pick up the canisters too. I just wonder if the same persons were involved. If you have any idea . . ."

"I cannot tell you anything of that kind, sir. You are the investigator."

"Still, there are some odd connections. The mother of one of the three who were murdered—"

"That is Mandirra, mother of Parender."

"—fell from a cliff three months later. We didn't investigate that one, it was treated locally as an accident. But Magundir, who was killed by burning, was the other son of that woman Mandirra, and—"

Etrem rose yawning and opened his startling blood-red eyes. "Do those matters connect by any evidence with the slaughter of our people last night, sir?"

"Not yet, but—"

"Are you conducting some kind of trial or official inquiry?"

"Of course not! We're only looking for information and we've got little enough of that."

Etrem shot his claws and stretched his tail. Haynes sat very still. "Someone kills our cousins and friends, sir, and we cannot even mourn them or burn their bodies. My cousin Bren's brother and sister disappear. We tell what we know and that is not enough for you, but far too much for us. A little chance leaves both of us dead and you have no one to tell you anything. Can you let us alone now?"

Haynes pursed his mouth and said, "I realize the turn the conversation was taking began to imply that I was accusing you of something, but believe me, I meant no harm. I don't want to add to your troubles."

"I acknowledge that," said Bren.

"Because there are still bootmarks in the snow, and Ungrukh don't wear boots. Or fire rifles at themselves."

"Or skin themselves," said Bren.

"Yes. I won't bother you anymore now."

Not quite sure whether they were being protected or imprisoned, the Ungrukh found themselves back in the hotel room, eating—very carefully prepared food. The sun was turning to the west and its light reflected from the eastern wall; deep blue shadows gathered in the snow.

Bren was very tense. Never in her life had she lost contact with the twins for so long; in defense mode, she was esping at full range. "I *tell* you they come to put fingers together."

"Haynes is not our enemy," said Etrem.

"How do you know? He is blocking very well."

"I see his face through your own eyes. It is not as blank as he likes to make it. But our tragedy is a damned big embarrassment to him. It shows that Solthrees do not take care of us as promised when they invite us here. He is Continental Security, and are not State and District authorities all involved? Even the world?"

"I don't think all the eyes of the world are on us exactly."

"It is still a big continent. If he can show we are negligent or disobey some kind of law to bring on our troubles the authorities lessen their own responsibility and that is what he is thinking about."

"If nineteen of us are murdered—slaughtered—in one night, with two still missing—it is hard for them to charge *us* with irresponsibility. But think what happens if the murderers are found. Their defense helps Security match all his fingers and find things to discredit us. Then possibly they turn many others against us and are hardly punished. If no one finds the guilty the people here invent some excuse to call us a nuisance; *our* world blames them *and* us, and especially *me* if we lose that stupid Tugrik and Orenda." She meant the twins. "Then no matter how innocent I can see them shunning us, and that is one good lick from Firemaster's tongue."

"I never expect anyone wants me home again," said Etrem.

"You are part of my family, Etrem!" But she could not say much more to counter his bitterness. Bren had spent most of her life as a full-time mother—to Etrem, the twins, whoever else was in need.

10

Bren was daughter of Emerald, whose mother was Prandra daughter of Tengura. Prandra and her man Khreng had been the first to make contact with Galactic Federation and journey from the world Ungruwarkh. Once returned to their Tribe on the Plains, Prandra worked at investigating the formation of the mind and its esp faculty, and Khreng set himself to bring agreement, if not peace, to tribal rivalries and spread the limited technology Ungrukh wanted from GalFed. This was in the areas of food production and medicine, for which the people paid with their only wealth, the brains of class-one ESPs, to be preserved for centuries of use.

Both adventurers were in their forties by now, very old for Ungrukh. Prandra was seriously ill with kidney malfunction, a common cat disease there were few means to treat even if more doctors had been available. Khreng stopped work to nurse her. His task was nearly done, the tribal network relatively stable, and this modest success was all he had dreamed of.

But their daughter Emerald had developed leucoma, like her grandmother Tengura, and was losing sight early. Since the umbilical cord with GalFed was cut and the last Observer long gone she had, like her mother, small chance of treatment. Raanung, her man, was a Hillsman who had stayed on the Plains when the easterly branch of his tribe had disintegrated with the death of his warrior father, Tribesman Mundr.

He and Emerald had taken leave of their world once; that was enough for them, and when Prandra became ill and Kreng was kept busy tending her, Raanung maintained the structure his father-in-law had created.

The Hillsmen pulled themselves together. They no longer needed to be marauders and terrorists; improvements in health, food supply and organization had cooled some of their fire. And Emerald's son Engni grew closer to his family there. In a surprise move, perhaps to forestall renewed bickering, Engni, though only fourteen, was offered the Tribesmanship of the Eastern Hills. He was not a bad choice: a capable, intelligent and rather stolid family man with irreproachable ancestry and an obviously patriarchal future. The Plains gave Engni their blessing: had not Khreng himself put out the first peace feelers to the Hills? Engni's young sister Bren, a small volcano of energy, helped care for her mother, grandmother, and those afterthoughts, the twins.

Trouble was developing in the Eastern Plains where Prandra's sisters Ypra and Ygne lived. Ypra's daughter Embri had been facially disfigured in childhood by accident or attack. Always reserved, she had become twisted into rage with frustration. The Observer, by great effort, had found surgeons to repair her scars, but her disposition improved only slightly: Men still feared it. It was a wandering Spotted Pink of uncertain temper himself whom she attracted. The tribe of Pinks do not have polka dots, or rosettes like Solthree cats, but are a variation marked like the clouded leopard, a deep pink in background with shadings of maroon in oblong or marbled patches. They are usually equatorial and slightly smaller on average than Northerners. This one was out of favor with his Tribe and obviously a poor risk, but was accepted for Embri's sake, because she was mad for him. Their one child was Etrem.

Embri had inherited a dark strain of crimson from her father; unlike the usual pale infant Etrem was born this color. When he turned darker with every new hair the Pink flew into a great rage and swore the child was not his. No matter that Embri was untouched and everyone knew it. On a world where descent was matrilineal and population increase more important than paternity, jealousy was still alive. Though Ungrukh did not know that the black variation turns up spontaneously among leopards on Sol III, they did expect something rather unusual in color from the union of a dark Northerner and a

Spotted Pink. But pure-black Etrem was too unusual—for everyone. When the Pink took it in mind to attack mother and son he was banished.

Then Embri turned truly mad. She tried to follow him; her body was found, self-starved, by a Scrublander hunting party. The Spotted Pink had vanished.

Etrem was tolerated. Since his parents had not even named him, his relatives gave him the name of the last Observer, Ephraim Tarvainen, and called him Etrem because they could not pronounce it. That name, and the food he was given, were his only connection with his world.

Then the child Bren came with her elder brother Engni to visit her cousins and found the shrinking Etrem, who could vanish in a shadow. She pulled him into the light and surrounded him like a ring of fire. She could not leave things alone, and her family got no rest from this small creature's nagging until they adopted Etrem. She was a year younger than he, but he was her baby and her toy. Bren, small and vivid as the flame that lights a fire, and big clumsy Etrem were one unusual pair.

And the twins. Oh, the twins! They were something else—not mischievous or openly disobedient. They simply stuck together like glue, and as the babies in a preoccupied family were either pampered or let do as they please. So they grew, hardly speaking to anyone but each other and Bren.

Ungrukh, like all sexed creatures, make the arrangements that seem suitable to them. A pairing may not be lifelong, but as long as it lasts it is monogamous—what else when jealousy lives and women are ESPs?—and the aim is for no fertile person to be deprived of coupling. The great social sin on Ungruwarkh is to die leaving the space of one's life unfilled. If Tugrik and Orenda had wanted to live together, unusual as that kind of mating was, it would have been tolerated as long as each produced children by other partners, to keep variety and strength in the stock. Someone muttered, *What do you expect when they are called Tugrik and Orenda?* for Tugrik was the namesake of Emerald's brother, who had been killed trying to avenge the murder of Tribesman Araandru's daughter Orenda, whom he loved.

But probably what bothered the Tribe most about the twins was that they actually seemed to like each other.

Sol III, which had killed off most of its big cats, reminded itself that there was a whole world full of them out in space. Through GalFed they invited Ungruwarkh to send a group of its own choice, not exceeding one hundred, for an experimental period up to three years, to settle in any parkland that suited them and its government. They would be (1) allowed to hunt game preserves that needed population control, (2) receive food supplements, medical attention and legal protection, and (3) be permitted to live by their own laws as long as those did not encroach on the rights of regional citizens. The price of this offer was that they let themselves be observed untouched by scientists, tourists, or anyone else who did not break any law, local or Ungrukh.

The reaction on Ungruwarkh was mixed, mainly negative. The people did not care to be the tribal exhibits some Solthrees enjoyed. The Council of Tribes certainly did not. But there were some young Ungrukh bored with peace, and these were the ones who pored over maps and pictures of the New World. Surprisingly, they came mostly from the Northern Tribes, which had always been the most stable. The Scrublanders and the Spotted Pinks were continuing thirteen-year-old negotiations. The Tidesmen were trying to stifle the usual internal squabbles, and the people of the Hills were shoring up what they had so painfully built.

So the majority of volunteers came from odds and ends of Plains Tribes. Mandirra, the eldest of all, had no family but her two quarrelsome sons. Emerald's twins believed that they would have more freedom and less harassment on another world. Their family did not agree, but Bren, responsible for so long to so many—and perhaps needing a new world for herself—elected to look out for them; they were fond of her and there were plenty of cousins to care for the elders. The family found her defection the most disturbing: It hurt to be forced to admit it to themselves that they loved her best—and that perhaps they had worn down her love.

Everyone expected Bren to drag Etrem with her; he surprised them all by volunteering before he knew she had done so. He was tired of all the staring eyes of Ungruwarkh. The volunteer list settled to thirty-six, and their choice was the great chasm where the stones are as red as Ungrukh. Nine backed out on the day of lift-off.

Now there might be four left.

You are part of my family, Etrem, Bren says.

Perhaps. They had never copulated with each other, though Bren at eight and Etrem at nine were old enough for Ungrukh to have several children of their own. Bren took lovers when she was not fertile. No man had yet pleased her. She was aware that her responsibilities were self-imposed, and that she was not sure what *would* please her. Etrem had had one sexual experience, moderately successful, but the fear of fleshly closeness stemming from his wretched childhood sparked an anxiety attack that threatened permanent impotence. Bren had quietly taken the problem to the best therapist she knew, her grandmother Prandra. She did not worry about privacy for once. Prandra had eased the agony for Etrem, but she could not cure him. Only he could do that.

As for Bren + Etrem, they were much like brother and sister, and not at all like the twins.

I never expect anyone wants me home again, says Etrem.

Authority could say, or if the killers were found, defense could say: Here is a world that has sent us its unwanted. Is it any wonder that things have gone so badly?

Bren did not say that aloud. She scanned for the Ranger, lying peacefully in his hospital bed; he had refused help to peel a tangerine, was doing it with one hand and his teeth and watching a deep-space shoot-em-up on tri-V.

:What are you watching that stuff for, Bill?:

:That you, dear? I just want to know how the other ninety-nine percent does it. You got trouble?:

:Maybe.: She told him of the interview with Haynes.

:Tell me exactly what got said.:

:By Firemaster, Bill, I already tell you—:

:Claws in, honey! I want to know what he asked *that I didn't!:*

:About the three dead of poison . . . : She gave him word for word.

:He's wondering why you didn't make a big fuss with the higher-ups when the investigation got nowhere. It was a terribly serious business. And the accident with Mandirra. I wondered too, and thought you were just toughing it out. You'd been here less than a year. You done something crooked?:

They had judged each other very carefully and it spoke for their mutual trust that he felt free to ask the question.

:Someone does something crooked, Bill, but I swear I don't know whether part of the blame belongs to us or not. Do you think we need a lawyer?:

:It wouldn't hurt.:

:I do not know one.:

:You sure as hell don't want one from around here. A case of mass murder involving GalFed e-t's means you go to the top and that's Solthree GalFed Headquarters.:

:We have no currency for that.:

:Good Lord, woman, you got a liaison to handle those things! They should have been in on the poison case. Haven't you ever been in touch?:

:Once, when we arrive. After that there seems to be no need.:

:That's what you think! I'll take care of it.:

:Thank you, Bill. I check in later, in case you find the twins.:

Her shoulders sagged and she looked out the window at the bloody horizon line and the brightening stars above.

"Trouble to come," said Etrem.

"What is worse than that slaughter? By the Blue Pit, if those twins of mine are alive I tie their tails in a knot for them!"

"Maybe it is time to untie a few knots," said Etrem quietly.

Bren reminded herself that Etrem had volunteered to come here *before* he knew she was going. She muttered, "First I want to know they are alive."

"Some world," said Etrem. "We are nearly murdered and we need a lawyer. Do you think there are spy-eyes here?"

"What does it matter? Mostly we eat and sleep, and very few here understand the Eastern Plains dialect of Ungru-'akh." She felt a familiar pressure in her mind. Someone trying to communicate. One she recognized.

:Bren? Bren?:

:Yes, Tom.:

:I've heard from my Navajo Ranger friend there's a couple of his people with rifles standing guard over a cave where they think your twins are holed up—don't get excited—they aren't troublemakers! Just want to pick up a few coins showing off the Cats to the locals.:

:Does he tell them—:

:He has no authority over them, Bren. Those men are on their own territory and he's not too keen on . . . :

:Getting them into trouble with their police. I see.:

:Look, I can get hold of the skimmer and take us—:

:That is risky for you.:

:Not if I'm careful.:

:How long to reach the place?:

:Three-quarters of an hour. I could meet you in twenty minutes a half km due north of the Lodge.:

Something in that voice . . .

She looked at Etrem. Without taking his eyes off her he flicked his food-bowl off the floor with one touch of a claw and leaped to catch it in both hands. Of course no drop spilled. He would not leave a drop.

:We see you then, Tom.: She said to Etrem, "A good trick."

"A little thing. But I am fond of it."

"I hope they leave him alive."

"I think so far it is cats they mean to kill. Otherwise Bill is dead." He was reaching for his knife harness. "Due north I know, a half km I can pace off, but how are Ungrukh supposed to measure twenty minutes without chronometers?"

"Be thankful they don't think of it."

"Does that mind belong to Tom?"

"Yes . . . under drugs or . . . or—"

"Best not think of *that,* woman."

Bren's harness carried two knives, both hideous, like all those used by Ungrukh. Their handles were wide flat plates with deep indentations for thick cat digits. Though she had been taught to do so she had never used a knife for defense; her personal knife was for butchering the kill: Ungrukh did not eat live off the bone like animals. The other was a heavy sawtoothed combination fish-gutter and crowbar made for her grandmother Prandra by the Forgemasters of Chlis. It was a marvel of balance, and she could also have cracked a skull by throwing it. Neither was much use against guns. "One day we may need . . ."

"Pray to the gods of Tide and Mountain that we never do."

"I am afraid my shield is not strong enough."

"It is good enough to pass the examination."

Yes, but only because through the ESPs in the family Bren had access to the storehouse of her forebears. Her life's experience was not broad, and her ESP-one status had no gold stars or oakleaves hanging from it. "I am surprised they are so clumsy. Tom is the first to call the police in such a case. And why are two men standing with guns in a freezing night waiting for their friends to come out of their hogans and shower gold on them?"

"We are ignorant, impulsive and childlike. They depend on that belief."

"That's just how I *feel.* I don't even know if they *are* alive."

Etrem was sick of the twins and said nothing, because he knew Bren felt the same. "To the rescue," he said, and bared his fangs briefly. He had never done this before, and the gesture startled Bren; his eyes were very red in the dim light, his teeth very white. "At least it is good to try a different style for once."

They had turned on no lights in the room, the door slid open very quietly, and they were on top of Security before he had a chance to turn. Bren stunned him with a padded hand and the two were off and running down the bright hall. The light was momentarily confusing to their nocturnal eyes, but they were outside in the cold night soon enough. Cloud had swept the sky and snow was floating down in dimness. The Pueblos had been dancing for it night and day and gotten it. Tom had once said, less than half jokingly, "Navajos don't get so much snow; they raise sheep." More than likely the Pueblos got the snow because they lived up on the Mesas.

Thick-furred Northern Ungrukh do not mind snow, and Bren and Etrem might have rolled in it if their time for play had not passed forever. It was not very deep and they loped among the piñon, scattering flakes from branches without caution. There was nowhere to hide among scraggy trees and scattered rocks.

A skimmer hummed. Bren could not tell from where.

And no weapons but knives.

Or, perhaps . . .

"Etrem, please become a rock."

"Why not?" He rolled lightly in the snow and curled himself to his tightest, eyes closed, limbs tucked, tail wrapped.

A few meters away Bren did the same. There were plenty of rocks about; why not two more under the dark gray sky?

Before Bren's shield was strained to its tightest she directed one very short penetrating mind-burst at the skimmer. She received an instant of confusion and took a careful moment to untangle and examine it: a flavor of Tom Green Corn worrying about cats. Fair enough. And a pinch of something else. Someone else. She would discover.

She did not have her mother's noisy and maddening esp shield, nor her grandmother's powers of hypnosis. She could not flick her food bowl in the air and catch it. But she had one modest trick of her own.

On Ungruwarkh, when her parents were arguing and Engni snapping at them both, and the twins mewling, and Embri howling and Ypra wailing—she had learned to withdraw to a cave or niche, curl up, press externals from her thoughts, bank her fire down to a spark and become, as far as anyone knew, nonexistent, insentient, invisible.

A rock.

She could not maintain the effort long, nor did she want to; there was a fine line between keeping sane and becoming catatonic. She had taught Etrem, and sometimes he could manage it; he needed it more than she.

She waited. Usually she kept track of time unconsciously by pulse; now by Etrem's hot and thudding heart.

The skimmer lowered and hung overhead for a moment,

dropped and hovered three meters above ground.

She watched through slitted eyes and thoughts forced through those openings to sentience: it was possible that Tom Green Corn was waiting to take her to the twins, that he had them on his mind; barely possible.

If she were wrong she would be horribly wrong.

The dull shape, darker than the sky, hovered idling. No port opened. No voice called.

From the east she heard the whine of another skimmer above the cloud. Its minds were penetrable, at least to her.

Here down below, the bay doors, where Tom should be, opened before her. Very near now, the floating bulk. A muffled voice called, "Bren! Bren!"

The second skimmer began to scream descent.

:Keep still!: she told Etrem, and jumped to her feet, tail lashing, jaws wide, roaring like a demon. Etrem, startled, uncoiled. She did not want that but there was nothing to be done about it. The bullet skinned her ear an instant before the rifle's sound slapped the air.

Two mopeds sputtered, one over a hillock from the west, another from the south. The Security man on the first one, gripping foot controls, fired two gas grenades through the bay doors.

A moment later Tom's beat-up old skimmer dropped on its belly and crunched the rough ground. Security, in quilted suit and plasmix body armor, untangled his feet from the moped, dropped the launcher and approached cautiously with his flamer.

"Don't bother setting the world on fire!" Bren snarled. "The sham Ranger is a local who is gassed out and knows nothing anyway. The ESP is dead of the gas or some poison."

The other moped squealed to a stop. Its rider, though no ESP, was shielding so well that she did not recognize Wallingford Haynes until he switched on his lantern.

Skimmer number two was hovering high now and barely visible. Haynes flicked his radio. "Safe now and all clear. Come down."

All clear. The room guard, who had allowed himself to be overpowered, was sitting on his bed back in the lodge holding an icepack to his head and drinking whiskey neat; Haynes, Big Chief Security Man, had turned back the edge of one gauntlet and was wiping sweat off his face with the lining. He did not bother telling her how nearly she had become another dead cat.

Etrem said, "You have a notch out of your ear and blood all over your shoulder."

"So I have." The pain hit and hit again, so that she stumbled. Etrem ran to help her, but she growled, "Leave me alone. I want to see those whelps."

She stood trembling while the Police skimmer lowered and disgorged two Navajos with flamers. They were taller and leaner than the Pueblos she was familiar with and their quilted jackets were marked with the insignia of their Tribal Police, but the incongruous and ubiquitous black stetsons seemed to have been weathered over a thousand years. They were followed by two shrinking, fawning red cats, whose eyes shone in the lantern beam. They slunk their way toward Bren and dug their heads under her belly as if they were butting for her teats. They were half again as big as she.

She whacked at them with her tail. "You damned troublemakers!"

One of the Navajos said firmly, "They are very young, Madam, and very frightened."

"Take care, man, she is hurt!" cried Etrem.

"Never mind that," Bren said. "You do not have to tell me about them, Mr. Policeman. They are my brother and sister and they are bold enough to run a hundred kilometers with death in every one!" She took breath and said more quietly, "They know I love them, and I thank you, Spotted Horse, and Son of Two Spears. You are more help than we can measure and braver than you know. If we are not waiting here they are dead and so are you."

"I thought these were George Watson and Oliver James," said Haynes. "However, I'm glad to see them and now we can get you some help. Also," he blinked at her thoughtfully, "I'm glad you and your cousin decided to go by the book for once and bring us in. I'd heard Ungrukh were very impulsive."

"Most of the time we are and the rest it is profitable to let others believe we are." Then the trembling increased and she began to sink. "I really . . . do not feel . . . quite all here. . . ." and things became very confused. The side of her head was numb and she could not hear out of the sore ear, images superimposed themselves: Security and his icepack, Etrem saying over and over: "her ear, her ear, ear, ear," the twins licking her nose with rasp tongues and whining, the unconscious body of the unknown man being taken somewhere, lantern-light on the dead ESP, a vaguely hominid blue-feathered woman (?yes), slender, graceful perhaps, deadly graceful, who had been implanted with a myoelectric instrument (transmitter? receiver? control?) which had stopped at death—Bren had understood that much in the last instant and was trying to tell all of it while she was being carried on some kind of stretcher the men had made or found and—

She opened her eyes to a vertical band of noon light; the drapes had been drawn back a little.

She blinked and saw Etrem licking a bowl. A full one was waiting for her beside it.

"Your head feels odd because of the bandages but do not try to claw them off. The bullet skims your cheek and breaks the skin a little. That leaves no mark but you can expect to have one strange-shaped ear. You have plenty of hairs to cover it—"

"Shut up."

"And all of your teeth to bite the head off anyone who makes remarks."

She and Etrem, son of Embri Scarface, glared at each other. "*I* have no complaints. How is Green Corn?"

"They find him alone and drugged in the lookout. It is kind of our friends to let him live since they are ready to kill two policemen to skin us four cats."

"Is he hurt?"

"No. He believes they attack him to keep us from outside contacts because we are already wary of the Continental Police. Where is the logic in that? *I* think that is a very stupid makeshift construct for an intelligent man's reasoning, and probably a plant. But it is better for him than finding out how they use him—until he is ready to learn. Therefore I ask," he licked his whiskers, "Mister Wallingford Haynes to leave him alone."

"Do they want to kill us now, or scare us home?"

"Is all that drama with the bullet in your ear a scare?"

She grunted. She felt slack, but she was pleased that Etrem could take up the slack.

The lawyer was a Lyhhrt. Bren had had vague recollections of Lyhhrt among the liaisons but had never met this one—or if she had could not tell. She did know that he had been attached to the Forensic Division of MedPsych at GalFed Headquarters on Sol III.

"Are you some kind of doctor?"

"No. No need to be uneasy. I *am* a lawyer, but we mediate in all cases where esp is a strong factor."

Lyhhrt were very powerful esp brains in starfish-shaped lumps of protoplasm whose home was a dark and boggy planet where they lived in layers, joining pseudopods to reach their God by the powers of their meditation. GalFed, the disturber, had brought them into the light where they discovered an affinity for metalwork of astonishing artistry. A few went mad; many simply very eccentric. Offworld they moved about in nutrient baths inside workshells of various kinds, usually of fine or precious metals formed in the shape of the prevailing sentient. Or approximations of the shape.

This one wore a dress armor of burnished gold and jewels, but its classic face was set in a solar disk with flaming rays shimmering from its edge. In full light it would have been blinding.

"Only to impress the locals. Dealing in legal transactions I go much more modestly."

"According to my grandmother Lyhhrt are ESPs who do not speak."

"We never lacked the technology. Now we find it more expedient to appear less elitist." The voice, though neither male nor female, was not robotic, but natural and expressive. The voice of an angel, perhaps. "We still prefer to speak to ESP-ones."

"Ha," said Etrem. "You have nothing to say to me, then."

"I am here to listen." The Lyhhrt fitted himself precisely to a chair and placed his glittering hands on his knees.

The Ungrukh were impressed by craftsmanship. As a people they were seldom awed by beauty. "What is your name?" Bren asked.

"I have none. I am Lyhhrt, fission-brother, legal practitioner."

Straightfaced, Bren said, "Man of Law."

The Lyhhrt, of a species nearly, but not quite, devoid of humor, nodded his sunburst head.

"And identification?"

"My fission-brother and I are third-generation descendants of those who knew your grandparents, Khreng and Prandra, in MedPsych."

"I suppose that must do. My grandparents seem to know half the people in the Galaxy." As an ESP-one she was supposed to be able to esp a Lyhhrt, but she had never tried it, and did not intend to make any clumsy attempts on this one.

"I can assure you we are not related to the mad creature who fought Khreng and Prandra inside the tiger, or his sibs. Those died without issue, and you are entitled to check MedPsych records."

"I don't think that's necessary. If you wish to destroy us you can do it with a thought. I am also sure you know everything about us. But by Firemaster, I hope you don't want us to tell the whole damned story again!"

"No," the voice turned gentle, "only the clouded part that has been making Security so uneasy. What you have been trying to shield even from yourselves—and will not be repeated by me to anyone. The story of Mandirra."

Bren had been expecting that request. But still she shivered.

"If you are upset I will come another time."

"What good? That is in the past and there is no other time."

Etrem said, "I cannot help. Do you want me to leave?"

"No. You help by being here." She breathed deeply, supported her body on forelegs, and pushed the words through her teeth. "Mandirra is a woman who . . ."

. . . had been a woman whose man was weak and sickly. Healthy in youth, he had developed a blood disease after the births of his sons and died young. After his death Mandirra gradually became erratic and unstable. The cubs were wild quarrelsome creatures she did not know how to deal with. She had come from another tribal branch, broken family ties for no good reason, made no friends and was not likely to attract another man. The Tribe did not shun her; she made only herself and her sons unhappy.

Parender, the younger, had been small and a late developer. He caught childhood diseases easily and healed slowly. Mandirra was terrified that he might die like his father, and doted on him. Magundir, cheated of attention, became wild with jealousy.

When the Sol III offer came, Mandirra believed that new beginnings on another world might bring health and calm. They had not. Parender had improved because he was able to separate himself from his mother and find friends among his peers. Mandirra stayed morose and sulky; she grew even unhappier because now she was the one who felt cheated and deprived. Magundir, an adult who should have been building his own life, allowed himself to become imprisoned in a no-man's-land where he had no parents, friends or lovers.

Because Mandirra kept lingering in the wake of Parender, to his annoyance, she was within range on the day of the three deaths, when the poison took effect. Down among the greens and flowers by a rapids that reminded her of a part of her own world in the calm days when she was young and gravid, and her man strong and vital. To either side of her were walls the rushing waters had draped and twisted into ribbons of stone, the emblems of her life now.

Agony speared her!

Parender was dying, his guts pierced and bleeding, pain lanced everywhere, he could not move, breathe, could not—

Two of the killers had been tracking with fieldglasses from one of the little skimmers that buzzed back and forth over the Canyon all day long. They had remotes monitoring the heartbeats and when the beats slowed to near stop, anchored the skimmer on hover over the trail where the bodies lay and descended to skin them. Neither was an ESP and they were not armed. They did not expect trouble on a seldom-used trail where the Ungrukh had ventured unusually far afield on a strange world.

When Mandirra leaped out, roaring, just as Parender died, one had managed to escape in the buzzer. He had no choice with the screams ringing in his ears while Mandirra's bloody jaws crunched and crunched again.

• • •

Bren's head sank; she rested her snout on her wrists. Nausea was pushing up her gorge and she did not want to lose a good meal.

The Lyhhrt waited.

"What can I say? Mandirra turns up among us with a bloody mouth and a mind full of bodies and screaming and . . . and eating. We try to make her calm, and take trackers and ESPs to find the bodies. When we reach the place there is no sign of a half-eaten Solthree except a puddle of drying blood, and the Ungrukh bodies are untouched, except by those creatures that like to have a dead body for the evening meal. . . . We cannot carry them. . . . Security discovers how they die before they give them back to us for burning. The killers take care of their own, and so do we. Nobody finds out more—and we don't tell them, either."

"It seems natural for Mandirra to wish to avenge her son's murder. Perhaps the . . . eating part was a hallucination in an unbalanced mind."

"No, man. It is unbalanced, sure enough, but you understand that we are leopards not so long ago by this world's time, and some leopards acquire certain tastes. When my grandparents first leave their world and come to places like this—well, it is a long time past when they have a good meat meal and they are somewhat nervous . ... . that they have feelings . . . about creatures with meat on them. But they find so many busy minds with so many new ideas that their thoughts pull away, they get good food that satisfies them and work hard to bring it home. But Mandirra"—she took a deep breath and got rid of it—"takes it in mind that Solthree meat is good and wants more."

"A leopard habit, then?"

"Beast-thinking! There is revenge and there is starvation and there is sheer madness! We can tell the police everything else and they are sympathetic, but they do not know where to look—and all the time we are half-crazy trying to keep watch on Mandirra. Every once in a while some kind of passion rises in her to hunt and eat some harmless person—a tourist or child. Magundir tries to appease her, hoping she gives him some of the feelings she spends on Parender—and she rasps him down by saying it is because he does not take care of his brother that causes the death—and the poor fool accepts this!"

"That's why you didn't call us."

"Of course. One ESP learns of Mandirra and the world believes it invites a colony of maneaters!"

"Then?"

"One day Mandirra disappears and we are horribly afraid. The search team finds her on the same ledge where her son and those others die. It is in her mad head that the other killer comes back and she is waiting with the appetite. Magundir cannot talk her out of it and she is ready to use teeth and claws to drive everyone away." She raised her right hand: there was a small star stamped in its ball-pad to demonstrate how ready Mandirra's claws had been. "You may know but no one can guess that it is my frightened sister Orenda who lies in her path to hem her in on the ledge—but when she tries to leap over she is half-blind with rage, and falls."

"Dead when you found her."

"Yes."

"No one examined the body."

"What need? Everyone knows she is behaving strangely, including the local police, and believes it is all from her son's death. No reason to talk of her appetites. Why do you ask? It is we who have the terrible questions: Is that death accidental? Do the killers influence us to murder her to trap us in some way, or are we murderers who want her dead because she is so much trouble and cannot admit it to ourselves?"

"If you Ungrukh killed her it was by accident. I swear it. Put everything else out of your mind. As for Mandirra's habits, there is no fleshly sentient species that has not eaten quite a lot of its own or another sentient's flesh."

"But we do not stop her!"

"You said yourself she was terribly unlikable. But evil thoughts and evil acts are different," he added to forestall her growling reply. "Please don't think because of your hot blood and our cold metal that I cannot understand you at all. Lyhhrt have their share of craziness."

"But it is the old story! Always someone to call us beast! Who cares who rids the world of killers!"

"But those other three were killed first and very differently. Why kill? Why skin? Were the killers practicing? And for what?"

Bren said slowly, "It is a terrible thought, but if we are all dead the killers are more vulnerable because they succeed completely and you find out what they plan more quickly—and probably it means more death. But there is greater upset on our world too. It is bad enough already. When Ungruwarkh discovers that of all, only my mother's children are alive, they think something *very* strange is going on. Besides, many people here know we are alive, as well as the killers."

"There are not that many people hereabouts who know you are alive, and most don't care. That is regrettable, but it works in your favor."

"I can't think what kind of favor that is."

"Better than being dead. Your people at home will be terribly upset about the murders, but I don't think they will blame you. I expect them to be at least as reasonable as you! I must ask one more painful question."

"Why, when you must know the answer?"

"Only a conjecture. I think Mandirra did not fall on her head. Is that so?"

"She breaks her spine."

"But you didn't burn the body immediately as usual."

"Of course not. By agreement we must have her brain removed to GalFed Headquarters to see if they can recover it for the converter."

"And you don't know what became of her brain?"

"Who asks?"

The Lyhhrt did.

An hour later he said, "It seems we do keep records at least. The brain was useless for bottling because of arterial degeneration. She'd already had several strokes nobody was aware of, and she could have died at any time. That explains some of her behavior."

"What a burden we consider the poor woman," Bren said. "That makes it all the worse."

"Not for whoever might have been the victim of her hunger," said the Man of Law. "I hope you don't have any more confessions to make."

"No." It seemed to her that he was warning her not to complicate matters further by mentioning the sub-legal business of the Pueblos. "I presume nothing useful is found in the skimmer?"

"Nothing. We can find out where the ESP came from, but she was obviously a neutral carrying no ID. The man who shot at you was an unconscious instrument—like Tom. The very last question: who gathered you together on that plain in the first place?"

"I swear I don't know. It is a rumor: go to such a place, we must discuss . . . by Firemaster, they herd us like sheep! If the twins don't run away, if I don't send Etrem . . ."

"Do try to keep staying away from death. Now I am going to prepare a statement for the inquiry. A short one, since there isn't much to say. Tom Green Corn is waiting to see you."

13

"You have some strange lawyer." Tom Green Corn, looking depressed, leaned against the doorway.

"Lyhhrt are strange to everyone. If they do not feel like ugly little things among other peoples they do not bother with all that foolish ornament."

Etrem said mildly, "They are much like many others. If I can change my skin to red with a black stripe I feel better too."

"You are perfectly handsome as you are," Bren said a bit crossly.

"You don't seem to be suffering too much, anyway," Tom said.

"When I get a look at my ear I see what that does for my vanity."

"I realize how I was used. I'm sorry. . . ."

"We are all used. We must find out what for and by whom."

When he had gone Etrem slammed his tail against the wall, snarling. "You are shaming and mocking me!"

"By the Blue Pit, how?"

"Speaking all that nonsense about how handsome when you know you despise me!"

She kept very still and did not tell him how weary she was of propping him up. "Yesterday I praise you and you know I speak truth. Today it is shame and mockery. Hell's blazes, I think the murderers are very near! Perhaps they mean us to kill each other! Etrem, my grandmother tells me I dash about so much to make myself feel bigger because I am a bit smaller than most Ungrukh. She has a fancy Solthree term for it: overcompensating. That may be true or a lot of silliness. But you are black and I am small and the Lyhhrt is a little slimy creature inside his workshell. Yet you don't see me as ugly even with my torn ear. People who admire flowers believe that naked Lyhhrt are quite as beautiful, and I damned well know a handsome man when I see one. Now I am going to sleep again, and about time."

Etrem did not know what to think or feel. He could accept praise and admiration only in very small doses; lately he had been given more than he could swallow. The mean and shrinking part of himself told him that Bren was trying to hold him fast not because she cared for him but because the others were dead. The solid rigorous part of his mind invited him to remember that she had rescued him from his disastrous orphanhood and—he strongly suspected—his depression. He knew that she had been at first puzzled and rather hurt by his unannounced decision to emigrate. Now she must realize his need to break out of comfortable dependency and, more important, his conviction that he could never be considered an Ungrukh among peers on Ungruwarkh.

He drowsed for a while, slept briefly, and woke to find himself swollen with sexual feeling. He was twitching. This had happened before in times of emotional turbulence and he had been too fearful to look for a loving woman; he had suffered. Now it was no surprise to him that danger might nourish the soil from which the sexual impulse grew—and there was Bren, two steps away, curled tightly in a circle like a great hearth cat, unthreatening. Oversize Etrem might take her even if she were unwilling, but his childhood had taught him that sex taken in anger grew from poison ground; his spirit would be more crippled.

Yet he longed so terribly. He crept from his bed and rested his forelimbs on the edge of hers. She was breathing evenly; her whiskers quivered. He climbed the bed quietly, even gracefully, until he stood pillared over her, she in his shadow. Perhaps her eyes flickered. His heavy penis touched her and he began to tremble. She stretched, drew in her hind legs and wrapped her tail around his body, red band on black, to draw him in. He had not thought that the joy drowning his fear might be so intoxicating.

When he was ready to withdraw she said, "What's the hurry? You have all that waiting in you for years. Surely there is some left."

When he woke again it was to the old terror, a thick glassy dome, through which all outside was blurred. He pulled into a fetal knot and howled. The Security man burst in with gun aimed, and he heard Bren's voice blurred, through glass. "No harm, man. Believe me, nothing I cannot take care of."

He stared at her, panting, his heart slammed against the bed. The barrier strained and cracked, he could hear it crack, he saw the veins of cleavage. It shattered, and he was Etrem, and Bren, on the other bed, yawned and lazily whacked her tail over the edge.

He growled, "Must I have that every time?"

"You feel better now, not so?"

"Yes," he said grudgingly.

"It is much better than last time."

"No!"

"Oh yes, man. It always seems as bad until it goes forever."

"And when am I to expect that?"

"I don't know, but you cannot stop loving on that account. At least this time you make love instead of tying yourself in a knot first. One day it is only a thin film of ice and when you breathe on it, it melts and never forms again."

"You are very sure of yourself."

"I have a very good teacher. This is the first time I try it all on my own, but I admit I am rather proud of myself."

Etrem might be less fearful and more satisfied, Bren more content with her control over her powers, but the two did not become insatiable lovers; they were Ungrukh, and two Ungrukh confined to one room are a couple too many. And the situation had not changed.

They wandered over the plain where the snow had melted and taken the blood with it into the ground.

"You cannot expect me to smell anything worthwhile when it is all nearly gone—and Security tramples all over it with their big feet."

"I always hope." He felt her jolt of terror recalling the figure bent over her with a skinning knife. The late sun cast their attenuated shadows over the mottled ground.

He said suddenly, "That is a woman!"

"What?"

"Your nose does not stop working because you are half out of your wits. It is a female scent."

"They say, 'That one's got Charley. . . . You'll hit *him*!' "

"You know that one is *called* Charley, and each is hiding *identification*. Name needn't be the only thing they hide. I also wonder whether if it is a man you can carry him that far."

"If you are right the masks may also keep *them* from identifying each other."

"And they may be killers for hire," said Etrem.

"Which increases the number to I don't know what, as far as involvement goes. And strangers to each other. It is hopeless."

"Except only that *you* know Five-scars when you meet her."

The shadows deepened. Down below the edge of the plain, in the hollow of a red stone tower shaped like a bicuspid, Moon's Woman, in plain rough clothes, long hair divided and tied with leather strips under the inevitable stetson, was earnestly listening to the twins telling the latest Ungrukh version of the Creation Myth, Qumedon and all. Many Harvests, the small, dark and very quiet man he lived with, was sitting with his legs dangling over an edge, playing a bone flute. It had nothing to do with religion, but was merely a shank he had reamed and cut into an instrument for making sounds. The two of them often camped near the Ranger lookout, even in winter; they were also uncomfortable with their people. The flute dropped cold clear notes into the chasm, like the ice-cold drops that fell from the tree branches.

The Ungrukh had liked the Canyon. Not because it was a great marvel for Solthrees; from their point of view, in part, it was homogeneous and could be counted on to remain the same, if only for their too short lives. Its limitless walls were layers of brown stone and gray, red stone and gray stone stained red, yellowish-gray and pink below them, often breaking and shifting, always returning. Among all the folds, crevices, creases, shafts and screes these layers repeated like the seasons and waited like the lava plains of home while thousands of lives, human, animal and plant, lived and died and were reborn. Sometimes this constancy almost touched boredom, but it was not peace. Not for Ungrukh. The Indian peoples claimed oneness with their lands; Bren did not dispute or even discuss their belief but did not share it; they propitiated too many spirits. For all that Ungrukh respected the roar of their volcanoes and the rip of their tides none would have been caught dead asking them for favors. A world was an implacable enemy, a beast of iron that broke bones when struck upon, spawned flies in the nostrils, worms in the skin, smuts on the corn; tossed great waters and blew fierce winds and twisted the limbs and spirits of its inhabitants. When this beast was silent there was safety in the moment—a truce.

She crouched on the plain's edge with Etrem, listening to the notes, slightly roughtened by wind and echoed by drops of water.

I like this place. I want to stay. Perhaps not forever, but for a while. When there is no worry after the bones are honored and the murderers punished. I like these peaks that savage the sky and the drops that plan their traps. Those ones that coast the rapids in little boats and squeal to enjoy fear can enjoy. I want to battle these towers and howl from the peak of every one. They are great adversaries for Ungrukh.

She sensed the radiance of Etrem's heat.

Nothing lacking in that one, by damn. It is good if he chooses like me. But let him find his own way.

14

The inquiry was a small private pooling of information of which there was nothing new to add, only a rehearsal of the bare facts. The news media had been kept at a distance, partly by the still intimidating personalities of the remaining Ungrukh. No one would dare ask Bren and Etrem how they felt about seeing their cousins and friends slaughtered. The news had flared around the world for a few days and subsided. In a teeming world whose basins of life had been scoured by slaughter time and again for thousands of years, what did a few aliens matter? They had been given their fair share of news for these days when the world was quiet.

"I'm afraid the best thing for you Ungrukh is to go home," Haynes said. "I can't believe the killers had no purpose for that guerrilla-style attack, and if they feel they've gotten rid of you completely they may start crawling out."

"Yes," said Bren. "Then maybe in a few years you find the one I can identify and I come back for a visit with my grand-children."

"You can't stay here waiting to be killed. I hate to sound callous, but there are several law agencies spending more time than they can afford guarding you. They'd be more useful—and you safer—if they were free to investigate."

:Don't argue with the man,: said the Lyhhrt. *:There are alternatives.:*

"What alternatives?" Bren's tail swung over the bed's edge like a clock pendulum.

"Why do you want to stay here?"

That seemed an odd question coming from a powerful ESP, but Bren gave it thought and presumed that a Lyhhrt lawyer, even one from MedPsych, might not be completely at ease dealing with mammalian reasoning.

"You can go back to Lyhhrt without your workshell and join limbs with your people and you are one. Me? I must shoulder a new space into my family. I can find a man and breed now, but I don't want to do that yet. My mind is full of the dead, and whatever man I give myself to does not find it comfortable. There seems to be no place for Etrem and he grows more fearful and depressed where no one is willing to look at him. It happens to his mother. For the twins there is nothing but shame and contempt because of the way they live. They needn't make much effort to mend the condition, and I think their faithfulness is misplaced, but I cannot change them."

"And avenging the dead? Leaving a task unfinished?"

"Surely I don't have to explain such obvious feelings to you."

The Lyhhrt nodded.

"Alternatives?"

"We'd shuttle the four of you to Moonbase, by the way you came in, then with some shifts smuggle you back to GalFed Headquarters here, where you'd be close to developments and perhaps even useful. Security is a lot tighter than when your grandparents were there."

"That is a lot of trouble and expense for you and small reward. And of course the news of our survival must go to Ungruwarkh."

"The news has been sent. We didn't think the four of you could bear the burden of carrying it very easily. This plan is cheaper than sending you home, keeps you safe, gets rid of embarrassment for the Continentals, and makes the killers believe they're rid of you. As for keep, GalFed has never had a chance to study Ungrukh in any depth, and if you were willing"— Bren had stiffened —"only if you were willing, we could do a few harmless experiments. Utterly harmless. Supervised by a Khagodi, whom you know is Morality Personified. Or not, as you choose."

Bren looked out of the window and thought of the cold clear notes dropping from the flute of that silent man.

"Of course it would be boring. But you have had a lot of excitement, and you would be bored alive, not to death. There is not much interesting here for you."

"We have living space. And we are not experimental animals with no friends and no freedom to run."

"Do you have the choice to stay?"

"I still do not care for experiments."

"Well . . ." There was a shift somewhere in the body that was not perceptible to the eye. "I suppose I spoke out of turn. I know there'd be curiosity, but I can't plan what might be done by MedPsych. I am a lawyer."

Bren looked at him and kept her mind very still. "I understand."

When the door slid shut behind him she said, *:Etrem, come fast, ask nothing.:*

Etrem, who took no interest in a conversation with a lawyer and picked it up in a desultory way, was exceedingly bored, and had nothing else to do but roam the corridors, eyed by bored Security men. Neither they nor the staff were now much disturbed by the red-eyed shadow; he radiated an innocent curiosity well reinforced by Bren.

He came in fast and calm. *:Shielding hard.:*

:How you know I want that?:

:Tone of mind, and,: he grinned, *:look on face.:*

:Ha. You think he acts funny?:

He gave thought. *:Inconsistencies. The Pueblos' Father Ramirez says, "Let not thy right hand . . ." You think so?:*

:The Father's Book says some useful things. But for a Lyhhrt . . . they do not fit.:

:What is the Man of Law doing now?:

She pushed at the mind for the first time: *Eavesdropping!:*

:That's not characteristic.:

:We need whitewalls.:

:Then we don't know what he's doing!:

She had to admit that Etrem's ponderous logic had its value.

:Where are the twins?: he asked.

:Sleeping outside, near the camp of Moon's Woman. No big animals about, and Security is cold enough to keep awake. No great help but better than nothing.:

:Only as long as we . . . :

Stay alive.

:Yes.:

:Then what, really?:

:You say already.:

:Inconsistency. Left hand . . . hah.: He hardly dared think further, and pushed the thought down to a depth where, even so, a Lyhhrt might reach it. *:((((Damn big workshell for one little Lyhhrt . . . left head . . .)))):*

:((((Right!)))):

:What chance against Lyhhrt?:

:Maybe . . . :

:Maybe all of this is foolishness and we are afraid for nothing.:

She burst out aloud, "When does a Lyhhrt in his right mind submit his moral authority to a Khagodi? Even a Khagodi can go mad, and Lyhhrt are nearly as self-righteous. At worst we look stupid, with no harm done. I am not afraid of that. I am having this out, by damn!" She called, *:Man of Law, we have a strange request and hope you humor it.:*

:Certainly, Bren.:

:Where is a quiet place where we can speak?:

:Not your own? That's unusual enough, but if you prefer another place I think the hotel won't mind if we use the dining room. No one eats there and the furniture has been put away.:

:Thank you. We are there in a few moments.:

"He knows," said Etrem.

"We find out." She, for once, was preparing for possible battle by shucking her knives and tags. "No use taking metal here. Any Lyhhrt can turn it against you."

"I am not afraid, but I hope there are no tigers. I am not a fighter like your grandfather."

"It is my grandam who has the good grip with the knife. But here are no tigers. Maybe a mountain lion."

"Thanks."

"And you are a match-and-a-half for any of those."

Bren slid open the door. The Security man, who had reacted to any noise, did not move or speak. Etrem shivered. "Why does it not do that to us?"

"I do not think it can. And we are coming to the den."

Etrem asked plaintively, "Why are we always walking into traps?"

"With luck it is a rescue operation—and it is one we set. It is no use going to Haynes now. He is sure to say we are either crazy or stupid, and serve us right."

"Maybe we are. Maybe it does."

The dining room was lit from the ceiling but empty except for the Lyhhrt, who was standing in its center, gleaming and immobile.

The Ungrukh could work in near dark, but Bren suspected that the workshell had infrared receptors as well as those for light—

"That's correct," said the Lyhhrt. —and that there was no advantage for cat eyes in darkness.

"Right again."

Did she imagine that this voice had a different tone or a different mind behind it?

"Find out."

"I expect I do." At least the room's light was not the sharp stab of the local sun that made Ungrukh need contact lenses when they stood directly in its light.

"But I make my own," said the Lyhhrt, and from its upper body ten knife-points of light stabbed.

Bren and Etrem narrowed their eyes and separated, not too near walls or corners.

"You wish me to dismantle and show you," said the Lyhhrt. "Very well." The hands lifted and wrenched away the solar disk, showing a neckless and near-featureless conical head, blued-steel in front and with a slot down the middle.

Hands flung the heavy plate at Bren; she dodged and it ran the paneled wall on its points to fall whirring to the floor. She stretched her tail to scoop it, tossed it to forelimbs and skimmed it, spinning golden knives that gouged the Lyhhrt between head and shoulder. "Na! Na!" the voice squawked.

The hands reached for the lower belly; the legs bent and the Lyhhrt sat down with a crunch. Steel knives sprang from the fingers and dug under the belly plates; two or three scales ripped off and flew glittering. The legs changed shape with the sliding of golden scales, became serpentine limbs, sprang three digits at each foot, reached upward and knocked aside the knifehands to wrench off the head with terrible force; the lights, all the while, darted spears in every direction.

The hands grabbed the head from the legs and tossed it at Etrem, who ducked in time for it to skim his crown and roll down his back and off his flank. He twisted round, bunted it with his snout, caught it with both hands and slammed it against what, in a Solthree, would have been the solar plexus. There was a sick sound, not all machine. The Lyhhrt body flattened. The lights went out.

The digits at the end of the legs turned red hot and drove at the area caved in by the head.

"Stop! Oh, stop!" Bren roared.

Arms fought legs then, twisting furiously, and both began to claw at the midsection. Parts flew—metal flakes, jewels, wires, cogs, power-cells, spools, springs, chip plates and coils —of gold, diamond, copper, steel, ruby, germanium. Upper and lower body wrenched, screaming with strain, pulled, parted. . . .

Except for one thin twine of protoplasm that raveled to a string, broke, beading at both ends, withdrew—

Free! Free! some mind-voice cried.

But the separated halves, dented, flaked, battered, still glittering in the scatter of their components, reached for each other once more.

Another voice screamed, "I dunno what this son of a bitchin thing is, but if it doesn't stop I'm gonna kill it!"

Alfred P. McNelly, faithful husband and father, long trusted Continental op, had come to and decided he was finally going crazy after all these years. He had let himself be punched senseless by the damned cats he was trying to protect, and hypnotized out of his wits by the one who was supposed to be helping them. Enough.

Staff were cowering behind him, Security men coming forward with Wallingford Haynes, who was fastening the gold frogs of a quilted orange nightrobe that gave him the look of a Monarch of Playing Cards.

But the Lyhhrt halves, deadly enemies, did not stop stretching toward the kill. Before knives and hotpoints made contact McNelly neatly shot their tips off with a machine pistol that was no beauty but quite as effective as a Lyhhrt workshell.

Upper gave in and flopped. Lower struggled to raise itself on limb stubs among the detritus of metal and jewels. Etrem, not quite sure what had been happening, stood watching. Bren, bandage knocked askew, was shivering. "No kill," she begged.

"I won't," said McNelly, and stepped into the room.

"But keep out of danger."

:No more.: The lower half tried to pull toward her. *:All done. No need of weapons now. I am your Man of Law, what is left of one.:*

"But what is he doing? Why do you divide?"

"That's not fission," McNelly said. "Fissioning they split clean down the dotted line in back. This was some kind of contact."

:Captivity. Please allow me to emerge.:

"Nothing funny."

:That was not funny to me. But there will be no more surprises.:

"Is that other one dead?" Bren asked.

:Not yet. He may be suffering terminal shame and frustration. He was—you say brainwashed, and he tried to do that to me.:

"He's stirring. I think he's too weak to come out."

:He has a strong inner shell. Right now I believe he prefers to stay in it, and I am content to take him back that way with me and send you another lawyer.:

"I prefer to keep the one we have. *He* does not throw his face at us. But first I like to be satisfied about what happens."

Man of Law, working from inside, cut rivets and unthreaded screws; more plates fell away until the outer casing cracked like a nutshell and a little glasstex box, edged and cornered in gold filigree, sprang tiny wheels and rolled out. Inside, the five-limbed orchidaceous Lyhhrt rested on a thin film of liquid, operating with a stretched tentacle the miniature control panel built into one end of its box. It was melon-sized, pink with dark red markings on top, and slightly translucent. It repelled no one. Fleetingly Bren wondered if the monster-image was as much of psychological defense as the workshell was a physical one. She turned to the other half. "Person, why do you want to kill us?"

The battered half rocked a little with outrage. *:I have nothing to say. I am a metal worker and you have ruined my work.:*

:Legally he does not need to speak,: said Man of Law.

Haynes opened his mouth and McNelly raised his gun, but Etrem was faster than both. "Whose lawyer are you?" he growled. "I want to go to sleep and hope I wake up, not stand here yapping all the night!" He ran forward, grasped the heavy upper torso in his forelimbs and lifted it, squatting on his great haunches and balancing on a circle of muscular tail.

"Mister Security Man, you can shoot me and this thing drops, and I find I can also throw things quite well!"

"That's mad!" Bren hissed, and put herself in front of him.

"Are you thinking of my mother? Damnation, I am angry! Get away!" He ignored the mental twitters of the suspended Lyhhrt.

The glassy box spun in a twirl of distress. *:This brother makes workshells for Lyhhrt who come here to work and cannot bring their own because of freight charges and import laws. The shell was assigned to me, and I did not know it was otherwise occupied until too late, and he had made contact. He was controlled by a Kylklad, a neutral ESP supposed to be here on cultural exchange. She is dead now.:*

"Blue feathers," said Bren.

:Yes. It seems she took an opportunity to do her work more quickly, but unsuccessfully. When she died he grew weaker; he is a bit stupid:—outraged twitter—*:but a good workman, and I learned much but could not break out. I had no contact with the ESP or would have learned more. This one forced me—not mentally but by controlling my nutrients—starving me—to make you tell the story of Mandirra, to use against you. Of course, there is nothing in it. He could not stop me from bringing that out, at least. When he began planning to finish her work . . . need I tell you I used all of my strength to make you suspicious enough to give me this opportunity? Do you believe how much it took?:*

"Yes," Bren said. "It is a wonder you have enough left for this battle."

:Desperation helps. Regard Etrem.:

Haynes did. "All right, Etrem, put the thing down and we'll get it all sorted out." There was a bit of a quiver in his voice. Etrem on haunches was still rather tall.

Etrem looked down at Bren. "This is a filthy stupid thing." He did not voice the question.

She said quietly, "You are quite right to feel as you do."

"But I am not a killer." He lowered the heavy half shell with arms trembling from its weight.

Haynes said, "McNelly, get this stuff together and maybe we can find out who made the electronics. Lyhhrt don't do that."

:I can tell you,: said the Lawyer. *:Sonotek Radio.:*

"Ahh," said Bren.

15

Senator John Tennyson Silver, known to friend and enemy as Long John, had a thirty-five year seat on the Continental Council. He was sixty-nine years old and in as good health as possible for a man who had completely indulged himself; and he was perfectly satisfied. Almost. He had free control of only one quarter of his Sonotek Radio, the rest in a blind trust. But everyone knew that he controlled everything within reach. Once he had burnt some fingers. Thirteen years earlier he had lent too much to a powerful businessman, Winston Horton Wardman, of WardRobotics, who was warped as a sea-soaked plank. Wardman, in his Byzantine way, was supporting the mad dream of a person named Thorndecker. But Thorndecker had used up his considerable wealth and owned nothing but a list of creditors. This discovery was particularly unfortunate for Wardman, who was eventually found in the bottom of his garden under a thin layer of sod.

Silver sent his best man to track Thorndecker, but Galactic Federation wanted Thorndecker for what it considered more compelling reasons, and Silver's man was stopped—permanently—by an Ungrukh agent. The humiliation did not end there: GalFed had done some tracking too, and for quite a while Silver found himself selling the Federation advanced electronic components at very good prices. He dared not complain. The investigations into the affairs of Wardman and Thorndecker had turned up some very grubby dealings under cold light, and Silver did not want that light on him. He was still very well off, very comfortable, in his tower in Phoenix where he lived with his family on the 33rd floor and kept an office and an apartment for his mistress on the 48th.

With surprise and pleasure he learned of the Solthree proposal to invite the Ungrukh, and endorsed it enthusiastically. It was perhaps coincidental that the Ungrukh chose to settle less than 200 km away, and complete chance that three of them were children of his enemy. It was by no coincidence at all that, while he was considering how to make the best use of this happy concordance, he received the invitation and the offer.

Silver's mistress was a long black woman called Ela Nkansah, who had cropped hair and the classic features of the finest African sculpture. She had been a model and earned a great deal during the few short periods her type was in vogue. When the next wave came she might be too old, but in the meantime she graciously let Silver take care of the rent.

It was she who received, in her apartment, the package addressed to J. T. Silver, care of. It was wrapped in opaque film, tagged without return address—no stampings, no carton, a soft thing shaped like a teddy bear. Red letters on the brown wrapping said: A PHUZZEE PHUNNEE™ FOR YOU. Ugly-cutesy, with Zs and Ns warped and slanted to resemble each other. It was not hers to open, but she noted that whoever had sent it knew of the relationship between her and Silver.

Eventually he popped out of the elevator with his yell of "Hi-hoo!" followed by his valet-bodyguard, Boris, a man slightly shorter and much broader than Ela; he bulged in the unnatural places of the armed.

"And what's new?" The cry of every day.

She stooped to kiss Silver's damp pink forehead. His thick white hair was all his own, and so was his considerable belly; the grogblossom would have been grosser without surgery.

"Something for you, today," she said, with the mildest curiosity. What would be new with her, when she sent out for what she wanted or shopped in the cool underground malls? The bills came to his desk, and she did not send or take outside messages on public carriers.

He looked down at the package on the thick glass table between the icebucket and the bourbon bottle. He blinked and gave Boris a look. Boris went to push buttons in the kitchenette. He picked up the package, a bit gingerly, and let himself drop to the sofa. His wife, "the old girl," was used to late meetings.

He muttered, "Funny they'd send a thing for me here." She shrugged. She did not know what "it" was or who "they" were.

"Ain't regular delivery. You see the messenger?"

"No. It just dropped in the chute around noon."

He took a little rod from the inside of his belt, pointed it at the package and pushed a knob at one end. "Not a bomb, anyway." He dug a finger in the wrapping and it peeled, almost melted away, to a shred like a burst balloon.

The thing was some kind of stuffed toy, not a teddy bear. More like the cub of a big cat, but covered in red furry stuff, a black stripe centered with a white line down its back. It had red bead eyes and no claws, but looked more like a real animal than a plaything.

"Something for your grandchildren?"

"This? No! Oho, no! This is for me." He grinned suddenly and his eyes narrowed in fat. "Yeah. Just what I wanted. Just like real."

She touched it. The red fluffy surface was just like real, firm, yet soft underneath. It was vaguely familiar, a nag in the memory for an instant before she realized what it represented.

He began to laugh, took a gulp of bourbon and sobered. "Boris, cancel that order! I want some of those Cornish hen things, and a filet with. And the right wine. And I'll have my shower now. This is gonna be a night!" He heaved himself up and trundled away.

Boris emerged, muttering. "What's with him? Spent an hour this afternoon deciding what he'd stuff himself with and—what's that?"

"Something that got delivered."

"Ugly lookin bugger. Now he'll want me to clean up on my night off. Lucky my girl's workin anyway."

She said sweetly, "You don't have to screw him, Boris."

He pulled up his shoulders. "What kind of salad, you think?"

"Greens and lemon juice. He's on a diet."

He snorted and went back to the kichen.

She picked up the toy cat in a very gentle way. It was not ugly like some dearly loved toys. It actually had a kind of beauty. But it did give her a wild feeling that it did not want to be touched. She blew off a shred of plastic wrap, and noticed in the breath's hollow that the hairs paled toward the base. She held the object under the lamp and, parting the hairs with her thumbs, peered closely. There was fine pale down beneath the glossy red. The PHUZZEE PHUNNEE™ was covered with real skin, undyed. She smoothed and replaced it, swallowing, as Silver came from the bathroom wrapped in a big turquoise velour robe, face flushed with heat and moisture. Fuzzy funny.

He grinned. "Don't bother dressing." She was wearing a narrow silky red gown with spaghetti straps and little underneath. He poured another bourbon, leaned head back, feet on the table, watching tri-V and idly playing with whatever part of her he chose.

He was a liar, thief and murderer. She did not like him, but she had never despised him. He was not cruel to her, and in perhaps a perverse way she admired his very grossness, his vitality in determination to be what he was. She was sure his wife knew about the competition, and that he was genuinely fond of the woman in a lackluster way. Ela wondered why he was content with *her*, when a comfortably pillowy blonde might have suited him better. Perhaps he had one. Probably not; he was too old and self-consumed. Or he thought the long skinny type would expect less, sexually.

Now the red toy, color of her in her red dress, red toy, stood between. The foulness of the outside had seldom come into this privacy. The delivery of the package had dangerous implications for her.

He ate heartily and gulped. She picked and sipped. He had never noticed. He had nothing to talk about with her. He giggled at the porn on the channel, finally noting with surprise that the dishes were empty, and turned to her with his greedy look. She smiled. One of the corners of her mouth began to twitch uncontrollably, but the movement was very fine, and of course he did not notice.

"I really, really like you," he said thickly.

"I know, honey. I know."

• • •

He heaved and puffed. She kissed, pinched, tickled.

After a final heave he grinned, a rictus, and collapsed over her. He was so heavy she had no room for a sigh, could hardly breathe. "All right, lover?"

He did not move. His eyes were open, his face purple.

"Lover?"

She dug a thumb in the fat below his ear and found no pulse. He was dead. She was terrified. A dozen times in this situation she had thought: one day you'll die like this, you poor damn fool, and the hideous thought had comic overtones. Now there was only irony and terror. He was fearfully heavy and she could not get out from under. A sickening comedy cliché: The self-indulgent slob dying on top of the wrong woman. She pushed and shoved, freed a shoulder and caught breath. A little blood was running from one of his nostrils. The waterbed heaved with her in waves; she fought down nausea and shrieked for Boris.

He would be in his den, watching tri-V, probably wearing earphones. She screamed again, without hope, struggling.

No. His steps were running down the connecting hallway and he slammed the door back and stared. There was a greasy rag in his hand; he had kept himself busy polishing weapons.

He began to giggle.

"Shut up, damn you! He's dead!"

He gaped. "Chrissakes, you sure?"

"Damn right I'm sure! Now help me!"

He stood, swallowing. He was good with guns but a bit dim. She had got a leg free but could budge the doughy heap no further.

"Get him off me!"

He dropped the cloth but his hands hesitated, curiously squeamish. She yelled, "Oh, for God's sake, *get*—no, wait —have you got grease on your hands?"

He stared at them. "Just the stuff I use to—"

"I can smell it and I don't want it on him. Trash that cloth and wash up." He was so damned slow. "Hurry!" She wrestled with the body to keep the blood from settling permanently in its front. She was of methodical mind and had made plans long ago.

Finally he hauled off the body and turned it face up; she lay panting, rubbing one numb leg. Then dragged herself off the bed. She was naked and, though far from Boris' type, grateful to pull on a nightgown.

"You went and made *me* wash. What're we going to do with *him*?"

"I'll wash him. You take his suit and shoes and put them in his office on a chair like he took them off for a rest. Then you help me put his underwear and robe on and we carry him to the office and dump him on the couch."

"And then what?"

"You go back to watching trivvy and I get out."

His face turned sly. "Just like that? Once I get out of the room—"

"But I *don't*. He died of natural causes and I want to keep it that way—but not connected with me. You've got an official existence but I don't, and I'm not gonna run around in my nightie. You're the one that's in his will, not me."

They stared each other down. He was wearing a light zip, obviously was not armed, and she wanted him to stay that way. Slowly he picked up the clothes. "What do you get out of it?"

"I got to live good while my savings piled up interest. I'm not greedy." He lingered, and she yelled, "God's sake, we'll have a stiff on our hands! Get on!"

He plodded down the service corridor connecting the apartment to his room, which opened to the office. His regular quarters were down below in the big apartment, and she wished he was there. She did not dare close the door, but when he was out of sight shook a wire spool out of a rouge box in her makeup kit, pulled away the adhesive-backed casing of the spy-eye in the trivvy control box, picked out the spool from it and slipped in her own. This would show her sprawled on the bed watching tri-V and trying out new cosmetics. She returned all to order with practiced silence and swiftness. Boris reacted quickly as a bodyguard, but did not think much on his own. She hoped he was not beginning now, and thinking in the direction of the guns. When he came back, unarmed, she was washing the body with a wet cloth, and she carefully did not notice that he checked the trivvy. Whatever he thought he had on her, he didn't.

Together they pulled on underwear and robe. She had not touched Silver's face; it was paler now, and she did not want it to look tampered with.

Boris said, still beetle-browed, "You got all that jewelry and stuff, rubies, emeralds."

"Honey, in my line of work you don't get to keep that stuff, you just get the borrow of it. He's got it all registered. He wasn't *that* generous. His wife'll get it—his anniversary surprise, I bet."

"I don't believe you."

She hissed impatience through her teeth. "Okay, we'll divvy it. Just don't try to fence it—and *get going*!"

"Maybe I can sling him over my shoulder."

"I don't want the blood in his head! Grab him under the arms. I'll take his legs." She did not know exactly when a corpse's blood coagulated, and she very much wanted an eye on Boris, and herself between him and the guns. She was still bruised and aching; she staggered, picking up the heavy legs. They lugged the body down the corridor, through Boris' den with its neatly laid-out guns, into the office, arranged it on the couch, clothes on the chair, shoes on the floor. "That's as natural as it'll ever get to look."

In the bedroom she touched a spot on the wall and a thick door swung open. She pulled out a brass-bound chest with a curved top, pirate's chest, set it on the floor, lifted the lid, removed a tray with two bottles of rum, and let the sapphire and emerald glitter reflect in his eyes.

"Half, remember. Half." He could have had the lot, for all she cared, but that would have made him even more suspicious.

"Awright, awright!" He chose his pieces, dumped them in a pillowcase while she stripped the bed, pushed the mattress-cover into the disposal and the rest of the linens down the laundry chute.

"Okay," he said.

"Give me fifteen minutes to get out of here and you can do whatever you think is good for you."

"I'll bring the service elevator up for you."

"Thanks."

No good-byes. Each had belonged to Silver in a different way. They did not impinge.

She locked the doors, threw a coverlet over the bed, pulled off the nightgown and sent it after the laundry, and took a very fast autobath. Then reached into the bathroom disposal tube and pulled out a nylon net bag which had been hanging from the inside on a hook. She took a very small camera from the bag.

Boris had forgotten the toy cat but she had not, and photographed it from enough angles to make a rough but recognizable picture cube. She attached a magnifying lens, switched on the flash, held the camera in her teeth, picked up the cat, parting the hairs to show the down, and pressed the stud with her tongue. She clipped off a few hairs with manicure scissors and brushed them into a specimen bag. She took another very small instrument from the netting, a minicord (manufactured by Sonotek), which contained a spool record of all Silver's activities during the last three thirty days; she had not gathered this information directly, but in her capacity as a drop during her shopping trips in the mall. She finished the spool by recording the events of the last hour.

She cut up the toy over the toilet bowl, found nothing inside but inert foam, and dropped the pieces down the chute, with the net bag, the priceless camera and minicord minus film and spool, and everything else that did not belong in a model's kit. She dropped hairs, film and spool into a small strong envelope and sealed it.

She did not make up, but put on a thin rust zip, straw sandals, and a cloud-colored weathercoat that did not look expensive. She ignored the open wall safe and the gaping chest with jewels pouring over its lip. And paused at the connecting door. The corridor housed the service elevator, and Boris' room was too near. She pulled a silver locket from round her neck, pushed the clasp in her ear, and the opened halves against the door.

Whine of metal; beat of heart.

Boris wanted the rest of the stuff. Or simply wanted her dead. Easy enough to find an excuse, huh, Boris?

She pulled away, painted a rough whorish face on herself, drew on a close silver-mesh cap and a light fur coat suitable for hyper-cooled restaurants, and used a very private key-card to unlock Silver's own express elevator.

A moment later, in the mall, glitter and flash, she used it twice more: once on a CommUnit to reserve a ticket to Marsport, ship leaving in five hours, in the name of Ela Nkansah; again, to get into a first-class wash cubicle, where she let hat and coat drop to the floor and card down the toilet, and washed her face. Her hair, in its natural color after shampooing, was a bit gray around the hairline: fine platinum wires twined among the black. These, and her scrubbed face, made her look a little older and softer, extremely good-looking rather than arrogantly beautiful. She knew she could not disguise herself; she hoped to make herself a little less noticeable.

She came out without a swagger, undecorated, and walked a kilometer to the lineup for a shuttle to Moonbase, leaving in an hour. At one point in the line, so subtly she could not tell, the envelope in her pocket was replaced by an ID card. She used tokens to buy a second-class ticket in the name of Marion Jeffries. She had spent her mall days planning these moves, though she could never be sure when they would be necessary.

She sent her small case on through and walked past the scope in perfect confidence, boarding immediately. She was not relieved or comfortable. There was something yet to do. Or not, as chance might have it.

At takeoff everyone would be locked automatically into couches for twenty hours; she accepted the quick diuretic. Except for emergency there was to be no rolling about in weightlessness for untrained people. Each passenger had a small individual V-screen with choices for programming and earphones for music. During the waiting hour, stretched as usual by half, three of the flight attendants played stringed instruments and sang to encapsulated babies.

Nothing happened on this voyage except that the woman named Marion Jeffries became more and more bored, too bored to be frightened, and did not care to look at the dramas played out on the fingernail screen or the reading matter displayed on it a few words at a time. There were no ports to look out of. After the low-residue meal, and before the lights dimmed to let passengers get some sleep to face the lunar "day," attendants came around with sleeping pills; she chose a mile endorphin, pretended to unseal and swallow it, but dropped it in a glove. She did not want sleep.

She thought there was something odd about the black man who offered it to her. He was wearing the usual black zip and red tunic, but it seemed to point up his extreme blackness. He was much darker than she, eyes like chips of coal. Did his look rest longer on her? She returned his blink of mild inquiry.

His skin: The light did not reflect from it properly, nor catch the translucence he should have had in the creases on the backs of his hands; the demarcation line along the paler skin of his palms was too sharp. He was narrow-nosed and thin-lipped, but his head and body were as typical as her own. Why should not a black man disguise himself by making himself blacker? Bright red hair and a big mole worked fairly well for whites. She did not think she knew him.

The lights lowered to near darkness; Marion Jeffries dozed off for a few moments once in a while. Awake, she thought of her dead parents, her divorced husband, her daughter. The kid would get the money. Her life was squared away. She turned on her smoke cone and rolled a stick of kif. Given the choice, how many memories would she want to keep?

It was after the shuttle had landed with lights up, in that last irritable hour when it was waiting to be cleared, that she gave in and slept. She woke to the voices of attendants trying to placate passengers who really did not want any juice or coffee until they were offboard and could empty their bladders. A melody flowed down the aisle; the black man was plucking a mandolin to a song she had never heard before:

> . . . and when
> the Devil hammered out that brute
> of brass and pitch and flame
> he pumped the bellows, forged the chains,
> twined the sinews, fired the brains,
> twisted its tail to make it roar
> and laughed to bust, it was so cute
> when the souls all shrank on the farther shore
> and thumped on Heaven's door:
> Hey Pete, go get me Willie Blake!
> Now Willie, come on down
> see what I made just for your sake
> just for your sake, old Willie Blake!
> It's called Tiger, man,
> Tiger! Tiger!

and as he came abreast of her, he smiled down. She was locked in, and far from the exit doors. His hand with the plectrum dipped in and out of his pocket and the sharp point on his finger flicked her neck. She looked up at him, blinking . . . and then her heart and throat and brain seemed to swell and explode.

"What's the matter, Madam!" he cried, bending over her, and whispered in her ear: "Charley sends love," but she was already dead. The buckles were unlocking row by row and she fell half out of her couch.

"Lady? Lady? Something's wrong!" Jabbing the button for the nurse. He made a show of loosening her clothes to avoid constriction, while passengers climbed over both of them, hurrying not to become involved. He did not expect to find anything on her; she had gone through the scope, sent her kit through the scanner; his confederate would check it out, probably find everything in a tube of some radio-opaque cream.

But there was something. She had one glove on, was holding the other in that hand, and there was an odd lump under the leather over the ball of her thumb. There was no one else who cared to notice; he fished it out.

A bit of paper wrapped around an object: her sleeping pill. By not taking it she had grasped a few half-hours more of living awareness. And on the cigarette paper she had scrawled words with an eyebrow pencil:

DON'T YOU KNOW A
DECOY WHEN YOU SEE
ONE, MISTER BONES?

He whirled about, swearing. More than half the passengers were gone, and among them, no doubt, a very anonymous fellow, with a package.

And she had known this would happen. That was what he had seen in *her* eyes.

He stood still, mandolin crushed at his feet, without trying to push forward, or call for aid again, or look back—though he felt, he thought, the breath of Tiger on his neck.

16

On Ungruwarkh the Tribes snarled and rumbled. GalFed had dispatched a Khagodi with news of the slaughter, and the Ungrukh were both too proud to show their feelings and too aware of the consequences of picking a fight with 600 kg of female Khagodi with esp equal to over a hundred class-ones.

Tribes who had sent no members had little pity for those who had taken such risks; others who had lost friends and relatives wondered where to lay blame; the Northerners, who were most stricken, expressed their grief by quarreling, and when a meeting of Tribal Council broke up in squabbles Raanung was in despair.

Emerald said, "That slaughter is terrible, but we lose more from one battle in the old days. The world cannot tie a knot in its tail over this!"

"It is the deliberate slaughter and skinning as if we are beasts! And it is by chance *our* children are safe. People look at me sideways and I know the feelings. How can I go endlessly among these fools to make them one people?"

"For a start, do not call them fools, and consider how they feel. Also, you do have helpers."

"And right now *they* are all busy quarreling! I do not know what to do."

"And you are tired." Emerald considered the young and savage Hillsman she had chosen long ago. "I doubt whether there are many things to learn from that old warrior father of yours, but at least he does not surrender."

Still so far to go: For all the Ungrukh had learned from

GalFed, of themselves, their world, other worlds, they were painfully limited yet. They had finger prostheses but not fingers, hand substitutes but not hands. They could not do delicate operations, and even GalFed could not cure some of their stubborn organic diseases.

Emerald's corneas became more opaque; Prandra grew ever more weary of taking pills, gulping water, trying to flush her kidneys: she lost appetite and grew increasingly weak. Khreng did nothing now but tend her.

She spoke and moved slowly, but her head was still hard. "You and I cannot help here," she told Khreng. "Nor Mra'it." She still referred to Emerald by that name. Only Khreng insisted on pronouncing it properly. He had chosen it, and labored to say it. "Those children must act for themselves. And I too."

Khreng looked at her. Long ago he had said that she would make a terrible fuss when she died. He had been wrong. She was beyond it. "You are not giving in, woman!"

"Old man, big man . . . dear man. I no longer want to eat or drink or take the damned medicine. I can hardly move or stay awake. While I sleep I can feel my brain decaying. The medics must remove it before I—"

"No!"

"Because when GalFed first comes it is my head we make our bargains on even if it is not the first they collect. You cannot deny I live long and well, and I want to give what is still useful."

And she closed her eyes and mind. There was no answer for her argument; the medics agreed that they could still save the brain. No one else tried to dissuade her in the face of her suffering, and it was Khreng who gave in.

He came out of the back of their cave and down the hill in time to see the pyre being poled across the river by a raftsman on one of the old wattled fishing barges and touched off by a burning branch at the farther shore. The body could scarcely be seen under the twigs, and he did not allow himself to think of the empty skull, or its brain in stasis in the stone block building a kilometer away.

Her family watched the flame, and they were not a great many. Telepathy and all, Ungruwarkh's people have much in common with others: they remember what they have learned, but not always who taught it; their heroes are most often legendary and less than half real.

While the flames still devoured the pyre Khreng went back to the cave. He did not build a supper fire or eat an evening meal, and everyone knew better than to approach him.

When he stood in the cave-mouth at midnight an Ungrukh blocked his way. His eyes were not so sharp now, but he knew the scent of Raanung, and waited for him to move aside.

Raanung said, very gently for this once-savage Hillsman, "Where are you going, my-father?"

"Hunting."

Raanung did not ask what for or why now. "My good father, my-mother tells me before she leaves us that if any Ungrukh decide to visit Sol Three over this matter we must send Mra'it."

"I know."

"She wants care for Mra'it's eyes, but I worry about the dangers. Of course, Mra'it must know, but I am afraid to speak of it."

"I don't blame you," said Khreng. "I don't know what is right, but I know Emerald always makes her own decisions, and you cannot change that." He added, speaking even more quietly than Raanung had done, "She chooses you, and I cannot think of better. You are as good and dear to me as one who comes from my own body."

"Thank you, Father," said Raanung, and was gone.

Father . . .

Tugrik . . .

Khreng sniffed the air for the last vestiges of Prandra's scent on its trembling currents and padded out of the cave.

Before his first mating Khreng had lost both parents and his brother in an epidemic; after that his family had been Prandra's. His only other living relative was his cousin's granddaughter, who was now Tribeswoman—Tribeswoman indeed!—and elected with only a few muttered grumblings, so quickly had conditions changed since Khreng leaped out of a split in the lava field to confront the explorers from GalFed. He was alone in his generation.

The embers glimmered from banked fires among the rocks and caves; Khreng knew the smells of all the sleeping, the restless, the lovemakers around him. He did not pause, even where his daughter lay dreaming, but went out southward past the cattle pens and storage bins. The night watch did not question him.

He turned east and swam the river half a km downstream from the burnt-out pyre, and when he rose from the water shook himself out of unconscious habit. The night was mild and autumnal.

He followed the path through the cultivated swath of the south bank, but it did not go far, and on either side lay only the stubble left from reaping. After meandering through a little scrub the path faded, pointing toward the desert strip between mountains and tidelands.

He loped on, not as quickly as in youth, still with some grace, among thorny growths and odd lava outcroppings as the plain became roughened and swept with low heaps of sand blown from the banks of streams that fed the tides. The weight of age, with all the ache and weariness he had forced back in caring for Prandra, dropped on him like a fall of hot lava. He went on.

Presently he was alone in the desert land with the three red moons at his forehead and the stars misty above, the silver diamond of age covering the crown of his head.

He wondered if now for once in his life he might see the Plains Companion, that hallucinatory cat who came to solitary desert travelers. Prandra's grandmother, Tengura's mother, had been the first to realize it was neither ghost nor spirit but the formation of a deprived mind. It was not seen often now, because there was so much more contact among tribes who journeyed in groups or on aircraft, and far fewer lonely hunters.

Even as he was thinking of it Khreng saw the outline of an Ungrukh shape in the dull light of his moons. He stopped and sniffed the air. There was no scent.

He waited. The phenomenon moved forward and he saw by its shuffling seven-toed gait that here was no hallucination but his old enemy-ally Kriku/Qumedon. He snarled and a star of pain broke behind his breastbone, sending rays burning through all of his quarters. He realized now how familiar that pain had become.

Kriku stopped before him and he saw the eyes open briefly on chaos and turn red again in acknowledgment of an old relationship.

"Don't be angry with me, Khreng," said Qumedon. "I am not here to insult you with the offer of an easy death."

Khreng got his breath back. "Good." His voice rasped and he despised his pain. "Then why are you here?"

"To wish you good hunting, friend." The cat shape stepped aside and was gone.

Good hunting! says Chatterjee from her bottle, oh, long ago. And Espinoza, bottled. Prandra in her bottle to come.

The star did not burst again in his body but the heat still burned.

Khreng hunted.

Finally he found a hillock of lava, half-shored with sand. He lay down in its slope, turning until it accommodated his shape. He lay there, eyes slitted, sore within the ribs, breath rasping. He slept a little, dreaming for a moment that Prandra had come to lie beside him with her head on his shoulder in the old way. Dreaming or waking he did not open his eyes to look, not then nor when the star exploded through his breastbone and its fires collapsed in darkness.

Raanung sulked about the house for three days, getting up intermittently to pace and lash his tail.

Emerald cried, "Raanung, cannot we mourn my mother and father in peace?"

"Not when the whole world falls apart without them," Raanung growled. "Mourn in peace. I am going."

At Tribeswoman Nemer's cavemouth he roared.

She stood square in the opening. "I am not going to ask what is on your mind!"

"That is because you know very well! Where is that damned lazy incompetent man of yours who is pretending to call himself my helper?"

A growl rose from the back of the cave and Nemer dodged as Berend came running full tilt, eyes flashing enough to light the dull sky. "Look what is calling *me* incompetent! Perhaps you like to lose a fang or two!"

Raanung purred, "I am glad to see you so full of vitality. Now maybe you come with me to visit the Hills where my sister Nurunda still has a claw to spare, and young Mundr a good set of teeth?"

"For a good roll in the dust, or a battle, brother hothead?"

Raanung laughed, hissing. "Neither. For a raiding party of

a new kind. Beginning with *your* brothers among the Tidesmen."

And Raanung began his own last battle. He spat out his weariness, used all he had learned from his headlong father and thorn-tongued mother, gathered his troops from the Hills Tribes and the Tideslanders, bullied and blackmailed, threw away half a lifetime of painful lessons in diplomacy, threatened and bribed. He had never been a Tribesman, and he had no title, but he had given his word to finish the work Khreng had begun, and finish he would, even if Khreng's ashes rose in a whirlwind of outrage against him. With his rasp tongue he drove the Scrublanders and Spotted Pinks and Herder tribes of valley and tundra back to their Council fire, snap and growl as they would.

There were no roasted fish or haunches of raw meat to be eaten at this fire, and no drowsing on full bellies.

Raanung stood with his fur risen to catch the light of the fire as his father had done to rouse his warrior Tribe, but he was careful to keep his tail curved along his flank, and his fangs covered. He looked one by one at two-score sullen faces, and listened to the occasional rumble of some empty belly.

"My people—and I call you my people because I belong to you and no other loyalty claims me—I see how angry you are that I bring you here by threat and insult, and I am ashamed of that. But maybe you better remember that I am the warrior son of Tribesman Mundr in the days when the Eastern Hills are the fiercest of all. I swear to finish Khreng's work, and if I cannot do it his way I unlearn it and use mine.

"I think you resent that the Northern Tribes are the first peacemakers, and wrongly believe we get a larger share from Galactic Federation. It is obvious to me that when you find the terrible slaughter on Sol Three affects the North worst you feel a little smug about our grief and confusion. Do I exaggerate? Not much. Now you can take up your old quarrels and struggles for supremacy again.

"No, Ungrukh, that is not so. Whether you see it or not you are no longer a straggle of tribes squabbling over a few barren lands.

"I am a Hillsman and my woman comes from the Plains. Nemer's man Berend is a Tidesman and my sister Nurunda's a Scrublander. And you, Tribeswoman Ghemma, herd caribou and antelope in the Tundras and your brother Medor is the first official delegate to Galactic Federation. *And all of us on the Council elect him!* Try to break up now and you tear apart families and bartering agreements, and soon you lose food supplies and the implements that make your lives a little easier."

He waited while the Council muttered and shifted. Finally Menirrh, the Scrublands Tribesman, said grudgingly, "I admit truth in some of what you say, Raanung, but *must* you bring us here first by making us ill-tempered and then further insulting us?"

"I try everything else and it doesn't work. I rather have you spitting at me than clawing each other." He paused again and turned to look at his own people of the Hills and Plains.

"My family and Tribes, I have another ugly feeling, and that is you believe I have some way to save my own children while many of yours die. I do not ask you the shameful question whether you prefer my children slaughtered as well."

"Damnation, Raanung!" Berend roared. "You know that is not in our minds!"

"I tell myself it is not. Because my daughter Bren just escapes being skinned alive, and even so someone shoots and wounds her. I lose a cousin and niece as well. Now I think all that happens on Sol Three is a horrible insult, not only to a few tribes but to all Ungrukh, and I intend to go to Sol Three and demand why their world's law cannot protect our people as they promise. You know I want Mra'it's eyes mended, but if you think I am going for that reason alone I invite any of you who choose to come along with me and learn what we can do."

Emerald, who had been sitting quietly on the edge, growled, "I want to go find out what is happening, not as some damned handicap because of my eyes."

Nemer said, "Mra'it, *you* are never a handicap, but if you go on that way you get to be too much like your grandmother. Raanung, you make a proposal to go with Mra'it into great danger, and I wonder what use that is."

"We who go offworld risk our lives many times in strange places. It is not our habit to let others slaughter us and keep still—anywhere. I don't know how this happens on Sol Three and I want to know. I want to spend what strength I have on that. There are others here as brave as we or more. Let them come if they choose and no harsh word from me if they stay. I say what burns inside me, now I shut up and let all us hungry ones get to our dinners."

"A masterly performance," Emerald said. "Any day now they start calling you an elder statesman."

"Not anywhere I am around to hear it," said Raanung.

Raanung filled his belly and slept for a day and a half. He woke to find Emerald's marbled corneas fixed on his. "What now?"

"The Council are still in their camps across the river."

"Good. They find more things to argue about. They can do that without me."

"They want you to help decide who goes to Sol Three and coordinate whatever group does go. Now they agree they want justice too they are arguing about how to go about it."

"Damnation! Berend can handle that if Nemer twists his tail for him."

"Just the same, they want you to do it."

"Then they say I am taking over everything, and who do I think I am, President of all the Ungrukh?"

"They still want you."

If the Council members had been arguing they quieted when Raanung and Emerald returned. Raanung crouched a body's length from the circle's edge and did not open his mouth. Nemer glanced at him a bit desperately and said, "Please help us. How many of the rest of us must go, and how are we to get justice? Sol Three is a sophisticated world with devices we know nothing about and cannot use. It has its own ESPs and its own hunters. Where are we to stay? and what are we to do?"

Emerald had found a place among the press of bodies and did not worry about Raanung. "Most devices we don't need and the rest we have brains enough to use. One trouble is, most people on that world are uneasy about big cats, because the ones they have are few but savage. Those we send out earlier, we don't prepare for this in the right way, so we must be sure to show ourselves strong without being frightening."

"But Mra'it, who gives us justice?" And Prandra's daughter realized for the first time that there was no Ungrukh left to call her Emerald.

"Does not every world have those who form and administer the law? Maybe after all it is better to forget the dead—and hardly a Tribe does not lose at least one—and keep delivering our best ESP minds to the worlds of Galactic Federation—dead or alive? We cannot tell GalFed to go away. We cannot make war on anyone. But GalFed and Sol Three guarantee to keep our people safe from theirs—and let the guarantee break. We can surely bring charges against their authorities for that."

"And where are we to go?"

"Where else but to that great Canyon, to remind that ignorant world it is not so easy to kill cats?"

There was a stirring about her.

Emerald continued placidly, licking a flake of stone from between her claws and spitting it out, "And send many more. One hundred are invited, not so?"

"By Neap and Flood, Woman!" cried Berend. "We send only twenty-seven from this whole world of near two million! Do you think ninety-six wish to risk their lives now, even if Sol Three allows it?"

"If there is justice—or shame—on Sol Three . . . it is allowed."

Berend said dryly, "I am sure they kill more than a score of themselves any minute of the day."

"Even the most savage do not usually skin *persons*. I know it is impossible to gather so many—and even if we can it suggests we wipe out the memory of the dead. So, one hundred less twenty-seven leaves seventy-three—and even that is an intimidating number. But that man of mine there who gathers this Council is too angry to speak. You, you Scrublanders and Spotted Pinks, Tidesmen and Hills People and Herders of our foodstocks, *you* are the Council with the authority to recruit. If you agree to demand justice, why not go and gather *your* peoples?—and good hunting!"

She turned away in one liquid movement to leave fire and Council, and Raanung followed. After they had gone a short distance he began to hiss with laughter. "Madam Diplomat!" he snorted, and kept laughing even when she bit his ear for him.

17

Xirifor is a chilly wet world whose ocean surface is broken by thousands of marshy hummocks; when its amphibian people visit these to light their fires and pray to their gods they see no sun, and can barely imagine it. Their planet is covered by a cloud layer that hides it always, and before Galactic Federation came they had no concept of *star*.

The Xirifri are low-grade telepathic hominids with hairless skins of dull bluish or purplish gray and huge branching dark red gills that lace their armpits from elbow to hip. Their speech is primitive because the Xirifri mouth is an almost rigid tube with a leathery tongue and spikes of bone on its roof for teeth; the seaweed they eat is very tough.

Tourists on this world are few, and all divers. Sometimes they come to see a mother swimming, the movements of her arms circulating oxygen as they pump milk into the gorges of one or two infants whose tube-mouths, not yet spiked, clamp the teats ranged vertically on her belly. More often they watch the great blue pearls being harvested in the oyster beds, under the eyes of armed guards, though there is little to see but big ridged shells.

Traders are many, and concerned only with pearls and mother-of-pearl. Xirifor's pearls are unique, and it is lucky that an intrepid GalFed Surveyor team considered the world worth exploring. When they did they found the population dying, like the Ungrukh—but not from starvation. Like Ungruwarkh, Xirifor had many quarrelsome tribes, but they did not fight each other. Bitter feelings were so powerful they kept to themselves in small groups until the recessive gene that caused hereditary gill-rot flooded their numbers and shrank them year by year. The people had no use for the pearls; a few were worn as decorations by priests. They had no Khreng with a dream of union. Only a desperate and compassionate Gal-Fed Observer named Berringer with a schoolboy's memory of lessons in elementary biology who realized that the tribes must join to create a viable gene pool or die out.

GalFed had use for the pearls. They brought in a new trading partner and created a thriving community that enriched both parties. Both still hotly debate whether the Xirifri would have lived without the pearls, but a hundred and fifty years later they are still alive.

The only significant landmark on Xirifor is the one created by GalFed to support the Observer Station and landing field. The Station is now a port with a customs house, refinery and trading center where all legal planetary buying and selling are done. The rest of the world is a vast expanse of ocean never completely explored and impossible to guard securely. There is nothing to stop an amphibious shuttle from hiding in its depths and becoming a smugglers' base.

The one definitely known to exist was believed to be run by a consortium of neutrals; they could always find some local hands to help them; payment in powerful spearguns was always good. If some religious group, climbing an islet to light a fire and worship, found a speared half-rotted corpse banked by the tide, they were not surprised. Xirifor's governing council, the Assembly of Tribes, plagued by too many reports of such bodies, smugglers or pearlfarmers, set up radio stations to report disturbances as quickly as possible, but these brought no evidence of sources. There was no official police force except a cadre of guards on oath to the Assembly, but it was easier for farmers to take on cheaper locals.

In desperation the Assembly sent out an agent, a brave and clever young man named Ungrav. Ungrav followed a trail of bodies and rumors for a hundred and fifty sleep-times; then he became a thief of oyster beds.

He did not find this difficult. He had been a supervisor of one of the largest. He tracked the worst area of blight, and, being an efficient thief, soon joined a band of others who were also murderers. His life became harder; farmers were on guard against thieves, and smugglers against informers.

He was never let into the shuttle station and never saw those who operated it. There was no way to determine its exact position because it shifted irregularly, and such information would be useless by the time it reached headquarters. Its guidelights were just sufficient to show the craft's markings—but Xirifri do not read or write: They count and tally. But Ungrav had the trained supervisor's mind; he recorded the markings on the tally-sticks of his memory.

That task completed his mission. If he had not been given a particularly heavy collecting quota, he would not have made one more visit to the base; but if he had missed this delivery he would have been pursued quickly.

His sortie had been dangerous, but he had brought the usual good take. He swam his way toward the distant wavering lights among a tangle of weeds and small sea-creatures wriggling between his limbs. Xirifri needed no personal light but were directed by sound, smell, current, pressure and magnetotactic sense. He was weary and wanted home.

Instead of his usual receiver he found a group of hovering figures blocking the lights. They were not his people, but suited aliens of strange shapes.

Perhaps, in his weariness, he had let down his shield. Perhaps they had been suspecting him for some time. He realized that this was all he would ever see of the smuggler crew; he knew these minds clearly enough. Death. And they knew.

He dropped the oyster sack and reached for his weapon. Before his hand touched it a spear had pierced his lungbook, a second his neck, a third his eye.

One smuggler grasped his body in its cloud of blood, another dove for the oyster bag and brought it up.

:Best not let these go to waste.:

:No. They will look good on him.:

Silent laughter.

Two sleep-times later Xirifor's Headquarters received a message that something interesting could be found in a certain place, coordinates given. The fast shuttle found Ungrav's body speared to a sedgy bank, washed by the neap tide. The skin about his hips had been flayed and replaced as a belt with a buckle of oyster shell nacre and studded with pearls.

The corpse was brought back to the Assembly and the incident might have ended in fury and frustration. But one of its members was Ruvik, who had been an Embassy official in GalFed Central, and whose sister Uivingra was a Sector Coordinator in Administration. He provoked greater furies when he refused to let the body be properly weighted and sunk with its hideous decoration.

:What do you mean, evidence, you sacreligious fool? He sent no message! He should have been buried before decay touched him! Every angry god in the sea will fling us smothering into the sky!:

:I have been flung beyond the clouds, brothers, and there is nothing to fear. Let the gods tear us to pieces if it soothes them. They cannot do worse than has been done to poor Ungrav by the bloodmen, and there is plenty to fear from them. They do not know it, but they have sent us a message. And it must be deciphered.:

There was no moving him. He would have insisted until the oceans dried. The Assembly gave him the belt in fear and trembling, and buried the body with multiple honors in a great hurry.

The landmass had been built up considerably since the old Observer days, and the market and sorting sheds were extensive.

Ruvik put on a waterproof suit—to keep the ocean in, not out—and went to the sheds, where he found Riungh, Supervisor of pearl sorters, in her little office surrounded by scales, magnifiers and samples. She had opened the seal of her old patched suit to pull back the hood, and plugged her nostrils and smeared her face with aqueous gel. On Xirifor skin dries out quickly, even in damp air, and tearducts and salivary glands are almost vestigial. Her membranous lids blinked often, and every few moments she dipped her hands in water and squirted her eyes and mouth. Her status was lower only than that of an Assembly member; she could have idled in great honor, worn a new waterskin every day, covered herself in pearls if she chose, but she lived for power and passion: the power of one with a great skill and the passion to use it well. Ruvik knew them: he found them in himself and his sister Uivingra.

"Eh, sister's son, you have work for me?"

"I think you know that well enough, Riungh."

A Xirifer's mouth leads only to the stomach, and the air drawn in comes out in a language of whoops and whistles. No one finds it pleasant, not even Xirifri, but to Ruvik it was actually soothing after his brainbeating with the Assembly. He removed the belt from where he had tucked it under his knife-harness, a ceremonial decoration with connotations of more sinister days.

"Ugh." She dipped her hands in water, touched the pearls, examined the rough back of the shell buckle. The fingers were nailless: the palmar tips had concentric oval ridges for grip. "You rather not remove the pearls."

"I think it's important not to."

"Unnecessary. Eh, by Gissh and all other gods this is an ugly, but the pearls are lovelies."

"They are all the same blue pearls to me, mother's sister."

"Heh." She got up from her water cushion, hobbled to a murky tank, dug about in it and pulled out a triangular oyster bigger than her hand. Without looking she reached to her bench and picked up a thin round-tipped steel spatula, pried gently, slipped in a finger to widen the gape of unwilling shells, gently winkled out a pearl, rolled it between finger and thumb. She replaced the spatula exactly where it had lain and dropped the oyster back in the tank where it shut gratefully. Then she dipped her free hand into a bin of unsorted pearls, shook them in the closed box of her two hands and held out a palmful. One, the smallest, was spherical and almost white; the rest baroque, lobed, polyhedral, darkening by grades to the big trilobar blue. She thrust her hand at him and he picked the treble wave-ridged pearl. "For all your experience, you have not worked on the farms. *That* is *blue*, Master Assemblyman!"

He matched it with the pearls in the belt and handed it back to her without a word.

She said, "I will examine the shell to confirm, but it is hardly necessary. Only two farms breed them, and they are quite close together."

"You know where they are."

"Of course." She dumped the unsorted pearls in the bin, reached into the bowl and smeared fresh gel on her face and head. She looked up at him with underwater eyes big as pearls. "We have rumor of a message from the smugglers: *Open your markets, Xirifor, and there is great advantage for all of us!*

What do you think of that, sister's son?"

"What do *you* think of it, Supervisor of Pearl Sorters?"

She pointed at his knife. "Eh, first there is a lot of using those, and then the great loneliness and the great sickness. And after, men beyond the world help the sickness shrink and the trades grow. There are still sores on the body, and even I know how to use a gun, though I have not killed anyone yet. Perhaps with free trade I can learn to shoot with a gun in each hand, ahi?"

"Maybe we can heal the sores first, mother's sister."

"The bloodmen are dangerous and very swift."

"But I doubt they will stray too far from the truest of the blue."

18

GalFed Center is in the Twelveworlds, the system of the sun Fthel. In spite of its name it wheels safely outside the blinding chaos of the Hub. Of its six useful worlds the cool fifth houses Central's administrators, and in one of ten thousand-odd conference rooms a group had gathered to deal with an abscess, the kind that plagues all sentient groups. The one in question had spread and was now erupting from sectors in several divisions. Director Dunbar Macpherson Kinnear's division contained Xirifor; therefore he had a seat. It did not have connection with Ungruwarkh, but Ungrukh were concerned, and he knew them longer and better than any others in authority.

There were several objects on the table, and it would be hard, knowing their sources, to say which was the most disgusting. Kinnear was staring at two of them: a red toy cat covered with Ungrukh fur and a picture cube showing one much like it. He was knotting his fingers trying to crack his knuckles, and he had never in his life succeeded. He was near retirement; his face had become a bit lined and drawn; he had lost much of the bland look of his old Security past. His pale hair had begun to thin at age seventeen and grown thinner during forty-seven years without leaving him bald.

A Junior Assistant Secretary, still smooth-faced, said, "Too bad about Jeffy. She was a damn good operative even if she was getting a bit long in the tooth for—"

"Shut up!" Kinnear snarled.

Uivingra of Xirifor, Coordinator of Kinnear's old Sector 492, said quietly, "This is no way to begin, Kinnear."

"Sorry." Again he tried to crack his knuckles. "Where

begin? One more outbreak of terrorism?"

"Going on at one level or another everywhere," said the Junior Assistant Secretary.

"They never spend a fortune sending us samples. This," he flicked the cube, "came—I won't say by luck—came by chance, and that—ugh—skin with the pearls because whoever made it knew Ruvik would send it, but with all of the sources we got the Free Trade blurb. And in one Supervisor's territory." He nodded at Narinder Singh, in mauve turban, white lines running down his beard now. "Could be coincidence."

Medor the Ungrukh, whose physical appearance was much more authoritative than his actual status, said, "In twenty-five years of GalFed membership we hear nothing of free trade in bottled brains until now."

Uivingra said, "When your Observer Berringer brought us into GalFed a hundred and fifty years ago he told us raiders might come from beyond the clouds and this organization was supposed to protect us from them."

Kinnear spoke carefully. "We can't put a force-field around the entire globe, Uivingra, and you have more than enough credit to put up a few spy-eye satellites. I know you and Ruvik can get around your superstitious Assembly."

"Kinnear, I am not worried about superstition." Her voice, which sounded through the suit-mike like a miniature Fingal's Cave, trembled a little, and she pushed the belt forward. The color of the skin was much like her own, and in such a setting negated the beauty of the pearls so powerfully that they looked like suppurating boils. "This represents many deaths, not one."

"I hope you will not consider this less serious," said the Kylkladi man in his high thin voice, while he tapped the last object with a blood-red talon. A block of lucite enclosing a bronze hand ending at the wrist, young girl's hand, gently curled, platinum ring set with a big star sapphire on one finger. He lifted the block and shook it; it rattled. His green feathers rose in fury, the vestigial wing-plumes down his shoulders stiffened as if he might launch himself. "Clever of us to dissolve the flesh and leave the bones," he whistled. "Eight dead. Three Solthree."

"A party of traders in a fight for no reason we've discovered." Narinder Singh, who held the chair, sighed. "When the only trade of yours GalFed protects is in ceremonial feather-armor to three worlds, ten percent of your exports, and you spend that conserving the species—why, Ti'iri'il?"

"I don't know, Chairman! A citizen went mad for no reason anyone could think of and swore a group of traders had killed his wife and family. But nobody knew him, he'd been living offplanet and come in on a supply ship with a friend and . . . they caught the first one, the killer, but the second disappeared with"—he could not make himself say it—"what he wanted. The first one arranged to die before he could be questioned. We found a device inside him like the one I have heard of in the—the Kylklad on Sol Three. That is all we have." The sense of impotence he gave off was painful.

Kinnear said wearily, "I've waded through scumpots on many worlds, and this doesn't smell like any of them. I have also chased many terrorists and caught some. Whatever crafts they use are on weaponry, not samples like these. The Free Trade Association is a blind. A fake. That's what I think."

"And where does that leave us?" Medor asked.

"Pushing investigations wherever we can, hard as we can."

"Not on my world, I trust. Even the worst of us Ungrukh do not skin and stuff ourselves."

"Right enough, Medor. Not yours."

Wallingford Haynes was at the CommUnit yelling at the Security Chief in GalFed's Solthree Headquarters. "What answers? Where answers? We got those four cats, won't move from the Canyon, one nearly skinned by somebody called Charley—try following up on that! Kylklad implanted with a communications device, fused into a lump when she died. You got another one? My God! The Sonotek business with Silver's a dead end. Dead, ha! end. Old pol, backslapper, fleshpresser, wanted it done all right, hadn't the guts of a mouse to go out in the field and do it! Everything's raveled. Of course whoever did it knew everything, had their network in the Mall just like our Security. Jeffries' murderer cleared out—probably they wiped him out—he didn't get the stuff, only did half the job. We knew about Silver's business—three Continental senators just resigned, we haven't forgotten them but they aren't moving a muscle.

"Me? I'm doing every dumb thing that can be done! Digging up all the Charleses, Charlenes, Charlots, Charcots, Sharmans, Shirlies, and you don't have to tell me it's halfwitted. Yes, Enbhor, I know you don't say things like that. But most people who change their names don't let go a whole identity. No? I'm sorry I don't know your world as well as you seem to know mine, but that's the only thing I can think of right now, and I'll let you know when I find a better one!"

Singh noticed the blinking light and picked up the mike. He looked at the ceiling and shook his head. "I don't know what to make of that and don't need to until I get formal notification, thank heaven! But I will let you pass it on to another interested party." He muffled the instrument with his hand. "Medor, sixty-three of your people have applied for temporary residence on Sol Three. Any comment?"

Medor took the mike in his tail, made grave salutation, listened, and said respectfully, "I am very willing to discuss that with whomever is concerned, but I believe it is better to reserve comment until that time. Thank you very much." He returned the mike, blinked slowly, slowly swung his long tail to and fro. "Ha. GalFed and Sol Three find themselves sharing fares plus reconstituted catsnacks and legal fees for sixty-three Ungrukh or they can forget about half a million ESP-ones in or out of their damned blue bottles." His mouth widened in a fanged grin. "There *is* only one way to skin a cat and by damn they are not doing it more than once!"

Uivingra flared. "Are you too full of your own affairs to remember anything else?"

"Don't misjudge me! I don't forget any one of those ugly things, and if they come from a common source it is absolutely necessary for us to work together and stop it up so it never flows again."

When they were alone Singh said to Kinnear, "Now you can tell me what smells like rotten fish."

"You must have been esping unconsciously. That sounds Ungrukh."

Singh started. "Well, it *was* unconscious."

"He's not stupid either. First this doll thing. Then three Standard days later the cube—and a thirtyday later the other two, nine days apart. That's close enough together by our time, but the Free Trade thing has to be a fake. We don't trade in converted ESPs. Or live Ungrukh for that matter. We send fewer conversions into the field every year, because they're clumsy and need maintenance. The long use reinforces neuroses; it's better to look for new sources. With the Ungrukh especially we've been trying to prolong the life span and get more use from them alive. I wouldn't be surprised if the Xirifri had pearl thieves before we got there, and they've still got so many pearls they don't know what to do with them; our interest keeps the world alive and healthy, even if they won't admit it. The Kylkladi trade their moneymakers on the free market; they just like the status they get from having us handle their fancy feathers."

"I agree. Then where does that lead?"

"The Ungrukh have lost most in this particular matter—all those lives—and that's not just my prejudice."

"I wasn't even considering it. Then you don't think the bodies were taken for the brains?"

"Hell, *we* have enough trouble working with Ungrukh—bottled or not. They skinned them on the spot! I think the bodies were just dumped. What's wanted were *skins*." He reached out to touch the doll, and pulled back his hand. "Just for that purpose. The way we used to collect scalps and ears in the bad old days."

"If that's so it makes the other two acts misdirections. Perhaps there might be a settling of some old debt or grudge? It's been thirteen years since the last business we know of, that affair with Thorndecker and Qsaprinel. Why not attack the world? They've got less population than most cities."

"It's still very big and very expensive. Thorndecker found that out on Qsaprinel, which was a lot harder to defend. If the grudgers are on Sol Three, the Ungrukh dropped right in their laps . . . with their skins. The Ungrukh have been on Sol Three, Fthel Four, Yirl, Qsaprinel, and points between. I wonder if every grudge-collector got one. . . . And as for thirteen years, we don't know what could have happened in that time."

Haynes' face was as red as an Ungrukh's. "Sixty-three? I'm packed up and ready to leave here! My men are deployed where they ought to be, and—oh, I don't have to? I'm glad you said that or I'd be in shit with this district when they find themselves supporting sixty-three more Ungrukh with appetites. I'm relocating in Phoenix. I'd rather go to the North Pole and shove my head in the ice, but I'm going to sit in a refrigerator and follow this hunch I don't even dare tell my own superior about or I'd get laughed off the Continent. Good-bye, and good luck to you, too, Enbhor!"

19

Bren, Etrem and the twins had located in a side-canyon off a side-canyon 30 km east up the Colorado where they found the ruins of an ancient two-family pueblo that might have been a summer home or storage camp. Bren had picked up its location when she was esping the wanderings of the twins. It fitted under a cliff protection inaccessible to Solthrees on foot with the narrow ledges and heaps of loose rock impeding it; there were four small rooms and two kivas. Security did not like it because it was hard to keep watch on, but the Ungrukh refused to budge. "We bother no one." Nobody could think of good arguments or actions against them short of tranquilizing and hauling them out, with embarrassing consequences.

Authority thought of archaeology and Indian religion. No archaeologists or Indians backed them. The Park sent a work crew to dig out: in the heaps of rubble they found three undistinguished potsherds and a heap of turkey bones. The Ungrukh were pleased with their home, and the Park arranged to drop food packages twice a month because they did not want the Ungrukh out hunting under enemy gunsights.

The location's real disadvantage to the Ungrukh was that they saw little of their Park and Pueblo friends except when Green Corn could borrow the skimmer and deliver them. The small religious society could not reach such a place, and were afraid to use the old one; they had disbanded.

On one rare visit Many Harvests roasted fish in the firepit while Moon's Woman looked up through the T-shaped doorway where the rim-tops burned in the last light. "My people lived here and grew corn down there for a thousand years. This place has been dead for that time and half again. I think soon we will be forgotten."

Bren blinked in the dim light, much more easy on her eyes than the bright daylight sun of Sol III, and regarded the two eating-bowls and three pinched-coil jars her visitors had brought for collecting water from the little falls past the ledge outside. The place seemed well-furnished to her, and she had a radio for outside contact. "Your people are growing and healthy, you do your best, and there is no shame when others help you." But she did not work to convince him; Ungruwarkh had also learned the hard way.

When they were gone she said to Etrem, "Now they have schools of their own, and doctors and rights. They can work for each other at their trades, or for the white man at the white man's wage, or hire the white man or the Navajo to work for them. If they want to live in the old way they can tend their corn and raise sheep and turkeys. *I* think that is a damned good life, compared to Ungruwarkh."

Etrem was remembering Chief Sun Rising High sitting cross-legged by the fire-pit, face and body marked in ceremonial paint, telling stories in an ancient chant of how his people had emerged through multiple worlds to the surface of their Earth. "They have a history and a culture, and proud feelings about them. We do not."

If Ungrukh did not have much appreciation of beauty, there were some who took pleasure in their beauty.

One morning, in the twilight of dawn, a being slipped out of a small hovering skimmer and stood in the air watching through the T-door while Bren slept with her head resting on Etrem's black shoulder, her tail a great red whorl around his hip.

Two pairs of red eyes opened. Etrem stared. Bren gaped sleepily.

"Hullo, Man of Law. I never know standing on air is a Lyhhrt talent."

"Would that it were," said the Lyhhrt. "But we do have workshells for reaching difficult places. Unfortunately we cannot stay aloft very long. May I come in?"

"Please do so."

He cut the air jets of his shell and stepped on the rock floor.

He was not encased in great metallic splendor this time. His hominid figure was much smaller, with a surface that looked like brushed silver. But Lyhhrt in their right minds could never look like anything but works of art. The metal eyes seemed to see, and the metal lips to speak. "I am quite willing to dismantle myself to show there is no evil stranger along with me."

Etrem grinned. "Not necessary, Lawyer. If Bren does not trust you I think you are somewhere else by now."

"I will be somewhere else very soon. I have some news to deliver officially, but I thought you might like to hear it informally first."

Bren looked hard at him. "My parents are coming."

"Not yet, Bren. They have asked to come, along with sixty-one others. They feel a great injustice has been done."

"Yes. It has."

Man of Law said, "I think you will get used to the idea." She could have sworn there was a hint of irony in that steel voice. The skimmer moved close in and he stepped into it without any display of Lyhhrt virtuosity. It slipped away like a drop of mercury in the early mist.

Etrem growled, "Why does he bother coming to us first?"

"Our people are on their way, without any maybes, and he is their liaison as well. When he meets them he opens his mind to let them know we trust him, and they trust him too." She yawned and settled back against his big shoulder.

"The damned fool wakes us for that? When is it time for breakfast?"

"When your belly growls. Right now it is only grumbling. Sleep."

It had been a night when Bren set out to supplement her packaged food with a quick scurry after rats and mice. She and Etrem took turns at this hunt, and neither ventured beyond her esp range. The heights and depths added distances that were beginning to tire her after a couple of hours, and then she would sleep deep and long.

That noon when the sun shot its beam through the doorway, angling on one closed eye, she woke suddenly and scrambled into shadow to confront Etrem, red corneas alight, pinhole-pupilled, red-white marking folded into a pleat on his forehead, fangs bared and glinting, nostrils wide.

"You are pregnant, woman!" he roared.

"Harrgh!" she snarled back at him, then collapsed hissing with laughter. "What kind of crime is that, you stupid?"

"You are the stupid one! You stink of it for a kilometer!"

"Is it so offensive you cannot bear it?"

The twins shoved through the inner doorway together, spitting and snorting, tangling each others' limbs and tails as usual. "Why do we have to live with these idiots? It is time to go away again."

"Then get away, all of you, if you are so childish!"

Etrem calmed down. "Oh Bren, it is you who are childish. No wonder you are not eager to see your mother and father. You do not think! After all that happens it does not occur to you to take whatever keeps you from having babies, and . . . and when you give me love it is very generous to me, but a danger to you. Your smell of childbearing is one I know all my life on Ungruwarkh but never here, and I only think of it now."

"But Etrem, what is so terrible?"

"Inside you is something very small that grows much and quickly to be a baby you must feed and care for, and if there are ones who come after you with weapons . . . Bren—we must call the Solthrees to take you and remove it."

She did not answer at once. "Your child, Etrem?"

"Even mine . . . most of all, mine."

"We have five thirtydays to work in before it is born. That need not slow me down."

"Bren! I do not want you to have it!"

"I am old enough to have many. My mother waits . . . my grandmother waits—too long, and loses two at the end. Etrem! You are not thinking only of my danger, and I am not even esping you. Are you afraid to be a father? I don't want anyone to cheat me of having a baby, even here, and even now. If you feel so strongly we do not have to stay together."

"Damnation, woman! Think what color it can be!"

"Is that all? I don't care if it is light or dark or a Spotted Pink. You do not have to love it. I don't care if it has red and black squares like Bill Gonzales' checkerboard! You do not make yourself sterile earlier, so why curse me?"

"Because I am stupid too! I don't think of it and I am sorry not. What makes you feel so differently now? Thirtydays ago you tell the Lyhhrt you don't want to go home and mate!"

"Not with some strange person, Etrem. You are one I know and love most of my life. An intelligent man becoming braver every hour by battling fear. The more I think of it the more I want to bear your child."

"The more *I* think of it the more fearful I become." He did not add: I am not fit to be a father; the thought hung like a raincloud over his head.

"If it ever occurs to me to think *I* am fit to be a mother I do not have to get so angry at my poor brother and sister . . . perhaps that is why I wait so long. Now chance pushes me." She stood and the twins peered up at her like cubs. She snorted and gave each a lick on the snout. "I have a lot of practice in doing things wrong."

20

Haynes did not search out the mist-shrouded Charleys of the whole world, but began with the records of Sonotek—dead end or no—shareholders and employees, Continental Government and staff, and also that of Southern District, in search of local grudge-holders. When he came up with the birth certificate of Phoebe Charloe Adams he stared at it in disbelief. She was the widow of Senator John Tennyson Silver, and had a seat on Southern District Council, a strongly independent body which often set itself against Continental. She had an excellent record for prudence and economy, particularly during the term she had served as Secretary of the Treasury, and was on record as having agreed to the original importation of the Ungrukh only if taxes did not have to be raised to provide the partial support required of the District. She was sixty years old and had one son, a criminal lawyer in Northeastern District, and one younger brother tending the import business which had made the family rich over two hundred years.

She always maintained herself very much apart from her husband's affairs of state—even his enemies admitted it. No breath of scandal had ever touched her, and she had no visible facial scars. Haynes researched the Charloe and found in an old record that it marked a line of descent from some royal French bastard. He gathered up the documents, sighed, and shook his head. This was simply too barefaced. Then he went on with his computer search through the rest of the alphabet without finding any other Charlene, Charcot or Shirley connected in any significant way to Silver, the Ungrukh, Kylklar,

GalFed or Xirifor. He shrugged and presented the file to his superior, head of Continental Security.

"But she's clean as a hound's tooth," said Kovarski.

Haynes did not think the Ungrukh would appreciate the simile, but said, "You can't disconnect her completely from what she married. She might well have considered she was doing Silver a favor by taking a whack at some old enemies—and herself one by getting rid of his mistress."

"The cats weren't bothering her and Jeffries had been in place a couple of years. If your witness got a sniff at her and called her guilty it still wouldn't be evidence. Even the Ungrukh have always agreed on that."

"A woman called Charley is still the only lead we've got. There must be one somewhere."

"You can't prove it's this one. Nobody on record has ever called her that name."

"Maybe not. But the Charley we know, she knows a lot about money and power. And loves them. And being married to old Long John, maybe she learned something about weapons and killers too."

She was sitting to the back of the box in black mantilla with mask and widow-black watered silk. These were relieved by the deep breastlet of garnets with a diamond center that flashed at every breath. The diamond-shaped mask, adhering to her face, pointed upward to her peaked hairline, down the bridge of her nose, laterally to her temples. Her eyes, through diamond slits, did not flicker. They watched the actor playing God in a golden mask:

> "I am gracious and great, God without a beginning;
> I am Maker unmade, and all power is in Me:
> I give you all life, and all grace worth winning;
> I am foremost and first: as I bid shall it be!"

The man beside her muttered boredom. He had black clubbed hair and heavy brows; his lower lip was thick and almost pouting. A sullen face.

The woman smiled a little; her lips were lightly colored with a pale orange tint that matched her hair, still a strong red between sweeps of white at the temples. The woman at her other side wore shadow-gray: her secretary and distant cousin, whose hair was gray-blonde, her cheekbones and pointed chin much like her employer's.

The woman in black heard a faint beep in her earpiece and took the little radio from her purse. "Yes, Boris?" she murmured.

"Council page reports special session oh-eight hours tomorrow for discussion and vote on application of sixty-three Ungrukh to visit and settle—"

"What?"

The rough voice repeated patiently, "Special session tomorrow—"

"Never mind! Did they say why so early?"

"They have to get together with Continental and GalFed. The Ungrukh are in a hurry. I recorded it for you."

The man in the golden Godmask said:

> "First when I made this world so wide
> from whirling wind and waters wan
> in endless bliss to be and bide
> with herbs and grass thus I began:"

"Ma'am?"

"I'm here. Do they want an answer now?"

"Yes, ma'am."

"Say I'll be there. I'll corroborate later."

> "I did not then My Godhead hide
> for in My likeness made I man
> the lord and sire on every side
> of middle-earth I made him then;"

"Anything else?"

"No. Just wait in the float."

Sixty-three. She felt the blood draining from her head.

> "Since then men wield so woefully
> and sin is reigning now so rife
> I do repent and rue that I
> created either man or wife . . ."

I have one vote. No time to talk to anyone. . . .

The black-haired man looked at her dully, but did not dare

ask, or much care, what all that was about. He pulled an engraved silver flask from a pocket, uncapped it and swigged.

Let me have men about me that are fat. No! Impervious. Boris was, and so was the pouting man. She had chosen both because they could not be esped: the one for Long John, the other, and others, for herself. They had not failed her, yet.

Boris had also escaped without making any serious mistakes. When Ela Nkansah slipped away and he checked the spy-eye for items that should be tampered with in case they implicated him, he found the substitution. That gave him to think. It was the woman who had the goods. He saw that she had left without the jewelry, had never intended to take it, and considered that his fingerprints were probably on the chest. He immediately shifted allegiance, dumped his sack of goodies, and sent out the warning.

A piece of luck for Boris. The black bitch had told the truth. He *was* in the will, for more than he could have gotten from the fence he dared not go to. So he kept his salary, and his guns. He was safe. Silver had made him take a blocking job; the Madam had it reinforced; he kept his secrets.

So he did not mind waiting in the land-car for Adams and her retinue, like a menial. It was a relief that she did not need the same kind of body guarding as Long John. There was a screen beside the dash and he was flicking models of new guns. A stinger he—

Knock.

He switched the port light. The black-haired man, the current Julio, Diego or Raul, he forgot which. They all dressed like the gaucho-types she fancied in white and black with boots no gaucho had ever put to horse or even afforded. They all went with boys, but her choice wasn't his business. This dago was standing there with empty hands hanging. Boris let the door slide open a crack. "What you doing here?"

"Intermission. But I'm not going back."

Boris grunted. He did not want the fancy-man's company.

"I mean, not ever," said Julio, Diego or Raul.

The recorder button was on the side of the pilot's seat. Boris widened the doorway. "Better come in."

The dark figure hesitated.

"Listen, I ain't gonna shanghai you. I want to know why. *She'll* want to know why."

The man slid in. "I don't want to tell her. She makes me nervous."

"Huh." She made them all nervous. "Anything in particular?"

"No. She provides and doesn't ask too much. But I'm some kind of windup doll she takes out of the box when she wants to play—"

The black woman had done more than that with a life of the same kind. Boris could almost admire her for it. Too bad she'd been a double. But this kind—

"—and it's a one-person game. Hers. You have something to do at least."

Boris agreed. He had spent a lot of time keeping an eye on this one. He wished he had the ability to ask the right questions, appraise the man for risk. But he knew his limits: reflexes and guns.

The dark man twisted to get his hand into his pocket. Boris tensed and began to move his own hands very slowly—

And the hand came out with the silver flask, *Luis* engraved on it. Yeah, Boris recalled. Luis.

Luis put it on the deck; it gurgled a little. "I cleared my account, and I'm wearing the diamond studs, but I can't get rid of a thing with a name on it. Figure I've earned this stuff. Okay with you if I leave now?"

Boris hesitated a moment, decided Luis had an empty head, like all the others and their friends. "Okay."

The door hummed open. Luis slithered out. They all slithered. Free outside, he paused, hands in pockets, and grinned crookedly, first time Boris had seen a smile on him.

"Tell the Black of Diamonds good-bye for me," and was gone.

Boris shrugged, popped the flask open with one thumb, and emptied it. The whiff of greaser perfume on it didn't spoil the brandy.

Half an hour later she came out with her rustling shadow. "Where the devil did he go?" A bit nervous. The secretary clambered in and gave her a hand up. Cozy, the three of them. Missile-proofed.

"He flit," said Boris. "Left a message, thanks for everything. Took his pay in his pocket. Guess he figured he wasn't getting to play the big man."

She snorted. "Did he say anything—in particular?"

He did not ask what about. "Only what I said. I got it on the spool, but it's nothing." He did not want to play the spool; he had a vestige of loyalty to his sex, as much of it as Luis represented. "You want me to track him, or . . ."

She pulled off the mask and rubbed her face with a square of linen. Then examined Boris in the overhead light that turned her face and hair very pale. The look drew his eyes to her. They understood each other. He would do what she wanted to keep his job. But if he casually destroyed one who had been so close, and was so harmless, it was too close for his own comfort.

"No," she said. "Let him go. He's a flea."

He dropped his hand and silently pushed the erase.

She picked up the flask and traced the engraving with a finger. "He emptied it, anyway."

"Naw. I did that," said Boris. He was honest about small matters.

She gave him one more speculative glance and turned away. Her mouth was tight. She really was antsy this evening. "Let's go home."

Like Nkansah, who was dead, he suppressed a shiver. Black of Diamonds. Too right.

21

The Ungrukh, setting out for Sol III to find cause, demand judgment, and secure justice, would have liked to travel on several ships; they had good reason to be uneasy about grouping. But even for them it would have taken twenty-five Standard years of work, embodied or bottled, to pay their share of what they wanted. They got, after hard bargaining, one converted battleship-cruiser, the *Blue Guitar,* and fifteen armed crew, who had their hands, talons and tentacles full decontaminating, loading and settling threescore-odd cats. Ungrukh look much alike, will insist on milling about, and do not care for administrative procedures. Most needed contact lenses against Sol III's bright sun and many required nose filters for the heavier atmosphere.

Between Ungruwarkh and the inner world of its system, Anax I, there is an asteroid belt. No one noticed when a strange object placed itself on the rim where it did not move in the swarm but remained in place, keeping a sharp telescopic eye on Ungruwarkh. It was a new superfast cruiser, small and neat, with all modern conveniences. It had been prepared and sent out very shortly after news of the Ungrukh application had reached Sol III.

It was positioned with plenty of time to spare, thirty-five days Standard before *Blue Guitar*'s scheduled landing and departure, in a wide orbit right above the lava plain where the landing field stood. The crew then set the monitors going and put themselves in stasis for twenty-five days. All was prepared. Nothing needed doing; if it did there were alarms, and if not there was no use wasting supplies. *Blue Guitar*'s flight paths were well-known.

When the timer woke them, the little ship's crew spent a comfortable ten days eating, exercising, checking recorded messages and receiving new ones.

Blue Guitar approaching, landing, loading with confusion and complaints. The little ship's neutral spacelight transmission was garbled, but the target came in loud and clear. The crew could not see the departing ship, but they were very close to its flight path, and soon after the walla-walla of cat growls, crew grumbles, pilot orders, they were on the track of the long powerful shape, transmission shielded, launchers tracking.

Automatics registered optimum and fired.

In half an hour there was a most satisfactory burst of flaming shards.

Small and Deadly fired retros and withdrew to enjoy the radar fireworks. The crew party lasted an hour before the spacelight erupted out of the garble with an explosion of its own.

"—hell you think you bunch of snotheads are doing?"

"Goddammit, we just blew up—"

"*Blue Guitar* left five days ahead of schedule and must be a third of the way home! We picked up their signal and couldn't reach you!"

"That's impossible! We've been—"

"Out of your skulls! Where *have* you been? What the fuck date you think this is?"

"We got 2135 Standard—"

"You—you—oh, you idiots, it's 2147! Who in blue bleeding hell stopped the clocks?"

"We had them running all the time! How could we lose twelve days? We picked up everything *Blue Guitar*'s done—"

"While you were conked out! Somebody played Foxy Grampa with you, but you deadheads aren't going to be playing *anything* when you get home. Not for a lo-o-ong time!"

The crew did not agree. They were a hardy lot; several had killed and skinned a few Ungrukh. But they had contacts of their own and they agreed unanimously to go AWOL and sell the ship to a friendly neutral. Still, before they coked and sauced themselves back to insensibility they ran an analysis of all receptions and decided that they had been hypnotized or drugged somehow and by the trick of delayed broadcast records, blown up an asteroid resembling—designed to resemble—*Blue Guitar*. They did not know who had conned them, and did not examine the question much because they were inexplicably seized with a fear of finding the answer. After that they blipped off and knocked themselves out.

In a corner of space not too far away, hidden in a gas cloud created for the purpose, was a ship the color and shape of an old bell clapper; it belonged to the most ancient class in the universe, and was still the most powerful. Its occupant had planned most and watched all, and if it did not laugh in any ordinary sense it sparked and crackled a little more than usual before it sent a few messages of its own, reabsorbed the cloud and also blinked out of the continuum.

22

She did not know what more to do with her rage except submerge it like phosphorus in the ice water of her surface. Still it did not stop burning. She worked faithfully by day, and on some nights; on others a Diego, Julio or Luis pleased her in the limited ways she chose—as John Tennyson Silver had chosen for himself. The defection of her playmates no longer bothered her, but the discovery of Silver's first ones had wounded her in a depth that was almost disembowelment, for she had served from the beginning as his vitals. She healed herself at the start by force of will, and then by acts designed to turn him back toward her in loyalty if not in passion. She rid him of his enemies, at first subtly, and subtly let him know. But he hardly seemed to notice; he took everything for granted from the loyal old girl. If their political connections never tangled—and it was she who made sure they did not, for he would have grasped at anything—they had at least remained together all these years.

She had married a young passionate athletic man whose body and passions disintegrated as his power grew. At the end she had arranged one great savage act to reach him directly. So savage she dared not tell him until it was complete. And before she could tell him, without thinking of her, he had celebrated with the self-indulgence that killed him. The black woman in the red dress had very little to do with this, for her, Phoebe Charloe Adams Silver. That one had died because she was a spy.

After that, she saw him. In white light on a metal slab, a

grayish mass of unleavened dough. From the few moist kisses, the occasional almost absent-minded fumblings in near darkness, she had hidden from herself what the young hero had become, and how the inward corruption had overripened into the rotten flesh. She had been almost as blind as he. After all, she too looked at herself in tinted mirrors.

The secretary-cousin combed and braided her hair for her while she watched herself. The woman was also an Adams, Mercy, of all names. They shared the good-boned face and strong capable hands of the family, though Mercy did not have the Creole strain reputed to have descended from the wrong side of some Duke's bed, Charolais or Charleroi. Phoebe Adams did not care about royalty or its bastardy. She had enjoyed in private the euphony of an unusual extra name. There were few private things to enjoy.

While she observed herself she was almost astonished that the rage did not burn her into white ash. For she had kept striking, striking.

And the ship was gone. Her most essential and very expensive ship. Some overbearing fool had frightened the crew.

And *Blue Guitar* was on the way with its damned cats.

The strong hands, having parted and braided one half of the long gray-streaked hair, were brushing the other half. Mercy Adams was quiet. She was well-paid and paid hard: She had submitted to hypnosis and chemicals ensuring that she did not speak of certain matters. And she was her employer's shadow in more ways than one: She was the veiled face avoiding the news media and appearing in dim ports and windows when Phoebe had business elsewhere. She was twenty years younger, but minor surgery had strengthened the resemblance and makeup aged her. Her independence of mind had not been stifled; if she did not speak unless spoken to it was her own choice. One that suited Phoebe Charloe Adams very well.

23

O BEST BELOVED I SANG TO AND PLUCKED AT THE INSTRUMENT
TO QUICKEN THE PACE OF ITS MELODY AND WHEN THE UNSEEN GRASPER
REACHED OUT TO DESTROY IT I GAVE IT A STONE TO BREAK AND ALLOWED
IT TO WITHDRAW
NOW I GO TO FOLLOW THE SONG IN THE PATH OF VIRTUE
BUT REMAIN AS EVER YOURS FAITHFULLY KRIKU

This message came over Kinnear's interoffice terminal. He pulled hard copy and stared. Nobody he knew in the office used quite that mode of expression, but somebody far away did. And trust Kriku/Qumedon to send it that way, with brows twisting and mouths pursing at every relay. He suppressed his impulse to crumple the flimsy and fling it in the disposal. He was stuck with it. He had received it probably because he was the only GalFed official the Qumedon knew personally, O BEST BELOVED. At least, if he interpreted it correctly, it explained a little of why the *Blue Guitar* was stacked in orbit around Sol III over Fiji for so long, sending the crew into fits.

He studied it. NOW I GO TO FOLLOW THE SONG . . . Was Kriku suggesting that he was on his way to Sol III? Kinnear wanted that damned Qumedon to keep his devil's mischief away from the Ungrukh, especially in that form. AS

EVER YOURS FAITHFULLY KRIKU. He could warn Kwemedn and bring down its wrath—but Kriku, the one Qumedon Kinnear truly knew, was so shameless he had never bothered to tell a lie—and he claimed to have saved seventy-eight lives.

Kinnear, of the Six Toes he had once been called by Prandra, sat scratching the scars where the supernumerary little fingers had been removed from his hands fifty years ago, and after five minutes of that took the message to Singh.

"Look, it's none of my business. I'm going to retire in two years, and I'm *not* getting tangled up again with that bloody Qumedon!"

Singh looked at him wisely. *Or the Ungrukh either.* Far too many memories. "Why would he send this to you?"

"Oh, he knows he'd have to tell somebody or burst. And *I* know *him*."

"So it's not just some story."

"Oh no, I'm sure of that. What bothers me is his using the name Kriku, what he called himself when he was taking on the shape of an Ungrukh. I don't want him following them. And I haven't the heart to set Kwemedn on him."

"Well, it *isn't* your business, and I don't think you should go out in the field again. You'd be retired by the time you got back."

"I agree, but I don't know whether to warn them, or how far to spread the news. I'm sure plenty of people have seen the message, but they don't know what it is."

"I think the Ungrukh will find out by themselves sooner or later. . . . You know—since I know what you know—I have the feeling we'd just better leave it. We're both pretty sure by now the Qumedon won't hurt the Ungrukh. I believe those two parties somehow belong to each other, and in the end they'll have to settle things with each other. With our help, if they ask for it—and if not, then alone."

24

On Xirifor:

Ruvik, having sent his findings to GalFed, sensed that if he did not finish this business quickly there might be a knife slipping between his ribs when he was on his way homeward in some dark pit of the waters. A few sleeps later he passed Riungh's pearl-sorting cubicle on his way to the slightly larger one of the Manager of Trades. There were maps on its composition walls drawn with grids of latitude and longitude by GalFed makers, and beautiful if inferior pearls embedded in them by Xirifri workmen to mark the locations of the biggest farms.

He touched two of them. "Those are where they reap the big trilobar blues, are they not?" he asked the Manager.

"Yes, and where we've had the most trouble," said Gnarg.

"Who in Port is buying them now?"

"Everyone would if they could afford them." Gnarg, like Riungh, squirted his mouth and eyes and renewed his gel with one hand; the other was busy with a fine wire abacus tallying shell-disks. "Two of the three this last eight sleeps, the Mandu and the Iremi, bought many powers of eight to sell wholesale. The Durbhast bought only one or two powers of eight but they make much of their jewelry from gemstones."

"They have the shuttle of a fast cruiser. They must do well. . . ."

The Durbha captain was waddling toward his shuttle on four stub feet. A short thick cylinder of deep but penetrating orange—a color he assumed when he did not wish to be disturbed—he was using two of the tentacles that emerged from his neck, or rather from the differentiation-line between his braindome and his body, to fan the bundle of tally-sticks, a Xirifri bill of lading, so that he could calibrate them with his band of eye-cells.

Ruvik approached in his clogs—all Xirifri on land wear clogs, for they are almost heel-less—squelching a little in the mud and closing his water-suit out of caution, and said quietly in *lingua*, "Shipmaster?"

The Durbha stopped but did not turn. His eye-cells ran their focus around to Ruvik. "Yes, Assemblyman?" The words came from the slit above the foremost tentacle. Durbhast speak from four sides of the mouth, and always the truth, but they also speak carefully: Their saliva is so important a part of their digestive system that if they spit in fear or anger they burn holes in the surroundings.

"You know me?"

"You are Ruvik, hm? Some of my crew are familiar with you, but don't feel they have the right to make themselves so. What do you want of me?"

"Do you have good divers in your crew?"

"My three divers are the best."

"Are you willing to let them risk their lives for me?"

"Not particularly."

"Not for eight by two eights of the best trilobes, and eight by four eights of the next most valuable, for you to sell or use, and four each of the best for yourself and crew members?"

"None for myself, Assemblyman, but if my crew agrees, an eight for each of them."

"Good."

The Durbha said, "Let me call my divers." He paused and added, "Why did you choose me?"

Ruvik opened his mind and spoke carefully so that he would be completely understood. "First, I need the use of a fast cruiser. Second, I want offworld witnesses for what I intend to do. Third, and most important . . . because the Durbhast are said to be almost as honorable as Khagodi."

The captain was not offended. "Some say that the other way around."

"Whichever satisfies me."

"Things must be in a poor way on this world."

"They will be if we don't hurry."

"I will speak to the crew then." He reached into one of his mouths, removed a minicom and took it from its thick film bag. Ruvik was about to leave him in privacy, but the captain's color had darkened to brown, and he said, "Stay. My people must meet their employer."

When Ruvik saw them, he cried, "Why, these are Solthrees!"

"Why not? Sol Three is a good place. My landsman and friend Enbhor works in GalFed Security there."

"But these worked for me at our market in Central." The three gray-skinned, spine-headed amphibians, results of genetic experimentation, had been part of the Frog Squad that helped rescue Qsaprinel. He recognized them; they were perhaps in the late thirties of their years now, and looked little changed. "Good pickings to you, Esteban, Sheva, Samson."

They nodded sullenly. The air, dry to Xirifri, was so moist for them that their faces glistened from the secretions of their warted skin, and they wore absorbent ventilated bodysuits under their zips. They had always been sullen and frustrated. Only Settima and that ESP Quattro, whom Ruvik had heard of but not met, had had flashes of humor and mischief. Ruvik was one of the few Xirifri who had learned to appreciate such qualities, and after working offworld he was drearily aware how lacking they were in his people.

"Ruvik has work for you," said Imbhi of Durbhat.

"I remember the last time he told us that," said Esteban. "It wasn't any party either."

But Ruvik repeated what their captain had told them, and its price.

Only Sheva spoke. "And this price, what happens to it if one or all of us dies?"

Ruvik was a bit startled. Esteban had always been the greedy one. "It goes to your next of kin, of course." But what next of kin could they—but they were looking at each other, minds open, and he realized that they were lovers—no, mates, and that they had a child. So Esteban was odd man out now.

"I believe I will take my share," said Imbhi. "For the little one. God knows I have enough pearls."

"Agreed," said Ruvik. "I will call on you very soon."

Honest and capable was what Kinnear had wanted for

Qsaprinel. The memory drove Ruvik to an act of honesty he had not planned. He told the Chief of the Tribal Assembly and his two associates what he intended to do, though not exactly. They were excessively harsh and superstitious people, but they deserved his trust, as well as a little of the back talk he had gotten from them.

:And where do you expect to obtain the pearls with which to fulfill your promises?:

:If many weights of stolen pearls are returned to the farmers, they had better be ready to part with a few in payment,: said Ruvik firmly. *:If the pearls are not returned you may do with me whatever you choose, but the people I take with me will be my choice, because I trust them.:*

He volunteered himself and accepted the service of his daughter, because they were both good with knives. Of his friends and their children he collected five: a spear-holder, three knife-handlers, and a shuttle pilot. He gathered this crew with the Solthrees and said, "Spears and knives. No flamers. We want closeness and silence, so the spears are mainly for show, the knives are for use."

With the ink of one sea-creature he drew a small piece of the grid map on the dried skin of another. It was a perishable chart, but he did not need it for long. He had sent the Master of Stores away for a heartier meal than usual, and closed the storeroom for use as a very short-term headquarters. He checked the grid against the wall map and knelt on the floor to flatten his frail chart with one hand.

"Here is the place where Ungrav was found, and here are the two farms." He drew a line with a reed pen from the first location to a place just between the two oyster beds. He tucked the pen under his thumb and, using two of his three fingers for calipers, measured the distance between the two farms, added it to the line and drew a small circle at the end.

"That will be the search area. It looks too simple, and I do not presume that the smugglers are, but I make the grand assumption that they believe *we* are, and did not bother with subtlety in their last move. If they have missiles they will not use them because there will be nothing big enough to home on. Our boat will be hovering well above the sea; when the operation is done we will gather on this islet here and call it down by radio. You Solthrees will use no lights but be guided by us at all times, because you do not have our directional sense. I hired the Iremi to hoist the underwater ship with their grapples so we can gather some evidence for Captain Imbhi to give his GalFed Headquarters. I have arranged with GalFed to pay for this because the Assembly certainly will not, and I want enough pearls left to return to the farmers."

Esteban said, "Suppose the smugglers come out of that station of theirs with flamers?"

"We will make sure they die before they are able to use them."

"Simple."

"And if the danger to us is so great that we cannot take all of them I shall certainly be demoted and possibly killed, but not before I know the identity of that craft. Do you feel easier now?"

"Grandmother's son, I don't," said Ruvik's daughter Va.

Samson said, "Let's just get on with it."

"Since we always get stuck anyway," said Esteban.

"Not if you keep out of the way of our knives," said Ruvik. "I presume you are all good shielders."

All offworld and many local divers were GalFed trained shielders. They had dealings with ESP neutrals as well as GalFed.

The expedition dropped from the boat over the target area into high seas. Xirifor's three unseen moons are medium-sized, and in conjunction produce high tides, but Xirifri do not sail. There was no great activity below to disturb the Solthrees. They had gill filters that screened unwanted chemicials and added salt, so they did not mind the composition of the waters; but they were used to carrying lights and moving in shallower seas when they traded at pearl farms. Ruvik's arbitrary target was very deep; they went slowly at first to get used to increased pressure and greater darkness, and they would have to surface rather more slowly than Xirifri to avoid the bends. But they had been built for strange conditions, and began to feel the magnetotactic sense given them by the combined esp of the Xirifri.

Twice the company met guards. One was known to Ruvik; the other judged trustworthy. He warned them both away. Once they confronted a startled thief, who brought his speargun to bear, and was distracted by the Solthrees while knives worked from behind and clouded the water. Xirifor served very rough justice. One of the knifers fastened the sack of stolen oysters to his hip sheath, and the party veered in the direction the delivery man had been going. They stopped a short while for rest and food; the locals ate weed-cakes; the Solthrees, ravenous on land, did not feed in offworld waters.

Soon after, they began to feel vibration. The station was breathing: The inhabitants needed atmosphere.

:These we try to take alive,: said Ruvik.

Their bodies angled through the water scarcely disturbing a weed or a creature. When they first saw the dim glow of lights they moved very slowly, shields down hard. Ruvik, who had worked in Market Administration offworld and had seen many shuttles, caught the first sight of the markings on the submersible. *:I have seen GalFed and neutral symbols, but never those.:*

:Perhaps they aren't idents at all,: Sheva said. *:Only scribbles for disguise.:*

Ruvik was abashed. *:I had not thought of that.:*

Esteban said, *:You think they've got Mother waiting in orbit upstairs?:*

:Not when they have run such a long operation,: Ruvik said. *:Perhaps they surface two or three times in the Standard year and call in to bring supplies and take delivery.:*

:They'd need them more often—and they could do it by way of your ordinary traders,: Samson said. *:I can tell you* we *don't.:*

Ruvik did not argue with him.

There was nothing to do then but hide in weed clumps and wait for the next delivery. Ruvik was prepared to hang on for several sleep-times, and the Solthrees were willing to starve themselves to a reasonable limit, but Esteban calculated almost two Standard hours until the next swimmer stirred a current. This would make the Station a very busy place if there were four or five deliveries in every thirty-hour Xirifri wake.

The thief hovered. The lock was hissing open, a grotesque figure emerging. Esteban, Ruvik, Samson and three others moved forward to surround them; Sheva, Va and her cousin watched in back for escapers.

There was a sudden blurt of explosion in the top of the vessel and a figure burst from the opening. Va, who had quick reflexes, ducked the hot shards and with a wrist-flick hurled a weighted net over the escaper as if she were the retiarius in a gladiatorial combat; she hauled the twine on the net's edge and drew it tight, bagging the prey. Samson grabbed the delivery man and took away his sack, slashed him lightly down both gills with his own knife, and gave him a hearty shove with his foot. *:End of operation! Warn anyone and you all get flamed!:* He had no sympathy whatever for the thief, and Ruvik had said, *:Take alive,:* but, knowing Xirifri, he thought torture and death would be likely.

The suited alien had time for one short flame burst that caught Esteban in the shoulder; his silent pain and outrage rang in the heads of everyone. Then the smuggler, finding the gun knocked away and him—no, herself surrounded, ripped open her faceplate and smothered. When the attack crew rushed the flooded station they found one unsuited Solthree in the throes of drowning. There was no way to save him.

:Kylklad in the suit,: said Samson. *:You all right, Esteban?:*

:Scorch. Only a flesh wound, huh.:

:Who's in the bag?:

:It is one of ours,: said Ruvik in astonishment. *:An Assemblyman! Lords of all Waters! I warned* him *and he sacrificed* them!:

"So much for a consortium of neutrals," said Ruvik. "A Kylklad, a Solthree, and a Xirifer."

In deference to Imbhi and the Solthrees, the Chief of Assembly and several of its members had made a Council chamber out of the storeroom Ruvik had used for preparing strategy. None of the aliens spoke very well under water. A tank with one glasstex side, kept for sleeping shiftworkers, was the prisoner's temporary holding area. No one had criticized Samson's treatment of the thief. He had put himself at sufficient risk. He and the other Solthrees leaned against a wall; Durbhast kept good medical supplies, and Esteban's shoulder had been dressed with skintex, a strange pink on his gray skin. Imbhi stood patiently in a corner, his surface a dark quiet brown. The Xirifri crew squatted beside him. The Assembly members sat on water cushions except for Ruvik who had been doing his expounding while clumping back and forth in his rattling clogs.

"This was the one who was so enthusiastic about appointing

Ungrav as the agent. Assemblyman, you knew! Why did you not tell the smugglers?"

:You were closing in, too near. I planned an escape I considered well-thought. I did not know there would be so many of you . . . and I expected that inevitably other smugglers would come.:

"Not for you."

The Chief of Tribes stared at the imprisoned man whose eyes were huge-pupilled and expressionless, his palms pale four-point stars against the glass. His skin was a beautiful deep-purpled gray, his features fine; any of the Frog Squad would have been happy to look like that, even with the enormous gills.

"Ungrav was not complicit," said Vorg, Chief of Tribes.

:No, he was an innocent,: said the prisoner.

"Like us," Ruvik said.

The Xirifri anointed themselves; the Solthrees wiped away excess moisture. The Durbha stood still.

"Why did you behave so, Arvir?" Vorg asked.

:For power.:

"You would have had many opportunities in election, even as I. The pleasures are limited."

:Yes. I wanted power on other worlds as well as this.:

The Durbha, a shade lighter, said, "Please ask what you choose of my crew. One is in pain." He was ignored. A streak of yellow began to rise from his base.

"Why did you choose these aliens, Ruvik?"

"I wanted offworld witnesses of whose honesty I could be reasonably sure."

Vorg condescended to look at the captain.

"*I* am a Durbha." Quite deeply yellow now, he passed a bulb of distilled water from one tentacle to the next until he had squirted into all his mouths. "Also, my name is Imbhi, Chief of Tribes. Captain Imbhi."

"Please allow the others to speak," said Ruvik.

Samson spoke without permission or salutation. "All of our crew agree that the ship is Kylkladi. Its lines are imitation—or maybe even genuine—a medium GalFed Surveyor, but many of the interior fittings are reinforced or composition wood, because the Kylkladi like to use it a lot. It's a well-known and unique feature. The ident outside is a composite of three or four similar ones of different worlds. You look at it and see what's most familiar. Now, will you let us finish quickly, please? Aside from the inconvenience to Captain Imbhi, you have a roomful of recovered pearls and oysters to take care of next door, my friend is hurting, and—and I don't care to see your justice done on this prisoner here."

"We are not quite as barbaric as you seem to believe, Aquaman. He will be deposed and exiled, not killed."

"Not an Assemblyman," Esteban muttered.

Samson said, "Excuse us, please. We worked for Xirifri on Fthel Four and found you just and fair. But we've gone into danger in strange waters, and we're tired and sore—and hungry. We'll take a report and the Kylkladi electronics back to GalFed Headquarters on Durbhat as Captain Imbhi promised, but I doubt we have any more information, and we'd like to leave."

"Go in pure water." Xirifri did not thank. "You shall have what Ruvik promised."

"Wait," said Ruvik. "The Kylklad was shielding too hard to be esped, but," he indicated his nephew, "this grandson of my mother caught the last thoughts of the drowning Solthree. They were only so long as—" He looked appealingly at the Solthrees.

"A minute or so by my time," said Sheva.

"I don't know if they are significant, but I believe they ought to be told." He said to the young man, "Go ahead, child, tell."

"Assemblyman, I cannot speak *lingua* well enough."

"By Gissh and all gods, he is capable of killing smugglers and his tongue dries out to speak a word! Give your thought to this kind woman, then."

The boy's pupils closed with gray irises, his translucent lids came down. . . .

omigod i'm dying dying bugger these
fish bastards pearls i'll never get to keep for
gambling away every only just got here oh
mother fuck them all promises shit if only goddammit
i'm dying oh help if only i hadn't
got mixed up
with that
bloody

• • •

"That's not all," Sheva said. "What—"

"I think—"

"Only one more word," said Ruvik. "What?"

"Perhaps a name, but I cannot pronounce it. . . . 'Tchur—' "

"Think," said Sheva. "Try hard. Shirley?"

"No. Tshar. Tshar . . ."

"Charlie?"

"Yes. . . ." Relief.

"No last name, and you didn't get the name of the drowning man?"

"No."

"Huh," said Esteban. "Charlie what? Charlie who? I dunno what good that'll be."

"Shut up. We'll have to take it anyway," Samson said. "Thank you, knifeman. You did well."

Sheva said, "But how the hell can we take all that? I didn't expect we'd need a recorder."

"No worry," said Captain Imbhi. "Whatever room is not crowded out of my brain by honesty is pure memory. I will give it to you intact. Now we leave. Go in peace, Ruvik." He waddled, dull orange, out of his corner and as he passed Vorg said, "Many thanks, and," making some kind of salute with his tentacles, "much good eating of lugga-beans to you, Chief of Assembled Tribes."

25

When the Committee gathered at GalFed Central under the chairmanship of Narinder Singh, one person was missing.

Medor, who had just taken a place, said, "Am I late for this meeting? Everyone is grave, and Ti'iri'il is not here."

"He has committed suicide," Singh said quietly.

"That is terrible! Is it because of the information the Durbhast send you?"

"No. He has been dead a thirtyday. He was spared this kind of anguish, but that is no consolation."

"Supervisor, you are ESP-one!" Medor growled. "You know he is not guilty of anything!"

"I can't see how he could be." Singh glanced at Uivingra, who was sitting tightly pulled into herself. "I have also been trying to explain to Uivingra that it is no disgrace that her people were responsible for the death of a Kylkladi criminal. Ruvik behaved with great bravery and in self-defense. But GalFed has to take some of the blame for Ti'iri'il's death, even though we meant no harm. We asked the Kylkladi Port Authority to hold their merchants in port long enough to be questioned. Of course that cost them time and money and they were very angry, and the whole thing seems to have been flung at Ti'iri'il. He was too proud to make excuses, he considered it begging, and by the time they were cleared and sent off, really without much delay, it was too late."

"Excuse me for seeming brutal, but if that is true I think the man is a bit of a fool. You are sure it is suicide?"

"It's a Kylkladi tradition. Some Solthree cultures have had it. *Seppuku* is the nearest word I can find." He gave a grisly picture. "I am told he composed a song of death."

"You heal one sore on Xirifor, if there is only one, and there is certainly one as bloody yet on Kylklar."

"It's hard to know what to do about that," Kinnear said, "but at least we've given the Solthrees one more connection with that Charley they've been grinding their teeth over. Now let's see what can be done to connect all that to the suspect."

"And 'all that' is no great deal either," said Medor.

"So this no-name Solthree was hired by some Charley," said Kovarski on the Comm. "That's all."

"It helps a little bit," Haynes said. "It's just too bad so many risked their lives and others died."

"The death list is lengthening, Haynes, and you've been the one to put this in motion."

"Kovarski, don't put guilts on me. I've worked at this job twenty-five years and you ought to know how I feel about keeping live people in that condition. What I see in that Ti'iri'il is a foolish vain man trying to be honorable. The Xirifri, crude as they are, didn't set out to kill anyone."

"All right, I admit that's not our job here. We're not GalFed and we don't work on other worlds. You're in charge of this operation."

"Yeah, and all the shit that goes with it."

"That's as may be," Kovarski said evenly, "but you've got to have some idea what you're going to do."

"I have some idea. I'll let you know."

He broke off and popped a tranquilizer and some pills for his high blood pressure. The discussion had been so level-toned Kovarski was probably doing the same.

Alfred P. McNelly watched this and said, "If you have anything, why didn't you tell him?"

"Maybe I've gotten paranoid and don't trust anybody." McNelly blinked. "Oh, don't worry, after all these years I trust you. Hell, I didn't mean what I said. He's all right. I'm just tired of having him tell me anything I plan to do won't work. All this time he's been leaning and muttering, and now he passed me the full crock; I don't feel I have to open it for him. What I have to do is try to introduce Bren to Phoebe without making the fur fly, and hope to get some identification, thin as it would be. But not just yet. If Phoebe *is* my Charley, she's probably been knocked off balance hearing all those Ungrukh are coming. She'll lay low. When they get here . . . we'll see."

26

On a mid-afternoon in late spring the Ungrukh arrived at Port Royal in three military landcars. Here the air was cool and thin, southernmost at the North Rim. They expected to spend a week settling themselves before tourists were allowed back. The investigation, having moved away, still had a few Security buzzers scouting the Canyon to spot-check Bren and her household. On landing day a helicopter collected all four and brought them to the debarkation point.

Supplies had been dropped on ledges and sandbars below, where the Ungrukh requested them. They wanted to keep out of sight until they had time to see and smell their world. Though wintertime business was never crowded, in a few days when tourists returned the very stones would breathe easier under the welcome shower of money after a long dry spell.

The four Ungrukh in the helicopter were very tense. They were not sure how they felt about meeting sixty-three more Ungrukh at once, especially the parents of three of them.

When the sixty-odd cats clustered themselves at the Rim the landcars backed away a little and stopped. The drivers came out to bid their Big Reds good-bye, and three designated Ungrukh thanked them gravely for their help. The drivers saluted, and every Ungrukh hunched the shoulder bearing the knife-harness in acknowledgment.

Courtesies accomplished, the landcars left humming. The Ungrukh sniffed the air, pronounced it good, and started down the trail in single file, pausing every few moments to take note of the folds and pleats of their strange long shadows in the rocks.

But Emerald lay down at rim's edge and curled her tail about her as if she did not intend to move, and Raanung sat himself at her hip.

In three minutes the helicopter landed in the space the land-cars had occupied. Bren, Etrem and the twins jumped out. The pilot waited. The four did not intend to live in the Canyon.

Emerald stood to face her children. Her eyes had not clouded much more since Bren had last seen her. There was no shock.

Raanung gave Etrem his ritual cuff and touched his teeth gently to Bren's undamaged ear. Emerald licked Bren's snout and bit Etrem's ear lightly. "About time," she said. Then her mind rested on the twins, and her shield went down with such a burst of white noise that the Ungrukh women going down the defile stopped and looked up for an instant. She found it difficult to speak. "Do not shrink from me, children."

How could they avoid it? She terrified them. But they came, haltingly, and she nuzzled their necks. She coughed and turned her head to Raanung. *:One day I think they run off again and I do not see them anymore even if I get my eyes back.:*

Etrem pushed words out. "Mother—my-mother, we do our best to make sure you see what is good." He said something else to Bren silently, and Emerald caught that.

"She does not have to do that if she does not wish. Everyone always says I get what I want, and this is another one."

Bren snorted. "Etrem is right, Mother. Tonight I stay with you and Father."

"That is too dangerous. Go home with your pilot."

"No. There are many of our best ESPs here. I am not afraid. My belly is no great load yet." She followed Emerald and Raanung along the path without a backward look, down and around the twisting trail into shadow and darkness among the great points of rock named for the temples of alien gods.

The Ungrukh had had their supplies packed in wooden crates because, in common with all peoples who have access to wood, they liked it. On Ungruwarkh they made rafts of woody shrubs for fishing, and had just discovered the arts of doweling and mortise-and-tenon when Civilization descended on them in the form of GalFed. They had not found the wheel because there was nothing on Ungruwarkh to suggest it. The seas were shallow and the winds light; erosive forces were slow and weak. If the mountains cracked or spewed boulders, the pieces fell in slabs or blocks and stayed where they were. Catches of fish were dragged on sledges or poled on rafts which were sometimes pulled along shores. They realized that rough-edged knives made saws, and so learned a little about woodwork from the crooked trunks of their scrubwood. Aside from the wheel, their greatest mechanical lack was of the lever: They had no way of making a bar of wood or iron long or strong enough to pry a great rock out of the way. They did not have the muscular opposable digit, and a prehensile tail is good but not as good as a strong fist.

GalFed came in flying machines and used treaded vehicles or hovercars, and so Ungruwarkh passed right over the wheel and the lever.

Ungrukh found most useful the materials that extended the development of their own culture: nylon ropes that did not scrape and bite as fiber ones did; casters, carpentry tools of strong steel, prostheses that fit their digits properly—unlike the old whittled ones—and useful implements. Radio was a marvel, but so was a good strong abacus with steel bars and nylon beads. They learned to read and write after a fashion, to handle whatever GalFed technology they thought necessary. They had neither fear of nor contempt for machines, but they trusted their mind pool best.

So it was on Sol III. They pried open the crates, fitted the prepared dovetailings of their parts and made sledges and barges. Some of the leftover wood they put into a great fire and gathered round it, not for eating but for reassurance. With esp they warned the local life forms to stay away until they were ready to observe them.

They grunted and snorted among themselves. There were Tideslanders, Spotted Pinks, Scrublanders, Northerners, and Hills people, who must forge themselves to become one.

The stars came out blazing; they were strange. The rapids roared downriver; those were familiar. The stone peaks surrounded them. They knew something about those, but not the history of their names: Deva, Brahma, Venus, Jupiter, Apollo, Vishnu, Zoroaster. They would learn—another day.

They began to growl. Someone roared:

Firemaster!

The walls called back;

burns through blackness

the stones rang

losing flame in the cold and lonely
searches for a world to save his fire!

Bren began to feel at home;

Ungruwarkh
has no god!
all is lightless
cold and dark and hard!

the walls rang back: *and dark and hard!*

no Tidemother brings water!
no Firemaster brings heat!
he swims the void for the world to hold his flame!

minds echoed: *his flame, his flame*

People, he finds Ungruwarkh!
dives deep into the stone alone
sets the sky burning, sets the world turning
spits out Sun brother
gathers up Icemother
tells them: see the light now, see the light now!
foam into rapids! grind the sands down!

they were home and alone in the great spaces:

I make children, make children
red as hard rock
sharp as stone truth

Bren had heard this one time before, at a meeting of many

hundreds to prevent a battle; it had done so then—after thousands of years of battles;

Firemaster forms them
Tidewaters move them
they cry: Fire and Tide, we live!
no more alone now, no more
I go sleep in the deep of the world
you know where I stay by my breath of flame
and when you see it name my name
Firemaster!

Echo in silence and dispersal.

The voices were not beautiful, and the story was not Qumedon's; it was a gathering of old beliefs put into form only a few years earlier, but it had been made on Ungruwarkh and belonged to Ungrukh. Their first stumbling attempt at art.

Bren, about to become a mother, slept alongside the flank of her mother Emerald and near the bulk of her father Raanung, without the importuning of the twins or the screaming of Embri, the unuttered longings of Etrem, the sense of pain always emanating from her grandparents. She slept deeply and quietly, as did her parents, conscious of the groaning and belching of one arthritic elderly man, the twitching and tail thrashing of a young woman's nightmare, without being disturbed by them.

She woke before dawn while the stars were still flaming, and, content, began her thirty km walk home. She felt safe, as she had said, and shared her mother's dislike of flying machines. Emerald did not waken, but she was one of the few Ungrukh whose esp never slept, and it reached to touch Bren:

:Your son is a Stiller, my daughter.:

:Thank you, Mother.:

So he would be like her uncle Tugrik, one of the big brave handsome males who did not need to compete, whose presence in his Tribe was a blessing to calm quarrels. She hoped he would live happier than either of the Tugriks, her uncle and her brother.

On the second night Bren sent the twins down to stay with their parents. Both parties had dissolved their bitterness; there was nothing else to do: All lives were fixed, and all must salvage something.

Etrem did not visit in this intimate manner. He was not the son of Bren's parents nor anyone else, and he did not care to thrust his incongruity among the people who had repudiated him.

Nevertheless, two days later Bren insisted that Etrem come down with her and walk among his people.

"I am afraid."

"Of what? You are brave enough at other times."

"These are the people I come here to stay away from."

"You lose your fears of sex and love. The ice melts. Etrem, you are soon a father with a son to teach many wise things. Once you are brave in some ways fear in the others does not matter. Come along."

Etrem went down among the shrines and temples. In the depths it was he who matched stone and shadow, and the other Ungrukh who did not. And Bren was at his shoulder, their child forming in her belly. He had never ventured down so far, and the heat settled in his black fur; in a way this discomfort was a blessing because it distracted him. He saw Tideslanders, Scrublanders, even Spotted Pinks, and the fear did not jump out of his loins. His people had learned, through Emerald, what he could do, and had done, and if the respectful greetings he got were subdued, it was because black Etrem had become the least of Ungrukh problems. Like all Ungrukh he appreciated irony.

In a few days tourists came back to hotels and resorts. Security became more subtle and the Indians went back to their more complicated lives: tall vigorous Navajos herding sheep and making blankets and bracelets with the left hand, mining uranium and building power plants with the right; the Pueblos, chunky quiet people, farmed and traded, made pottery and jewelry, sometimes with materials imported from across the world and from other worlds, their private dreams put aside.

27

McNelly said, "When the first group of Ungrukh came a couple of years ago wasn't there an official reception by some District and Continental officials? I seem to remember they invited five or six Ungrukh as representatives and the Cats elected them."

"I should have thought of that," Haynes said.

"I haven't heard anything like it on the slate yet, with feelings running as they are. But there should be some kind of acknowledgment."

"We can blow a flea into somebody's ear, if they're just planning to let it sit. I wonder who was at that first meeting. . . . Hell, Bren's got a radio!"

"No, Mister Haynes. The twins are too young, and Etrem shy, and I don't care for that sort of thing. The meeting is in the Legislative building and it is too hard to bring all of us, but I remember Mandirra makes sure to go and takes her favorite Parender. I can't remember the others, or who they meet."

McNelly dug into the media files for SOL III WELCOMES UNGRUWARKH, and Haynes called Legislature down the street to ask whether Security knew anything about plans for a reception.

"Well, they're fighting over it," said Security. "Some call it elementary courtesy and others bad taste."

"What about Phoebe Adams?"

"Keeping her mouth shut."

"What do you think?"

"They can't just ignore sixty-three—plus the other four."

"Sol Three didn't welcome the first Ungrukh with much fuss," said McNelly. "I don't think we were standoffish, just cautious because it was an experiment. Adams was there because she was Treasurer then, and naturally Long John had to be invited on the Continental side. There were three others from each branch, plus aides, and they look clean."

"Probably be the same kind of show again," Haynes said. "They'll have to invite Bren and Etrem as survivors. I don't think those two can duck going this time, whatever they feel. We've got to make sure Phoebe's there. I've run checks for both Silvers on Murder Night. He was with Jeffries/Nkansah in a restaurant he thought was dark enough, and then home. She was at a late session of Council till twenty-three hours, and that gave her enough time to be on the spot in the Canyon."

The vote went in favor of the reception. Phoebe was invited, and accepted immediately, with courtesy and grace.

"I dunno why, but that makes me nervous," said Haynes.

"What about the Cats?" McNelly asked.

"They haven't decided—but they'll come. They better."

28

Ungrukh were neither humble nor easily intimidated, although they knew their limits. But they had withstood the threats of Qumedni and the spectacle of a strange living universe bursting through their sky. So the Grand Canyon did not make them feel small. But the world containing the canyon did astonish them. Here was a sun that was a blazing star so bright it could barely be glanced at with the naked eye, not the dusty orange ball they knew; and even their own selves blazed with red, not the washed-out pink of Ungruwarkh. The sky was a strange crisp blue; flowers vermilion, orange, yellow, purple; leaves and conifer needles vividly green: colors, tints, shades they were hardly aware existed, the sparkling white band of the Galaxy at night, the deep black of its voids. In four days they had seen two thunderstorms, one that roared and crackled down the Canyon while the sun shone on them; and one overhead that drenched them briefly while the sun burned in a clear sky to the west—that one followed by a rainbow. Perhaps not even a third of all Ungrukh had seen a thunderstorm, and many fewer a rainbow, though, rarely enough, they saw in thin lenticular clouds all the same colors in paler tints. They marveled, sniffed and explored this world, keeping out of sight of the curious until they accustomed themselves to differences in air density and pressure. Then they decided to make themselves more comfortable in thinner and cooler air near the Rims, slowly moving their supplies and maintaining their esp network.

• • •

Emerald was feeling uncomfortable. She did not like the seasonal heat, but that did not make her tense. She was not sure of the reason, or perhaps not sure she wanted to know.

One night she woke under a cloudy sky feeling feverish and irritable. Raanung was snoring beside her peacefully as usual. She felt his sister Nurunda stirring to her other side.

"Forgive me for saying so, Mra'it. I never esp you without permission but your sleep pours out the thought you do not like, and it is a dangerous one."

Emerald knew then. "Bren's belly is showing far too early. She is due to bear in two thirtydays but not show until next."

"Bren is unusually small, and Etrem a big one. If the child is a Stiller it is at least as big."

"It is a mistake for me to let her walk those thirty km."

"She is very willful." Like her mother.

"I wonder if she realizes."

"I think she is very tired," said Nurunda. "But perhaps does not want to know either."

"I don't believe she can give birth normally." Emerald shuddered. "Solthrees have ways to open up the belly and take the child, but I don't like to think of that."

"It can save two lives."

"Yes . . . I am very hot and cannot sleep."

"We are on the wrong side of the flank here, where the sun sets. Let me guide you up to the flat and find cooler winds."

"I am afraid of these rough places. I bring Raanung too."

"Why wake him? Young Mundr seems to be stirring."

"Nurunda, please do not let Etrem know. He is too fearful."

"If he is that fearful he is not fit for Bren."

To the top of Wotan's Throne was a great stiff climb and scramble among loose rocks that tired the Ungrukh sufficiently for them to fall asleep at once, and the low trees were good concealment, but Emerald's sleep was still restless, and before dawn her esp alarm woke her.

"Nurunda, it is too far to see well, but there are enough wakened ESPs to show me that under the ledge over there north at the scarp of the Cape a Solthree male is letting himself down to hide in a little clump of vegetation. His clothing is the color of stone in twilight, and he believes himself invisible. But he has an illegal shield I can lift like a potlid. He also has a very good rifle with a silencing mechanism and infrared sights which gave him a blink of us even in these trees. I warn everyone, but I am saving him for you if you want him." This was not an invitation to risk, but a compliment. Nurunda, of a hunter Tribe, was as capable as her mother Nga had been and far better natured.

"Is he connected with all that is going on here?"

"I think only in the sense that he wants a nice red fur rug for his hunting lodge."

"And how does Security miss that?"

"His companions have hypnoformed their van in the piñon; they are not daring. Security is up northwest and anyway cannot see him or them through camouflage. The Park police are helping with a small fire and cannot be here for half an hour. This hunter expects his friends to pull him up after. . . ."

"He seems to be taking his time, so let us take his too. I esp he has a strong line with a hook like something for catching fish."

"It is."

"And is hanging a slab of meat on it to let down for some young male to smell. He wants a big bright male."

"Yes. He surely does think we are stupid."

"Animals."

Young Mundr rolled over with a huge fanged yawn. "I am a big stupid young male animal."

Nurunda tapped his rump with her tail. "The rest is good. Stupidity you do not need."

"Are you sure you want to do this, Nurunda?" Emerald would have rejoiced in the action but for her eyes.

"I am only an ignorant Hillswoman," Nurunda grinned at her personal joke, "but I do what I can."

"Do not be too rough on him."

"Trust me."

"That surely is a good piece of meat," said Mundr.

Nurunda hissed with laughter.

"I mean the bait."

"Do not eat the hook."

The morning wind coming down off the Rim brought a few micrograms of raw meat scent to his very fine nose. He rose, yawning, and scrambled over the side of the Mesa, slithering down along the ridges, but never losing balance, and moving very quickly without much effort.

Emerald knew that many had wakened salivating, but also appreciated the danger. She had made sure they did.

Mundr, having reached bottom in twenty minutes, now took his time. He was not one to rush headlong like his Tribesman-warrior namesake. Perhaps this was why Nurunda, with Ungrukh irony, had given her son the name. He stalked, sniffing around rock and scree as if he were after live prey. Hunter, hypnotized with watching, did not notice that Nurunda was no longer on the flat. Emerald made sure of that as well.

The big male cat was clear in the dimness through infrared. Beautiful. But time was running a bit fine. There was a good three kg of meat in that chunk, and Hunter did not expect to let the big cat put a tongue on it. Cat was a few meters away now, coming up the rockface. Crosspiece aimed between and above the eyes at the point of the black V, such good resolution he could see the very thin white line in the center of the black. But a shot through the eye might be best . . .

And the cat lifted his massive head, looked up at him and grinned just as a very hairy red limb came round his shoulders, his hood was pulled back and a hot wet rasp tongue licked the nape of his neck. Every hair on his body stood up.

The *lingua* was low and rasping as the tongue but very clear.

"That is my son down there and I am sure you do not want to break a mother's heart."

He stood in paralysis while the prehensile tail plucked the marvelous expensive piece of technology from his hands and smashed it against the rock.

"Now, I am not harming you in any way. The police are coming in one minute, and I think there is a trivvy news helicopter about, because they seem to get here quicker than the police. We just stay as we are until they come, and I doubt there is a charge against me for defending my son by smashing your gun, because it is illegal in this area, not so?"

"Unh," he said, with the arm against his windpipe and the hot breath in his ear.

The trivvy people got a good shot, and were refused an interview, politely. "You see what there is to see," said Nurunda. "My knife is in its sheath and this man has no scratch on him. I am content to give him to the police."

The police shouldered the media people aside and removed Hunter. They were a mixed group of Rangers, Park, District and Tribal police. Some had surrounded the van.

Bren's old acquaintance, Oliver Son of Two Spears James, had been drawn in by the emergency call. He pulled up the fishline and said, "There's only a shred of meat on this hook."

"Originally it is a good three kilos," said Nurunda.

"A very good three kilos." Young Mundr scrambled up licking his jaws.

Nurunda laughed. "He takes the risk, he gets the meat."

"That *was* a risk, you know. It could have been poisoned."

"We know too well. But even curare doesn't work without ground glass. We are with him on every bite, for taste, smell and texture."

"Yes, I think I can hear everybody swallowing out there." Son of Two Spears looked thoughtful. "We found the van with the other hunters where you told us. We can't prove they had intent. . . ."

"No. They try to persuade him not to be a fool."

"I suppose they'll plead that. Um . . . we did haul in a hefty lot of unlicensed venison they'd have to prove they took outside the park, and since they *were* accessories once they gave in and brought him here . . . maybe we can bargain and confiscate. I'll have to talk to Security."

He came back in half an hour, grinning. "They decided not to hold a hearing over it. We can ease up on those guys. They've sweat themselves into jelly already. Just say where you want it."

"You take care of that very well, my-sister," said Emerald.

"Yes indeed, I am very circumspect. I do not say I can lick his scalp off with my tongue, or crack his skull with my teeth, or even think of slitting his belly to let the tripes fall out. I truly restrain myself. And by damn I am hungry!"

Emerald, forgetting her troubles for a moment, snorted with pleasure and closed her cloudy eyes to remember the younger self, the Plainswoman who was long and rangy like the Hills people, and who loved to hunt with them, shoulders to Nurunda and Raanung, sheath slapping flank behind Mundr and Nga. And remembered that they were so fierce because some chemical in their spring water took fertility from fish and women, until they must battle others for water and food, and live endlessly suspicious and destructive among themselves. Not a joyful life, looked at closely, old bully of a father scared of the snarling mother, failing and dying ignominiously . . .

"Do not worry, Mra'it. We never become like those."

"Everyone says that, Nurunda."

29

A Security gun in a buzzer collected Bren and Etrem to meet the skimmer with the other Ungrukh at Cape Royal. Bren was so cross as to be almost cross-eyed.

"There is no use in it. It is long ago and I can make mistakes in identification. I know why my mother is worried and I do not want to be carted about everywhere like a nursling and I am perfectly sure my baby—"

"Bren," said Etrem, "enough."

"—can be born perfectly nor—"

"Bren. If a hundred and forty-five kilos of Etrem can admit fear so can eighty-five kilos of Bren."

Bren shut up and bit the end of her tail.

There was no question of food at the reception. Ungrukh did not sit at tables and eat off dishes or drink from cups. Neither would they take refreshment from bowls on the floor of the Legislature. They passed along a receiving line of officials separated by a meter, necessary to accommodate long cat bodies, convenient for isolating Solthree scents.

One by one, Bren and Etrem, witnesses and representatives of the Plains; Raanung for the Hills; Ghemma the Tundra herders; Menirrh from the Scrublands; designates of Spotted Pinks, Tideslanders, Valley herders . . . There was a grand confusion of scents because so many men and women wore artificial ones—perfume, cosmetics, deodorant, salve. Each Solthree reached out a hand palm upward and every Ungrukh looked up and for a second rested a forearm on it. The Solthrees must have found it unnerving to allow that scarred padding and raw fur, even with claws retracted, to touch the vulnerable inward skin.

Phoebe Adams, red-white hair braided round the head, wearing plain-cut black with a faint glitter, smelt least of perfume or cosmetics. Bren, smaller than the others, could not raise an arm as high except by rising on haunches, a position Ungrukh used but did not favor. She did not rise, but lifted her forearm even rather lower than need be so that Phoebe must bend a little to greet her. Red eyes and gray looked at each other.

Bren had pushed down her fear; except for the small deliberate act intended for observation rather than provocation, she had set her mind firmly on neutrality in meeting a stranger suspected of murder. What she took away was a subtle confusion of scent and perhaps something more than self-assurance in those calm eyes, though she could not define it. She resisted the impulse to give a twitch of her notched ear before she passed.

After everyone had been received, the Solthrees made a short formal speech of regret for the tragedy and hopes for a new beginning, and the Ungrukh made a short formal speech of thanks for permission to visit the beautiful world of Sol III. These hypocrisies committed, since there was neither food nor other agenda, the parties separated. Bren and Etrem were carted downstreet for debriefing in local Security Headquarters, and the rest of the Ungrukh went to wait for them in the skimmer.

In the office they faced Haynes, McNelly and Kovarski, the last a tall thin man with an olive face and black curly hair. In one corner Man of Law was standing with arms folded, like a switched-off machine.

Etrem found another available corner and spiraled himself into it. Bren sat, with hind legs tucked and tail wrapped, and said, "That is not the woman I leave clawmarks on."

Kovarski barked, "You sure?"

"There is a dog's breakfast of scent in that place, but Adams is relatively free of the artificial. I make her bend to get close to me, and as far as I can tell in those circumstances she never comes near me before."

Kovarski rolled his eyes to the ceiling and Haynes turned

brick-red, but when he opened his mouth to speak Bren overrode him. "Do not bleed at the nose, Mister Haynes. I do not have much skill for an Ungrukh woman, but I know that is one damned hard Solthree woman. She is tough enough to stand straight as a pine tree for a year until I rise, but she is sure enough of herself to bend and give me her personal scent. If I think there is something in her eyes more than she plans to show, it may be my imagination."

"Leaving us with nothing!" Haynes snarled.

"And there goes your Charley," said Kovarski.

"Maybe *your* Charley," said Bren. "Mine has five scars and this has none. This one has no fear, but I bet you mine does, even as I do. And there is a smell of *my* Charley about this woman."

Kovarski made a dismissive gesture, but Bren went on calmly, "I think Phoebe Adams—like some other persons—considers me stupider than I am. Skills or none, I am smart enough to value Etrem more than anyone else does, and his nose is a very good amplifier of scents."

Etrem raised his head and opened his eyes, two disks of eyeshine swimming with colors like those on soap films.

"Mr. Kovarski, your wife is pregnant, but I cannot tell the child's sex from hormonal scent."

Haynes was inordinately pleased to see Kovarski turn magenta.

:By the Blue Pit!: said Etrem. *:The man is so upset—is it possible the child is not his? Or the wife?:*

:Tcha! he feels it is private business and fears seeming vulnerable by discussing it. That is all.: "Mr. Kovarski, Etrem is trying to tell you that people smell not only of their own bodies but also of those who touch them, as inland air smells of the sea it sweeps over. It does not occur to Adams that the sweat or oil of whoever helps her dress or arrange her hair stays on her. Even though I am quite sure of it, I cannot call it evidence, and I am sorry to be of no help."

Kovarski sighed. "Madame, there are sixty-three of your world's people waiting for us to give them *something*, and even if it turns out to be nothing we'll have to work on it." He said to Haynes, "Who all hangs around Adams?"

"One of them is a shadow that goes in and out with her. Mercy Adams: cousin, secretary, slave. Subs for her in a veil getting in and out of flyers when she wants to be elsewhere."

"Does her scutwork, okay—but murdering? Skinning?"

"Even without what Bren says, we know our Phoebe's one tough article. Blocks, hypnosis, what-d'you-want."

"As far as meeting *that* one again, I do not want," said Bren. "Nor the other."

"You've already suggested *she's* probably scared of you. But we can take over on this for a while and leave you alone."

"Good."

Haynes scratched his chin. "Doesn't mean Phoebe couldn't have been there all the time . . . in the moonlight . . . watching the slaughter and laughing her head off."

Bren closed her eyes. "Man of Law, why are you here?"

"To observe the official reception by esp and collate whatever may have been found."

"Supposing you find something you call evidence, what do you do for the sake of justice?"

"Whatever is necessary. An inquiry, or a prima facie case locally, likely appeals to Continental because she has too much power in the District. I will not be arguing any case, because I am Liaison; you would have a prosecutor in whatever court tried her. If I could I wouldn't want to do it locally."

"And all of what you are saying, to use a local expression," said Etrem, "is sweet bugger-all."

"Exquisitely put. But I agree."

Haynes said patiently, "Phoebe Adams is the widow of John Tennyson Silver. She knows what he knew. She controls what he controlled. His servants, his contacts, his influences. She had the 'Charley' tag, possible opportunity, a fair-sized motive. We have to push. Especially now, when Ungruwarkh wants it."

"Ha. One day I say I come back and visit with my grandchildren to see your justice. At this rate I do not think I even have to go and come."

30

When you see the dead they look like things that were lit up and got burnt out. Some insight. Did I see that in those cats? Things. Him on the slab? Thing. Was there light in him even half the years I knew him? Half the years I thought I knew him? Did he know me? He knew I was loyal, knew when to come in out of the rain. Not when it was raining on me. I cursed him for not caring. Wrong. He didn't know. Stupid-cunning. When I miscarried he was away screwing some whore. I lost the one who should have been like me, taken my place. Beautiful redheaded kid, perfect except she was dead. My body killed her, cord around the neck. Never knew light. I got stuck with the other one like him, baby nearly forty years old. Fat around the jaws, fat belly, married that sharp little thing, wonder he got in her long enough to make two kids without being cut into pork chops. Graying around the edges, he'll look like—and I won't be able to stand the sight of. Him. *Why don't you come oftener and stay longer, Mama?* Sappy grin stops at the eyes. Him. At least she has the sense to shut up. Either of them goes for politics it'll be her. He has the sense to know what he hasn't got, brains, and what he's happy with, money. He was always thick and dim. That rotten slob I took had light in him once, magnificence. Like a flare, meant to flash and burn out, and I saw the stains of light in my eyes for years when it was gone. Poor Phoebe, you stupid cunt.

Nobody to talk to but you in the mirror, shadow-Phoebe, combed by shadow-Mercy. Dim. Dim Boris, gun for cock. Bullet head. Useless. Wonder if they ever get it on, like to see that, nah, their beast with two backs exciting as a kitchen robot. And look at you! Saving the place for him, took those dago faggots because he had it, like an old lighthouse, maybe once or twice a year and a son of a bitch of a job to fire up.

Nobody, nobody to tell what I did for him, waiting for one look straight in the eye. Never even looked at that black bitch, on those tapes, hands on, yes, eyes in the mirror—couldn't you tell anyone either, you old pirate?—eyes in the food, eyes in the bourbon, guzzle and slurp. Eyes turned in, who to stab, who to suck up to, where to kick ass, how to squeeze it out of the business like a pimple where nobody'd see. And I did all that for him, so what? What did he care that a few cats cost him a packet over Thorndecker, and GalFed tapped him a couple of years? It came back, he grew money like weeds. Did him no good, my doing.

Me. Me it did. All that was killed in me, I killed back. With the poison nothing to see—but in the moonlight, with the white snow, all of them there for me with guns, from the ratholes, snake pits, black cellars. And you, red on white, with the blood ready to burst out of you, red on white. For me. Another kind of power.

And I'll have both kinds when I sit in that seat of his, faithful widow, prudent careful manager of District Treasury. That seat to begin with. Because I've also lost a lot, spent a lot, know where to get more, where to sink my teeth, what arm to twist, what ass to kick and where to put the knife.

Those ones who think they know and can't prove. Like Zeno and his infinite dotted line, Achilles racing the tortoise can never occupy the same dot, the number of dots never ends, and my line stretches over the Galaxy. I've paid my debts, I'll call in his, I will consume him until there is no shred, no memory of him left.

And you two, you with the red eyes and you with the sharp nose, who think you know, I will have your blood and consume it, and him, because there is infinite space between the dots, and there will be nothing left in it. Nothing.

31

The ad hoc Committee at GalFed Central gathered to confirm that there was nothing much doing.

Kinnear said, "As long as we're calling ourselves Ad Hoc, I wish we had some hoc."

Singh was glum. No matter how he turned it about he did not know how he could have solved the Kylklar problem or saved Ti'iri'il. He had held a position like the Kylklad's in his younger days and struggled through the same difficulties. The difference was partly one of culture, probably; but Singh, every bit as moody as Ti'iri'il, was not the kind of person who committed suicide. "Business on Xirifor a hint, no more; Bren meets the putative Ogress: a faint sniff. Perhaps we should be glad things are quiet. At least we haven't heard anything of your friend Kriku, Medor."

Medor grinned and refused to bite. "If he wishes to be a friend, let him show it. Otherwise let us not hear from him."

It was no fault of Kriku/Qumedon's that he had not been heard from. When he broke into the continuum with his course set for Sector Heliones and aimed at Sol III, he found himself in a starswarm on the rim of a magnificently flaming galaxy which was certainly not his destination. He was about to be caught up in the orbit of a planet he did not know, but he was knowledgeable enough about the area to recognize in that blaze what the locals in Heliones called the Andromeda Nebula. It was a good feast for energy consumers, but it held many deadly traps in a maze of turbulent forces far greater than those of his homely little spiral. Qumedni are not immune from fear. They usually call it caution.

He quickly pulled himself back into subspace and wrapped himself in a time-bubble. There he carefully examined his vessel. He discovered that the degausser had been activated for some nonexistent planetfall without giving a signal, probably while he was congratulating himself on the exploding asteroid. Repair needed only the replacement of a few silicon chips, but he was annoyed that a piece of equipment only a few millennia old and quite new by his standards—Qumedni made things to last—should have betrayed him. Perhaps a cosmic ray had hit the instrument and warped direction; he would not bother with molecular analysis. Perhaps it was time for Qumedni to make ships of nonferrous materials that did not have to account for planetary magnetic fields. A new idea to take home. But why bother? He would get no credit for it, and in another few thousand millennia some bright new sparkler would jab the old ones into doing it. He made repairs and continued on true course.

For several blessed days nothing happened. Bren felt the stirring in her belly and did her best to go on living as usual with Etrem and the twins, trying to disregard the increase in Security buzzers. It would have been more convenient for everyone if she had been content to move down among the rest of the Ungrukh instead of maintaining a doubtful status as a source of worry to Etrem, her parents, and Wallingford Haynes. Sometimes she even wondered if she had inherited only the flaws of her forebears: Emerald's dangerous stubbornness, Prandra's impetuosity, Tengura's crankiness, instead of their talents and powers. But she could not give up the independence she had worked for, no matter how small and foolish it might seem. Etrem, gaining bravery and a sense of self-worth, had kept patience and kindness.

And what do I keep? she asked herself.

"The love of these twin children," Moon's Woman said quietly.

She opened her eyes into the dusk. Eagles were screaming after mice. Many Harvests had prepared the firepit and was spitting bronze carp the white man had brought to the river hundreds of years ago. Now Many Harvests guided the white man on the river and took a few fish sometimes for his Ungrukh friends. Etrem and the twins were dozing in their rooms waiting for supper.

"Moon's Woman, am I speaking to you unconsciously, or are you an ESP?"

"Perhaps a little of both. I like to believe I have a few powers. At least I have a paramedic's certificate! No one can prove cornmeal and tobacco rituals don't help antibiotics." He added shyly. "Nights ago I heard your chant of Firemaster."

"From where you camp twenty km away? You know the story from the twins. . . ."

"Do you know all the words, Bren?"

"Not without help."

"Firemaster!/burns through blackness/losing flame in the cold and lonely . . ." She caught even the rough harmonics under the words.

"Forgive me for doubting you."

"No insult."

"On our world it is!"

"There are insults and insults."

There was some bitterness in his voice. Some of his people came to him only when they had waited too long for the white man's doctor. She turned the subject. "You call the twins children." They were, for him, because he loved them best among Ungrukh and they returned his love.

"You can see yourself that they are . . . stopped. They can reason and act like adults, but they shy away to play and love, play at love, demand love—childishly."

"Yes. It is a pity others cannot recognize that. Tcha! They are surely jealous when my son is born."

"I will try to make it up to them."

Many Harvests looked up from the firepit and down again. Another jealous one. Another who had searched in the cold and lonely.

And nothing to be done about it. She dozed with the smell of grilled fish resting pleasantly in her nostrils. The Ungrukh would have eaten the fish raw, but the cooked meal was a gift shared with friends.

Moon's Woman first heard the hum of the skimmer. "That can't be Green Corn back so early."

"No!" Bren jumped up. "Get back! Away!"

But Moon's Woman, crouching, gaped in a paralysis of astonishment.

Lights flared into the window and split the dusk, half hiding the bulk of the vessel, armed figure standing in the open bay doors.

Many Harvests sprang to knock down Moon's Woman into the shelter of the wall and caught the exploding bullet in his left shoulder. The slow fire bit and he screamed.

Etrem came running, Orenda howling after, "No! Stop!"

The skimmer moved sideways to the door. Moon's Woman pulled himself up to reach for Many Harvests. Bren tripped him with her tail and whipped after, but the burning man, screaming, "No! No!" in pain and fury, had kicked the fish off the firepit, pulled off his hat with his right hand, plunging it into the pit to grab live coals. He ran to the doorway and shoved the coals and his burning shoulder into the belly of the figure, the armed man, stepping over the sill.

Screams joined; both figures fell outward, the intruder's head knocked against the edge of the bay, rocking the skimmer, before both buckled and dropped flaming and screaming. A black streak passed Bren; she howled, "No, Etrem!"

A woman's voice yelled, perhaps only in her mind, "We'll crash! Get out of here!" as Etrem launched out the door into air.

The skimmer pulled away and was gone; the screaming, the burning, fell, paled, echoed.

A few coals glowed in the pit. The fish lay scattered, their smell of roasting overborne by that of scorched flesh. Bren lay unable to move with the pain of burning, the sounds of screaming in her head diminishing into silence and death. Her belly cramped, but still she could not move, her mind full of fire and agony.

Etrem pulled himself over the sill, panting. His fur was thorn-caught, his feet bleeding from the slides and tumbles he had taken before he found a ledge to hang on. "A few branches catch fire, nothing to spread. Best not go down there."

Moon's Woman said faintly, "He's dead, isn't he?"

"Both," said Bren.

"He died to save me."

"Us."

"You would not let me help him,"

"If I do those ones come in and kill everyone. It is Ungrukh they are after, and they need no witnesses either." The pain in her belly licked at her, one spasm, and ebbed. Not this time.

"Do you know who they are?"

"We believe, but cannot prove."

Etrem rubbed his head against her neck. "You are unhurt?"

"Yes. A cramp for a moment. Gone now."

"Good. Bren, my hands are sore, and I am too clumsy anyway to use the radio."

"I call," said Orenda, and did.

"Bren," Etrem said. "It is time to move."

Bren was thinking of the look in the eyes of Phoebe Charloe Adams. Anticipation.

There was a bowl of water in the corner. Etrem drank some, dipped his sore pads in the rest and licked them dry. The twins groomed his fur with claws and tongues. Bren watched Moon's Woman, crouched staring into empty darkness, mind clamped like an oyster shell. She did not have the strength to pry it open and draw out the grief.

Haynes rubbed his eyes and heaped the pillow under his arm. "What in bloody hell happened with Security?"

"Mr. Haynes, sir, all the credit that can be spared has gone into it. Six men in three buzzers can't pass any particular place more than once in two hours even with extras and overtime. And the skimmer had a tourist ID, probably rented by Anonymous. Those four Ungrukh know they have to move out now, but we couldn't sit at their doorstep like a terrier at a rathole!"

"All right, all right! Did you find out who the dead killer was?"

"We're working on it. The bodies were still hot and charring when we . . . they—they'd fused. . . ."

"Oh God, don't give me details! I'm sure you've got cell records and samples—if there's any cells left. No use my coming down there with the magnifying glass. Nobody else got hurt at least."

"The other Indian fellow, Moon's Woman, is in shock. Etrem tried to go after attackers, lucky not to land head first. Some abrasions, needed cleaning and shots. Bren had contractions, we had the doctor check her. I—I think what we really need is a vet."

"Better not say so! The Ungrukh have their own paramedics and know where to send her if she needs treatment. Call me again if the Tribes get excited, but I think their Lyhhrt will probably handle them better than I." He broke off and called Mall Headquarters. "Trouble in the Canyon—you got that? Okay. Gimme all-staff and night-owl alert on Adams and her building, especially the Mall: stairs, ramps, elevators, turnstiles, cans and wires. Don't lay a finger. Just who's going where." He deactivated the bedroom unit and rolled in a blanket on the study couch for his wife's sake. He did not expect to sleep through the night.

32

Boris did not know whether the world was pressing on him or receding from him. Phoebe Adams was keeping him on tight rein, but giving him less and less to do. Her cousin and her maid took care of her person; the longtime cook who had served both Silvers provided the meals. She had hired a new pilot and another bodyguard, no fancy-boy; there had been none since Luis. Boris was being kept on as a house watchdog and he did not like the job, but he doubted he could quit it easily. His room was cramped, he missed the space of his den and the apartment he had shared with Silver and Nkansah upstairs. Now it housed the pilot and ambulant bodyguard, and if the rumors he had heard were true, Adams was going to use Silver's office for her own reach for his seat on the Continental Council.

He had the feeling he was going to be dumped—in the worst way. As a judge of the soft ones, the pretty boys, he was unsure of himself. The murderous and larcenous he knew. He had saved Silver twice from assassins, killing both, and convinced still other pests that they ought not to blackmail him.

Adams was a hard one. He had not pleased her by allowing Luis to slip away on his personal decision, and what he saw in her eyes since then made him uneasy.

Unless he could think of something to save himself he was done. He had no—dared have no—connections who could clear his mind and give him strong blocks for his own protection. He had no trustworthy ESP to warn him when a rifle shot might pick him off from a distance or a knife slip between his ribs in a crowd—to do the things he had done for Silver because he was savvy enough not to need esp.

And no one would worry about his disappearance. His type was expendable; he was forty-four, his reflexes were slowing. He would be going down rungs in the employment ladder—falling right off if he were being hunted. Under his grandmother's surname there was a bank account no one else knew of, for emergencies, nothing fraudulent, all he dared siphon off from his salary, check and double-check secret from *her*, all-seeing Eye, because his main savings and inheritance from Silver went into the bank Sonotek dealt with. His only other secret was an illegal weapon, a heavy-duty stunner he had seldom used because he did not need it.

Everything else had been taken from him; his woman had given him up because he was kept on so tight a leash. He crept out once in a while to find somebody, but most of the time was too scared to feel horny. All the time he had felt put-upon guarding that old scumbag Silver, kitchen duty and cleaning up after a man with unlimited appetites—that had been paradise compared to this, the tension something he could bear. Now it was pure danger.

He sat brooding at trivvy images, sound turned down, door slid open a few centimeters: on alert. He had always drunk little, to keep what wits he had, and now had given up that little. Adams had no bourbon; she took a little gin in public and herb tea in private. Because his room was near the entrance he heard the fumbling at the lock: somebody having trouble with the key. Adams maybe, but not drunk.

No alarms ringing; he reached the door just as the key fitted properly and the veiled figure came in.

"Hullo, Boris." She turned back the veil. Mercy Adams in red wig streaked with white. She pulled off both together and shook her hair out of its knot.

He grunted. "Thought it was her."

"She had business and I had to use her opera ticket. Fucking *Jason and Medea*. Hero deserts woman. Woman kills kids. Ugh."

Her eyes were blue, not gray. Her lips, unlike Phoebe's thin ones, were curiously fleshy, more than Nkansah's, lips sometimes seen on narrow-headed Caucasians and looking odd because they did not seem to fit. The cheekbones and chin were Phoebe's, the high forehead was not.

"I gotta get out of this stuff. Will you check for messages?"

That was not his job, but he shrugged and went to her cubbyhole of an office and punched keys.

BORIS GET THE CONSTITUENCY FILE FROM OFFICE DESK UPSTAIRS NEED IT TONIGHT P ADAMS.

"Why didn't she mention this earlier?"

"Probably reminded herself." He followed her down the corridor a bit and rubbed his dark-bristled jaw, listening to her zip, zip, rustle.

His brows drew down. "Who brought you home?"

"Tragg." The new bodyguard. "Why?" Her voice was muffled from pulling Phoebe's silk and taffeta over her head.

Phoebe didn't take me, didn't take him. . . . "He's up there in the office, ain't he?"

"She told me to give him time off. It was only ten. What's with you?"

"I coulda used the time off."

In the wardrobe now, putting away clothes. "I. Guess. She . . ."

That muffled voice.

"What'd you say?"

She came out, walking like an automaton. "I. Guess. She. Needed. You. He . . ." Her mouth gaped. Her eyes were filling.

"What's the matter with *you*? You on something?"

She blinked rapidly. "Noth. Nothing." She closed an eyelid with one finger. Something in the eye? No. Spy-eye. I spy. "She'll be home soon, she wants it." Trembling.

"Something else first." He took her by the arm, very carefully, led her into his room, and closed the door. "It's not locked. See?" He slid it open and back. "No spy-eyes either. I know about them. She gave up on me." More ways than one.

"She wants . . ."

"Tragg's up there, waiting. Ain't he?"

"I—I—ca—" She clamped her mouth to keep her voice from rising into shrieks, straining against psychic blocks. Her shoulders shook, her eyes ran.

"Isn't Tragg up there?" He did not touch her, for fear she would lose control and scream for the servants.

She nodded, both hands over her mouth, tears running over her fingers.

He scratched his ear. "I just don't understand. Whatever

she's had against me I did what she wanted and never looked at her cross-eyed."

She sat on his bed and whispered, "Sometimes she talks to herself. You know, she really loved Silver—"

He snorted.

"Oh yeah, with everything . . . but since he died she's turned . . ." She was scrubbing her face with a tissue.

"She didn't have to hire me."

"It looked like the big gesture. Didn't want you talking either."

"I don't think I could. Like you."

A light scrape at the foyer door.

"Omigod, she's back! I can't face her!" Her eyes were reddened, her skin streaked with smeared makeup.

He closed and locked his own door. "Give a bit of a screech and tell her I tried to—"

"No, no! You'll get in trouble!"

"Trouble! Who you kidding?" He pulled at the tag of his zip. "Forget the attack and just pretend we're—"

Phoebe was yelling: "Mercy! *Mercy!* Where in hell are you?" There was a tinge of hysteria in her voice now. All he needed. Two of them in full cry.

"Forget it then. Wash your face over there or *you'll* be in trouble."

She sobered fast. Then giggled. First time he'd seen any kind of laugh out of her either. "Like to give her a surprise for once."

But it was he who got the surprise when she pulled his zip all the way down with one hand and hers with the other. So much the more because she'd always been shy of her body. Like him.

He worked out in the building's gym odd moments when he could get away; his torso was like a wall of roughcut blocks, thick-haired as if dark ivy were growing from the midline. He was wearing nothing under the zip, not even the usual armory.

"Boris! Mercy! Where the hell are those two?"

"I dunno, Ma'am. They were here a few minutes ago."

She was forty years old, but her body was white and smooth with unused flesh. She lay back on the bed and pulled at him. Crazy, crazy. And he went willingly.

"Her room's empty and his door—"

"Boris!" She was pounding at the door now, shrieking.

Something had put her in a tantrum and who cared?

He had not believed he would be capable, but he was, such a thirst, with the mildly perverse pleasure of being in the heart of a storm, bolts of lightning flashing about them.

When he withdrew her spirit went with him. "Face the music," she whispered.

"Some music." He took a deep breath. "That was damn good anyway."

She smiled faintly. "Likewise."

The pounding had slackened. He grinned and said in a voice dripping with insolence, "Just one minute, Ma'am, and I'll get you that file."

Mercy whispered, "Oh Lord, please take care!" and said in her high light voice, "I'll be right with you, Miz Phoebe."

"It seems I missed the Late Show," Phoebe Adams snarled. "Come out when you're ready."

But he paused to look at Mercy Adams. She had tried to warn him, had succeeded in her way. Yet he had done nothing for her except perhaps to draw away some of the filth that was always being dumped on her. She had a few light scars at the hairline. He wondered if they had come from Phoebe's nails. But she was safe enough here. Phoebe had a lot of use for her. "Give me a minute to wash up and you can have the bathroom."

When he came out she was still sitting on the edge of the bed, disheveled, hands folded in her lap. Her head rose.

He said, "You probably won't see me again, whatever—"

She surprised him again by jumping up and kissing him lightly on the mouth, then shut the bathroom door again before she would allow herself to say more.

He dressed in clean clothes and took what he needed. There was not much to leave. For all his love of guns he was no pack rat about them either.

He found Phoebe in her study, foot tapping. "I'm glad you found the time. Here's the key. The tape is beside the terminal, clearly labeled." *If a dummy like you can read,* the tone said.

In the hall light he looked at the key. It was a magnetically coded perforated plasmix card, like any other key. But this one did not lead to the office upstairs. It opened the door of the apartment's private elevator in the foyer leading to the living room. To reach the office he would have to pass through the living room, the service corridor, and his former den, where he had watched trivvy and polished his guns. Perhaps she had given him the wrong key by mistake. He thought not. She did not make mistakes like that, and he did not think it would be wise to bring it to her attention. He did not know what would be wise.

He used the key in the elevator slot and stood aside. The door opened into an empty cubicle. He stepped inside and the box closed on him. He touched the DOWN button and nothing happened. And the OPEN button. Again nothing. No surprise. All had been prepared. He was not completely trapped. He had key templates no one else knew about.

UP then. He kept his eyes on the door, not the lights flashing 34, 35, 36, 37 . . .

The door opened. No hiding place, but no one in the foyer or, through its inviting door, the living room. Hands in his pouch-pockets, he crossed the carpeting quietly with heavy-shouldered ease. The door to the corridor was unlocked, carpet cheaper here, worn. Door to the den open a crack. He slid it very slowly, keeping his body behind it as long as he could.

The den had not changed much except for a new red rug on the standard tiles, and Tragg sitting at his old desk with a gun in each hand. Cowboy.

"Well, hello, Borisko."

"Borisov," Boris said mildly. "Anton Borisov."

"The things you do learn."

"Kind of late for that, Tragg."

"Too bad, ain't it? Now just slowly, Boris, take the hands out of the pock—"

He died on a syllable, head slumped forward, hands falling dropping guns.

Boris withdrew the snub of his heavy stunner from the slit-open placket of his zip. "Bigmouth," he said. "I should've been dead the second you laid eyes on me. Shmuck." Worse than that. Amateur.

He dropped the stunner down the disposal. Nothing to explode. It was expensive, the ammunition hard to obtain, and illegal. He did not want it taken from him or used against him by anyone. He did not touch the body.

Behind the desk there was a chronometer telling the time in twelve cities on Earth and mean time on twelve other worlds.

He opened the latch of the glass and the fingernail slot of the face, to reveal the innards where a spy-eye stood in for World 12. He plucked out the spool and dropped this in the disposal as well. As he had expected there was no tape marked CONSTITUENCY FILE. If there had been he would have trashed it too.

At the moment when his heartbeat was beginning to slow he took a look at the rug and the roots of his hair tightened. A red cat-skin on the pastel squares, very red, very big; black chevron flaring from head end to flank edges above the hind legs. There was no gaping toothy head with beady eyes. He was thankful for that. Down in the unconscious, hidden or pushed, he had, he must have, suspected. Now he really knew.

As Mercy must know.

The CommUnit chimed, and sweat burst over his body. Tragg hung dead on the desk and he felt nothing. Three melodic notes turned him to water.

He dared not speak, and he dared not leave without answering. He cut off the recording tapespool, flicked on and gave a wordless grunt.

"Tragg?" It was Mercy's voice, and he sagged with relief. It would be Phoebe's little twist, to make her call. In the background he heard Madam screeching at the maid, so she was not eavesdropping; she still trusted Mercy that far.

"Me."

"Everything okay up there, Tragg?" Her voice began with a tremor, quickly suppressed.

"Under control. Too bad Tragg can't talk. Smear your record down there if it's on. I gotta go, because I don't want to be one of the bodies they dump. Good luck."

Slaughtered and flayed red cats. Red fur toy cat. Red rug. Critical mass.

Oh he was in the shit now, deep. Lonely and afraid. Like Nkansah. Red dress, humming about the place. *Boris, honey . . .*

She was frightened of him, had good reason to be, but he didn't know that. He had not seen her as a threat to Silver, would not have killed her. He had helped rearrange the body so that Silver wouldn't be shamed. The man was a slob, but he had treated Boris well, and Boris had rung the bell on Nkansah when she ran out so fast out of the same kind of loyalty. He had not thought about sending her to her death; he could not escape knowing the probability. He had always thought of himself as having some kind of moral code, even if only defined in terms of loyalty. Now there was no one to be loyal to, and he was lost.

Before he had surrendered his 48th floor key to the public elevator, which did not open there except to its inhabitants, he had a copy made, for emergencies. He could not use it from 33 under the eye of Phoebe, but he did now. He took no backward look. His loyalty was to his life.

Though a few stores had staggered hours, the Mall was open all night. Everything was available somewhere. It had its habitués like any place of its kind, many quite respectable-looking citizens who lived off stolen key-cards in Eatamats, Autobaths and Laund-R-Alls. Some straight-arrow insomniacs, some wealthy eccentrics, some shoplifters. It was a high-class place, not one of the scurfy pits where living civil-service automatons looked for wild relief, though it too had its wildernesses, mackhouses, bartermarts.

One blue-rinsed red-eyed old lady with a blue poodle under one arm, big pockets popping with knitting needles and crochet hooks, and a spring-harness police stunner up her sleeve, nuzzled her dog and said to the mike on its collar, "Something up. There goes Phoebe Adams' man Boris, Ring two-seven crossing F/H west, trying to look like he's not in a hurry, shoulders forward, something on his mind."

"Got that. Will track."

Boris had the sense of eyes watching, and the sense to know that not all eyes were watching him. Security did not bother him much; he recognized Blue Rinse and one or two others. They would not have hurried to grab him for popping Tragg even if they knew about it. The worrisome ones were Phoebe's: She would have cleaned out Silver's crew and strengthened her own. If she'd done it at home she'd do it here.

"Heading for Jha's Joint. Old crony of Silver's. Maybe thinks she'll take him in."

"Her? He's really desperate. Wonder what he did to deserve her."

"Better track?"

"Yeah."

• • •

Jha was not the kind to give shelter. She sold services: gaming and women. Boys on the side. She was a brightly lit spot in what would otherwise have been a grotty cul-de-sac which, because of her, blossomed with shops selling sex aids and gambling machines. Silver was an occasional gambler and had eventually come to protect Jha from blue laws because she had offered him Nkansah, who had applied and was considered unsuitable. Silver had investigated Jha to his satisfaction and found no connection with Security; she was kosher. Unfortunately he had been too taken with Nkansah to be so thorough.

If Boris gambled alone it was never at Jha's. Her women made him uneasy. They serviced the tables and the clients, but they were not ordinary. A few were hominid extraterrestrials, but all had been surgically altered in grotesque design to increase sexual excitement, and dressed—or decorated—to show off. Nkansah would never agree to that; Boris, whose tastes in food and women were straight as his cropped hair, stayed away.

Jha herself looked like an anorexic flamenco dancer: thin, ivory-colored, black hair knobbed tight and shining as if it had been enameled on, black tight flicker-gown that flared below the knee. She was intimidating. The bouncer, Sukey, was very differently grotesque, but she did not disturb Boris, possibly because he felt at a level with her. She was built like a sumo wrestler, but her round face was pink and sweet, her blonde-white hair tightly curled.

"Hey, Boris, haven't seen you around awhile."

"Boss lady don't gamble." Not at games.

"You playing tonight?"

"Business. I want to see Jha."

Jha was circulating to make sure all wares were being promoted with enthusiasm. She was smoking a cigarillo in a sapphire-studded holder the length of a conductor's baton. The weed was some neutral tasteless herb; like Phoebe she maintained an image.

Business was moderate: an off night. Boris folded his arms and waited at the corner of a sparsely occupied craps table until she noticed his plug-ugly face: the prole among the perverse.

She looked him up and down. "Haven't seen you since the old man croaked."

"I need a favor."

"I don't lend."

"I ain't borrowing. I want a fund transfer, form of a gambling debt, from this bank here," he produced the cards, "to this one."

This was another of her specialties, and a profitable one. "Twenty-four-point-five percent house cut."

"I won't bargain. Don't take your time."

"I need twenty minutes. Grab a fist of chips and hit the tables."

He expected to take four-fifths of the holdings out of the Sonotek bank—he was afraid that a complete cleanout would prompt immediate investigation—and tuck it into the private account. There were no marks on the cards except bank logos, and Jha handled thousands of them.

Sukey was at his shoulder. She walked on little cat feet. "Hey Boris, you going to win a fortune?"

"Do I get to keep it?"

"Why not? And you pay if you lose."

Gambling had been Silver's one moderate appetite. Boris had followed him in moderation. He did not know the parable of the servant with one talent, but he lived it; his employers preferred it so. He played with his usual prudence, keeping every raddled gambler in sight, and left with his savings under his control and the value of his chips, plus ten percent, in cash tokens. And a hearty pinch in the behind from Sukey.

Also alone, in darkness, among enemies, for the first time in a long while. The feeling stuck at the back of his neck long after the pinch faded.

"Hullo, Mr. Man."

"Yeah, Sukey, where you calling?"

"Scrambling on PubComm 1877. Your fella Boris left Jha's with his funds transferred from Southern Continental to Western National, dunno what branches. Think he's heading north but I can't tell from this blind alley. Stuck a rover-dot in his armpit so you'll know where his clothes are traveling for a while."

"Damn good. I'll be on him in three minutes."

"Guess you won't be coming round for a spin."

"I'll do you a favor and stay away. Thanks, Sukey, and good night," said Haynes.

• • •

He asked himself: why's Boris running? Naturally because he's in danger, or thinks he is. He was Silver's faithful servant, and Phoebe chose him herself. . . . Maybe too faithful to Silver . . . and she's hiring new staff. Whatever, he must know something interesting about one or both. See what Phoebe does about that, hm. . . .

And that guy burnt to a crisp. And the skimmer, gotta be hired or bought from somewhere. And . . .

Haynes had set three chases running and did not expect results within minutes. He went to sleep.

Sukey arranged her weight in the lounger of her cubby and lit a dopestick. She had done her part keeping things calm in the Mall. She wondered mildly whether she should have let Haynes have one more bit of information. She had picked out the two glims tracking Boris, mainly because they were relatively new customers. Phoebe was being a bit subtle: These were not the usual harnessed beeves but more sleek and knowing. She could have decked them and flung the remains in a can, but she'd got one of the girls to crook a finger from the shadow of an alcove where she herself had tripped them efficiently enough to bash their faces good and hard, and disarmed them. She just felt too damn lazy to dispose of bodies tonight.

33

Moon's Woman refused to go to the hospital where he felt the doctors would look at him askance, or back home to his uncle's house on the Mesa, and Security refused to let him camp out in the place he had shared with Many Harvests. Tom Green Corn took him home to his wife Rosa, a nurse who had worked with Moon's Woman in off hours. She washed him and dressed his abrasions, then doubled up the children and put him to bed with a sleepy drink.

The four Ungrukh settled in dispiritedly with the rest of their people and next day Tom brought Emerald with Bren and Etrem to visit the grieving man.

Moon's Woman looked glassy-eyed, but was aware enough to be keeping his mind on his hands while, with a thick nylon cord he had spliced, he did the figure Lightning almost as fast as the bolt itself. Green Corn's son Steven laughed and reached for the string. He did not know how much Moon's Woman valued it, but Moon's Woman knew how much he owed his friends, and let Steven show him the Apache Door, which gives a figure of great beauty with a minimum of effort.

No one paid special attention to Emerald. All were used to Ungrukh. Distracted for a moment, she watched the string figures through Steven's eyes. She enjoyed looking at hands because they were such beautiful instruments, and would have loved a pair of her own.

Though they look pretty silly on me, you bet.

"We saw you on the trivvy," said Steven.

"That is Bren's Aunt Nurunda."

"Yes. Your eyes are different . . ." He paused.

"Yes, love. I see through the eyes of others."

"Oh. I know. You're an ESP too."

The first thing Bren noticed was that Moon's Woman had had his hair cut by Rosa, in the old way, but straighter, so that the bangs did not fall into his eyes and the rest hung gracefully below his ears. He had a narrower jaw than most Pueblos and sometimes looked as if he truly did not belong.

He was silent and she did not urge him to speak.

"How long will he stay like this?" Green Corn asked.

"He cures himself eventually." If he lives. "Let him smoke tobacco, but better not give him a drug for the mind even if he asks."

:He may try to kill himself.:

:We must try to watch.:

Sun Rising High came in without knocking, a plastic sack slung over his shoulder. The room was crowded now; Green Corn and Rosa went into the kitchen with signs for the children to follow. Moon's Woman gestured for the children to stay and went on with his string figures.

Sun Rising High looked at Bren and Emerald, learned what he wanted to know and took bundles out of the sack. He offered the white buckskins and Moon's Woman shook his head. They were wrapped and replaced. He produced a pile of clean clothes: brown denim pants, a lighter shirt, underwear, a belt with a hunting knife in its scabbard. Rosa had laundered the clothes he was wearing, but Moon's Woman did not want the ones that reminded him of death. He folded the string and put it in his pocket, accepted the clothes, but removed the scabbard and knife from the belt and returned them. Bren's ear twitched involuntarily. Moon's Woman glanced at her and smiled faintly. The Chief removed three skin-wrapped packages from the last bundle.

Moon's Woman put two aside without opening them. Bren knew that they contained a prayer stick and a Corn Mother with multicolored kernels, and it was clear that they had nothing to do with whatever he was planning. He unwrapped the last package, a pouch made from the skin of antelope testicles, and tucked it into his shirt. He nodded thanks, and Sun Rising High replaced everything else in the sack, unfolded himself and went out, an old withered man bowed under a great weight, head bound by a kerchief with one downy feather tucked in it.

The eyes of Moon's Woman widened; he spoke, finally, in agony, but low-voiced to keep from frightening the children.

"There is too much evil here!" A terrible cry. "Can you not take me with you to the Fifth World? Are my sins so great?"

Bren said gently, "Dear friend, whatever kind of kachinas or Eyes we may seem to you, and though we see in what some others call darkness, our world is a place where people quarrel—and like yours are trying to learn not to kill. We know of only one world where people seem truly good, and I think if we visit there we find sinners among them too. *We* are not fit to help you be reborn."

Moon's Woman thought about this for a moment, nodded, smiled faintly once again, and returned his hand to his pocket and to putting all his soul into the fingers looping the gleaming cord into the shapes of stars and fishes.

Green Corn stood in the kitchen doorway. "We'll keep him as long as necessary, but what can we do for him?" *:Working days we can't keep watch on him.:*

:Everyone is most grateful. Give us an hour to think.:

A helicopter pilot was waiting for the Ungrukh in decreasing patience in rising winds, but Bren was much more worried by the storm in Moon's Woman. Emerald sent an apologetic thought to the pilot: *:I am afraid to leave this place until we decide what to do.:* She settled in the shadow of a crumbling adobe wall and the others huddled with her and became as rocks while she spread her white-noise shield.

:It is clear he has some knowledge of this woman whom all suspect, and believes she takes part in the murder of his friend. How does he come to find out about her, and why does he think he can punish her with a bit of feather and some pinches of vegetable matter?:

:He catches what is going on because he is some kind of ESP, but not the usual Solthree type. The materials are important to his rituals and he is a priest among his people. He feels he has special powers. The belief is fueled because he is angry at us when we seem to stop him from saving his friend. We all know of angry warriors who consider themselves invincible.:

:You are therapist. Why can you not turn him aside?:

:Mother, can you make that knotted tree branch over there

grow straight by bending it back—without breaking it first?:

:I see him going after that woman with no defense and someone kills him first.:

:The police must set guard on him,: Etrem said. *:He is a witness.:*

:Of what?: Bren asked. *:They don't know more than we do.:*

:Still,: Emerald said, *:if he can pick up our song at twenty km—:*

Bren said, *:I am not sure he is quite that powerful. Even a Lyhhrt is not. I think what he does is gather snatches from listeners nearer to him, and passers-by in aircraft. Then he collates and integrates. That is still truly remarkable, and—:*

"Bren! Etrem! Where the hell are you? Moon's Woman—he's gone! The bedroom window's—"

"So much for the hour of thought," said Etrem.

"Yes, I know, I have him now, running for the hoverbus," said Emerald, "and that is half an hour away. Yes, into the bedroom to change clothing and—"

"You're just sitting there!" Green Corn yelled. "I don't want some strange police picking him up for a crazy Indian!"

"Tom," said Bren, "we send home the helicopter and you have the skimmer. The day is free, if you don't mind spending it with us."

"Jesus! What do you think I am?"

"The skimmer, Tom," Bren said gently. "Lead us."

The Cats had disappeared outside, the children watched trivvy, Tom and Rosa were in the kitchen. Moon's Woman reached into the skin pouch and took out a sliver of flint. He put it into his mouth under the tongue, where it lay cold and hard as determination. It had no religious significance, but was a personal talisman. As an adolescent he had known already that he would become a priest who would dress as a woman and be a source of perplexity to his family and the people who lived in new ways. In his one effort to look for other directions he had adopted the old Plains custom of taking peyote and going out to find a vision. At one level below the conscious it was no surprise—it was perhaps even desirable—that Moon should withdraw the man's bow from him and offer the woman's spindle. At the level of aching boyhood he had wept, and saved the stone fragment that scratched his shoulder while he lay in the piñon, to keep as a promise to himself that he would become a healer with a single heart who had no dealing with witchcraft.

It was not in his mind to kill the murdering woman. That was not the work of healers. He wished to give her fear, though he might be killed. His death would demonstrate that he had truly given her fear.

He dressed quickly, neatly in inconspicuous clothing. Even his old hat had been brushed and steamed for him, his boots polished. Very faintly he heard the laughter of children, the yelping of clowns on the trivvy and dogs in the alleys who smelled Cat, the clink of pots in the kitchen. He himself was a center of quiet, as if the whole world were in his mind. Of his discarded clothes he took only the jacket, because he had no other, and he needed pockets for his pouch and money.

He knew that fifteen minutes of hard running, even through scrub, would bring him to the place where the bus descended. His mind was so far away that he did not feel the ground beneath his feet. Perhaps this sense of oddness was caused by the drug Rosa had given him to make him sleep. He had slept, but he had not changed his mind.

And yes, there was the bus riding over the plateau, dark against a hot blue sky cleansed by winds whipping the storm away. Yet he was not weary or sweating. The bus would take him precisely where he wanted to go, and he had enough money to reach there.

Most of the passengers were Pueblos or Navajos who did not recognize him or chose not to. Some were taking packages of artifacts to boutiques in the city.

A young woman in blue with ribbons binding her braids was watching him with lively interest. Her snapping brown eyes reminded him of Rosa, and he had a jolt of fear. But she was not Rosa, only a young woman interested in a handsome man. He pulled the hat down over his eyes and adjusted the belt so that he could slump in his seat. No one sat beside him or spoke to him. He radiated touchlessness.

He closed his eyes and seemed to see through the lids the bus's shadow crossing buildings, water reservoirs, irrigated fields. Inside was cool but the ground and sky sang with heat. They sang rough counterpoint to the voices of Ungrukh and the cool liquid notes of the bone flute Many Harvests had

played, perhaps charred and broken in the burning mass of
He shuddered, but not at that image.

He had not loved Many Harvests with the same intensity the small dark man had given him. He loved Emerald's twins because he had been given little love and was incapable of giving much to his own kind. The twins were careless of the love of others and he loved them for that too. If they had attached themselves to him he would have pulled away. He was ready to give up his life not for his own fury, but for his guilt in accepting the passion of Many Harvests, who had saved his life.

It was the first time this realization had come to him clearly, but he saw the truth of it. It was the body of a song for which the chorus had been: Nobody loves, nobody wants, nobody cares, so why should I? So why should I?

Another thought spoke: *Surely you are doing yourself an injustice. You have many friends and you care for them and their children. Green Corn and the Chief are sad for you, and so are the Ungrukh. Your feelings for Many Harvests are the strongest possible for you, and who can expect more?*

How do I know he did not expect more?

But it is true. Perhaps I should get off at the stop and go home.

Then he felt the scrape of the flint beneath his tongue.

No. I will avenge Many Harvests.

It must play itself out.

Why did I think that? No matter. I'll sleep a little and the bus will land.

He descended into the burning heat of the street surface. The dark towers were taller than when he had seen them before, and they leaned over him. Of course. They are curious and want to know who I am. They will know soon.

He passed through the nearest entrance, where a mild force field kept most of the heat out. The cold inside was startling because it was of greater intensity than that of the bus, and there seemed to be some mild amusement in the structure of the building at his reaction to it.

His resolve weakened again for a moment, and again the scrape of flint on membranes strengthened it.

Then a thing happened that seemed strange even to him. The stone grew hot. Without thinking he took it out of his mouth. His own fingers felt alien to his tongue, but once the flint was in his hand it was cool again. He put it in his breast pocket, as near his heart as could be, and as hard.

There were few people in the lobby. As he wished, they did not notice him among the basalt pillars. He discovered the directory, pressed the index button for A and found Adams: 33A.

But he must ask permission of the guard to unlock the gate. This seemed ludicrous as well as impossible; he hesitated because he was not sure what to do, and leaned for a moment against a pillar, weary now, but it was as warm as flesh, and he drew away.

What now?

You have many kinds of power. Why not use them?

An armed guard was coming toward him. He looked straight at her through the gate lattice and told her in his mind to open the latch and turn away. She did so, vacant-eyed.

Surely I do.

He took the mike, touched the comm toggle, and the harsh voice of Phoebe Adams said, "Hello? Hello? Who's that?"

He had the power. He said in a woman's voice, "It's Mercy, ma'am. I've forgotten the key."

"Damnation, you idiot, you're always doing that! I'll let you in."

The elevator enclosed him like a seed pod and raised him as if he were being lifted on the wind.

The door slid back. Phoebe Adams stood before him, red-white streaked hair, dark gown. She smiled grimly. "Welcome, Moon's Woman." She tilted her head and added, "Come here, Mercy."

The woman with the dark-blonde hair and fleshy lips came to her side. White scars crawled from her hairline like worms.

He reached for the skinning knife, and armed men appeared to either side of him.

"No need to take it," said Phoebe. "He won't use it."

What the devil is going on here?

Still smiling, she backed into the room, lay down on a chaise longue without looking to see if it was there, and began to pull up her skirt and open the steel gates of her thighs.

"Is this what you want?"

"No!"

She was standing before him then, holding the knife pulled from the sheath with its blade edge lying along his throat.

He smiled and grasped her by the neck with his thumbs on her trachea.

Madre de Dios! What's happening?

Help, Mother!

Nurunda, Grenna!—networking—Ygne, Ghemma! hurry and join, please! Orenda!

One black hundredth of a second.

He was standing before the door. It slid back. Phoebe Adams was waiting framed in it, red-white hair, black gown. She said, "I didn't really believe you were Mercy. Did you come to kill me? or to make love to me?"

Moon's Woman looked at the person he believed responsible for many horrifying murders and saw her in her daily flesh, a creature of Earth, without hate or terror in his heart. There was no knife or sheath. They had disappeared with the other feelings. "I have always been incapable of both, Madam. I made a mistake in coming, and I wish to go."

"Go then," she said.

Darkness covered him.

Thank you Mother, sister and friends.

Moon's Woman felt the rough cool cloth wiping his sweaty face and opened his eyes.

"What have I done?" he whispered, and looked into the sharp brown eyes of Rosa, while she kept on sponging his face, her blue dress bright in the shaft of a late afternoon sunbeam, one ribboned braid hanging over her shoulder. He reached into the pocket of his shirt and touched the flint sliver.

"What have I done?"

"Nothing. You haven't hurt yourself or anyone else. Better take another rest."

"I am a stupid dolt," Bren said.

"The man is alive and sane," Emerald said. "What more do you want? A victory fire on every hill? I think there is some kind of interference."

"What kind?"

"I am not sure. I must think about it."

"What on earth were you doing?" Green Corn asked.

"Trying to create a full-scale hypnodrama by myself for the first time in my life and I fail miserably." Bren was still sulking. "I do not like having to erase that ugly part. Does Mercy Adams really look like that? How can he know? Does she really have such scars, and is she truly the one?"

"Bren, I truly don't know," said Emerald. "And kindly stop wallowing. I think that is foreign matter and as for the rest, you succeed."

"Foreign matter?"

"Just let me talk to your father first before I say more. I may be wrong."

"I'm sure Moon's Woman doesn't think very kindly of us."

"That we leave him to deal with for himself. He still loves the twins, so maybe we let them explain to him. They are childish, but certainly not stupid."

Moon's Woman felt a massive head nuzzling each armpit. Each of his hands rested on a furred shoulder. He opened his eyes again and the heads rose, four wide black pupils rimmed in Ungrukh red watching him calmly. He was in Tom Green Corn's bedroom. The first lamp of evening had been lit.

"What happened?"

"You set out to find the woman called Phoebe Adams," said Orenda. "While you are waiting for the bus we pick you up in the skimmer and bring you back to keep you from harm."

"But I did go! I went—"

"You do *not* go. Bren—and the rest of the women—make you believe you go. You mean to force Phoebe Adams to kill you, Moon's Woman, and we don't want that. We care for you."

"No. Only Many Harvests cared for me, and I failed him."

"We are not as good at loving as he, but we love you as well as we can love anyone. We do not even love Bren more than you. Can you accept that?"

"Yes. It is all I will ever have."

"We think it is quite a lot," Tugrik said, not as sharply as the words suggested, because he did not wish to frighten the man.

"Oh friends, I *am* grateful, and I love you best in the world."

"Then promise you do not try to do foolish things that harm yourself," said Orenda.

"I promise."

"I think he is as safe now as we can make him, and I am sorry to behave so foolishly," Bren told Green Corn.

"Bren, even your mother says you're wallowing, and we're thankful—so why don't you just stop it?"

"We are very well aware how much *you* do to help—but you cannot take care of him forever. In a day or two he is probably ready to go home. I'm sure he doesn't get on as badly with his uncle as he believes, and he has more friends among you than he is willing to admit. Of course he is free to visit the twins as often as he can come."

"But is he safe from attack?"

"I doubt anyone recognizes him when he lives among his people and behaves like them," said Emerald. "None of us is immune from attack, but he is probably safest. That is all we can say now."

Phoebe Adams woke shrieking from a nightmare of being strangled by a faceless man. She took another sleeping pill and tossed the rest of the night away sweating in broken dreams.

The weary Ungrukh were returned to their people.

"Raanung," said Emerald, "you think back to the story my parents tell of how they meet Qumedon in that time warp here."

"Yes, and at home on Ungruwarkh when that other one comes, and . . . and—"

"My brother dies trying to fight him. Yes. So what is the meaning of those things that happen when Bren is working hypnodrama today?"

"Why do you ask *me* about such meanings, woman?"

"Because you are not altogether a fool and I want to know whether *I* am one!"

"You are good at setting up a case in which *yes* is wrong and *no* just as wrong. No, I do not consider either of us a fool, and yes, there is a sense of Qumedon in what happens today, particularly in the twisting of feelings in the wrong direction, which is a specialty of Qumedni, and also of Kriku/Qumedon's misguided attempts to help Ungrukh. There is no other evidence."

"We must find out."

"You can ask Man of Law, who probably does not know, or you can send a message to Kinnear at GalFed Central, and the answer comes too late."

"I do not want to involve Kinnear in our affairs at his age. Nor Security here. Man of Law seems trustworthy, so let us send a message through him to Medor, and maybe it goes fast enough. If he knows nothing, we have one more thing to watch out for by ourselves."

"More than one. We must call a meeting to let everyone know what we suspect. We owe that much to all the women who help you today, even at the cost of making them more fearful."

The Tribal representataives on Sol III *were* fearful of Qumedni interference, but they were also inspirited at the prospect of doing something, anything, rather than mill about waiting until governments decided how justice was to be accomplished. They sent, through Man of Law, a short scrambled message to Medor: PLEASE INFORM OF ANY INDICATION OF QUMEDNI MOVEMENT, PARTICULARLY OF THAT BEING CALLING ITSELF KRIKU.

34

McNelly said, "The dead gun in the Canyon was a man named Ignatz Scharf, an aide of Senator Dorema Bibacz. The lady's only connection was that she tried to ring the bell on a couple of Silver's grimy deals and was voted down on the issue of an inquiry at the push of Silver's cronies."

"Ignatz?" Haynes was bemused. "Did Phoebe put a watchdog on Bibacz's team, or is that stretching the imagination?"

"I wouldn't think it was. Scharf's molecular analysis showed the esp configuration in his genes, but he's not marked ESP in any of his records."

"Some ESPs don't realize, or don't bother, or prefer not to be registered . . . most are innocent . . ."

"And some not."

"Yes, I had figured that out for myself, Alfred. I'm sorry he's dead—because I wish I knew what he knew."

Phoebe had sent out a garbage disposal company to help Tragg dispose of Boris. The body had not been described, and when the team found one they disposed of it as instructed, and reported that they were disconcerted at not having found Tragg to confirm directions. When they described what they had found and gotten rid of, Phoebe turned so cold with rage she nearly splintered into icicles. But she had paid them half in advance, and completed payment without comment.

Mercy.

Mercy's door was closed and locked. Her heart beat within, like a fluttering bird. Phoebe did not scream or pound the door. She needed Mercy yet. Oh yes.

She went up to 48, found the fallen guns and dumped them. There was no blood; Boris' bullets, whatever they were, must have been poisonous, not explosive. The rug caught her eye. A piece of stupid bravado to have kept it. The garbage collectors would make nothing of it; they were competent non-locals who kept their eyes to their work. It would have to be cut up before trashing, and that could wait a short while; she had no knife or scissors with her. The owners of half-a-dozen other skins, and toy cats, did not know their source.

Then she saw the clockface standing open, spy-eye capsule empty. Boris. Stupid-cunning Boris. Yes, he and Mercy, they did make a pair. Boris would take a little more effort, but she was not afraid of hard work. And a lot of work had to be done on Mercy.

She stood in the middle of the living room. Some of the furniture had been removed, the vulgar overstuffed clutter for overstuffed Silver. She rubbed her arms, cold in the center of emptiness, in the dead place. Silver dead. Tragg dead. Nkansah dead. Scharf. Ungrukh. Kylkladi. Xirifri. She felt a trickle on her chin and realized that a drop of blood was running from where she had bitten her lip.

I too have sharp teeth.

I would have made a good one of *them,* jaws in the live throat and blood running down my breast. The best one of them.

The CommUnit chimed. A call rerouted from 33 told her that two agents tracking Boris had wound up flat on the floor with bruised faces and no guns, quite unable to tell what happened. The news hardly moved her. She left a message for them to clean up and stand by.

She expected Boris to run, jump, flea on a hot griddle. Let him.

Mercy Adams' father had been an asteroid miner, handsome, strong, silent. Eventually too silent and too long absent for his wife, who worked at a dull clerical job in the company's base, while their child was cared for in a lackluster way in the company's crèche. When Mercy was ten years old her mother ran off with a fast talker, leaving Jeremy Adams embittered, and more silent. On holidays he brought his daughter to Sol III and spent the time in game parks, killing and skinning wild things and sitting around fires with other hunters who did not have much conversation. Mercy never learned other kinds of life except through books and trivvy. Her father never discussed her mother's family, if any, and of his own he told her only never to get mixed up with the snotty Charloe branch. When she was sixteen a flying rock shattered his air hose and killed him. The company managed to extricate itself from most of the blame, paid small compensation and added an offer for training in a job like her mother's. She took the training and the job until ever-advancing technology forced her out.

She was thirty then, gawky, ill-educated, ill-conversed. She had the Adams bones and strength, which suited her awkwardly, few and quickly passing sexual experiences with lonely married men much like her father. She came to Sol III determined never to live in silence again. But there was little place for a woman of at most modest attractiveness in a world of tertiary and quaternary services.

In desperation she sought out the Charloe branch represented by Phoebe Adams. Phoebe, newly elected, already bored with formality and ceremony, recognized the family resemblance, coarse as it was, had it reinforced and refined by minor surgery, and Mercy became a drudge again. Secure, but a drudge, in silence and shadow. Long John looked through her; Boris made her uneasy—he shied from her because she was too much like Phoebe—and the toy-boys sneered at her. The servants, drawing their own caste-lines, avoided her as well. Whatever spirit and passion left within her compressed like a neutron star and only just managed to avoid implosion. The characteristic Adams hardness maintained her in homeostasis.

It was becoming unstable now.

She crouched in her bed in the windowless room where the clock told her dawn was near. She did not know what had set Phoebe off earlier in the evening, but she did know that Boris' escape and the discovery of Tragg should have done it later. So Phoebe had gone into one of her cold rages, and Mercy would not be spared from it. Phoebe could not quite prove conspiracy; Mercy had claimed that background noise (Phoebe's screaming) and a poor connection had misled her. But there would be no chances taken, and that meant a visit to a stocky woman in a blue smock, who called herself a doctor because she had a needle and a repulsive apparatus.

Mercy had no keys, no templates, no guns.

Phoebe did not ask Mercy to braid her hair. The maid combed and coiled it and fastened it with clasps. She forsook her faithful black for a dark red like dried blood and went to Committee meetings and to open a hospice for the latest fashionable disease. Mercy was sent on no errands, ate by herself under surveillance by servants who did not need to be told. No one mentioned Boris or Tragg. There were spy-eyes and alarms on the doors. She spent the day in her office compiling reports of no urgency. There was nothing in the news about anything that ought to concern her. Not Tragg, not Boris. She assumed that if there was no news Phoebe had ordered it nonexistent. In the afternoon she spent an hour lying on her bed with her thoughts clacking off the walls of her skull like ball bearings, and then an hour in unrefreshing sleep that felt drugged.

Phoebe came home for dinner and summoned Mercy to eat with her. She was calm, almost cheerful. She remarked on Mercy's pallor and advised her to get more fresh air. "Tomorrow we'll take a little trip," she said.

"Yes, Cousin Phoebe," said Mercy. The barest hint of . . . something?

"My, we're getting familiar," said Phoebe. Her lips tightened.

The night was another of those horrors. Phoebe went out again, briefly, without taking anyone from the household. Mercy tested. When she tried to leave the butler told her very courteously that the Madam requested she stay in and finish a few tasks. She could have broken the elderly man like a stick, but she knew that there would be stronger hands beyond the doors. Phoebe had let too many get away, had thrown away too many like crumpled tissues. There must be a limit even for her.

Mercy retreated. Did the appointed tasks quickly. Shut herself in her room again. Tried to read, smoke dope, watch trivvy. The horror was in the powerlessness that corrupted. She was not descending the employment ladder, like Boris, but at the bottom. Her one talent, her only resource, was in her slight resemblance to Phoebe. The ricocheting steel bearings threatened to crack bone.

• • •

Phoebe came home without fuss, listened to the murmuring of the butler, laughed a bit, lightly, and went to bed.

Mercy lay rigid and let the hours pass.

Until she heard the shriek, and after that a moan. The noises were muffled; soundproofing was good, even in that close environment. It took her two minutes to realize that the sounds had come from Phoebe. God Almighty, the Black of Diamonds was having a nightmare!

She opened the door a slit and listened. The maid came without summons. There was a mutter, a croak, a cough. Silence.

No freedom. Spy-eyes, coercion, blows, guns. An ugly past, a sickening present, no future. But escape! The neutron star imploded. Death was escape.

In silence she clothed herself in the best she owned—hand-me-downs of Phoebe's, with her only jewels, a necklace of jet beads her father had given her. The wig. A light dotted veil. A lace muff to hold cash-on-hand and a bus pass.

Away, even if no farther than the outer door, kicking and screaming. The hours again added to dawn.

She closed the door of her room behind her forever. Like Boris, like Nkansah. Down along the dim hall. No butler, guard, alarm. No challenge. Ghostly. The ease made her uneasy. Trap? The foyer was even dimmer, lit by wall panels like early dawn windows . . . and in one corner stood . . . a shadow?

Ghost?

She wondered if terror and sleeplessness were warping her mind further, but the semitransparent figure did not look like any possible projection of her imagination. Some kind of Indian with bangs cut at the brows and hair falling to the earlobes, worn dark stetson, plain light brown shirt and pants, gray jacket, hiking boots like those her father had worn. He did not at all resemble the hard weathered men who sometimes guided her father's trips.

She thought she saw him blink. She thought he took one hand from his pocket and sprinkled a line of coarse yellow meal from her feet to the outer door. His eyes gave no sign of seeing her. While the lump of hysteria rose in her throat he changed, or did not change, to shadow. There was no line of grain. Nothing.

She flung open the door to the stairs and ran down three flights to the public elevator.

• • •

The bright Mall seemed even more unreal, because it was normal. But if she could be seen, she could at least see—whatever existed. She did not know Phoebe's new regulars any more than Boris had done, but she steered away from dim corners and breasted the swells of light from the shops. A couple of Mall guards gave her respectful nods, though she was not sure they took her for Phoebe: she did not have the retinue. She recognized an old Security plodder of the type who tried to appear anonymous, and of course Blue Rinse, maundering along blearily while she knitted something white and fleecy without looking at it. But she had seen that old fraud in the gym, straight-shouldered in leotards with the body of a sixteen-year-old PanGalactic champion. Mercy had quite good eyes too, wise enough to avoid those deceptive ones.

A quick step came up behind her, something flicked glittering over her neck, terrifyingly like a noose, and in reflex she opened her mouth to scream. Another figure stepped in front of her and said harshly, "Mercy Adams?"

She was confused. "What? Yes?"

"We're making a citizen's arrest, Madam."

She stood with her hands caught in the lace muff clutching money and pass. The man confronting her, dark-haired and bearded, had a most peculiar complexion: nose, forehead and chin patched with pink skintex that did not match his dark skin. And when she twisted back for a blink at his partner she found a smaller, fair and clean-shaven man similarly patched and ill-matched by some cheap doctor. But she hardly troubled to think of that when she looked down and saw that what had been flipped over her head was no noose but Phoebe Adams' complicated garnet necklace with diamond clasp and center. "What the hell—"

"Does that belong to you, Madam?"

"Of course not! Its—"

"Exactly. Mrs. Silver gave warning that you were seen taking this item surreptitiously and sent word to—" His voice had turned low and unctuous while he pulled the wisp of veil from her head and slid a finger under the widow's peak of the wig. The other hand rested almost elegantly on a holstered weapon. He was supple. Both were; Phoebe did not hire the kind of oxen Long John had favored. All the while fore and aft lightly pushing, softly pulling her toward a shadowed and uncluttered aisle near the doors.

"One moment, gentlemen," said an old whiskey voice. "You are bodily coercing the subject and may be charged with assault."

None of the three had noticed the old lady with blued hair gliding and dipping in soft-soled shoes, but those wise old eyes and that sharp new earpiece had missed nothing. The V-shaped smile sent angled wrinkles rippling over her face, and the blunt snout of the stunner poked beneath a scalloped-edge of baby jacket.

"Ma'am, this person has admitted—"

"To nothing. I saw you guys planting the stuff and called in. Now—"

"Leave me alone!" Mercy, past breaking point, ripped off wig and necklace and flung them aside, clutching at her beads. "That stuff's not mine and I don't want it! Let me go!"

"Dear, I am trying—"

A cheerful burbling voice said, "Do you mind if I handle this one, Debbie? We need her more than you do, and your people can have a go later."

Heads turned and a very odd person vaguely familiar to Mercy came into the light. Her maroon zip and breast-pocket insigne—gold triskelion superimposed by silver lightning bolt, denoting ESP-three—were regulation Continental. The material required to cover her 140-odd kg frame might have made three for Mercy, large-boned as she was. The woman wore no gun. Mercy doubted that she needed one.

"Oh, it's you, Sukey. Didn't recognize you in that getup," said Debbie.

"Ho ho. Jha's Joint got clipped yesterday and bust my cover."

Mercy stood in paralysis.

Sukey, with the toe of a little shoe that did not seem to belong on her body, flicked up a loop of the fallen necklace, snatched a handful of its dark glitter from the air and tossed it to Blackbeard; he had to take hands off both Mercy's arm and his gun to catch it. "Vasquez, hm? and Billings? You give that little thing back to Herself, and I'll take good care of Mercy here. You know," she flicked a finger at the nose of Vasquez, who flinched, "you fellas look like you got tripped in a dark corner one night. Just shuffle off, now."

They shuffled.

She touched Mercy's shoulder very gently. "Come along,

dear. You really are safe. See you around, Debbie."

But the old woman was staring resentfully at a smear of lubricant the stunner had left on her hand, and transferred to her knitting. "Goddammit, I tell myself and tell myself, *don't* work in white on the job."

A few steps away, outside in a one-star dawn that was already heating, Mercy, teeth chattering, was ushered into an official aircar. Sukey said regretfully, "I really should have chopped those two right down when they were after Boris." She did not pay attention to the increased rigidity of Mercy's already taut body. "With Jha's network buzzing I'll never get another soft cubby in a joint on this Continent." She shrugged. "Rio'd be nice."

Mercy said in a flat voice, "I'd rather be dead."

"I don't think so," Sukey said quietly.

"What right have you to make me go with you?"

"Warrant, dear. Material witness."

"Arrest."

"Would you rather have gone back to Phoebe?"

After a moment Mercy said, "Tomorrow, I mean today, she was going to make me . . . to make me . . ."

Cropped gray hair. Blue smock. Electrodes.

"Yes."

"Why would she do it that way?"

"Don't *you* know her?"

"A lesson. She enjoys watching that. Then takes the fallen sinner unto her breast, half the brains burnt out. She's noted for humanitarianism."

"That so?" Sukey covered the raw-knuckled hand for a moment with her own chubby one, its wrist braceleted in a fat-crease like a baby's. "Then, sweetie, don't think of it as arrest. Think of it as rescue."

"Dammit, Chief, why the hell'd you have to close up Jha's Joint now just when we need her?"

"Wally, I couldn't help it! The Mall Director's been pushing for it all these years; Jha's been getting injunctions, and they finally ran out. She's been accused of laundering money through fund transfer God knows how long. *I* think she's been running an unlicensed banking operation for customers at the highest rates, and *I* think somebody whose name doesn't get mentioned kicked the Director into crunching it."

"Betsy, I hope to God you're taking good care of the records."

"Where does God come in around there? We can't find the bloody records! Jha claims the fat broad—her words—she hired on for a bouncer wiped them when the tip came in, and if that's true she won't go to jail—maybe. But I know what a liar she is."

Haynes said darkly, "In this case I'm afraid she's telling the truth."

"Sukey, you did a great job bringing in Mercy Adams, and I'm gonna send you to count the penguins in Antarctica *if you can't give me a good reason for wiping Jha's records!*"

"Golly, Mr. Haynes, the Mall Director would have got them for Phoebe to give her a line on Boris. Why do you think he busted the Joint?"

"Why didn't you ca—"

"I did call in—you'll find it on record—but I couldn't get hold of you or McNelly, and I wouldn't talk to anyone else. I also wanted to mention I shunted off the same two goons trying to pick up Mercy when they were after Boris. If I'd known how hard he was running for it I'd have put you on to them earlier—"

"Yeah, yeah, you did your best—"

"—but they were tracking him on spec, so I had no authority. They're Joe Vasquez and Bobby Billings. If you look at their sheets you'll find they have a lot of lovely talents. I'd have picked them up today, only Mercy was trying to climb the wall, and I was afraid they'd be too slick for Debbie. . . ."

"So get to the point."

"Um, when I pulled their feet from under them the other night I collected their guns and put them in cold storage to compare with what they're carrying. . . ."

"Yes, thanks, Sukey. I appreciate that a lot, but I've got to have Boris! There're three Western National branches in the five km northwest quadrant we tracked before he lost the dot, and none have an account in his name. Sure, I know he'd have an alias, but what would it be? We've been staking out the last couple of days."

"Aw, sweetie, you know about names! Didn't you pick out Phoebe? I wouldn't have to be an ESP to figure Boris would never invent one, he doesn't know how! You've got the file—look for an old family name, especially in the female line. All those muscleheads love Mama or Grandma. And if your stakeouts don't work it means he's using a messenger to deliver the handcash in that name. Just follow the footprints."

Haynes snarled, "Thanks for teaching me my business!"

He went after family names.

"Mother, Janusz," said Haynes. "Grams, Gödel and Paryniuk."

"Gödel," said McNelly promptly, "I'd pick it. Damned if I could spell the others."

The name was Gödel.

35

"I'm not ordering you," Haynes said. "I'm asking."

"Yeah," said McNelly.

"Sukey wants to go, but she's not only too damn conspicuous—if I put her in the buzzer with two Ungrukh it wouldn't get off the ground."

"I never said I wasn't going."

"This is irregular, like everything else I've been doing on this case, and if it doesn't work I'll get the axe."

"And I'll just get my head beat in, like usual."

"The Ungrukh are familiar with you, at least. I don't know if they like us—and I don't care much for them—but we're responsible. I mean, Kovarski and I—"

"I don't suppose you've told him about this."

"Don't suppose. I want you particularly because you're never noticed."

"I know. I don't look like anybody."

True. Somewhat in the same way as Bill Gonzales, McNelly was the median of North American Caucasian male: Saxon, Celtic, European, Slavic, Scandinavian, Amerindian. Hair, eyes, skin, features inconspicuous and unmemorable. His only mark was a scar down the left ribcage from a knifeslash, always covered by clothing. Disappeared in a crowd or picture. He might have been a perfect criminal. He was an almost perfect op.

Haynes played a chord on his keyboard and brought up two pictures on the screen. "Vasquez and Billings. There'll be somebody hunching around, and I don't know if it'll be them, but they'll have to do something for Phoebe to keep their jobs—and maybe their lives. We can give the Ungrukh their scents from the guns Sukey kept hold of, but I don't know which belongs to whom. Those funny patches are temporary repairs from the job she did on them, but they'll probably be cleaned up, Vasquez will get rid of the beard, and I figure they'll look like this." Two doctored pictures.

McNelly said, "Vasquez looks like he came in slashing with Coronado a thousand years back, and Billings like one of the Gold Rush boys. Got a heavy beard shadow for a fair man."

"Probably grows in red."

"Red . . . I don't mind the risk, but we could start a battle if any of the cats got hurt."

"They want justice. I don't think they're afraid to work for it."

"Of course we are not afraid to work for it," said Raanung. He and Emerald were crouching, Haynes and McNelly squatting among ragged junipers in the village near Tom Green Corn's house, where no one had bothered to plant bugs or spy-eyes. A combine spluttered in a noontime field nearby.

"Good. Before I say anything else I want to tell you that the witness we have and the one we're after both worked for Phoebe Charloe Adams. Now—"

Emerald said, "Mr. Haynes, before you say more, let me mention that we understand what you intend. Mercy Adams perhaps kills some of my people, under duress. Anton Borisov is perhaps responsible for the death of one of your agents; but both probably have important evidence, and we are here for justice, not blood."

"Settled. Then all I have to say is: you have the greatest concentration of ESPs and trackers there is in the world right now, and we need one of each."

"There are many willing to volunteer. . . ."

"One," said Raanung. "I am going, and I volunteer Nurunda. She likes a good bite at whatever is running."

Haynes opened his mouth to speak, but Emerald snorted, "Just because you feel you have a reason for going is no reason for going."

"You think I am too old and decrepit, woman? I am the same age as your father when he is dashing about among the worlds."

"Your trouble is you think you are the only big nose in the lot! We can't endanger Etrem, but there are Mundr, and Tengi, and Kshuni, and among the women Togru—"

He read the look in her eyes, clouded as they were, by the way the lids and brows formed around them: If you die what is left of me?

"My love, I cannot lie about Council fires as a wise head nodding itself to sleep. All those times I snarl and howl at our Tribes you tell me I must go. Now that *you* are afraid, I must not be."

After a moment she twitched her head and shoulder in the movement Prandra had taken from the first Solthree she had truly known, the brain-in-a-bottle Espinoza. "Then go, and take Nurunda."

"No," Haynes said. "We don't work that way. We're sending you back to your people, and if you want Nurunda, you *ask*. You can't volunteer her."

"Yeah," said McNelly, and snickered.

"You have an hour."

McNelly watched the buzzer diminishing in the steely sky and said, "I think they have the biggest collection of egos as well as ESPs around here."

"I can't judge Ungrukh as well as I do Solthrees, but I doubt ego's pushing Raanung. He has some other reason."

"I hope it isn't revenge. They've said not. And they've been careful to keep the claws sheathed."

"We have to trust them. I presume you have what you need," said Haynes.

"Guns, ammo and my usual nerveless daring."

"Want an ulcer pill?"

"No thanks, I have my own."

The buzzer circled the small cluster of towers and the sprawl of lower roofs shimmering with solar collectors. The street canyons were dark, the bridges among towers twilit. A star or two rose where the limb of the world was turning toward darkness, and a few flamingo plumes of cloud drifted above the red sun.

The buzzer, crammed with pilot, McNelly and two Ungrukh, was a heavy-duty vehicle and did not falter. Raanung was asleep. He had not eaten heavily, but had no reason to stay awake yet. Nurunda was scanning the area below. Unlike Emerald, she was never travelsick, and she was intensely interested. The people she was picking up led strange and extreme lives quite unlike those she had learned from the tourists and Indians in the Canyon. Beggars, politicians, thieves, business executives, killers, clerks and whores were all new to her.

She picked up a faint salute.

"What does it mean, 'Tell McNelly, hello from the fat broad?' "

McNelly laughed. "Sukey. If I called her that she'd sit on me and I'd be a puddle."

"She knows what's going on?"

"Only that we're after Boris. Lots of people are."

Spaulding was a small satellite town northwest of Glendale, which had sprung up with great expectations of contracts in electronic components fifty years before. Most of these had drifted away through competition to other communities, and the place had become a rather shabby collection of small industries and apartments, augmented by an art colony of glassed-in boutiques hoping to attract tourists. Boris had demonstrated a certain shrewdness in picking a hideout just a bit askew of his character.

The buzzer cut speed and became quieter, lowered to quarter its sector, pendulum-wise.

"Dark in half an hour," said McNelly. "If the way's clear we'll go down and fish him in."

"Several people with murder in their heads," said Nurunda. "One with intent, but not against your man."

The pilot said, "Give me whatever you pick up on that one. I'll warn the locals."

"Fast and neat," said McNelly. "I don't want a swarm."

For twenty minutes the craft swung and swung over Boris' head down below in one of the cramped spaces. He was impervious; he might not be home, except that no one had seen him leave.

"Something down the street."

McNelly focused the infrared. "Landcar, big, some kind of van. Popkin, get over the roof park to let me see, but don't touch down . . . gently, keep her running—Nurunda, what do you read?"

"Storage compartments whitewalled, the driver—probing

—hound? some kind of dog? And—bugs."

"Bugs? The two don't go together. And tracking dogs haven't been used for—oops, they're swinging around to the lane for underground parking. Popkin, we're jumping. Anything funny you see, use the cannon on metal and the stunner on meat. Raanung, up and going!"

"I am awake," said Raanung, and was first out.

The cooling system was faulty, and Boris, naked except for the holstered gun, was lying on his bed with a sheet half over him, watching blurred images on the old trivvy. The water in the hot tap was a lukewarm drizzle, and the food was awful even by his modest standards. Since he was renting by the week in the cheapest apartment-hotel for this rather pretentious area, Boris would not bring himself to attention by complaint. He was both fearful and bored, trying to keep his reflexes honed sharp in a dull atmosphere, fighting to keep his mind from drifting to times when life was easier. His lights were out, his two corner windows clear. Luckily the immovable bed was placed where he could watch both.

First he saw the buzzer on an arc of passage. He trained the telescopic gunsight on it; a flicker of late sunlight caught Security markings. No indication it was searching for him. Another sweep. Maybe. Yet, there were no crimes in his file; he wanted none.

He glanced down into the street in time to see the landcar making its turn toward the garage. He had driven one much like it, an expensive model. Surely she wouldn't use the same—but the sweat flowed. And he was three floors from the roof—close enough to hear the buzzer hovering: pincered.

He was too drenched in sweat to pull on his zip. He wrapped himself in a towel, rolled the zip and stuffed it under his arm, ran out the door to the fire-elevator, peered down and saw the cab rising. He dashed back into the room, double-locked, darkened the windows, flicked off the trivvy, and crouched in a center of deadly quiet.

Down in the street there was a *crump!*

The roof door was locked, but McNelly had his own kinds of keys. Then he stopped for a second. "Oh God! Bugs, hound! Mechanical sniffers, home in on molecule combinations—just like that nose of yours!"

The pilot said in his ear, "They usually use tranquilizer darts."

"Not for Boris they won't! You still see that car?"

"Sure do! I whacked it. Two or three guys jumped out."

"One is your orange-beard man," said Nurunda.

"Local pop. around?"

"Nah. Monday streets rolled up."

"Keep on it!"

"That's what I'm doing!"

McNelly, Raanung, Nurunda ran down the spiral escalator. "No racing, Ungrukh! You won't get in without me!"

Another *crump!* from the street. Footsteps down the escalator. Thumps from behind the ventilator grilles in bedroom and shower stall. Heavy blows popped out the flimsy screens, hordes of tiny metal things poured through the openings, clattering, and in one instant all sprang alive, whirred, buzzed, hummed, clicked. Boris was dizzy and almost paralyzed by fear, but in some vestige of rationality realized that these things, which could not be shot at, *knew* him, *recognized* him. In a spasm of terror he grabbed sheet and blanket and rolled himself in them, cocooned, enwombed, shaking.

Two pistol blasts, the door slid open, a voice cried, "Security! Don't move, for God's sake, we're here to help!" McNelly switched on the dim lights. They were bright enough to show hundreds of whirring beetles, coated dull gray, each with a tiny sponge-tipped antenna rising from its back, a needle pointing from its snout.

McNelly groaned. "Shit, what do I do with these?" The bugs ignored him, and when he saw that they were still pouring in hundreds from the open ventilator he holstered his machine pistol and crouched to shoot stunner bolts into the shaft.

Nurunda leaped on the bed and covered Boris with her body. He struggled and freed one hand that twitched helplessly. "Be still, man! I am protecting you!" She whacked her tail about, sending the bugs flying.

But it was Raanung, blazing with anger, worry, long-suppressed sexuality, who found himself lifted on hind legs by an instinct older than his species.

Schpritz!

Under the hissing stream a hundred tiny monsters, systems

shorted, whirled like dancing bees for a moment and stopped.

"That's it!" McNelly ran into the shower stall and, knowing cheap hotels, shoved at the cold tap and directed one nozzle into the ceiling ventilator where bugs were still dropping, pulled out the shower hose to sweep down the bedroom and everything in it.

In two minutes there was a great mess and a thousand dead mechanisms. Boris was gasping and Nurunda pulled the bedclothes off him. He was pale, bluish.

"Christ," said McNelly. "Raanung, did you pick up any unfamiliar scent when we got in?"

Raanung scoured his memory: yes . . . a faint smell . . . Nurunda amplified it.

"Cyanide! He can't have got much—Popkin! get medics!"

"You giving mouth to mouth? Don't bother. I've got an ambulance."

The empty street had suddenly filled out with a deep circle of the curious around a landcar with a dent in its reinforced roof and an engine battered into fragments among mashed power-cells. A blaring ambulance bullied the watchers aside.

Nurunda pulled down the emergency switch to lower the plasmix pane and let in paramedics hovering on an air stretcher. One silver-suited figure jumped in to push McNelly aside and give Boris a needle. "The cure's almost as bad as the disease, but he's still breathing, so I guess he'll live." A woman's voice. She tipped back the hood and looked around. "Big party. Anybody else need help?"

No complaints from the Ungrukh. "We seem to be all right," said McNelly, and added, "We're Security, and we'd like to keep it that way."

"Not my business. *You've* got to tell the landlord." The loaded stretcher floated away.

"I'd better be right about cyanide," said McNelly. "Whatever, it would have killed him, and the antidote won't. God almight—Security!" he yelled at the redfaced landlord. "Keep the door closed and seal it after we get out. We'll pay for everything. More than it cost him," he muttered as he crawled into the ventilator shaft and pulled out a groaning figure. "Bobby Billings, howdy-do."

"One got away," said Popkin in his ear.

"Probably another still crawling around in the air vents, but I'll leave him to the locals. Let's get out."

• • •

"Yeah, cyanide," said Haynes. "Nurunda, you said he shoved his hand out of the blankets—that's when he must have gotten those seven or eight stings. But then he couldn't have stayed under forever. Luckily a weak solution. Thirty or forty of those would have done him."

"I should have smelled it myself. I dunno why not," McNelly said.

"Because it was weak," Haynes said. "It takes a Big Nose." He glanced at Raanung, who was coiled in a corner, moping. Nurunda was asleep on the couch, snoring heartily.

Haynes rolled one of the bugs between thumb and finger. "Nobody uses them anymore—nobody's supposed to. It was the dazzler of four or five years ago, the techs couldn't begin to trace it to Phoebe's outfit. Five or six firms in Spaulding were making them, thought they'd have a good start on a new thing. Find a stray kid, pet, zoo animal, by homing with sensors to pick up characteristic sweat, skin-oil, saliva molecule patterns. Nose. Nobody recognized how fast it could become dangerous: crime and piracy got into the labs and turned it into the murder weapon you just saw demonstrated tonight. As a legitimate business it had to be shut down. Except . . . what the devil's the matter with you, Raanung? Got a chill from your soaking?"

"One good shake warms me. Mr. McNelly has chattering teeth even in dry clothes."

"Pure fear," said McNelly.

"Something is bothering you, Raanung."

Raanung stood up. "I spend most of my life trying to make a civilized man out of myself, and end up behaving like an idiot!"

Nurunda woke to grin and hiss with laughter. "Long ago you are angry at yourself because you must kill a Solthree to keep on living, and tonight you decide you must save one. And you do. Whatever debt you believe you owe you pay. So shut up." She closed her eyes and resumed snoring.

McNelly snorted. "A few hours ago I made the mistake of thinking you Ungrukh had big egos, but you're just guilt wallowers. If you hadn't behaved that way I'd never have thought to use the shower and Boris would be dead. Stop the tail-thumping. The lady is right."

• • •

Haynes was wiping his bleary face with a wet tissue when McNelly brought him the flimsy.

"A present from Mercy Adams. She actually asked for a mindclear when Sukey delivered her to District, and it's on record."

Haynes pushed aside a heap of spools, papers and fruitpits. His hands were shaking from weariness.

"I think you need a holiday."

"Hah. What about Boris?"

"I've sent Lundberg to the hospital. The antidote makes you feel so sick I'm not sure he could talk if he wanted. This thing is a rough, but I thought you'd want to see it."

Haynes squeezed his lids, blinked and read:

. . . make this statement willingly after mindclear, which on oath I asked for. During the ten years I worked for Phoebe Charloe Adams Silver I was given mindblocks and hypnosis regularly. I am now able to give an account of the material covered by blocking.

On a night in January last of which I don't remember the date except that there was a full moon, I was given warm clothes and a balaclava and taken by Adams and another person I can't identify, both masked, to the Canyon in a commercial skimmer. On the way we stopped twice and each time picked up nine or ten persons with the same kind of mask. I think they were all Solthree. I'm not sure of that, or even how many were men or women, though I judged from the voices that there were some of both. Somebody said my name was Charley. I don't know who. We were set down some place in the Canyon, I think on the North Rim or some projection of it. It overlooked a level area. We were given guns and told to shoot to kill. After a few minutes one Ungrukh led the others there. I had never seen Ungrukh before except on Tri-V and knew nothing about them except of their presence.

I hesitated. The same person who told us to shoot struck me a blow in the shoulder and said, "Get on with it, you dumb bastard." I think I was unable to speak. I used to hunt with my father when I was a girl and am a fairly good rifle shot but never used handguns. I pulled the trigger several times, but don't know if I hit anyone or even if the ammunition was real. I was standing in for Phoebe Adams, but I wonder if she trusted me with the real thing; I was hardly aiming. But I was drugged and docile, and I can't prove anything. After all that killing there was one left alive, I think the Ungrukh who led the others, and that one was flamed. I don't know why. I was one of those sent to skin bodies because of my hunting experience. The one called Bren was the first I got to, and I was shocked to find her alive. She grabbed my arm in her jaws, pulled my mask most of the way off, scratching my face, and dragged me by the arm some way before she dropped me. Whatever happened after that is confused, except that I had a few scratches that healed with light scars and needed no special treatment. I can't swear I didn't kill anybody, but I do swear that Phoebe Adams had me drugged and took me out to kill. That's all I remember about it. . . .

Haynes put the paper down. "That one who led them there, that was the Magundir Bren identified; he managed to set them up somehow. He got flamed and that was his reward." He sighed. "Something. I don't know how much. District seen it?"

"Yeah. If you get something good from Boris, think Phoebe can be brought to trial?"

"Maybe."

"Convicted?"

"Of course not! Not on her home ground, and she'll manage to duck the scanner. But it'll keep her busy and quiet for a while, and that's a beginning."

36

At GalFed Central, Kinnear, summoned by Narinder Singh, encountered Medor in the corridor. He stood aside to let the big Ungrukh pass, because Medor's fur was standing on end from whiskers to tail tip, making him look very large indeed, and his brow-drawn eyes seemed about to shoot lightning bolts.

Kinnear was careful not to esp, but took the risk of saying, "Hullo, Medor, how are things?"

"Not good, and I am sure I do not look as if they are good either."

"Sorry, Medor. I didn't mean to pry, or disturb you."

"*You* are not disturbing me." Kinnear would have passed, but Medor paused and said, "It is Rrimi."

Kinnear understood. Rrimi, Medor's daughter, was a young woman of seven or eight, big and powerful like her father. On Ungruwarkh she had competed for the favors of a very desirable male. She had won the battle but lost the man, and her only memento was a crescent-shaped scar over the right eye. Medor and his woman Argha had brought her with them to help her forget her woes: a questionable solution.

"The apartment is small, there are no other Ungrukh here; we must get permission to use the parks and gymnasiums at night when the cleaners work because we make other users nervous; we make the cleaners nervous; my woman and daughter are driving each other mad, and they already drive *me* mad!"

"I suppose she wants to go home. Surely she can find a man worthy of her there."

"Surely, and we all want her to go home. But no ship passes for several thirtydays. Solthrees, Kinnear, have useful proverbs: 'God provides, but let Him provide until He provides!' " He snorted and passed on.

Kinnear shook his head and went to find out what Singh had on his mind. He had a sense of déjà vu, though the expression in Singh's eyes was one of pain rather than anger. Again he kept his thoughts to himself. "New development?"

Singh blinked the pain away. "Message from Kylklar." He pushed forward a holo cube, the smallest in commercial use, 7.5 cm. "Nice conventional portrait of Ti'iri'il's daughter Pai'ili'ot." He pushed the stud. Trilling voice in *lingua*:

"From Pai'ili'ot ni Ti'iri'il of Kylklar, Port Na'at, greetings. A memorial service for my father Ti'iri'il will be held in order to welcome and thank friends, on date: 09.26.78. With honors and respects to all."

"Announcement? Invitation? Call for help?"

"Look."

Kinnear picked up the cube. "Portrait of a young Kylkladi woman dressed in all her feathers, pink with red crest, quite pretty by Solthree standards, small beak, eyes calm, intelligent, in control of herself." He pressed the stud and listened again. "What have I missed? Ring with red stone. Necklace. Those usual?"

"Kylkladi are not strangers to adornments."

"Ring red, matches crest. Necklace . . . blue. Blue what?" Singh passed him a magnifying glass. "Xirifri pearl?"

"So it looks. Setting and chain of white metal. Could be platinum, chromium, steel, silver, tin, they don't care." Singh lifted a piece of multicolored silk. "Vendor's wrapping inside the packing. Fancy letters: *Yglar & Co., Artists of Fashion and Refinement*. Tourist nonsense. Also: *We make attractive enlargements*. Lab says that's been added by hand—or claw, so . . ." He rode his chair to the cabinet and took out a 25 cm cube, "I had Lab do an attractive enlargement. Good resolution."

"A trilobar pearl of the kind we saw on . . . that . . . skin."

"Exactly."

"You know, the metal setting looks kind of—"

"I thought of that." He produced another cube. "This is a holo, not the original, you'll be glad to know."

The star sapphire on the finger of the chopped-off hand was set in a white metal of a whorled design similar to the one holding the pearl. "Traders buy Kylkladi work," Kinnear said. "Still . . . that date she gives is local. When about?"

"A thirtyday and a half, roughly."

"She knows something, or needs someone. Or both."

"Yes. I imagine she's hoping someone will come. She's put the date back far enough."

"You want to send someone?"

"I'm not sure, and I don't know who. Of course, one assumes the worst."

"What's the margin?"

"A couple of days."

"I'll put my mind to it."

Singh smiled faintly. "Thanks, Dun. I knew you would."

Kinnear left almost gratefully, but not before seeing the film of pain come down over Singh's eyes again.

On the way home he paused at Stores for a fresh Dewar clip.

"These things are ingenious," said Ordnance. "Ever use one?"

"Never had to, I'm glad to say."

"Snarks are pretty thick in your Terrarium sector."

"I've managed to avoid them."

"Hear one of Singh's kids runs with a gang."

Kinnear fitted the clip in its case and dropped the weapon in his pocket. "I don't pay much attention to gossip."

"You may have to. I think they ought to fumigate the place, like for roaches."

"You want a job like that?"

"I'm satisfied—and I'm qualified here," Ordnance said quickly.

"Good. I hear there're some vacancies in Waste Disposal."

Pertab, Narinder Singh's youngest and eighteen years old, had grown up in an overcrowded Civil Service community; overcrowded further by five siblings in the largest apartment available: three rooms. Singh had saved hard to send all his children home to Sol III for education and religious training as they grew. Most were established now, one or two in ways that did not please him, but they were beyond his control. The expense was great, even for a man in his position high on the ladder, and the children had to be sent at advancing ages. Pertab would be the oldest to leave, probably too old to profit from Singh's hopes. Singh at the top of his ambitions, Medor barely starting, were in the same position. Medor had only one child. It hardly seemed to matter.

Kinnear walked along halls where he had once been greeted by guards and now avoided maintenance-and-alarm robots. A robot in good condition *might* bring help with a call.

Up elevators, along halls; up escalators, along halls; up ramps . . . Robots did not notice grimy corners. The carpet, almost napless, had not been renewed in twenty-five years. The Civil Service had increased, and were paid well but got little service. In the grim lounge the tea, imported from Fthel IV, was at least still good, even in disposable mugs.

Kinnear disposed of his mug, took one last elevator, walked one last hall, hands in pockets, slowly.

Snarks are thick in your sector.

Three doors from his apartment they burst from the Supply Room, Snarks, ten or twelve, in their teens, all Solthree, because this was the Terrarium, all shapes and colors, because they came from a world of them. They had their own brand of knife, a steel skewer that did not spill much blood. Kinnear stood still, mouth agape, shielding hard because many here were the children of ESPs, ESPs themselves, some better than he.

"That's right. Just keep still," said their leader, a small wizened girl with red hair. She looked fourteen. He clapped his hand to his mouth and kept it there. "Good. Keep it quiet."

Cockroaches? They were boys and girls, bored, bitter, frustrated in overcrowded and stultifying conditions. They would not kill, but torment. Jab, jab, jab, leaving scars for life.

These were unfamiliar, except perhaps for one, came from different floors, distant corridors; they did not work home territory, and the remarkably well-organized gangs avoided each others' provinces.

The girl was ill in some way, mentally or physically, manic —or on drugs? Her parents, if they thought of her, were too busy, or maybe helpless, like Singh and Medor.

Kinnear retreated slowly, waiting for the one who would come round, needle knife quivering, to get at him from behind. Artful Dodger.

"You, Foxy," the girl said. A little pointy-chinned kid, Kinnear would have guessed twelve, but likely they were all older than they seemed. Growing up here they got stunted.

Kinnear waited until the child was abreast of him, then lurched sideways, knocking the fist holding the knife, which flew in an arc to the carpet; he grabbed under the armpit and flung the small body into the knot of his fellows. The time for pity was gone.

Before they could regroup he opened his mouth. A hundred tiny needles sprayed from it, pierced cloth to sting first and then numb. The children yelled, scrambled and ran, limping.

Kinnear had been very careful to aim for the legs. He took the gun, which had been molded to fit against his teeth, out of his mouth, opened it and the vacuum case to shake one last carbon dioxide needle to the floor, where it vaporized in a tiny cloud. He picked up three abandoned knives and chucked them in a disposal.

Then he opened the door of Supply, which lit up, and took the slender neck of cowering Pertab Singh in one big hand. There was no pressure in the fingers; the gesture was almost one of love. "Lion of the Punjab"—he had given the nickname to three-year-old Pertab—"why didn't you warn them? You're a better ESP than I." Pertab had passed his ESP-one exam a thirtyday earlier, *summa cum laude*.

This boy too looked younger than his years; his beard was pubertal. "You are my father's friend. You would have told him." Streaks of dark hair fell sullenly over his eyes.

"I don't discuss you with your father. I can see by his face there's little to say. I wouldn't have told your father. I won't." He took his hand away.

"You will do something," said Pertab.

"I'll think about it. Get home now. If you're late for supper you'll have a hard time making up a story."

Pertab gave him one malevolent blink, fetched his comb from his waistband where it was tucked beside the knife, fastened his hair with a quick twist, pulled out his folded turban and began winding it neatly around his head. "Your weapon will be out of fashion now that it's known."

"I'd have been out of fashion if I'd hit anybody in the eye. I never expected I'd have to use it. Close the door when you go."

After supper Kinnear answered the CommUnit; his heart sank at the sound of the familiar growl, but Medor was oddly diffident. "Director, my daughter is taking her ESP-one exam at fifteen-thirty hours tomorrow. I like to invite you to sit in, but I understand if you are too busy to come."

"Medor, I'd be absolutely delighted. Give me the room number and I'll make time."

"Thank you, Kinnear. . . . I don't know if this makes any difference, but perhaps . . ."

Kinnear's heart ached: Medor was so demoralized that he had given the invitation on short notice to make it easy for Kinnear to refuse—and it would make no difference. *Pertab.*

He poured two fingers of scotch and looked at it. Then he called Singh's number. Pertab answered. "My parents are not in. You said you would not tell." His voice was clear and firm. He was alone.

"I'm not telling. I know your parents are at the shadow-puppets exhibit. I called to speak to you."

"And what kind of punishment have you thought up for me?"

"I've never punished anyone and never will. Only, make sure you're in my office at fifteen hundred hours."

After he rang off, he thought long, and drank too much, and slept badly. In the morning he overdosed on antidotes, eyedrops and coffee.

Pertab appeared on time in white puckered cotton shirt and pants, sandals, lightly bearded and tightly turban-wound, in the same pale green his father had preferred many years ago. The bones of his face were those of Narinder Singh. Its expression was not.

At 1530 both were sitting in on Rrimi's ESP-one exam. It was as silent as usual, and for non-ESPs as excruciatingly dull. Prandra's exam was the only really exciting one Kinnear had attended—because he was risking his life—and that was long ago and far away.

Some changes had been made in the rules as applied to Ungrukh. *Forms—optional, Category: illusion* had been made truly optional, and the Cats, with limited imagination, had no longer to torture themselves trying to produce astonishing visions.

As her party-piece, Rrimi, notwithstanding many thirtydays of isolation and bad temper, was constructing a mosaic of pleasing youthful memories, carefully chosen not to embarrass or invade privacy, drawn from, and for, everyone in the hall.

Kinnear lay in a meadow of heather and buttercups under a lightly showering sky; observed Khagodi's bursting volcanoes against the background of its deep sky of noonday stars from just below the surface of its seas; raced four-legged through the foamy edges of Ungruwarkh's Tidesland; swam with dolphins; shared Cosmic Thought limb-twined among Lyhhrt . . . a construction that only seemed simple, for it was simultaneous, and considering the nature of Ungrukh, and of Rrimi, a masterpiece.

Observing the rule of silence, Kinnear nodded toward Rrimi and said to Pertab, *:What do you think of that one?:*

:For what? My father is sending me to Sol Three to find a bride. Or so he thinks,: and before Kinnear could stop him sent Rrimi a thought that should have shivered the image into fragments.

Rrimi did not twitch, but Pertab opened his mouth in a silent scream of agony. Rrimi's accuracy was worthy of a Khagodi, and her control so great that no one noticed Pertab at all; Kinnear picked up the exchange but not the blast, as he supposed was meant, and the display completed its course without ripple or buckle.

The pain subsided as quickly as it had struck. Pertab shook his head and blinked. His lips were trembling. Kinnear resisted the impulse to put his arm about the boy's shoulder for comfort. Pertab had brought it on himself.

Rrimi got her *summa*. Kinnear would have added stars and bars. She met her fond parents, accepted a lick on the snout from her mother and a love-tap from her father that might have decapitated a Solthree. Then she ran after Kinnear and Pertab, who were filing out slowly in a clump blocked by a large Tignit trying to balance a pressure-pump with four tentacles while working cramps out of three others. "Princeling," she said, "I apologize for giving you pain."

Kinnear assumed that she knew where her father's meat got cubed, but Pertab smiled and murmured, "Not so, Kinnear. I am also one who does not tell." To Rrimi he said, "I am not a good enough ESP to harm you, lady. You are too good an ESP to harm me."

"You speak graciously, master." The term was used not in deference, but in respect to the new ESP status of both. Kinnear surmised that neither of these persons had ever spoken so politely to anyone, but he kept that thought very far down.

A weary Kinnear dragged himself to his office to make a stab at clearing his decks. There was another message from Singh.

"What now?"

"Medor passed this on, from Sol Three."

PLEASE INFORM ANY INDICATION OF QUMEDNI MOVEMENT, PARTICULARLY OF THAT BEING CALLING ITSELF KRIKU.

"Oh God, I knew that would catch up with us. I'd better answer it. Just let the bloody fireball mind his own business."

"And . . ." Singh pinned Kinnear with his sharp black eyes, "it *is* a good idea."

Kinnear sat down and covered his face with his hands. When he pulled them away the effects of eyedrops and antidotes went with them. He was haggard and bloodshot.

"I have also been an old Security man, Kinnear, and will not apologize for esping without permission."

"I fought with the idea all night," said Kinnear. "It seemed too much like throwing a couple of troubled young people in the garbage."

"No, Kinnear, no! I came here directly from school at sixteen, and by eighteen I was out in the field. Pertab is willing to go and so is Rrimi, and they can use authority if they choose or be innocent travelers. Best, they are strong enough to help Pai'ili'ot and young enough so that I hope she will find them sympathetic."

"That's not a word I'd use, exactly," Kinnear muttered, and Singh laughed.

"No, they are not exactly delighted to go together, but they must get along together if they want to go." He added more slowly, "I doubt if this will cure their spirits; perhaps it will improve their minds."

If they succeed . . . "Well, I'm damned glad that's been taken out of my hands."

"I am checking ship lists for a fast cruiser within five days. They can train while they are being starved and dehydrated for deepsleep. That will make them angry at us instead of each other. For shuttle we want a good small lifeboat, and then they are on their own."

Pertab and Rrimi looked out through the Port window at the little boat. It was tough; lifeboats are constructed not only to be launched but expelled under extreme conditions.

"If it's like the ones I've used it will do very well," Kinnear said.

"Better nowadays," said Mechtech. Pertab and Rrimi looked at her. Singh pulled his beard. Kinnear was thinking that in GalFed nepotism meant that one sent out those one loved the most. Mechtech ran her fingers through crisp auburn hair and said firmly, "You will have one night of sleepteach, and memorize the spool manual while you are training at moving about in the gravity chamber and acclimatizing to Kylkladi atmosphere. It is all simple."

"I am sure," said Rrimi in a voice of rough plush.

"I see the registry symbols," said Pertab. "I presume it has a name?"

It did not, but Kinnear, ever impulsive, stuck his tongue in his cheek for a moment and said in a voice almost Ungrukh: "*Snark*."

"Why not?" Pertab said coolly. "The *Snark* is going hunting."

37

Pai'ili'ot was, like *Snark*, gracile but not delicate.

Kylkladi adults were much of a size, though they varied greatly in the lighter tints. Instead of graying with age they darkened into deeper and richer colors that gave them an appearance of gravity and wisdom. They had strong horn-plated feet, thick of talon and round of claw like the grebe, but longer in the shank. They walked with great dignity, and their arms, though draped with vestigial wing-feathers, were fitted with hands both powerful and slender, three fingers and thumb.

Pertab and Rrimi were greeted by all they met with great courtesy, which characteristically made them uneasy.

Pai'ili'ot served them nectar in her summer bower where sun and shade flickered, a cup for Pertab, a bowl for Rrimi. Rrimi dipped her tongue gingerly. She liked stuff that was redder and saltier.

"You had better call me Pai, so you will not have to wring your tongues over my name. I am very grateful to have you here, and it was thoughtful of your parents to send you. Too much official interest would be dangerous. In two days—about sixty of your Standard hours?—it will be over, and nothing can be done. But someone will *know.*"

:It is dangerous for her already,: said Pertab.

:She is aware.:

"And I will tell you everything that happened now, before I choke on it.

"I went down with my father to the Port field—he was Portmaster as well as GalFed delegate—to make polite talk with the traders. We did that whenever there was some kind of convention."

"Did that happen often?" Pertab asked.

"About once a year. I don't care much for traders' talk, and I wandered. It is usually safe. Many crews are corrupt, but they are rarely violent, and the district is quite well policed. There was a neutral ship hired by Xirifor to bring pearls—no one seems to remember who owned it—and the documents were in order as far as anyone could tell. Remember this took place after that horrible murder and everyone was being careful. A young crewman from that ship, a Kylklad, approached me with what he said was a gift from his captain."

"The necklace."

"Yes. I was nervous, but . . . also very stupid. I was flattered. He was a handsome fellow. I know nothing of pearls, and imagined it must be flawed or cultured because it was so big . . . and when he asked me to wear it so that he could take a picture . . . I am no great beauty, my friends."

"Oh, but you are, Pai," said Pertab truthfully.

"Not for a Kylklad. The whores here dye themselves this color. My father was criticized for marrying my mother because she was such a color . . . but that is not my story—"

:Only half of it,: said Rrimi.

"—and I was affianced then, and a bit nervous. I was afraid the man might take me for—but . . ." perhaps a note of disappointment recalled, "he only said good-bye, and left, and when I showed the necklace to my father he astonished me by becoming very angry—even frightened—did I have no sense after that murder, he asked, and I was to take it off and throw it away at once. I could not see how it would have anything to do with murder, and it was surely not valuable, but no, no, I must get rid of it. Yet . . . it was a beautiful thing and I kept it. I was afraid to mention the picture."

"And you still have the necklace," said Pertab.

Pai slipped from her hassock, lifted its lid and took out a crystal egg. It seemed perfectly clear but at the press of some spot halved open with a faint tinkle of melody into a box. She held it out. Pertab lifted the chain on one finger and the magnificent pearl hung free.

"*Is* it valuable, Pertab?"

"I should think so, but I'm not sure."

Rrimi stretched her neck from the shoulders and her tongue from the jaws without leaving her own hassock and touched pearl and chain. "It is valuable. The chain is platinum."

"How do you know?"

"When you go to Galactic Federation to be educated you can learn unusual things."

Pertab asked, "Did it occur to you that it might be contraband?"

"There are things I am stupid about, but—there were many things kept from me. I was . . . sheltered. My color . . . My father was an honest man and took no bribes, but he could not choose his underlings. . . . I think they wanted to make sure he did not try to extend his appointment after end of term—and they succeeded. A few days later he received the holo of me wearing the necklace, and a threat of exposure at GalFed—when there was nothing to expose! Then that terrible fight happened among the traders being detained—and he broke down. He had gone to GalFed to try drawing attention to what was happening here, and I begged him to go again and tell everything, but he was too frightened. I always thought it foolish of him. He should have told the whole painful truth."

"What about the call for free trade?"

"Idiocy! No one wants free trade! That would drive prices down."

"Did your father know the contrabanders?"

"Like everyone, he knew of them. The law will not act against them."

"Did he know who they were?"

"He did his best not to know, because he had no power against them. I hate to confess I think that was weak."

Rrimi said slowly, "The young do tend to think their parents weak. And foolish. I know that much from my forebears."

Pertab asked, "Why did you call for help just now, Pai?"

"My mother broke down. She is in a . . . a place."

Cage.

"And my father's term will be up soon and the filthy will have *all* of the power. Forever."

"Maybe." Pertab swung the jewel. "Why hold on to this?"

"I hoped to use it as a weapon against my enemies. I don't know in what way."

"May I keep it for now?"

"Of course, if it will help. But how?"

"I'm not sure." Pertab, late a Snark, gave a grin worthy of an Ungrukh. "Still—excuse the expression—it may possibly make some feathers fly."

:Without breaking any eggs,: said Rrimi.

"He cannot have been that weak," Pertab said. "It must have cost him much control to behave the way he did." Pai was asleep in her curtained chamber while Rrimi lay on a reed mat and Pertab on a featherbed in his nightshirt beside her, both watching the great orange moon through the leafy branches of the bower.

"The Kylkladi are excellent blockers and very clever at many small things. They are certainly a complicated people."

"But he was still a fool."

"For trying to be honest?"

Pertab said coolly, "*I* would have poisoned those bastards. And kept the pearls."

Rrimi ignored the youthful bravado. "Until the money-collectors come."

"I would have made plans . . ."

"Indeed, Princeling. Indeed."

The peaceful sleep that followed was the gift of Pertab, who reasoned that two GalFed innocents, without obvious authority, would not be slaughtered during their first night on Kylklar.

38

The summer city was a resort community built mainly of reinforced saplings and other plant materials in groves some 20 km outside the Port. Although the materials were not expensive, the labor of arranging and maintaining them in grace and beauty was. Pai did not long expect to keep her bower on her father's pension, considering the expense of her mother's treatment and the difficulty of finding employment in her kind of society. But she spent as much time as possible at the bower: Her city quarters were no more spacious than Rrimi's and Pertab's; the memories were painful, and she did not care for her parents' friends and relatives; they had not treated her very well after Ti'iri'il's death.

And she visited her mother in the hospital nearly every day —a wearying journey. Kylkladi had exact measurements for everything except distance, which they reckoned by the time it took to reach a certain place, in such a vehicle, at a particular time. Therefore they were indifferent mapmakers. But since many Kylkladi peoples were migratory, and most had the same kind of directional sense as Xirifri, mapping did not seem to matter.

It is safe to say that there has never been evolutionary debate on the world where the reptiles fly, the mammals lay eggs, and the butterflies grow feathers. The Egg came first, and all grew out of it. It bred many great birds, the most useful of which were many species of *uku*. The smallest of these was larger than the greatest ostrich, laid eggs the size of Rrimi's head and had a kick that would send her spinning. The largest, over four meters tall, would have shivered her bones as she spun. Finely formed heads stood on their pylon necks, and their eyes were shrewd as a cat's. Even their narrow feet with spatulate toes were handsome, as was their plumage, dark gray or brown, with golden crests and flightless wings of the same color. They carried people, drew vehicles to a speed of 30 kph and pulled plows, all with studied arrogance.

Pai owned one of the smaller ones. She had hired a pair, small and great, for her guests; with the aristocratic presumption of Kylkladi, she expected them to know how to ride.

Pertab had ridden horses, sometimes bareback; at a zoo as a small child he had ridden an ostrich with hobbled legs. Rrimi had ridden only the backs of her parents as a cub, and she did not know how an uku would feel about having Ungrukh claws digging into its plumage. But the alternative was to run a total of fifty-odd km at a pace she could maintain for no more than fifteen.

Pai did, however, have a sense of proportion. While the three were finishing breakfast, hers of nectar and various seeds, theirs of reconstituted somethings reputed healthful—a meal she had served with as much dignity as if she had not been forced to discharge her servant—she said, "Rrimi, I have ordered a double harness for your uku, and if you can use your claws as we our talons, I think you will get along."

The liveryman was approaching with the two great beasts. and Rrimi thanked Pai gravely. *:It is a pity those creatures cannot reason,:* she said to Pertab. *:Then they can tell us who gives them posthypnotic suggestion to kick us to death when we dismount.:*

:Really? I hadn't caught that. Surely not Pai. She's no ESP, though she could have been hypnotized to—but that's too complicated and uncertain.:

:Or perhaps we are only to believe and be frightened away. . . .:

:No. Too twisted. We'd be trapped into thinking like them —and get our heads kicked in. We're different: Our strategy is not to play on their terms but against them.:

:Then you cook the strategy and I serve the tactics.:

:On that big son of a bitch I wish you luck.:

The exchange, unnoticed by Pai, had taken three seconds,

and she said, "I hope you will excuse me while I visit my mother. It takes only a short while, so perhaps you would like to tour the city."

"I really think it's better we don't separate, Pai. We'll go with you while you visit your mother, and wait."

Pai began to tremble. Her feathers ruffled and her hands fluttered. "I—if you please—"

:Her mother is in some shabby hospice,: said Pertab, *:And worse, she has another visit to make. She's promised, um, sexual favors to pay the people supplying the decorations for her father's memorial, and today is payday.:*

:I already realize that,: said Rrimi dryly. *:I don't worry about eavesdropping once in a while.:*

:How do we get by this without shaming her?:

:You of all people shrink and cringe, Master Snark? We do it in the usual way.: She drew Pai aside a few steps and said, "Dear lady, we are a couple of scrappy rascals who are probably not fit for decent company, but we mean no harm, and we determine none comes to you. We have generous vouchers, and the credit is no more than is owing you. Forgive our rudeness and accept."

Pai felt she ought to be scandalized, and was not. She decided it was better not to wonder why not. She calmed and said with her usual dignity, "Many thanks, best of friends. I do accept."

Most roads everywhere are hardened and weatherproofed; country roads in Kylklar's resort areas are tilled and harrowed daily to accommodate the thumping feet of the big birds. *Pit-pat, pit-pat*, went Pai's uku. Pertab's went *pik-pok, pik-pok*, and so did his heart. Rrimi's great beast went *plump-plomp, plump-plomp*; she cast her mind back through all the memories of her people who had ridden their parents' back as children, and accommodated the movement of her body to the one beneath her. The feeling grew quite exhilarating, and she also did not forget the perils of dismounting.

Kylklar has generous temperate and southern tropic zones, twined with fresh waterways draining into the northern salt seas, a comfortable 8.9 Newtons of gravity, and a 28 percent oxygen atmosphere, which is a bit rich for Solthrees, and very much so for Ungrukh. The trees grow taller and leafier, but there is nothing either magnificent or grotesque about its landscapes.

To one who grew up among landscapes it would seem only a different country; to Rrimi from her Tundras, and Pertab from his pot-treed Terrarium, it was the kind of world seen only in dreams and pictures. Yet they saw no great marvels except trees, flowers and fields punctuated by irrigation ditches, and a few high clouds roiling from winds coming off distant mountains. The long-winged reptiles flying overhead were delicate and hollow-boned, strong enough only to snatch fledgelings from their nests.

As they rode, the airs of their passing fluttered cloth, plume and fur, all pleasant on a fair day. Pertab and Rrimi, however, kept watch for little valleys with streams and groves, and when finally they saw one that looked right, they turned—"Pause here," said Rrimi—from the harrowed track.

"Where are you going?" cried Pai, who feared they had lost control of their uku.

"One moment, Miss Pai," Pertab called.

She pulled short on the reins and watched while the two hired uku backed into a grove of trees without perceptible command.

"I do hope these things have carotid arteries," said Pertab, reaching as high as he could to clasp both hands around his bird's neck and choke with all his strength.

Pai shrieked, "Come back! What are you doing?"

"Be calm, lady," said Rrimi. "We are only taming them." She slipped all four limbs from the stirrups to the creature's broad back and clapped the narrow of its neck between two paws. She had an easier time of it, for though her uku was two and a half of Pertab's, she was three of him. Pai, casting about in terror of being seen, jumped down and pulled her mount into the grove.

"Keep well away from the feet," said Rrimi. She did not waste breath explaining, but opened her mind, and Pai, trembling, pulled back.

The uku flapped their wings for a moment in great whacking beats, but Pertab was kneeling and Rrimi crouching above them. Then the eyes began to close, the heads descend to the ground. Broad toes and pillar legs kept the birds standing. Pertab skittered down the neck with a whoop; Rrimi descended the taper of her pylon, one foot before the other, at leisure. She came to stand beside Pai. Pertab gave a good pull on the reins, first to one uku, then the other, and ran like the devil fast and furious across the stream.

The uku opened their eyes slowly, raised their heads, turned tails in the direction in which their reins had been pulled, and kicked savagely; huge broad toes thudding against trunks, shedding dead bark, rattling seedpods, nuts and dry leaves on their backs.

Pertab jumped the brook and skipped back, laughing. Rrimi did not laugh. Pai said in a low quavering trill, "They meant to kill you!"

"Oh, perhaps give us a good shake. Now we teach them to believe they do their duty and they become gentle like little mice."

A couple of farmers were loping and squawking across the paddies. "What do you do! What do you do!"

"Give our poor beasts a holiday! Do you not think they deserve one? We do not harm your crops or charge for gardening improvements. Many thanks and farewell!"

They mounted and went on their way, leaving the yelpers behind.

:I trusted that liveryman for many years,: said Pai, with the desolation of one more loss.

:Do keep trusting him. It is not his fault that someone subverts his animals.:

Port Na'at was built of wood: wooden towers, aeries, shops, roads; fastened with dowelling and fitted with parquetry in its finer sections; plastered with wattle and clay in its poorer ones. At fifty thousand pop. it was the largest community on its migratory world, pleasantly spread out, treed and flowered, though its buildings were old and unspacious. Only the Port field was not wood, but paved with mixed and leveled composition, scoured black with takeoffs; its noise was kept 5 km from the city. The uku were stabled near it, for they did not mind the noise, and Pai exchanged them for a curiously antique rented automobile, a box-shaped wooden frame fueled by kerosene, to be ridden on the stone road leading to the city and the timbers of its streets. Pai was a competent driver of one of these simple vehicles which never exceeded 15 kph, and Rrimi and Pertab were able to identify their boat on the field—there were only four others—while their latex-rimmed wheels humped and bumped on the uneven blocks.

"Don't you wish to look over your ship?" Pai asked.

"The only thing valuable about it *is* the thing itself. If the force field's tampered with there'll be some devilish alarms only my remote can shut off."

Though the city seemed a pleasant place with its high peaked roofs just visible among the trees, the nearer she approached the shop where the memorial arrangements were to be made, the more nervous Pai became. Her ruffling and fluttering, no matter how justified, were rather annoying, but her guests recognized them as characteristic of the people, rather than of individuals; there was an inner spine to Pai that Pertab would have called steel if that metal were much used on Kylklar. Jouncing on the car's hard bench he was feeling more put upon than Rrimi, who was crouching on the floorboards of a very skeletal mode of transportation. "One might almost wish for rickshas or pedicabs," he said, sighing.

"There are plenty of them, see? just down the road, but they would not hold us all," said Pai. She meant, all of Rrimi.

:In the matter of weight, I think I will stay outside and let you go in with Pai until you make arrangements,: said Pertab.

:Yes.: Pai had stopped the engine in front of a small A-frame, but was still hesitant, and Rrimi said, "Pai, let me come in with you."

"Yes," said Pai, and still did not move.

"Pai, Ungrukh give rides almost as good as any uku's. On Pertab's world bird species are much afraid of cats, but you need have no fear of this one."

Pai looked at the calm red eyes, color hardly dimmed by the lenses. "My feet will hurt your back."

"Less than my child's when I have one."

Pai hopped lightly from the car seat to perch on the waiting back, felt the warm muscles moving behind the shoulder pistons, from the corner of her eye caught the continuous sine wave of the long tail, and lost fear for good. Inside the garlanded door she slipped from that accommodating back, facing the waiting greedy eyes that suddenly turned fearful, and stood safe in the fire-circle of the long tail, ready to haggle.

Pertab sat with legs dangling outside the car, drumming his heels and stretching his neck like any tourist.

A group of young people with variegated feathers, trimmed or dyed, gathered—it seemed materialized—before him.

"A puny featherless creature," said one. "He wears a metal band on his wrist. Perhaps he is a criminal on his world."

Pertab twirled the Sikh's steel bracelet clinking against his chronometer, drummed his heels and grinned. He knew this bunch. He had been one. And he was almost relieved. Courtesy was beginning to bore him. "A religious object." He lifted his shirt and pulled the ceremonial dagger from his belt. "So is this. On my world it is a crime to carry concealed weapons, so I am happy to show you mine."

Calmly he watched them stretching their sharpened claws. A dull knife-blade—or even a sharpened one—is not always effective against thick oiled plumes. That is why armor can be made of feathers. "But this," he pulled out his Snark's spike, "goes in and out very quickly, where the guts and the hearts and . . . other things are not well-protected." He tossed and caught it.

They backed one step but did not give way further. One to five was poor odds, but Pertab grinned again, because Rrimi was coming out of the shop.

Rrimi's pupils contracted quickly in the burst of sunlight, irises very wide and bloody red. Pai slipped aside at a thought. Rrimi snorted.

The young Kylkladi whirled and stood. Rrimi moved very little. Her tail was still and coiled. She observed the group, yawned with all her fangs, raised one forelimb, shot the blood-veined claws and admired them briefly before retracting them. The gang disappeared. The street seemed very quiet.

Pertab laughed. "That would have been an enjoyable fight."

"For whom? Everything settles nicely. Let's go."

"Why are we traveling so slowly?" Pertab asked. "Everyone is passing us."

"I don't know. I'm driving normally."

He coughed. "The air seems thick."

"The filters are working well enough," said Rrimi. She was luckily young enough to have missed the old stiff ones that made noses terribly sore, particularly convoluted cat nostrils; the modern spongy disposable ones were a small annoyance. But the air did seem heavy and ominous. It congested the lungs, weighed on the crown of the head, slowed speech, made fingers clumsy.

"Pai," said Rrimi, "perhaps you do not mind to go home now, and collect your mother for the memorial tomorrow instead of visiting?"

Something far beneath the words made it an order. "If you wish, Rrimi."

Traffic was not heavy, the light-framed car swung easily about. Almost immediately the air lightened, and spirits with it, and the wheels sang squeaking on the hard resinous wood.

Pertab said happily, "Ah, this is grand! Now that we know where what we are not supposed to know is, turn again, Pai, and prepare for a headache!"

:I don't understand.:

'Before, we suspect that the important thing comes with the memorial service tomorrow. Now we know it is in the hospital, and that is why we are going there.:

:But my mother—:

:I am sure your mother knows nothing and is safe—but Pai, we do not put you at risk against your will, and if you prefer, we go home.:

:No! You have done everything for me until now, and this is my turn.: She swung the car back into the syrupy air.

"There," said Rrimi, "is a poor soul visiting the hospital on foot. We stop and ask him if he knows the way."

"But—"

"You have policemen nearby, not so?"

Pertab removed the spike from his belt and tucked it in his turban.

The poor soul, a Kylklad of mild gray feather, had begged rides from the barren Northern Provinces to see his wife, and was pleased to get another and do a good deed as well; he had seen many outworlders in the City on his visits and they did not disturb him.

When the inevitable police constable stopped the car on the grounds that there was no night lantern showing, Pai produced it from its storage compartment and showed her driving permit, while the hitchhiker pleaded so loud and long in his shrill Northern accent that they were waved by.

"The hospital is only around the corner," said the stranger much more quietly, "but this often happens on the way. It is because of the political prisoners, I think."

:His wife is one, but there is no need to mention that,: said Rrimi.

Pai said, *:He might be a spy.:*

:No. Only a poor man who shares a cage.:

The city ended abruptly at a field of thorns and thistles. They were very thick and taller than the car; so regularly aligned that Pertab suspected that they had been planted. Even Rrimi shrank from these. The road leading through them was a narrow dirt lane. Eventually it was blocked by a timber gate, and the timbers were set with thorns as long as fingers. Through an opening, an official-type blue-feather guard asked for more identification, and when Pai held out a carved turquoise disk, pulled on the latches from inside with a long cord, keeping away from the thorns.

Twenty meters inward, the thorn barrier ended at a weedy lot straggling with wild flowers. In its center was a square wooden building, built with the same care Kylkladi lavished on all their wooden structures, but without grace or style. It needed none.

A guard beyond the massive door requested surrender of weapons. Rrimi gravely handed over the standard Ungrukh fish-gutter-and-scaler, perhaps the ugliest utensil in the Galaxy. Pertab's dagger was graceful but had no edge or point to speak of. His spike remained in his turban. Neither Kylklad carried a weapon.

Pertab was quivering now like a plucked string. He was feeling smothered by forces induced from without, surrounded by hostility in a dark cold prison-hospital on a world that should have been exotic because of the beauty and grace of its inhabitants, but was somehow more oppressive than his Terrarium, more ugly, shabby and uncared for than many places on his ancestral world.

:Take care,: said Rrimi. *:We do not need another inmate.:*

Pertab's teeth began to chatter, and almost without thinking Rrimi forced a synapse in his brain that released a natural opiate. After a moment he began to breathe normally again, and said, "You must show me how to do that."

"As soon as I learn how I do it, Princeling."

The place was lit by the dull glare of cold light; Kylklar imported what technology it felt a need for. Pai's mother was in a bright room, even a clean and comfortable one; she had a large oval mirror to admire herself in, and it was herself she spoke to, sang to. Pertab and Rrimi watched through the window a moment while Pai deceived herself that she was communicating with the woman, a beautiful creature they hoped Pai would never become at her age; but her mind was a shattered mirror, and they turned from that privacy to wander the corridors.

All at once Pertab's hair stood on end, and he broke into a

stinging sweat. Rrimi took a step back; she felt as if a spear of white light had pierced an eye—much as Pertab had felt during the ESP exam. Both shielded quickly, opened a slit for direction, shielded. They shouldered dense atmosphere once more, through water, through slime, through tar.

She was in no comfortable chamber, but behind a metal mesh wall in a large hot dusty room that had supplies piled in two of its corners. An attendant was trying to brush rubbish off the floor from under the mesh, while she did her best to savage him through the spaces with beak and talons.

:Low ESP, but a terrible will,: said Rrimi.

The attendant looked up and said in his local dialect, "Best not have anything to do with this one, friends, she's a terror."

"I can believe that," said Rrimi in his tongue. "We take good care to stay away."

"I'm responsible here." He was a very dull-minded person. He had to be, to bear the presence of Occupant.

"We take care. *You keep away too, please.*"

The attendant dropped his brush, looked about for it, found it on the floor and went away, blank-eyed.

Though it was a stinking hot place, Pertab was hugging himself, shivering. Rrimi's loose heavy skin writhed on her body. The two seemed almost about to be crushed between the force designed to keep them away from this imprisoned woman, and the repelling power of the woman herself.

:Who puts out the force?: Rrimi wondered. *:I think they use the madness of others and join it like the streams of a river to flow against us.:* She ignored the squawking and clawing of the woman behind the mesh. *:But they cannot use hers—:*

Pertab forced open his rattling teeth, "—because they drove her mad themselves, and want to keep her that way."

"They . . ." Rrimi looked up at the figure suspended on the mesh by hands and feet, and asked in *lingua*, "Red Angel, how long are you mad?"

The deeply red-plumed woman dropped from the wires, smoothed her black crest with black-feathered arms and said in clear *lingua*, "Forty-odd of my years. Fifty of yours."

Rrimi kept her eyes on the woman, red to black through the network. "Dear lady, that is more than the life span of one like me."

"I am ninety-seven of this child's years."

"Red Angel, are you willing to be my friend?"

"Yes. But I will do my best to kill you if you come near me. I cannot help it."

"I understand."

"Do you bring me a message from my White Bird? or is she as evil as the ones who gave her me to nurse?"

"More so, if that is possible."

The Red Angel leaped at the mesh, tried to tear it with her beak, hopped down and began gobbling pebbles and trash from the floor, screaming all the while.

:Stop that!:

Pertab took off his turban and unwound the pearl necklace from his comb. The madwoman spat pebbles and guano flakes. She stared at the pearl. "Why should I be shocked? They were horrors, those. She was a savage child with moments of sweetness and I hoped to change her, until they took her from me."

"Did you have children of your own, Angel?"

"The shells were too brittle and the yolks good only for feeding the nestlings of others."

"Who are *they*, who gave and took Phoebe?"

She jabbed her beak at the swinging pearl. "What do you think the fine old family she comes from is? Old money, I hear they call it! Oh! Come near! Let me tell you!"

Neither Pertab nor Rrimi moved.

The woman screamed, "Come near!"

They waited. Rrimi said quietly, "I like my eyes in their sockets. I prefer they do not go in your crop."

"I want it to stop! Make it stop. Please."

Rrimi looked at Pertab. *:Can we burn out the urge to kill?:*

The thought *Snark* did not come to her mind, but it came to Pertab's. He flushed. *:Sometimes one must kill in self-defense.:*

:Don't be so sensitive, Princeling. This is a case of induced madness. I ask if it is possible because I'm not sure either of us is able.:

:I'm sure as hell you are! But if it's seen to be missing she'll be in danger.:

The red and black woman clawed the mesh with four limbs and tried to pull feathers from her shoulder with her beak.

Red and black Rrimi said quietly, "Do not harm yourself,

Red Angel, and do not scream and bring the stupid guards."

"You are not friends of mine, not friends, not friends! You are here to make sure I am mad enough to keep you safe!"

Rrimi picked up on it at last. "The pearl-smuggling trade from Xirifor gives that family the old money, not so?"

"Yes! Yes! Two hundred years of it! Two hundred and fifty now! There! Kill me! Why do you not kill me? Why?"

"That's a good question," said Pertab. "They haven't been shy about anyone else."

"Possibly they believe they are repaying her service."

He stared at her, speechless. Then said, "Perhaps Pai's mother is also—"

"No. That is only a pathetic woman. Red Angel, I cannot take away your madness. Partly, I am not sure we can do it properly, but mainly because it is your protection. They leave you alive because it is their horrible way of thanking you for tending and loving the White Bird. But I promise you that if I and Pertab remain alive, or one of us does—within one year you are no longer mad."

"I will be dead by then," said the woman dully.

"No! You have too great a passion to live and be free." *:Pertab, this kind of brain and personality are more like those of Solthrees. What are we to do?:*

Pertab, unsure whether or not he was being insulted, took the remark and question at face value. *:She already has a kind of weapon. Why don't we give her . . . a kind of armor?:*

:Can you do that?:

:No, but you can, and I'll help.:

"Red Angel, regard me." The lashless black eyes fitted their pupils to hers.

"Your spirit is a blazing sun. We find you by its terrible light. Consider it: it is matter you can control. You can draw it from yourself with your hands, and form it in any way you please. Now you draw it from yourself with your hands," *and form it into burning gold wire*, says Pertab. "With this you can make all the images that bring to mind your life and hope." *Like the filigree of jeweled women.* "A design to remember that I am from Ungruwarkh, and my name is Rrimi," *and I am Pertab Singh from Sol Three.* "We are here to promise you freedom in mind and body," *and swear to keep the promise.* "Hope that we live to do it and form a shape for that. Remember the grasses, trees and flowers of your world, that the sky is blue by day, and red as your plumes by evening, black as your eyes by night," *and all other suns burn in it.*

"That is one more cage."

"No, woman. It is a shield you can break and destroy with a wish, or keep to protect yourself in the same way."

"My name . . . Red Angel . . . she gave me that. Perhaps it is one I ought not to keep."

"As you choose, but it belongs to you because you do what you can to bring out love—and it is not you who fail."

"Yes . . . I form the children I did not have, and the man who died waiting for . . . yes, womb-bearers, I understand . . .

"I am finished, I think. . . .

"Is it well done, my friends?"

The star blazed, and for a moment Pertab and Rrimi saw the gold filigree enclosing Red Angel in its light, celled like honeycomb filled with the strange shapes of her imagination.

"You make it very well indeed. Now show us its work." She crouched and pushed one padded hand beneath the mesh where the prisoner could touch it.

Red Angel said, "I am afraid. Oh, I am afraid."

"We are not."

Not quite. Pertab was terrified. But he knelt in the dirt and placed his hand beside Rrimi's.

Red Angel's eyes darted madly for a moment, but with the effort of conquering her own terrors. She bent down and rubbed her cheek very gently along Pertab's naked skin, more strongly against Rrimi's coarse fur.

"Fifteen years since I have given any embrace. Friends, I thank you quickly because you must go. Let it be our secret."

"It is." They turned to find the attendant gaping in the doorway. "*Forget what you see here*," said Rrimi.

He dropped his brush, peered about myopically until he found it and said, "There is a young woman waiting for you."

"We are coming."

Past the door they heard the thud of Red Angel's body against the mesh, and her screams and curses at the attendant. And underneath, *Remember, remember . . .*

:We swear. No other knows. Neither forgets.:

"I surely did not mean to make you wait so long," said Pai.

"I hope you were not bored or annoyed." *:And were successful.:*

"Miss Pai, there is nothing here to annoy us."

:And we certainly weren't bored,: said Pertab.

Leaving, they passed the Northern man embracing his wife by the doorway, but he was not ready to go, nor ever would be.

Pertab and Rrimi had worked so hard at shielding that they were very weary, and both dozed—on watch—during the ride across the city. The atmosphere was calm and neutral as the air. Deceptively so. Rrimi was not deceived.

Pertab stirred. *:Why should they be here with a big pearl shipment just now?:*

:Why not? We are here. Probably they always have enough pearls about for shipping. Solthrees talk about killing two birds with one stone.:

:Not around here.:

:Do not be insulted if I say we have the advantage of being a pair of brats their parents are glad to have a holiday from. We can put on ESP insignia if we choose and be Authority, but we need not, so they cannot jump on us directly.:

:No. Only sideways, like kicking us to death.:

:But we are now merely guests attending a memorial.:

Pertab licked his lips. *:It would be very nice . . . :*

:And even more dangerous.:

:We've gone so far . . . now we can dump this rattletrap. I'll just go along to the field to hop around and gape.:

"Oh, now what kind of terrible thing is he doing?" cried Pai. "I want to go home and make the evening meal."

Pertab was ostensibly surveying his own boat, but his eyes were darting about at the other inhabitants of the field. He found one of the ground crew, a cheerful innocent fellow, and asked, "That shuttle over there looks as if it belongs to a Gal-Fed Surveyor. Does it belong to anyone I could give greetings to?"

"I don't know, young sir. By markings, looks like Tignit to me. But a lot of neutrals buy up old GalFed vessels because they're so well built. A-ki-ki, Topi'it!" He hailed a mate before Pertab could stop him. "The Solthree lad wants to know who owns that GalFed shuttle. Are they Tignit?"

"No. They could be Yefni or Ungbar, though they have some of ours and Solthrees on board. Why does he want to know?"

"Only to pay respects," Pertab said quickly.

"I'd say, don't, young master. They're a surly lot who'd rather crack your beak for you than give a good word."

"Thank you, I've been warned," said Pertab, and dimmed their memories for their own safety.

:Don't see how to manage it.: "Ready to go now, Pai. Just take the long way around so nobody on that shuttle sees us."

Pai asked no questions.

When the party stopped at the market and collected two netfuls of fish, Pertab was careful not to ask what Pai must have paid to fill Rrimi's belly, but he satisfied himself that the food had not been tampered with.

The uku gave no more trouble, but Pertab and Rrimi would not let Pai go near her bower until Rrimi had used her nose and Pertab his detectors on it. The meal was cooked at the Community kitchen, a simple array of barbecues, bonfires and cooking pots; Rrimi, who like most Ungrukh did not consider fish a prime meal, found it so good that she ate her hearty share.

:Princeling, consider the next step.:

:Someone will set fire to the bower while we are inside.:

:That kills many innocent people by spreading.:

:What do they care?:

Pai said, "It's going to rain, shortly."

They stared. "How do you know?"

She stared back. "Don't *you* know what rain is?"

Pertab knew, but had never been in it. Rrimi thought hard over the experiences of her almost rainless planet. "My great-aunt sometimes complains of her bones. . . ."

"Just smell," said Pai.

They smelled it with her, through her nose. "It is something like wind from the sea," said Rrimi.

Pertab asked, "Do Kylkladi enjoy being in the rain?"

"It's refreshing for a few minutes. After that we use the shelters in the hillside."

"Good," said Rrimi. "Do you usually return these nets that hold the fish?"

"No. They're very cheap, and rot quickly."

"Do you think much rain comes?"

"Look there." The huge equatorial sun was setting quickly beneath a thick bank of cloud. "Why did you want to know about the nets?"

:If she's right, it rules out fire,: said Pertab.

:No. Only it is less likely to spread.: "Because whether it rains or not we are going to the shelters tonight. We stuff the nets with leaves and branches to make substitute bodies."

Pai considered this proposal coolly, without surprise or horror. "Garbage is being collected, and we have a lot of that. Why not use it?"

Rrimi laughed, hissing. "Because, my dear, it smells very much like fish, and not much like people. We can wash some of the smell off the nets with water, in case it does not rain."

"You think killers might come. Won't others be in danger?"

Pertab said, "If they didn't know where to look they'd be very stupid. But I'm more afraid that if it doesn't rain they're sure to set fire to the bower. That would be dangerous, and I don't know how to warn the others."

A drop fell on his nose.

"Ha," said Rrimi, "let us help the others clean up and do our own business in a hurry. I am not overly fond of water."

"Nor I of wet clothes," said Pertab, "but," he pulled a rainskin from his travel case, "I have come prepared. Let's get the furniture covered."

Pertab and Rrimi, from Pai's shelter, looked out at the sheets of rain. The shelter was cavelike, and made Rrimi feel at home. Pai said, "The bowers are treated with water- and fire-retardants. The flowers will grow." Pertab and Rrimi were both thinking that a flamer or a Karnoshky could be used on flesh under water. "If they were to come, as you think, they'd know we wouldn't be down there in the rain."

"The rain may stop—and we may go."

"Where?"

"I'm damned if I know," said Pertab glumly. *:Rrimi, we have nearly fifteen hours of darkness. A pair like us who just* *passed ESP-one exams very well should be able to think of something.:*

:Ungrukh are tacticians, not strategists. But I put my mind to it.:

:Ours!:

:The ship is there. I am almost certain pearls are there. All we need is an army.:

:Army . . . Rrimi!:

"Ha! Pai, do you know an honest policeman?"

Pai seemed to shrink inside herself. "I was affianced to one even though my father thought he was of too low a class—for me! But I broke it off because of my fathers disgrace."

Rrimi restrained herself from mentioning damned foolishness. "Does he still feel for you?"

"I . . . think so," she said in a small voice.

"And I hope he has a few honest friends."

"What are you planning?"

"Is it possible to reach him by radio?"

"Once he gave me a small transmitter. I returned it."

"Good, so you know how. Now, what we ask sounds stupid or crazy or both. Tell him to come here, now, because your faithless friends steal your jewelry and run."

"But that's terrible!"

"I assure you it is not!"

Pertab was unwinding his turban to remove the necklace from his comb. "Will he come?"

"I believe so, but—"

"Yes. You have so few jewels. Still, he gives you the ring with the red stone, and that you keep, not so?"

"I don't mean to seem greedy! I just couldn't bear—"

"Quite right. Here is the radio. Please make the call with a maximum of emotion and we explain later."

They were gratified to hear squawking and sputtering from the receiver. "Good. That gives comfort to our enemies if they overhear and keeps you safe. When he comes explain this to him and tell him, by our Authority as GalFed agents—which we put on just this minute—that there is almost certainly a shipment of contraband pearls, like yours, being unloaded at the Port. The shuttle is the GalFed one with symbols hard to identify. There is only one like that; ours is a lifeboat. He and his friends must go well armed, I hope he believes you."

"He will believe. He is ESP-three."

"Even better. May we borrow your uku?"
"Yes, of course, bu—"
"Do they mind rain?"
"Not at all, their feathers are heavily oiled. But oh, Rrimi! Pertab! where—"
"Just going to raise an army, Pai! Wish us luck!"

Kylkladi went to bed with the chickens. Pertab harnessed Pai's uku as he had watched her do it. Rrimi borrowed a larger one with no harness, but she would have to manage without it by force of will. She also collected all the others dozing stoically in the falling rain, with a simple order to follow:

Come, uku! Come uku!

She did not think much of having a group of uku behind her, but preferred not having them and their feet in front of her. She and Pertab herded their group aside and kept them quiet while two P.C.s galloped by, headed for Pai's shelter.

The ride was as horridly uncomfortable as she had expected, and she was forced to smack the unoffending beast on the rump with her tail, an act she found repulsive. She would never have hesitated to eat it if she were starving, but that was a different matter. The creature squawked in pain and outrage, and the squawk said: *Come uku! Come uku! Defend me from this monster!*

Thunder and rain screened the answers of dozing uku from sleeping Kylkladi. One or two waking citizens twitched and slept again. The tracks were mud, and so were the squelching uku, and so were Pertab and Rrimi, who cursed freely and with joyful exhilaration.

Come uku!

They came in tens, twenties, hundreds, sometimes pulling the carts or carriages of protesting Kylkladi engaged on errands honest or evil, who tumbled aside in flimsy wreckage. Thunder grumbled, lightning sizzled, rain slapped down in sheets and the hundreds of big splayed feet whacked and whacked at mud, like demons, like devils, like djinns to capture the monster—vainly. Wind howled, trees lashed, and Pertab the Snark would have howled with bloodlust if he and Rrimi had not needed all their breath and brains to keep from being overtaken by the walloping herd behind them. Their control was limited: They were only apprentice sorcerers.

At the Port nothing was visible on the field but red dots of light dim under the rain. The squawking stopped, by lack of breath, by esp will, but the uku stabled nearby heard the call in their minds and broke barriers.

The Red Angel woke in a passion, tightened the gold armor about her to keep herself from flinging herself at the mesh, and crouched twitching.

Figures on the field were wheeling, carrying, dragging crates and sacks, stumbling and crouching like trolls against wind and rain. A red-lanterned shape called, "Get all of it out, out! Come on!"

UKU! UKU!UKU!

But the cry was silent, the thunder snarled and no one heard the rumble of great birds until it was too late.

:Now! Kick, uku! Kick, kick, kick! You love to kick, uku!:

They kicked.

Pertab and Rrimi jumped down and drove their tamed mounts away.

The uku horde was confused for a few seconds by the hard surface and the red lights, but they kicked: The composition plates of the shuttle dented, the crates broke, the sacks burst, and crew screamed and ran. Rrimi, panting, herded the crew as she had herded uku because she did not mean to kill, but some were bloody, some broken-limbed, some hobbling and cursing, rolling and screaming on the spattering field. While uku kicked, oysters and shell-pieces scattered, unrefined pearls—good, bad, indifferent, baroque, polyhedral, trilobar—rose in fountains to meet the rain and fell bouncing like drops. Pertab watched crouching beneath the shuttle.

Shots slapped through thunder and the uku faltered. Shots again from a half-score police, hard put to control their own near-mad uku. Pertab put out his last burst of will and the wild herd fled screeching and the police drew back to let them go.

Rrimi leaped after one running figure, a man, flung herself on him, rolled him over with one slap of a paw, ripped the hood to let rain fall on the orange-and-gray streaked hair, the hawk features coarsened by age and dissolution.

His wrist was broken, and he screamed in terror.

"Don't!"

"O Adams, Mister Adams! Phoebe's baby brother, not so? Burton Charloe Adams?"

"What? What? Don't hurt me!"

"I do not mean to—"

:Are you joking?: said Pertab.

"Does the Red Angel nurse you too, or is she more lucky?"

"What? What do you mean, Red Angel? She's mad! She's mad!"

Abruptly, without slowing, the rain stopped.

A mounted Kylklad pulled in beside Rrimi. "Rrimi? Pai'ili'ot's friend from Ungruwarkh? I'll take care of that one."

"Indeed—Chief Constable Ka'iti'ol? Take very good care of him for Galactic Federation."

"I surely will. And thank you very much."

"Not necessary. We go back to Pai now, and relieve your second—before he steals her away from you." And she pulled herself off the fallen man, hissing, and went to reclaim her accursed uku without a backward look.

Pertab loosed the two beasts of his command to freeze.

Rrimi said, "Tcha! They have some time gathering up all those dirty pearls. It is a pity we don't think to pick up a few to show GalFed for evidence."

"I have a piece of their marked casing to hide in my waistband—and I also got three trilobars and a couple of others."

"Best to hide those too."

"I swallowed them."

"I leave you to recover them."

The Red Angel slept.

"What made you think of pulling in all those birds?"

"I have it from my mother, who has it from her cousin, who has it from her man's sister, who has it from her aunt, that Prandra daughter of Tengura, the first woman to leave Ungruwarkh, does something similar with birds of prey in a different situation on a world whose name I don't recall now."

"Yirl."

"Right."

"You have a great network on your world."

"Almost everyone on Ungruwarkh knows almost everything about everyone else. Of course, nobody agrees about anything."

The Port field was in no condition for use, and Pertab and Rrimi did not have to convince those in Authority that they would stay one more day. In the morning they discovered that an uku-drawn two-wheeler would not collapse under them, and visited the bazaar, where they actually found Yglar & Co., the artists of fashion and refinement.

At noon the memorial was conducted quietly and with dignity. Pertab and Rrimi wore their own signs of authority: Pertab the arrow crossed with the lightning bolt of ESP-one, Rrimi, the bolt twined with serpent—the old Cracked Caduceus—that indicated the therapist she would become when she finished training. Pai's mother, a nurse beside her, looked as if she knew what was happening.

Many formerly neglectful friends and relatives appeared out of the woodwork, but Pai, strength supplemented by a lover, did not look at them. Garlands of flowers and feathers were piled on the crematory slab.

At the end of the ceremony Pertab and Rrimi slipped away again. Pai was not offended. She knew of their errand, and that they wished to complete it before a debriefing that was bound to be fairly rigorous.

The Red Angel had a clean room of her own with water, toilet and bed. It was not a comfortable room like that of Pai's mother; she did not need comfort, but time.

Now she had a proper nurse, who was as nervous as the attendant. Angel was crouching by the window, watching the circle of sky.

They waited for their presence to seep into her consciousness.

She turned savage but controlled eyes on them. "You remembered very quickly."

"We tell you we swear."

Pertab approached her slowly, very slowly. "Red Angel, will you give me your hand?"

She raised one without asking why.

Pertab took the terrible cold and horny claws in both his vulnerable hands. "Rrimi and I argued a lot before we chose. I didn't care for green, though Rimi says emeralds can look very good on red. A pearl was out of the question; you are already beautifully red, and neither of us thought blue or yellow was right." He drew away one hand, fumbled in a little skin pouch around his neck, and took out a dark opal ring set in yellow gold. "When you look at this in the light you can see all the colors you wish—all there are . . ." He slipped it on the talon it fitted best, "and *you* remember."

Red Angel looked at the opal in its ring of gold, at the sky in its ring of wood, at Rrimi and Pertab, and bent to touch the back of his hand with her fearsome loving mouth.

Pai clasped her hands. "Oh, my friends, I have no gift to thank you with—"

"We don't need one, Pai. I think we have what we came for."

"—except this pearl, which is not a disgrace or evil any longer. My Constable will see it goes through customs easily."

"I cannot accept a gift, my dear," said Rrimi.

"Ungrukh don't care for chains," said Pertab shamelessly. "I will be happy to take it in that case, Pai. Pertab the Lion of the Punjab, the Snark, the Princeling—I have been collecting nicknames the way Rrimi's fur collects ticks"—he dodged a whack from her tail—"I'm not sure, but Pertab might possibly have a bride one day."

40

. . . I killed two people who were trying to assassinate Senator Silver—their weapons were in sight—and I punched up a couple of others trying to blackmail him. I never had any kind of record, no charge or conviction. I took all those hypno and drug things, but they don't work completely on me because I'm an Impervious. I rang the bell on Nkansah because I found she was an agent. Silver died when they were screwing and I helped her dress the body because I didn't want him found that way. I don't think that's committing an offense on a dead body. I had in mind to grab the jewelry he'd given her and do some running myself, because I was out of a job, but she ran first and I found out . . . I don't like what I did because I had in mind to stop her, not get her killed. I remember that stuffed cat but it was gone when she left. She'd told me I was in Silver's will, and I thought she was lying. I shouldn't . . . I never could figure out women. . . .

I guess Phoebe Adams kept me on so I wouldn't talk, but I think she wanted to get rid of the people around Silver. Mercy Adams saved my life by letting me know about the fake order from Phoebe. She had a hard time fighting the blocks. I was supposed to go upstairs to bring some file and get wiped. I had this illegal stunner, a Gothenburg 238, and found her man Tragg in my old office pointing two guns at me. A pair of Murmansk needlers. Them, they look like real hammers, but they're snub and only good close. I was real close, so I got him in the heart, didn't touch him. His head hit the desk and the guns fell on the rug. I dumped the stunner and the spy-eye spool that was in the wall chronometer. That was a mistake, maybe. You could have seen what happened. There was a big red cat skin on the floor. . . .

"That'll get thrown out too," said McNelly.

"Yeah, and there's no sign of Tragg. There was such a person, Mercy described him, but the name's not even on record. Well, we do have Jha, Sukey, and our lovely Vasquez and Billings, plus the pair of needlers Sukey held on to, and we'll have to make do with what we've got."

TO ALL UNGRUKH ON SOL III WITH RESPECTS FROM MEDOR, AND TO EMERALD, RAANUNG AND ALL OTHER UNGRUKH ON SOL III WITH LOVE FROM KINNEAR. KRIKU/QUMEDON SENT KINNEAR A MESSAGE CLAIMING TO HAVE SAVED *BLUE GUITAR,* PASSENGERS AND CREW, BY MOVING IT OUT OF RANGE OF A HOSTILE NEUTRAL PREPARING TO ATTACK. GALACTIC FEDERATION CANNOT CONFIRM OR DENY BUT BELIEVES THIS IS THE TRUTH. MESSAGE FURTHER SUGGESTS QUMEDON INTENTION TO APPROACH SOL III. CANNOT CONFIRM OR DENY AND HOPE THIS IS NOT TRUE.

Man of Law told the news to the Tribal representatives, and those who had had personal experience with Qumedni snarled, "Let that damned interloper leave us alone!"

"Do you believe he saved your lives?" Man of Law asked.

Raanung said patiently, "Yes. He is not a liar. Kriku likes to make grand gestures. If he saves our lives I am sure he makes a grand gesture of that too, and ensures we find out. Even when he wishes to help he is too capricious to trust."

"In the meantime it seems nothing else is being done," said Emerald.

Man of Law said, "In the meantime the Law is doing its best to build a case that will not fall apart among its ramifications. Ungrukh, this is a complicated and populous world, and there is not even a guarantee of trial. If there is, it may take many thirtydays to come to court."

Menirrh snarled, "Is that how justice works in the worlds of civilization? What do we give up such a great piece of our lives for?"

In a black leap and roar Etrem landed on the ridge beside Man of Law.

"My woman and I come to this place at will and risk, because there is little hope or comfort for us at home—and we suffer much from it. You come by shaming and bullying to do what is right with respect and loyalty—and if you cannot do it by the laws we accept, go home and know nothing beyond your rocks and dust and your stony dusty lives!"

He stopped in silence and lowered head and tail. "I apologize. What I say is not all of the truth. Some of those who come with me are fools—like me—and all of you take risks."

"Not altogether just," said Raanung, "but with much justice. Go ahead, Etrem. My jaws are sore from all the snarling and snapping I force myself to do, and I give you leave to take my place if you are ready."

"Perhaps when I am ready there is a place for me. I am not yet wise enough. But I *am* ready to wait."

"I wonder if I'll ever get enough sleep," said Haynes. "It's like we have twenty-five pieces from twenty-five Chinese puzzles and are trying to make one block out of them."

Still, on the strength of the depositions by Boris and Mercy, an inquiry date had been set for within six weeks.

Phoebe's son Adam Silver began to marshal his troops. Phoebe waited for the summons. She did not look forward to the inevitable prospect of huddling with lawyers and relatives as well as appearing gracious to sympathizers and well-wishers. She withdrew from Council sittings, but did not give up the seat.

No one drawing up the case considered change of venue. Phoebe held on to her territory with iron jaws. At the preliminary hearing there was some confusion over jurisdictions. The original agreement had been between Ungruwarkh and Sol III in the person of the Congress of Nations in conjunction with Galactic Federation.

There was first an argument over who exactly was plaintiff and who defendant. The Ungrukh were unwilling to have all Ungruwarkh stand for nineteen victims—as well as one wounded—when the poisoning cases did not seem likely to be solved, and Phoebe Adams' lawyers could blacken the visitors as malcontents, misfits, exiles or dump them in whatever ugly sack they chose. Nor, when the Ungrukh had decided to live in one narrow area, was it reasonable to put the onus on all of Sol III; GalFed by its own law took no court or police action against worlds. After the dust and rocks had settled, the Continent, which controlled National Parks and had conducted the investigation, took responsibility as plaintiff in guardianship of the Ungrukh. More precisely, Southern District Division of Continent stood in for its pro tem citizens, the Ungrukh, and pitted itself against Southern District Commonwealth in the person of Phoebe Charloe Adams Silver.

Defendant argued that Plaintiff was taking too broad an authority because the Ungrukh had been allowed the freedom of the Commonwealth, and the Commonwealth had been paying part of their support. Ungrukh/Continental agreed in principle to both claims but declared that the support of 9.5 percent agreed upon when Phoebe Adams was Treasurer was too small to consider as having weight, and had also been discontinued as soon as Continental had begun investigating the murders; as for the former, the freedom was appreciated, but upon arriving the Ungrukh had never left the Canyon except for the one occasion when the twins, Tugrik and Orenda, had strayed into Navajo lands before the crime and without knowledge of it. This statement was corroborated by Park Rangers and District and Tribal Police. So Justice, lumbering, fenced its grounds.

41

Moon's Woman, ignoring preparations for legal proceedings, continued living on the Mesa with his uncle, on fairly good terms. He took no other lovers, kept providing medico-religious services when requested, and did a little craftwork for tourists. He seemed to himself to be on hold, waiting for something he did not know of.

He had gone once to the city with Tom Green Corn to buy cloth, beads and wool, and one morning he was sitting cross-legged outside his uncle's house in the shade with a piece of buckskin laid out to one side with all his materials, and to the other the fishing-tackle box that held his sewing gear.

He made gifts for Tom Green Corn's children: a bead pendant for the boy and a Mudhead kachina doll for the little girl. The shadows had moved until the sun was standing at noon. Someone called him to take food, but he was not hungry.

He looked at what was left in his lap. Bits of cloth. Beads. Fine cord. Wool. On the skin a roll of foam stuffing. He reached for scissors, cut quickly, sewed cloth with invisible stitches as fast as a machine. Squat red body. Legs, arms, head. For hands and feet a bird's talons of fine looped wires wound tightly with yellow cord, a red bead claw at the end of each. Large black bead eyes, ocher beak, tiny bead nostrils. He feathered the arms and shoulders with black wool, built up a black crest on the head. He took three blue beads and sewed them in a triangle shape on the bird's breast.

He was sweating. He took off his hat to rub sweat from his forehead and looked up. The sun was at noon.

A shadow fell over his shoulder. "What is that?" Sun Rising High asked.

"Red Bird Kachina."

"There is no such thing."

"There was not. There is now."

The Chief shrugged and went into the house to have a smoke with Uncle without telling him his nephew was still crazy.

Moon's Woman sat waiting. A figure, outlines quivering from heat, came from the southwest. Moon's Woman watched it, without hearing the barking dogs, until he recognized himself.

Himself stood before him. His eyes were very hard to see under the shadow of the stetson, and a cloud moved on the sun so that his shadow became shade.

"I will deliver that for you," said himself.

Moon's Woman gave the doll without a word.

Then he was in the noon shade again, wiping sweat. Someone from the house called him to come eat; he packed away his sewing materials and went. He was hungry.

Two days before Phoebe's summons was delivered her informant in Continental's office let her know. The summons was no surprise; the surprise was in a kind of soul-shaking blow, looking back over so many years, that her marriage to that Roman candle John Silver could set her steps along this road. True enough, she had not been brought up gently, but her life had been a long series of subtle changes up to that death, and many harsh quickly shifting ones after: The realization that the risks she had taken for him were valueless; the displacement of her hatred and frustration onto the Ungrukh; the unsuccessful attempts against them; the painful letting go of all emotions connected with Silver. The cats, none of whom she could manage to kill; they truly seemed to have nine lives apiece. Put them out of her mind: one more step. Rid herself of Silver's apparatus and build her own to take his place and more.

Her family had been successful; she expected to be. But she had loved the man; had they loved anyone? And in some twisted way each of her acts instead of adding subtracted: love substitutes, companions, servants, guards, enforcers, sycophants. She seemed to generate more and more unease. She was secure, but walled by nothingness. She peered into mirrors, and found her mirror-self as always. Then what change? There were no probing ESPs around her in government; in law they had no legal standing. There were only about 750 class-ones in the world, and 500 worked for GalFed. The rest counted lower on the rungs than wiretaps or spy-eyes. As Ungrukh would say, no more than the testimony of a nose.

I am alone now as I chose to be, but in the abyss I believed I stood watching. Can I climb up again from this depth? I have still a few debts to collect and a power base among the people I gave bread and circuses to—not freely but cheaply.

When the clerk's messenger walked between her guards to deliver the summons—a small man lent strength by the power of Law, whatever that might mean on a Monday or Tuesday—she stood with hands clasped while the maid accepted the traditional paper document, until he bowed and left.

She took it without looking at it. "Why didn't Harcourt answer the door? Oh . . ."

The maid stared.

"Yes, Ellen, I remember. He went yesterday."

The old crock should have been replaced long ago. *I am simply too old and tired, Madam.* Without notice. Taking his month's wages without thanks. But there was nothing for him to know or tell. Maid and cook remained. Let the cook go too; delivered meals were cheaper. Money was better spent on guards.

Adam Silver was on his way. Important show of family support. He could not, nor would he want to, practice in Southern District. Yet his network would bring counsel she needed, even if she did not want it. And bail. After Silver's death she had directed that his Sonotek holdings, even if allowable under District law, were to be put in a blind trust. All the family money she kept openly was in government and municipal bonds; she lived on her salary. And she owned the two apartments. She would put up the extra one and some bonds, if she did need bail. No jumping. She would hold ground, and show it.

Adam called before leaving.

"Yes, dear. No, dear. I'm all right. Keeping up. Yes, see you soon." She switched off with relief.

"Ma'am?" The maid was holding a package, guard following.

"What?"

"This was dropped in the mail chute."

The guard said, "I used the detectors on it. Nothing explosive or chemical."

She examined it. Wrapping the same brown plastic as the PHUZZEE PHUNNEE™, but there was no lettering. Only, in black, the petroglyph of Pueblo Emergence, quartered spiral representing the Four Worlds. "Did you see who did it?"

"Yes, ma'am. Some kind of Indian with a black stetson and buckskin fringed jacket. Came through the elevator doors, shoved it in before I could stop him and went back through." He swallowed. "You won't believe it, but I swear," he swallowed again, "the elevator never moved. I dunno if the doors opened."

Phoebe closed her eyes and saw the face of the faceless strangler. After a moment of dizziness she said, "I see. Don't worry about it."

She took the package to her room and closed the door. Her body to head, limbs, toes, fingers, was a tangle of vibrating steel wires. She ripped the plastic with a fingernail.

A kachina doll. She knew them.

A red and black bird with the blue beads representing the trilobar pearl. She knew that.

She grasped the doll by the arms and bit off the beads of talons, eyes, beak, breast. She spat them into her palm and brushed them into the disposal, swallowing on screams.

From where? How? Not GalFed.

That one Indian who knew nothing. Some kind of visionary. Phoebe, no visionary, snorted in self-disgust. Coincidence.

Revenge for a dead lover, as I revenged? But he knows nothing and is helpless. This is just some kind of tribal symbol, an evil spirit. Be damned to you. She cast about for a knife or scissors to cut it up, as she had cut the incriminating red skin. But why bother with a mess? The stitching was so fine it was almost invisible, nothing inside but stuffing. Like Silver. The outside was all. She pushed it into the tube, one blue bead stuck to her palm. She flicked it after, slid closed the gape. So much for that.

She gripped herself against the cold and stood at her window, the only one in the apartment, pushing aside the cream lace. In the towers around, what windows there were looked aside, not avoiding, but unknowing, uncaring. She turned and found that mirror-Phoebe did not care. Some damned help I get from you.

Monogrammed silver brush in hand.

No. Don't smash. Put it down gently, so.

Touched the whorl in the wall's design that opened the safe, took a capsule from its film container and pressed it against the thin skin of her wrist until it absorbed. Closed the safe.

Lay down on the chaise longue to wait for the effect and buzzed the intercom for herb tea. Rest first, then hard thinking, Phoebe. Make all tight and secure. Stop shaking.

42

Haynes was holding wet packs on his eyes, which were inflamed in lid and membrane, circled in bruise.

Kovarski said, "I'll admit every one of these pieces is important, and you can nearly fit them into one shape, but however you try it there's a space. The guns used by Vasquez and Billings *are* Murmansk needlers like the ones Boris said Tragg was trying to kill him with, but that pair went on oath that they were hired for certain work by a firm not listed anywhere, and you can't pin them on Phoebe if they won't go under scanner. You *can* put them away for attempted murder and kidnapping. When they give serious thought to that they may loosen up—or they may give thought to what may happen if they do loosen up. We can be pretty sure that Mercy Adams was in a drugged and fuzzy state on murder night, but her situation is also fuzzy. Being ready to skin Bren in the belief she was dead is giving offense to a dead body, even if she killed no Ungrukh—"

"If she didn't skin her she didn't give offense."

"Attempt, anyway. Phoebe can't be proved to have ordered it. The testimony Boris and Mercy gave can be jumped up and down on. He thought of stealing and didn't. He killed, and there's no body. He might as well have kept the recording—"

"Couldn't be introduced."

"There is no Ungrukh skin—"

"Might not have shown on the recording."

"—if there ever was. There is no provable connection between Phoebe and what we believe she did: dead Ungrukh, dead Nkansah/Jeffries, dead Indian, skin toy—no recordings, documents, witnesses. Lots of crimes, no connection. No piece, no case."

"Right," said Haynes. "But we have some days between summons and inquiry."

"So you can afford to take eight hours sleep. Pop a pill. Hammer your head in. Anything. Sleep. An order."

After ten hours Haynes came back to the office. Kovarski and Lundgren were looking red-eyed from a night punching terminals to track the business activities of Continental members.

"I got it."

Kovarski crossed his arms and looked down his nose. "Eureka?"

Haynes popped a spool into the recorder.

"Psyche Demetriou recording apprehension of Mercy Adams, witness:

"Adams: 'What right have you to make me go with you?'

"Sukey: 'Warrant, dear. Material witness.'

"Adams: 'Arrest.'

"Sukey: 'Would you rather have gone back to Phoebe?'

"Adams: 'Tomorrow—I mean today—she was going to make me . . . to make me . . .'

"Sukey (insert: Witness thinking:) *Cropped gray hair. Blue smock. Electrodes.* (Witness speaking:) 'Why would she do it that way?'

"Sukey: 'Don't *you* know her?'

"Adams: 'A lesson. She enjoys watching that. Then takes the fallen sinner unto her breast, half the brains burnt out. She's noted for humanitarianism.' "

Haynes flicked off. "There's the contact. The thing Phoebe Charloe Adams Silver did in person. The one."

Kovarski said, "But Mercy Adams' head was a mess. So where do we find gray hair with smock and electrodes?"

"Mindclear might have jogged her. Hertzberg did it, and he's got the records."

"We can use only what relates to prosecuting Phoebe. The rest would concern Mercy's defense, if she's charged—and Hertzberg's tight-assed."

"What we need wouldn't incriminate Mercy. Why not ask her?"

"How do we do that? She's in a white-walled holding area, and I sure wouldn't want to tell the world."

"Mr. Kovarski, I've given you *all* the pieces and I'm not half woke up yet. Why don't *you* put the last one in place?"

Kovarski was leaning back in his chair with his feet on the desk. Haynes was rolling his red eyes from Sukey to Lundberg. "I'm tired of all these warnings about risk."

McNelly yawned. "Us spear carriers gotta carry the can."

Sukey said, "Bren's caesarean is due in ten days."

McNelly asked, "Did her parents climb up on a rock and give you thunder and lightning?"

"No," Haynes said. "I think they took their lawyer's advice to be patient with due process. That's what they really want. I have to agree with them that it would be a good thing if it would walk a little faster."

"It may walk too fast for us if Phoebe's mind runs on the same track as ours," said McNelly, "and I can't believe it won't."

"Then let's get on with it."

Sukey and Bren went down the length of the Hall of Justice, which had archaic arched windows to display beams and motes, and avoided the vulgar convenience of moving walkways.

Bren muttered, "You think this leaks as usual?"

"Maybe. She's got a plant somewhere in the office, but we don't know where to use the weedkiller."

Bren was trying to keep her mind on Mercy Adams rather than the conviction that too solid Sukey was a good slab of beef, and Sukey, the person Mercy trusted most, was trying not to think that Bren, in knife-harness and ID tags, and the first Ungrukh she had met, belonged chained up or behind bars somewhere.

Midway to the elevator banks, both heard the arrogant and spiteful *tik-tik* of sharp-tipped heels, and looked up from their concentrations.

Jha was on her way past them in a great snit. Sukey was mildly amused. She had never seen Jha in daylight street mode, flouncing in electric blue dress, shoes, hat—heels set with stones that caught and reflected darts of light, hat a mere dot foaming with lace. Plus a furpiece with a hundred wagging tails, a long amber holder, cigarillo unlit, and two red cheekbone circles like those of a terminal tb victim.

As she came abreast, Sukey said, "Sorry about all that, Jha." She was genuinely regretful.

Jha paused, eyes flashing, tails wagging, spitcurls quivering. "*You*," the word was a dagger, "had to bust me. *You*. Thought I had the best bouncer in the whole fucking world!" She did not even seem to notice Bren.

"I was on your side, Ma'am. I didn't bust you, I'm Continental. District and Municipal did," Sukey said mildly. "That cubby was the sweetest lookout I ever had. I never ticked you off, I was looking for different trade. I'm not in love with your business, but I wouldn't have stopped it."

Jha, defensive and also a little mollified, said, "Somebody's bound to do it."

"For sure. Think you'll get back?"

"Nah. They screwed me good. I'm gonna try Mexico City. They got everything there."

"I hear down that way they're running some big new stuff called Devil's Thumbs that gives users more holes in the head than they got now."

"I deal cards and meat, not shit."

"Then good luck. I liked working for you."

"Hey," Jha looked her up and down. "I don't care who you work for straightside long as they're not in my bailiwick. You want to bounce, come on down any time."

"Maybe I will."

The castanet clicks diminished. "I've never seen Jha in a getup like that." Sukey looked down at Bren, puzzled. "And I don't think she even noticed you."

"Light brings fears and she tries to fortify herself. I don't want her to fear me, so I stay in shadow and keep my mind to myself. If I don't wish, no one notices."

The holding area was clean, spacious and well guarded. Each room was cut off a quarter of the way in by a glasstex barrier in which the whitewall was embedded; there were several circular openings for speaking through the mesh.

"How's she eating, Yvonne?"

"Picky. You want the leavings?" Sukey grinned, and when the door was unlocked shoved herself into a chair near the divider. Bren stood beside her.

Mercy had a player and spools but was lying on the bunk with her arms folded back of her head. She was wearing a cream zip and looked, except for the jet beads which she had kept, as if she were coming new into the world. Bren, on fours, regarded her.

Mercy flipped the beads. "Psych doesn't think I'll strangle myself. Maybe I should."

"We've been through that," said Sukey gently.

Mercy came closer to the network and looked down at Bren. "You can't think much of me."

Bren inhaled deeply and said, "I hope my teeth do you no harm, Madam."

Mercy stared. "Oh, come off it! What kind of fat-tailed four-footed goody-goody are you? You know about my statement, I suppose?"

Without moving, Bren said, "Agent Demetriou, those mindclearers of yours do a sloppy job."

"They just bring back memories, lovey. They aren't therapists."

Mercy had turned away to look at what would have been a window if it were not a square of illumination. "Mercy Adams, I am not sorry to dissatisfy you by refusing to condemn you. There is still a deal of murky stuff in your mind that does not belong."

"What of it?"

"There are also things in it that can help."

Her mouth twisted. "I don't know what they would be."

Sukey looked at the wall-clock and pinched her lip. The power went off. Blackness struck; so did Bren's esp.

"Hey!" Yvonne had her penlight shining through the observation window. No one had moved. "Hey you, Chukker, what's going on there!"

From down the hall a voice called, "Short in the alignment! Just this block!"

"Fix it!"

"Yes, dear. Putting in new power-cells."

In ten seconds the light returned, dimly for a moment, then brighter. "We've had enough," said Sukey. "Let's go."

"Just leave the witness."

"We like her where she is."

The door, not quite on full power, scraped a bit. Sukey turned to speak to Bren, found no Bren and realized that the moment the door had opened the presence was gone. Oh my God, this wasn't in the program!

Sukey could run quite well, but did attract attention, and dared not try now. She walked away quickly; she did not want Yvonne to notice a lack of cat. But Yvonne was talking to Mercy through the intercom. "You all right, kid?"

Mercy, sitting on her bunk with head propped on hands, said, "Oh God. Yeah. I'm all right. I think."

Sukey pulled the radio from round her neck, thumbing the scrambler button: "Out through northwest exit, stopped there a minute . . . oh, oh, shielding hard now." *I stay in shadow and keep my mind to myself. If I don't wish, no one notices.*

Rock.

Etrem, in the landcar, caught the message. "Let me out!"

"You gotta have the others!" McNelly snarled.

"They can follow. I know Bren and how her mind works."

In the Japanese stone garden northwest in the courtyard, a tower-shaded square, a rock detached itself from the shade of another and glided into a corner where its dark red faded to gray. The black stalking shadow picking up a movement ignored by the few pedestrians followed, followed in the dark overhang behind the stone columns, mouth shut, eyes slitted, whiskers flattened.

:Bren! Bren! Wait for me at least! I don't try to stop you!:

:I don't dare wait! Follow if you can!:

She was around a corner by the time he reached it but he had caught her scent. The shadows were deep here in the late afternoon, but hot. He came abreast of her, gulping. He dared not pant and show a large pink tongue; his medallion was nonreflective and his knife-harness black as his fur. He could hide Bren by his size and shadow, but not from enemy minds.

Young Mundr and Orenda were with Popkin in the helicopter. The twins also felt they owed a debt. Both were brave, but Orenda was the ESP, and Tugrik paid his by admitting that Mundr was the stronger and better tracker.

"You got Bren and her man?" It was Sukey on the radio. Her sweat almost came through.

"Yeah, they're dodging. We're sending you a moped and you can go direct if you don't mind being a target."

"Shit, I'd rather be sliced by Phoebe's knives than Kovarski's tongue."

If Sukey were right about the leak, that was a liability. Phoebe would have had more time to plan. But Sukey's powerbreak had joined Bren's therapeutic power, and the sense of direction she had inherited from her father, to the expertise Mercy had picked up—even in her few hunting experiences—and translated into memorizing the routes to and from the woman who dealt oblivion; routes Bren had cleared for her. The other liability was Ungrukh impulsiveness.

Etrem was both fearful for and angry at Bren, endangering their son's life as well as her own. He stood shielding her in a dark corner while a clump of traffic passed. "Oh let me out, Etrem! I feel them coming from cellars like rats, from dirty rooms, from mouldy eating-places and whores' beds! They have quick machines to ride on and knives in their guns!"

Sukey whizzed by, bulging over her moped, picking up their presence without acknowledging it.

"Look, she is drawing them! I cannot have that!"

"You stay then!" He ran to the colonnade, forever a little clumsy but very swift, and with beauty in the black arrow of his passing, glancing Sukey's eye and mind when he caught up with her briefly.

"Bren still following!" Orenda cried. "Let us out!"

"Not now!" Popkin yelled. "The rats are swarming!" He raised City Police. "Chopper CP-one-seven-six, you got Betsy Widmer there?"

"Here I am, Pop."

"Cycle chase coming up Hohokam Plaza. Can you clear the intersection?"

"Whose cycles?"

"Who, Orenda?"

"They call themselves Rasputin's Raiders."

"Oh, not a chance, man. They're fast! You've got to go over the Tower bridges and they can skim under or use the ramps before we can beep. I'll send buzzers, though."

Popkin did not even take the time to swear. "Give me clearance to land on Hohokam Tower Five." Three km to go.

McNelly's landcar had turned off on a shorter route. The helicopter was above and behind Sukey; Etrem was dashing alongside her; Bren his in shadow beneath the overhang back of the pillars.

:Bren, the woman doctor is talking on the instrument,: Orenda said. *:Stopped. Now loading the weapon. Poison darts. Bren, are you with me?:*

:Where do you think I am running, Orenda?:

The cycler pack closed in, roaring. Bren dodged shooting knives: blades like arrows but spring-fledged with steel. She huddled behind a column. One of the Raiders skinned off to flush her . . .

:Help now, Orenda!:

. . . and found herself circling madly, pinned like a fly in the concentrated beam of two joined ESPs. Bren leaped out and circled with her, wrapped tail around neck, jerked.

The cyclist keeled over in the tangle of her wildly howling machine, the primed knife skittered away. Bren clawed it up between digits, did not hear shrieking pedestrians pinned by fear to the walls, hesitated a fraction of a second at the vulnerable skin under the ear. The woman, unhelmeted, one hand caught beneath her, was scrambling for another gun. Bren, as Etrem had once done earlier, decided that she did not have killer blood. She plunged the knife into the free shoulder and was not sorry to hear metal scrape bone.

The pack swarmed, and Sukey on her moped raised one hand to wipe sweat from her face and her little finger was sliced off. She controlled the moped with her feet and grabbed the kerchief from her neck to bind the wound.

Etrem saw this from in back and, snarling, ran harder to catch up. Popkin swore because he dared not reduce speed and had no room to maneuver. Bren, loping now rather than running, still mind-joined with Orenda, aimed disruption at the pack. But the two were against many; only five or six riders wobbled and fell away.

The front-runner grinned at the stupidity of Etrem, crossing his path, trying to swipe with his tail. He paused to aim, but Etrem had dashed away and he swerved after. Etrem swiftly yanked from its socket a flag set in the walk in front of a patriotic club and skittered down the service alley with the thing awkwardly clenched in his teeth and rippling behind him its circle of ten stars and border of ten state flowers. The rider laughed at the thought of the cat using the flimsy thing as a barrier to jam between walls. He had no time for another thought. The flag's butt end pierced helmet, teeth and skull, and while Etrem flattened himself to the wall like a skin the rider and cycle did a great loop-the-loop and landed. For good. Etrem let the rest of the riders pass and followed after McNelly's landcar, which was being pursued by yet another Rasputin. He stopped when he saw McNelly swerve to take the impact. The cycle was not flimsy, but neither was it armored like the car.

Police buzzers were whooping about the helicopter like gnats, but the Raiders had dispersed into the shadows of many colonnades where the cool air swept down from vents. And suddenly, except for those tangled and thrashing on their machines, or dead, there were none.

Bren was taking a tumultuous shortcut through the bank opposite the building she was aiming for.

Etrem shoved aside the mauled rider to free the landcar, which had suffered no more than a dent. McNelly yelled, "You idiot! You'll ge—"

"No," said Etrem. "They are no longer here."

Sukey had reached the fire escape elevator of the building housing Phoebe's mind-treater, Dr. Erna Kriss, and the helicopter was crossing the roof parapet when Orenda ripped out an earsplitting mind-piercing blast:

"Look out! There are two snipers on—"

The outburst jolted both snipers enough to send one shot wide and the other ricocheting off the heavy glasstex, leaving a melt-streak blossoming with cracks that did not keep Popkin's stunners from knocking out both man and woman before he landed on the roof.

Popkin and Sukey reached the office and shot the door down with a yell of "Security!" to find Dr. Kriss backed into a corner and aiming a gun with both shaking hands, screaming, "The cats! The cats!"

"What?"

"The cats will kill me!"

"Oh for God's sake, how—where *are* the cats?"

:Bren is lying in the street!: Mundr and Orenda were galloping down the emergency ramp. The corridors yammered with office workers whose heads were ringing and finding out that putting hands to ears did no good.

Two buzzers on the rooftop were disgorging police to collect snipers, three had blocked traffic so that four could gather loose raiders and call ambulances for the dead or disabled. McNelly was bulling his way through in the landcar trying to protect his shoulders from a howling Etrem's claws.

Quietest of all was Bren, whose body had given up at the building's entrance. She did not hear the exclamations of people around her; she was trying to control the spasms while the blood flowed between her legs.

She did not notice the hush when the four black pillars of Etrem's legs surrounded her or hear his howl of fear and anger, or feel Orenda licking her face, or notice McNelly's yell: "Chrissake, there must be somebody besides quacks in this goddamn building!"

In a short time an ambulance came, a stretcher hovered, as it had done for Boris. For McNelly, nightmare recalled.

43

"Why should you be afraid of the Ungrukh?" Haynes asked.

"Because of what—I don't know why."

Because of what. Yes, because of that. Neither Haynes nor Lundgren pushed it. The woman's face was as gray as her hair, her narrow lips cyanotic. Haynes at first thought she might have taken poison, but he had seen enough frightened people to recognize an extreme case.

"Who warned you?" he asked quietly.

She licked her lips. "You know. Why ask?"

"Who warned you?"

Sukey was away having her wound attended, but the esp insigne would have shut the doctor's mouth.

"Mrs. Silver," she said at last. "I did work for her. Everyone knows that. I'm a licensed practitioner."

"What did she say?"

"The Ungrukh had some kind of grudge against me, I'm not sure what, and I should get out of the way for a while."

"And you didn't think that was enough. You got scared and called the Raiders."

"They're a legitimate club. I'm not ashamed to have them for clients. Some of them have emotional problems." Like being connected with much less legitimate groups. And they surely had a Rasputin.

Lundgren, who worked for Continental Psych herself, said dryly, "A good doctor has all kinds of clients. Excuse me, patients. But you made another call."

"To tell Mrs. Silver I was taking care of it myself. I was too scared to run."

"And?"

"She was a bit annoyed at first. Then she was sending a couple of people to help me."

"Ah. It's a pity you didn't call the police, Doctor. The Ungrukh were trying to keep you alive, and if the Raiders had killed any you'd be in much bigger trouble. Or dead. The gunners on the rooftop were on their way to kill you."

"*Somebody* has got to get out of here," said the nurse. A technician and a cardiologist were watching the monitor; a surgeon was checking the drainage tube under the bandage running up two-thirds of Bren's belly; the house doctor adjusted the IV, the ventilator tube and the urine catheter. Emerald and Raanung were standing quietly in a corner with the veterinarian.

Emerald said, "He seems big enough. I guess it must be time for him to come out."

The nurse was massaging the big cub with a towel, because Bren was too weak and hampered to lick him. "Do you think he minds being rubbed the wrong way?"

"Not just yet," Bren growled.

The doctor said, "Her lungs are clear and her heart's pounding like a stone hammer. She doesn't need that tube." He pulled away the ventilator and swabbed the sore nostril.

"Good."

Etrem said nothing. His forelimbs were hooked over the protective bars; while the towel pushed the damp dark-red hairs this way and that he was staring at the cloudy markings beneath, the pink and red of the Spotted.

The veterinarian came forward and said quietly, "Some black leopards are pure black, like you. Some show basic markings in the light."

"What color is this one?"

"I'll never know. You'll have to watch him grow, and find out."

"I prefer black, myself," said Bren. "But we can dye him whatever you choose. If you like green trees on blue sky we do that."

Etrem snorted. He bent to sniff at the fresh new body of his son, touched Bren's nose with his tongue and left the room.

His heart was bursting with joy and relief, but he had some distance to go before he could express them.

Bren was lapping a dish of milk, hoping to prime the maternal dairy pump for the big Stiller. She lifted her head, chin dripping, and hissed with laughter. "It becomes interesting to watch the child in that man grow up with this one here . . . and now you can all see I intend to stay alive maybe you let me sleep."

"The case is neat, tight and solid as we can make it—with all its bumps and dents," Sukey said. "It'll go on trial I bet before Buster here sheds his fuzz and rides your back."

"What of your finger?"

Sukey regarded the skintex-capped nub. "Not enough left to regrow. My fingers were the only nice little things I had."

"Consider how the notch in my ear spoils my beauty."

"The kid makes up for it." The cub, nearly half the size of his mother, eyes still sealed tight, was lying on his side sleepily hugging and sucking a bulb filled with vitamins, bone meal and laxative mixed with his milk supplement.

"I am not a good enough provider for Embrin."

"Embrin . . . is that derived from your name or—" She flushed lightly and shut up.

Bren said calmly, "It is a masculine form of Embri, Etrem's mother. His choice, and I agree. The poor woman is bitter and unhappy, and we give her name to someone we hope brings joy."

Sukey was careful to keep down the thought that it sounded more like a curse—or at least a burden—to her. Ungrukh had their own ways of thought, and Bren and Etrem had borne their own burdens.

A formal inquiry in the New Court near Flagstaff (a short distance from the New District Capital—both branch-plants a century old and of stultifying barrenness) brought down indictments of attempted murder and conspiracy against Phoebe Charloe Adams Silver. Since GalFed had no legal rights it was granted a watching brief conducted by Man of Law and Enbhor, Captain Imbhi's friend, GalFed Security Chief on Sol III and a scholar specializing in comparative law.

Phoebe pleaded innocent on both charges. Mercy was

charged with attempted murder; she pleaded innocent by reason of diminished responsibility. Boris remained a witness, but could not be charged with anything because, in spite of his admissions of killing Tragg in self-defense, there was no trace of crime. Dr. Kriss, several Raiders, and Billings and Vasquez were heaped with various charges; there would be a long series of trials.

Flagstaff was not a difficult place for Continental Representatives to commute to every ten days or two weeks, when they joined their other colleagues three times a year rotating among Ottawa, Washington and Mexico City, but its Courthouse was too small and difficult of access to accommodate all the principals and public spectators anticipated—to say nothing of sixty-odd Ungrukh. By tactful negotiation trial was set in the larger Southern District Courthouse with half of its balcony seats removed and converted into a sweep of benches for the Ungrukh to crouch on. Ungrukh declared that they did not need or want the expense of carpeting; Authority determined that it was not going to appear to Sol III that they were being treated shabbily.

44

For the Ungrukh the days that were passing had the texture of those in the tropics, where the weather is balmy but marked regularly by brief fierce storms.

Emerald, with Raanung close by, went to MedPsych in the Siberian tundras where, under the same dome system in which her mother had passed the ESP-one exam twenty-two years earlier, she was given a new pair of corneas much superior to her grandmother Tengura's replacements. After some days she saw Raanung without thick mist for the first time in seven years. The gray was spreading in the V of his chevron, and as she had seen through his eyes, in her own. But he *was* Raanung, and like everyone else, fresh and young in her sight.

Ungrukh on Sol III no longer felt personally threatened; no Ungrukh death would benefit any Solthree now. The taste for rugs of crimson fur had faded. Raanung, because he had spoken most harshly to Menirrh, the Scrublands Tribesman, ceded him authority, glad to shuck his father's harsh mode. Menirrh responded by curbing his own.

The Ungrukh settled on ledges and in niches up the North Rim for cooler and thinner air; they spoke civilly to hikers, posed for pictures when asked, ate what was delivered without bothering about hunting or any other privileges, and kept private when they chose.

But Security remained watchful, if less obvious. With resignation Bren and Etrem wore radios and answered twice daily. The small new family was the object of attention among both Ungrukh and Solthrees. Embrin, firstborn on a strange world, acquired many new mothers before his milk teeth sprouted. Bren had been nervous about licking open the gummed eyes on a world swarming with strange infections, and Rosa bathed them. They opened clear and questing before they shrank against so harsh a light. Before his fuzz wore off his fur could be seen growing beneath it in the same color, darker than his mother's, lighter than his father's, and the pink and red markings were unnoticeable except when he got soaked in a cloudburst or, out of curiosity, under a waterfall. Etrem would lick him dry, and, as the wall of glass around him had turned to ice and melted, the stone of pain inside cracked into grains and dissolved, while with careful strokes of his tongue, he pushed away his harrowing past.

Emerald returned with her own new eyes; grandchildren were no novelty to her, but this was the first she could see clearly enough not to fear hurting when she played with it. Etrem was grateful for the warmth and concern of his family and people, and also relieved when they lessened with the news that three other women had become pregnant.

The twins caused a mild flurry by running away again. Bren damped it quickly with the accurate guess that they had returned to the place she would have liked to live in with her own family. It was out of the question then, as she suspected it always would be. Moon's Woman would not return to where Many Harvests had died. The pair were hauled back half abashed and half defiant; they too wanted a hold on some familiar aspect of life.

So Tom Green Corn and Bill Gonzales spent a weekend ferrying them with Emerald, Bren and family to the Mesa where Moon's Woman and Sun Rising High could comfort the twins and subject the baby to the beam of curiosity and admiration.

Moon's Woman let the oafish cub crawl over him with amusement at the one spark of jealousy emanating from the twins. They soon forgot that and everything else by wrestling in a dry dirt patch, raising a dust cloud and some bemused attention from passing harvesters. Then he felt free to give Embrin his gift.

Moon's Woman had wished to make a toy for the cub and was hard put to think of one. Young cats or dogs played mainly with pine cones, or things that could be chewed, or else chased their tails. Most of the young children he knew played with toys bought at stores, although his kachinas, when he felt like making them, were appreciated. But a kachina doll was not so much a toy as a lesson in religion and history. Yet he thought a very sturdy doll might be enjoyed by a young Ungrukh. As with string figures his creative abilities were a private matter between his hands and his unconscious, and at dawn he rose and took out his tackle box and scrap bag and waited to be told.

In a short while he found himself working with pieces of the strong red cloth he had used for what he called Red Bird Kachina. He had to work harder with smaller scraps, but his fine stitching made up for this liability. He made the black wool feathering shorter and without loops for young claws to catch in. He had plenty of beads but did not use them, or the wires, for fear they might be gnawed off and swallowed; he made tight stiff braids wound hard for talons; eyes, nostrils, beak and talon-tips were formed of cord knots well sewn down, and the trilobar emblem on the breast was embroidered. In all other respects the doll was identical to the one he vaguely remembered making earlier. Was this a kachina? He was not quite sure now, and for Embrin it would not matter. If the child wished to learn of such things his parents were capable of teaching him.

The gift was received with thanks and admiration; the cub rolled it in four paws and licked the cheek of its giver; his tongue's rasps were then no harsher than a domestic cat's.

But Sun Rising High frowned at the sight of the doll, and Bren and Emerald fell silent, unwilling to esp.

Bren's radio buzzed. "What is that?" She squinted at the sun. "It is not time for check."

"Better answer anyway," said Green Corn. He reached into her pouch for the earpiece so that she would not have to scramble for prostheses.

Bren, answering, grunted; she felt the hour was spoiling. "Yes, Man of Law. Come." She said to the Chief, "You know our lawyer from another world, not so?"

"Yes. That is one strange creature, but welcome."

"He says: wait one hour and he brings interesting news. That is not altogether welcome to me. I think I am tired of interesting news."

• • •

Man of Law found a place for himself and sat, crossing his legs and placing hands on knees with a soft clash. He said nothing, and by his attitude no one was disposed to speak to him, for his attention was directed at the doll. Then he said, "I came to tell you of the brave work of Ungrukh on a dangerous world, but now I wonder if you do not already know."

After a few moments Bren said slowly, "No . . . not until now," and with Emerald and Orenda turned heads to look at Moon's Woman. His eyes widened. He pulled the doll from the grasp of Embrin and raised his arm to hurl it away.

"No, man!" Man of Law's arm seemed to stretch out a great distance to restrain the hand. "That is not an evil thing! It represents a courageous person and a great blessing."

"And also a very dangerous being," said Emerald. "This double the priest is recalling must be a creation of Qumedon—or Qumedon himself. Perhaps he is among us now in his Kriku shape. Even you, Man of Law, cannot tell that." She said to the Pueblo friends of the Ungrukh, "I am sorry that there seems to be another strange one about."

Moon's Woman whispered, "Does that mean I am not mad?"

"Of course you are not mad! This being uses you for his own purposes. There is no harm done yet."

"Not if he keeps to himself," said Bren. "And we cannot charge Phoebe Adams for her part in a pearl-smuggling trade half across the Galaxy."

"Nor can we," said Man of Law. "We are already having enough trouble trying to keep Kylklar and Xirifor from cutting up her brother and dividing the pieces."

Emerald said with a sarcastic rasp, "You think Phoebe Adams is lucky not to be in the charge of us Ungrukh?"

"Do *you* tear persons apart for revenge? You are letting her people judge her."

Bren looked at Moon's Woman, draped by the jealous twins and at the same time hugging the squirming Embrin who was clasping Red Angel as he was clasped. (Image: double Moon's Woman, eyes occluded by the brim of the hat, eye-windows to chaos, reaching for Red Bird Kachina: *I will deliver that for you.*)

45

Phoebe's son Adam Silver had lost weight. He looked as if he had lost it too quickly, because there were drawn lines down the sides of his cheeks. The two hugged stiffly and kissed the air at each other's ears. He was dressed in sober blue cloth, as were his fellows, probably, but he had come alone and without documents. He was also an observer. "How are you, Mother?"

"As well as can be. Nella and the children?"

"Fine. She offered to come, but I didn't think it was necessary."

"Nor do I. You've put up at a hotel?"

"Yes." Neither of them wanted him here. He was looking about. "Where are all the servants?"

"You know about Mercy and Boris. I let the cook and butler go and have meals brought in. One maid is enough. I've hired plenty of guards."

"Do you need money? My inheritance—"

"No. I put the apartment upstairs along with some bonds up for bail, and cashed others. I have enough."

"Good . . . um, I never asked about the . . . business. I guess I thought it better not to. But now I do have to ask something."

She laced her fingers. "Ask away."

He took a deep breath. "Are you guilty of what you are being charged with?"

"Absolutely not."

He released the breath. "I'm glad." He kissed her cheek.

"Good night, Mama. Don't worry, now. I'll see you tomorrow or next day, latest."

In the great abyss where Ungrukh were absorbed with their own affairs it was difficult for them to assess the scale of those matters in a hugely populated world. The adventure of Argha's daughter Rrimi was a grand espisode for Ungruwarkh and its sector in GalFed, and Phoebe Adams' involvement in pearl-smuggling made a great stir in Southern District. She resigned her seat before she could be expelled. These occurrences made flurries in international and interworld circles like brief storms; no participant regretted that they were brief. The almost certain presence of a Qumedon, which might cause a much greater stir, a more powerful storm, was an item carefully left unreported by both Ungrukh and Authority. Solthrees at home knew little about Qumedni. Moon's Woman believed he knew more than he wanted.

The days went by and on the Mesas the people who chose the old ways, some of them clerks, police or civil servants, spent holidays gathering spruce twigs, made prayer sticks, painted and masked themselves into kachina forms and danced in blowing dust. Sun Rising High felt a stirring of hope for his Society, and Moon's Woman made more kachina dolls—traditional ones—and ceremonial bows for young boys.

The first corn was picked; eagles were tethered, but not to be sacrificed as in old days: There were too few. The round of dances ended, and the rest of the corn was gathered with beans and squash. The villages garnished themselves while the land waited for the last summer rains, and the clans sang and played flutes for the new planting and the coming of Blue Corn Girl.

The winds cooled and the Ungrukh, having learned to appreciate a little warmth, moved further down the slopes; they gathered around fires, discussed, and dispersed. And Phoebe Adams sat among her lawyers and spoke little.

When the women of the Mesas assembled for their autumn dances, the Law performed its own ritual dance of jury choosing and the trial began.

While the jury selection was going on the prosecution was making a last-ditch effort to connect the death of Many Harvests with the other charges against Phoebe Adams and for that purpose had called Moon's Woman as a witness; he spent two nerve-racking days waiting until they decided that the attempt was hopeless, and for all his sorrow and anger he went home with relief.

He found that the twins had persuaded Bill Gonzales, the Ranger, to let them stay in the old kiva where the Society had begun; it was protected from extreme weather, kept fairly warm with small fires instead of the cumbersome old stove, and was out of the way. The twins had nothing to do with the trial, did not care—and were minding the baby. Moon's Woman moved in with them temporarily, to the relief of Bren, whose trust in the twins had its limits. Moon's Woman had the company he loved best in the world, and did not have to stay in that city with that woman, or be pinned by the eyes of strangers.

The trial was trying to the Ungrukh in a different way. They were quartered in a hotel that was to be torn down for a new heliport; though the furniture was gone the rugs, water and toilet facilities were more than enough luxury, and the courtroom benches were carpeted; they brushed carefully and oiled themselves lightly in order not to shed hairs. And they got a breakfast of fresh meat every second day.

But they were also obliged to crouch in stillness for hours on end, and they became tense. Occasionally when they flicked their tails there would be great waves of movement sweeping the group. Fortunately most others sat with backs to them.

To help them understand, Man of Law provided mental commentary, with footnotes by Enbhor the Durbha on historical and comparative law. The event was something like an ESP exam, with inquiry, demand, accusation, riposte—but far slower for Ungrukh. Witnesses gave testimony in a white-walled enclosure that looked to them like a cage. Due process droned.

"Did you recognize any of those persons firing weapons during the attack on January 20 of this year?" Defense asked.

"No," said Bren. She had been given a bench because she could not use a chair. The hair had grown in on her shaved belly and the wound had healed without pain or infection. She kept her tail still by tucking it under.

"You recognized Mercy Adams only by the memory of a smell, or scent, some time later?"

"Objection," said Prosecutor. "It was agreed beforehand not to use this line of questioning. Ungrukh themselves do not use it in judicial process."

"Sustained," said the Judge. He was a large, wise, weary man who knew, like Plaintiff and Defense, that the question of scent had been slipped in to make Plaintiff look ridiculous.

Drone.

"Did the defendant, Councillor Adams, ever personally attack you?"

"No!" said Boris.

"But you claim she attempted to kill you."

"Not by hand. She left an order for me to collect . . ." and on. "The elevator was locked . . ." and on. "The man was waiting . . ."

Defense asked to cross-examine under scanner. Witness gave permission. "Agreed, if we can do so as well," said Plaintiff.

Allowed. Testimony repeated and confirmed. Then:

"Did you kill two men while protecting Senator Silver?"

"I did." Scan-op confirmed.

"Were they attacking him with weapons in full sight?"

"Yeah, unless they had more hidden. I'm no ESP."

"Did you commit violence against others in defense of Senator Silver?"

"I did."

"On what occasion or occasions?"

"Objection. That is irrelevant."

"Your Honor, the man admits to violent behavior. We ask the questions to discover if his acts of violence were gratuitous. If they were, doubt is cast on his claim of killing a man in self-defense—and on his whole testimony of an attempt on his life *by the defendant,* under scanner or not."

"Overruled. You may ask."

"On what—"

"I punched up two guys for threatening to blackmail Senator Silver like I said, but no other rough stuff."

"Confirmed," said scan-op.

"No further questions." Prosecutor did not bother. The scanner was not completely trustworthy on an Impervious, and nothing would shake Boris.

And on. The waves of tail-tapping swelled and receded.

Opinions among spectators ebbed and flowed.

Ear and nose twitching were added to tail-tapping. The Lyhhrt had intended to suggest that the Ungrukh take turns in groups attending and reporting on the trial, because day after day it had become their life, their weather. When sessions were adjourned they were transported to their hotel, where they took great care not to inconvenience the staff. But sometimes in the night they loped the corridors under the dim light-strips in silence: by pairs, threes, tens, to free their limbs and minds.

Man of Law gave up his intention, for in the courtroom they joined mind to mind to mind in a single unseen unfelt focus of intensity upon the trial.

Dr. Kriss admitted doing mindblocking work for Phoebe and on Mercy, but denied that there was any mention of Ungrukh in their dealings. Scanner confirmed. Yes, she had treated Mercy on the day of the slaughter, though no reason had been given. Yes, she had mindblocked many of the Rasputins and given therapy for anxiety attacks to some, using legal drugs and methods of hypnosis. She worked on the edge of the law but did not overstep.

"Why did you think the Ungrukh would attack you?" Prosecutor asked.

"Councillor Adams told me the Police—the Continentals—were spreading rumors that she was responsible for the killings and that I had helped her."

Scan-op confirmed, astonishing the Continentals, who had been told no such thing.

"Then why, if you really believed you were being threatened, did you not go to Municipal or District Police?"

"Why—I—I thought the Councillor was telling the truth and . . . and that made me afraid to go to any police. When I called the club president I hoped a few of the cyclists would come out and guard me and—and I guess I must have sounded very upset. I didn't expect the whole club."

A wrangle then took half a day that ended in summoning Continental Police, represented by Haynes, Kovarski and McNelly, to deny, truthfully under scanner, that they had spread rumors. But this delay proved a welcome slowing of pace for the Ungrukh to nerve themselves for the presentation of two new pieces of evidence: an Ungrukh skin found in the possession of one of the Rasputins (not a patient of Kriss), and a fur toy cat, owned by a member of an associate club, the Minotaurs.

The Rasputin would not go under scanner or admit to anything. He was charged.

The Minotaur testified that she had been given the toy at a club convention where she was too stoned to remember who gave it to her and it could have been any of the bunch she had been in, uh, intimate contact with and had never liked the damn thing anyway and stowed it away and forgot it. And that was the truth.

The jury separated into faces, intent and still.

The next day Adam Silver did not attend the trial.

In the evening he visited Phoebe. She had moved very little during the trial, and looked gaunt. Not expecting callers, she had put on a blue velvet housegown with silk-embroidered dragons. "What's the matter, Adam?"

He had spent the day reading transcripts in an over-decorated suite made bleak by his feelings. She put her feet up on her hassock and accepted a cup of tea from the maid. "Would you like something to drink?"

He sat and moistened his lips. "No. I didn't go today."

"Oh. I—"

"Didn't notice because you didn't look for me. I was reading hard copy of the testimony, today's too, after adjournment."

"So? Get it off your chest, Adam."

"Most of my life I've realized you despised me, and taught myself to accept it. I fought my way beyond resentment and even made some kind of excuse for you. . . ."

"You're doing very well. Go on."

"I will. One thing I never believed was that you were a liar. Now I do."

"Adam!" She put down the cup. "That's going too far!"

"Is it? I don't think so. You lied to the Kriss woman. A terrible lie that cost lives and injuries—"

"Nothing there touches me directly."

"That lie opens the way to a great many other lies. I can't stand that. I had enough of it from my father. I gave up on him early. But I believed you were at least honest, and I held on to that. But you are a liar and a hypocrite, and I am giving up on you." He stood. His eyes were red-rimmed. "You will have all the legal help I can give and all the money I can spare, and the company of my children, if you want that—which I doubt. But you will not have me. There will be nothing for you to miss."

The door closed on him.

She sat for a moment with arms dangling, then got up and went into her office where she unlocked the cabinet of her bank of scrambler comms. "Senator Hepworth's residence. Who is calling please?"

"Tell him Charley."

"Senator Hepworth is at his hunting lodge and taking no calls."

"Hello? Madame Narayan? Miki?"

"This is a recording. This line has been disconnected. This is a recording. This line—

"Pigott there? Where's Pigott?"

"He's runnin an I'm packin an you better do the same an don't call back because there won't be nobody here."

She stared at the silent phones a moment before she locked them. "I only wanted to talk," she whispered.

"Another cup of tea, Ma'am?"

"No."

The maid turned down the bedding for her. "Is there anything I can do for you, Ma'am?" She was silky with youth.

"*Would* you do anything for me, Ellen?" A dilation of the pupils?

"Oh yes, Ma'am." A slyness in that smile?

"No thank you. I don't need anything."

46

Prosecution believed that calling Phoebe to testify would be an exercise in recalcitrance, so it did not even consider putting her on the stand. And her defense did not want attention lingering on her. If she could be judged lightly her stigmas might fade. What did Sol III care about a few dead alien cats? Or Xirifor's pearls?—if her brother kept his mouth shut. A few years out of the public eye, a turn of the electoral wheel, might renew her. Stranger things had happened.

But Mercy Adams was required to testify, and neither party was eager to put her on the stand either.

Raanung said, "Why not? She incriminates enough with the statement she gives of her own will."

"It works in our favor that she lived with Phoebe Adams for many years, and knows her character," said Man of Law. He was sitting on the rug in the chairless room as gracefully as if it were a luxurious couch. "She swore Phoebe drugged her and took her to the slaughter, and force was used to make her fire the gun."

"But being drugged she might not have had a clear idea of what was happening," said Enbhor, who was standing, and always stood, even to sleep. "And the police might have put ideas in her mind, which even a scanner could not clarify from drugged memories."

"Unless Hertzberg tested her liquids for traces of psychotropics before mindclear—and that can be established."

"Ah, but," said Enbhor, "Mercy declared that Phoebe would not have trusted her, and the implications are that Phoebe was afraid Mercy might attack her. It is true she did *not* say, 'I would have killed—or wished to— kill her,' but she should have retracted that statement."

"Perhaps," said Bren, "her feelings are too strong for her to go back on it . . . tomorrow, we discover."

Mercy pulled herself away from past and future as well as she could, and listened to music. Her daytime guard, Yvonne, was a cheerful young woman who did not try to draw her out; she had been bringing tea and coffee for both of them. Her weaponry was intimidating, but to guard rather than threaten; Mercy had nowhere to go. Boris was, though not under indictment, in an analogous position as a witness. He was being kept in a low-security holding area for safety and also because he too had nowhere else to go. Whatever he admitted, however thuggish he seemed—and he did know a few thugs through Long John—he was a cranky loner with a stubborn loyalty, no more. He and Mercy sometimes glanced at each other in the courtroom, sometimes thought of each other. Neither reached out.

On the day before Mercy's testimony Caroline, her night guard, brought her a package; she was almost a clone of Yvonne. "This is the way it came." She produced a sack with a drawstring. "They knew we'd be looking at it."

"They?" Mercy hefted it by the string. "Doesn't feel like a file or crowbar. Who?"

"There's a note."

Mercy dumped the contents on her bunk. Candy, fruit, dope sticks about the strength of beer, music spools. The crinkled note said, FROM THE OLD MALL GANG. "Sounds kinda sentimental," said Caroline, "but you better be sure they aren't."

"But—who?"

"*You* know. Sukey, Debbie, some of the old clodhoppers who've seen you around. Hey—you're not bawling!"

"I—I don't think so."

"Better not. Water ruins the spools."

Mercy's voice hardened. "They feel sorry for me."

"Calm down, lady! They feel bad for you. There's a difference. And that's no way to take a gift."

Mercy bit her lip. "You're right. Can you thank them for me?"

"Sure."

"And . . . do you think I can give some of this to Boris? Anton Borisov? He hasn't got . . ."

"Why not? Divvy up and I'll send it with his supper." She grinned. "Any message?"

"Just say—I thought he'd like a share."

Boris sent thanks with the evening coffee. Mercy did not expect more, did not want more, because the effect of the modest gesture from people who owed her nothing had been paradoxical. The collapsing fire of her breast had turned outward and streamed with flame.

She had not had care, friends, love or gifts. A life. She was not self-absorbed or self-pitying; she had never allowed herself a teardrop of those luxuries. Not beside the burdened, the maimed, the starving, the mad, the tortured. But she had had nothing, and she searched back along the path for the branch-points where she might have turned toward something.

How to escape a world peopled only by companies that administered mines and processed ores? On a rung where survival traits were ignorance and stupidity. No looks, no money for education. Could she have asked her father to give up their half-fare vacations to save money for her future? Sacrifice his moments free of the dark wormhole?

If ever I get blown out here you stay away from them snotty Charloes. Where else then, old man? What else for someone so easily replaced by a machine, who knew so little she'd be laughed off any street she tried working.

Phoebe had made her shadow-Phoebe; not a sculpture but a flat gray cutout. Phoebe was her own self; shadow was nothing. Fed, clothed, lodged, a little something to spend, she did not want much, had not learned to want enough. But saving Boris, whom she owed nothing, had shown her how much she wanted to give, and this small gift from people she hardly knew, who owed her nothing. How much she might have enjoyed: friends, lovers perhaps; and still, from the ten years back, and the years back of them, she could not find the branch that did not lead into the shadow of Phoebe and the blood-pit that was not hunt but murder.

She dreamed: *Phoebe on the stand, calm, dignified, widow-veiled.*

Prosecutor: Did you on the night of force your cousin Mercy to?

Phoebe: No. I am innocent.

Prosecutor: Did you on the day of attempt to have Mercy Adams falsely accused of?

Phoebe: No. I would never consider such.

Prosecutor: Did you on that same day plan to force Mercy Adams to undergo?

Phoebe: Absolutely not. (Weeping.) She betrayed me when she was as dear to me as.

Mercy, waking, wept into her pillow unregarded.

"Dr. Hertzberg, when the witness, Mercy Adams, was given mindclear was there any trace of psychotropic drugs in her body fluids?" Defense asked.

"Only the mild tranquilizer we give all subjects on the previous evening."

"And is it permitted to ask how she scored on the psychological tests, which are drawn up and given by legal psychiatrists like yourself?"

"Perfectly rational—and of course resentful and rather angry."

"Why 'of course' resentful and rather angry?"

"Because she found herself in the position of being obliged to go through this process. Otherwise—"

"But isn't that degree of protest—"

"Otherwise," said Dr. Hertzberg firmly, "she would hardly have been normal. She grumbled but did not lose her temper."

"Would you like the witness to accept a scan?" the Judge asked.

"No. That's not necessary, thank you."

"On that note of harmony," said the Judge, "let us adjourn until fourteen-thirty hours."

"What happens after this?" Bren asked Man of Law.

"After Mercy testifies there will be a summing up by both parties and then the jury will go out on Phoebe."

"Do you expect they find her guilty?"

"I don't know about attempted murder, because they probably can't prove that she actually attacked or ordered an attack on the Ungrukh. But I expect they'll be able to patch together a guilty verdict for conspiracy. All this has nothing to do with her actual guilt; she's certainly not innocent. Would you feel badly done by?"

"No. This is what we are here for."

47

At fourteen hours the principals began to assemble.

In one of the balcony tiers where the Ungrukh were settled with Man of Law and Enbhor they found themselves crowded. The neighbors of the crowder whacked their tails against the tier's riser and began to request he move elsewhere.

At one look from him they fell silent. The hairs rose on every Ungrukh. "What is happening?" Enbhor asked.

"What is expected," said the Lyhhrt. "Qumedon is here."

KRIKU IN THIS FORM, IF YOU PLEASE. He who had pushed in raised one seven-toed paw and licked its pads.

"We do not please at all," said Raanung.

BEFORE YOU THINK OF CALLING ON GALFED—OR KWEMEDN—CONSIDER THE TIME IT WOULD TAKE —AND ALSO THAT I SAVED SEVENTY-EIGHT LIVES. SIXTY-THREE OF THEM YOURS.

"I believe that," Raanung said, "and you deserve thanks. Yet it is hard to thank you, Qumedon. You have an interest in us because you consider yourself our shaper—if not our maker—and you also believe that whatever mischief is about, *you* must make it."

OH, I HAVE LEARNED TO EXPECT NO THANKS FROM YOU.

"Then why are you here now?"

LIKE YOURSELVES, TO SEE THAT JUSTICE IS DONE.

That did not reassure the Ungrukh, nor their companions. Kwemedn had its own idea of Law—and Kriku had his.

They could not esp him, he could esp all of them, his powers were enormous and they could not get rid of him. They pulled their shields down as tight as possible and Raanung swallowed bile and said civilly, "Allow us to accept whatever justice we get."

Kriku grinned, nudged his neighbors further aside, and swung his tail to and fro.

Defense asked, "Ms. Adams, how long were you in the employ of Councillor Phoebe Adams?"

"Ten years, three months and four days."

"Um. And she also provided lodging, clothing and food. Is that true?"

"Yes."

"And salary?"

"Minimum wage."

"Did you consider that fair?"

"Yes, because of the other provisions."

"And you were on call at all times?"

"I had some free time for shopping, exercise, occasional amusements like theater."

"Did you consider yourself well treated?"

"Yes."

"You were never abused, criticized or provoked."

"Oh, I was criticized. Everyone is, I suppose. Once I was slapped."

"By the Councillor?"

"Yes."

"Did she apologize?"

"She said, 'I'm sorry I lost control of my temper.' "

Bren watched, and though she could not esp, recalled the little of Mercy she had glimpsed, a quite different Mercy. This one had learned control from Phoebe herself. Defense was hard put to show her the resentful beneficiary of a generous Phoebe.

"Did you consider leaving her?"

"No. I had little education or training."

"On the whole, then, you were treated well?"

"On the whole, yes."

"No further questions," Defense said quickly.

Defense had been very dainty about stepping over the night

of the slaughter; all of that could come later when Mercy was used to the stand. She and Phoebe, now, were co-defendants. Phoebe's stake was higher, but Mercy's case, no matter how it turned out, would be blurred about the edges, and her control was brittle. Defense's tactic must be to keep her strong and calm, because though Prosecution might break its fist against Phoebe's ice-wall, it could crumble Mercy's shell to slivers.

Some instinct made Bren turn her head to look at Kriku. His tongue caressed his teeth like fire lapping timbers, and she shuddered.

Prosecution was a tall strong woman in her forties, with dark wound hair and gray eyes. "Ms. Adams, you have said you were treated fairly by the Defendant Councillor Adams."

"Yes."

"Did you get along well in the household?"

"Objection. The ground has been covered and the question is irrelevant."

"No, your Honor, the ground has been touched on, and I can show why it is not irrelevant for it to be *covered*."

"Overruled. Proceed."

"Ms. Adams, how would you say you were treated by the rest of the household, including Senator Silver and the others who worked there?"

"Politely."

"Did you have friends among them?"

"No. That's not unusual."

"I presume your friendships and social life took place outside that establishment?"

Defense twitched in his seat and bit his tongue.

"I had acquaintances in the Mall gym and library."

Prosecutor paused for one beat. "At ten-thirty hours on January 20 you were taken personally by Councillor Adams for an appointment with Dr. Kriss, as established, for blocking with hypnotism and drugs."

"Yes."

"Did you receive any kind of therapy?"

"No."

"How often were you taken for these sessions?"

"Three or four times a year."

"Did you know their purpose?"

"To guard against ESPs for security reasons. Most officials and staff had them."

"Did you ever resent them?"

"I didn't enjoy them. I recognized their importance to the Councillor."

"When you took mindclear you also chose to go under scanner, and on oath. I remind you that oath still holds. On the night of January 20 the slaughter of nineteen Ungrukh occurred. Can you give us an account of that event?"

"Most of the time those sessions left me confused and disoriented for seven or eight hours. Around evening my mind would begin to clear—"

"By your own account, not completely, not on January 20. You were, as you said, drugged and docile, that is to say, suggestible, so suggestible that you allowed the Councillor to take you to the place of slaughter, allowed weapons to be put in your hands, and though you didn't know whether they were loaded, fired them. Yet you were clear-headed enough to think that the bullets might not be genuine because, I quote, 'I wonder if she would have trusted me with the real thing.' *Why* would she not have trusted you, Ms. Adams? Was it because—"

Bren had a sickening sense of déjà vu. Yes. Her grandmother Prandra in the synagogue with the Demon Rabbi, Qumedon . . . She saw with horror that this attorney, in her zeal to get a conviction, a zeal perhaps inflamed by Qumedon to show off his own power, would crush Mercy and throw her aside. None of the other Ungrukh, none the Ungrukh knew, were vengeful toward Mercy. Not even the police. The more they knew of the case the more they knew how shamefully she had been used and beaten down; they understood her better than she did herself. Phoebe Charloe Adams Silver had kept herself clean by using others like disposable cloths to wipe her own filth away, and of those Mercy was most victimized. She would be broken; there was no one to stop—

The Judge's lips moved: *You are leading the witness,* but no sound came from them.

because—

Phoebe's pearl necklace rose and fell on her breast.

"—because after living for ten years with a woman of your own blood who gave you no friendship, small wages, no gift or bonus, kept you at her call in an atmosphere where everyone looked through you, most words addressed to you critical, struck you and could only say that she regretted losing her temper—not hurting you!— took you to the murder scene with the intention of putting you in her place to do what she wanted to do, as a symbol or for whatever evil reason, dared to use part of her own name and attach it to you, expected you to take blame whatever the accounting, let you believe you were a killer whether you were or not? And you claim you were well treated? *Well treated?* And yet—you say that perhaps she might not have trusted you? Would she not then be in murderous control of herself at all times? Even as she used you for a substitute aggressor knowing that her savagery might rebound on her—and—"

Kriku stood. THAT YOU WOULD WISH QUITE NATURALLY TO KILL HER?

The Prosecutor, Madame Desrosiers, whirled with her hands out before her, pushing as at a wall of glass. *What? Where?*

MIGHT YOU NOT? AND WHY SHOULD YOU NOT KILL HER?

GET UP, MERCY ADAMS! USE THE STRONG HANDS OF THE HUNTING WOMAN!

Emerald roared, "QUMEDON!"

"Regard, Ungrukh," said Kriku/Qumedon in their own tongue. "The woman killed nineteen of you by slaughter and skinning, three by poison, and did her best to kill sixty-three more. And many others. The justice you have come so far to find will be that she is sent away to live in comfort for a few years and return to do more evil. You call me a mischief-maker, and yet I have killed far fewer, sentient or animal, and saved lives as well. Why are you so weak now? Look, Ungrukh!

"Look, look, Prosecutor, Lyhhrt, Durbha! Look, murderer! and look, witness, my instrument! I have taken us away from Time. We know, and no one else knows . . . need know . . ."

All others in the courtroom were silent and unmoving: one frozen blotting his sweating forehead, one smoothing her hair, one speaking a syllable into a recorder, one scratching an ankle, the Judge's eyes closed in a blink, Boris in a sneeze—

ALL THE REST OF YOU ARE FREE AND MOVING —AND CANNOT TOUCH ME! AND YOU, PHOEBE ADAMS, MAY LOOK AND BREATHE—FOR A WHILE—AND CANNOT RISE.

BUT YOU, MERCY ADAMS, CAN RISE, AND MOVE—AND KILL.

OPEN THE DOOR OF YOUR BOX AND DO AS YOU CHOOSE, AND IF YOU CHOOSE TO KILL—

Raanung howled, "No! It is *his* choice!"

—ONE WHO ABUSED YOU FOR SO MANY YEARS? ONLY *I* CAN GIVE YOU FREEDOM AND ALL YOU NEED TO BECOME FREE. NONE OF THESE COWARDS CAN HELP YOU. MOVE!

Mercy Adams, shadow-puppet, got up from her chair, pulled the door of her whitewall cage, came down the steps. Phoebe Adams writhed and could not scream.

The Ungrukh, fixed, thrashed tails and twitched ears. The Durbha had the will to move, but was too slow to go anywhere; fiery yellow streaks flamed up his body; his tentacles swarmed helplessly. Man of Law drew his legs together, his arms into his body, his head into his shoulders, his shoulders into his trunk.

Mercy took one step and another toward Phoebe.

Kriku leaped tier by tier. The Lyhhrt, a dull silver lightning bolt, darted after. But Kriku, on the floor, knew him and burst into his primary shape, the nothing-colored sphere blazing with sparks. STAY AWAY STAY AWAY OR I WILL BURN YOU TO A SHRIVEL WHO DO YOU THINK YOU ARE THAT YOU CAN TOUCH ME?

The serpentine shape paused and drew back.

The whirling sparkling Qumedon advanced down the aisle as slowly as Mercy on Phoebe, as slowly as her arms rose, strong hands around neck, thumbs on trachea.

"No," said Bren. The Lyhhrt's desperate move had in some strange way rectified her mind, which had been twitching madly like Qumedni sparks, stilled its confusion.

"Mother, no."

"No," said Emerald. "Nurunda!"

"With," said Nurunda. "Ygne?"

"Here," said Ygne. "Etrem?"

"Yes, Merra. Mundr."

"One! Menirrh. Raanung. Nogri!"

stop
here now
be here come
we come now be
now we can be come
one now we can all stop

the Ungrukh couched closed eyes tails still ears still Bren lent eyes and mind to Mercy Phoebe Prosecutor

NO NOW WE CAN STOP WE
ARE ALL ONE COME BE
ONE WE CAN STOP
NOW WE ARE
ALL HERE
ONE
STOP NOW!

There was an implosion of silence.

Qumedon stopped. WHO IS SPEAKING?

UNGRUKH

WHAT ARE YOU?

AS YOU SEE. *UNGRUKH.*

UNGRUKH opened its eyes. Twice sixty-five red eyes. Twice sixty-five lenses of one Eye.

Mercy's hands stopped at Phoebe's throat.

The Prosecutor Desrosiers stood still, hands out.

QUMEDON, YOU MAKE BETTER THAN YOU KNOW. CAN YOU NOW UNMAKE? Qumedon, sparkling, whirling, found he could not move from his place.

Only once, long before, had the massed minds of thousands of Ungrukh repudiated a Qumedon who offered them a marvelous world in a living Universe who longed for them. This, now, was not a collection but a being.

Qumedon changed to his Ungrukh shape and spoke softly, persuasively. "You do not know what you are doing. I have come to help you."

I KNOW WHAT I AM DOING. I DO NOT WANT YOUR HELP. I DO NOT NEED IT. I AM WHAT YOU MAKE ME TO BE WHEN YOU DO NOT KNOW WHAT YOU MAKE.

NOW IT IS TIME FOR YOU TO GO AND MAKE NEW THINGS IN OTHER PLACES. YOU CANNOT OWN ONE CREATION FOREVER.

"I defy you! Mercy Adams, kill that woman!"

MERCY ADAMS, USE YOUR FREE WILL.

Bren, with and apart at the same time, called, "Mercy!"

Mercy looked up. "Bren? Is that you?"

"Yes, Mercy. You are free to do or not to do. I/WE swear, as Bren/*UNGRUKH*, that you are always free of Phoebe Adams, no matter what happens. Qumedon cannot control you, and you are in no danger of revenge or control by me/US. You are absolutely free."

Mercy Adams pulled her stiffened hands from Phoebe's neck and stood back. She looked at Phoebe with no expression, then at the helpless Qumedon almost with contempt. Phoebe sat gasping, hand to throat, though there was not so much as a pink pressure mark on it.

Mercy said to Bren, "You thought you were pretty safe in giving me freedom, didn't you? I mean that Phoebe was safe."

"Of course."

Kriku howled, "Ungrukh, what are you letting them do to you here!"

GIVE ME THEIR JUSTICE. PAY ATTENTION, QUMEDON:

I, *UNGRUKH*, AM NOT ALLOWING *YOU* TO DO ANYTHING YOU CHOOSE TO ME. NO MORE. I LIVE OR DIE WITHOUT YOUR HELP OR HINDRANCE. I ACKNOWLEDGE THE ACTS BY WHICH YOU SHAPE ME, AND SHAPER, LIKE ANY CHILD TO ITS PARENT, I SAY, NOW, WITH WHATEVER RISK, I MUST LIVE MY OWN LIFE.

"Can you force me to go?"

I CAN IF I MUST. I MUCH RATHER ASK YOU TO GO.

"I give up on you! Ungrateful, stupid, foolish, idiot animals! Why did I spend all those hundreds of thousands of worlds of years!"

UNGRUKH was silent. It would not say *pride*. It dared not say *love*.

Kriku seemed to shrink a little, twisted his head toward his body in that old Jewish shrug that Ungrukh had learned mentally from the first loved Solthree, mind-in-a-bottle Espinoza.

He seemed about to wheedle, but he said evenly, "*UNGRUKH*, may I speak to one of your components, Emerald, daughter of Prandra?"

Emerald wrenched herself away. "Certainly, Qumedon."

"Emerald, I saw your father going out to die, and I spoke to him."

Emerald flinched.

"No, I did not offer him an easy death, nor give him one. I wished him the death he wanted."

"Then, Qumedon, I thank you with all my soul."

"At last! I have gotten a simple thanks from an Ungrukh! Then it surely is time. Good-bye, children."

He was gone, and the air popped faintly as it filled the space he had occupied. The last Ungrukh image of him was as one of themselves, rather strange with his splayed seven-toed feet. No more.

"Bren!" Mercy cried. "He's gone, but nobody's moving! What's happening?"

IN ONE MOMENT WOMAN, said *UNGRUKH*.

The flaming colors of Enbhor died away, the serpent pulled in his tail, bifurcated it into legs, contracted body, pushed out head, extended arms in the shape of Man of Law.

"Bren? Ungrukh? *UNGRUKH?* I've tried to understand all you've told me. I'm not sure I can, but—what do you want of me?"

"Tell your Prosecutor," Bren said quietly.

"Me? I don't know how—what—"

"As we tell you: tell her. You know."

Mercy stepped aside, to keep facing Phoebe, though Defendant Adams sat still in her chair, hands to her face; then turned to the woman, so strong and frightening a short while ago, now pale, hands clasped, white-knuckled.

"Madame Desrosiers, long ago Bren's father Raanung killed one of Senator Silver's agents, a hired murderer, in self-defense. In some complicated way that made a lot of trouble for Silver. This—this woman here really loved Silver very much. I don't know why. When the Ungrukh came she thought he might respect—even love her again, that dumb selfish bastard, if she killed them in revenge for that one act. I don't understand that either. I guess she took me along to cover the track. But she'd have let Silver know, all right.

When he died too soon and everything blew up she covered with that stuff on other worlds. . . . Phoebe, did *anyone* ever call you Charley?"

"That's not evidence," said Desrosiers.

"*I* know." Phoebe lowered her hands to her lap and smiled faintly. "*He* did, when we were young."

Mercy shrugged. "Now I'll talk about evidence. You were trying to show I wanted to kill her, and that she realized it. Maybe she didn't trust me with ammunition. But Madame Desrosiers, I hadn't touched a weapon in twenty-four years!—and then only rifles. I became a good shot to please my father, but I hated it—killing, skinning, stupid drinking . . . most of all killing harmless things we didn't even like to eat. She knew that. If she didn't trust me it was because she'd be pretty sure I'd aim *over* the Ungrukh or—oh God—maybe even at myself—and she's so damn stingy she wouldn't waste ammo. Hell, I wore her cast-offs for ten years. All I got new was shoes and underwear. But I'd *never* have turned a gun on her. I wouldn't have minded if she dropped dead, even if it left me out of a job, but I never thought of killing her. I *am* on oath. If you'd gone on with that line of questioning, trying to show she was so despicable she'd make *me* want to kill, you'd have hurt me and made yourself look foolish without helping the case. Do you understand?"

"Yes. I think I do."

"And—do you believe?"

"I believe."

"Good for you, Mercy," said Bren. "Are you ready?"

Mercy and Desrosiers threaded their way among statues, one to the witness box, one to the Prosecutor's bench.

Sound exploded.

Blink, sneeze, scratch, breathe. The hall was intense with small sounds filling dead air into which words had been spoken during stasis.

Desrosiers found herself saying, "—and you say you were well treated! *Well treated!* I call it shameful!" Then, breathing hard, she approached the Judge's bench and said, "Your Honor, I—I find myself feeling rather unwell. I would like to request an adjournment until tomorrow, unless you would prefer one of my associates to continue the examination."

"Uh, no," said the Judge. He rang the bell. "We will adjourn until oh-nine-thirty hours tomorrow . . . and do please have yourself attended to, Madam."

And the spectators filed out. But the Ungrukh were gone.

"I don't like that," said Emerald. "I don't like *UNGRUKH* at all!"

None did. The apparition had stunned and wearied them.

"I tell you one thing," said Raanung. "We don't get rid of Qumedon without it." Then rolled into dead-cat position on the floor and snored.

"Bren," said Emerald, "how can you be part of the *UNGRUKH* being and separate *all* the time, when I must take so much trouble to pull myself away?"

Bren said gently, "Mother, I have a lot of practice in pulling myself away from things when they are too heavy on my back. I am the rock."

"Lucky for you," said Nurunda. "I am afraid of that being. Etrem, why are you not so fearful?"

"I take so much trouble learning not to be afraid I don't care to do the work of unlearning," said Etrem and fell asleep.

"But what *can* it be?" Enbhor asked.

Emerald scratched her nose with her tongue-tip. "Many years my mother works on a mind-model. Since the time she first comes here. People laugh or sneer; even my father doubts, though he trusts her. So she stores it in her depths, and never lets anyone know. But . . . sometimes I get a hint. . . . People think she is trying to make a model *of the mind*—yours, Enbhor, or mine, Solthree or even Qumedon. Perhaps at the beginning she does . . . but I wonder if at the end she does not make some plan, map, chart . . . of a model *for a mind*—and if that mind is not *UNGRUKH*."

"I don't tell anybody about that in a hurry," said Nurunda.

"Yes. It may be a possibility she does not much like."

"But why not?" Enbhor asked. "That kind of joining would surely help a slow clumsy people like us."

Raanung sneezed and lifted his head. "Man, I spend a long time working to make our tribes cooperate. To think each one can form a quorum for itself and become *UNGRUKH* makes me shiver."

"*I* am a Tribesman and don't care much for it either," said Menirrh testily.

"Don't start the war now, gentlemen," said Man of Law. "People of many tribes joined to make *UNGRUKH*. Perhaps one alone cannot. If *UNGRUKH* is a king all the Ungrukh may be its kingdom, and many citizens have risen to destroy a king. Don't take it as an insult to a very strong and talented people when I say that you are very young. You have heard it before—and that you have developed exceedingly well. But most sentient peoples have millions of years of troubled history behind them—even, I suspect, the Khagodi. And particularly non-ESPs, like the Solthrees, who have their weapons and their angers. As for my people, why do you think we hold on to each other so tightly and turn our thought to the Cosmos? We have a rather high incidence of disturbance among individuals, and even more when we separate in groups."

Emerald growled, "It seems we have a long hard history before us."

"Mother," said Bren, "in every case we can remember using a network so far it is to save a life. That must be a hope."

"Yes," said Emerald, not much consoled.

"And, glad as we are to get rid of Qumedon it is often he who stirs us to save lives."

"If we want peace," Menirrh rumbled, "it is better to work for it without the help of that one. I mean either one!"

48

In Phoebe Adams' apartment foyer the guards changed early in the morning. In change and mid-shift they checked for her presence and well-being, with care not to disturb.

Next morning's shift found the maid drugged unconscious in bed and no sign of Phoebe. The service and private elevators were locked from within. Phoebe's guards were former police and military men, all capable, and since she had hired them she had never gone out unguarded. They called an ambulance and the police. The maid was given an antidote and questioned, but she knew nothing. Analysis showed her evening tea had been drugged and she had also been injected. The police sent out bulletins and examined the apartment.

The place for all its dimensions had always seemed cramped to those who worked there; they were not quite sure why. The good antique furniture and bric-a-brac had been well arranged, but never had so expensive an apartment been less open and spacious. All apartments had thick boundary walls for cooling, venting, disposal, wiring, plumbing and kitchen service. Here the walls separating the rooms were also very thick.

First the police found the safes in them. A half-score big wall safes, all empty except for a few heavy pieces of jewelry. While they were wondering over these they took a call on the CommUnit from the Chief Superintendent informing Occupant that the disposal in Unit Block N-23 has become overloaded, and kindly collect your own trash for twenty-four hours while repairs are underway: receptacles provided.

"There go the records."

The closets were full of tasteful rich clothing and furs, perfumes and cosmetics. Anything taken must have been small or plain. "Hey, Rita, you think anyone else did this? Knocked her off and cleared out?"

"All those safes, and all that disposing? Hell no, Pete, her underwear's gone."

"Jack, there's still a lot of thick walls these safes don't account for. I can spend the day looking for the magic button, or call the janitor who's gotta call the super, who's gotta call —we'll just melt a hole in this wall where there's nothing fancy and they can repair it easy."

They found a hive of very narrow passages, two coffin-sized elevators to the basement, a tiny spiral staircase to a hidden door in a service-chute.

"Not many vents here," said Rita. "Plenty of dust. Soft-soled shoeprints to the elevator . . . I think I can smell some perfume . . ."

"She had since yesterday between guard-checks, until they went to wake the maid this morning at oh-six. Now it's oh-nine-thirty, and the trial . . ."

The trial convened only to adjourn indefinitely until the return of Phoebe Charloe Adams Silver. The other cases on the docket would be tried upon notification as soon as possible, defendants to hold themselves ready . . .

Phoebe never returned. The search for her was conscientious but not urgent. Her son did not inquire after her. Her friends and associates were as silent as her enemies. She was never seen, or if seen never identified, on ground, air or space transport or any world. She disappeared completely.

"Ungrukh," asked Man of Law, "has the justice of Sol Three failed you?"

"How can it?" said Raanung. "The woman is alone and running, without power or wealth, friend or family, any kind of love, none to feed her, naked as any shivering soul who goes down into the Dead World, except that she bears the burdens of terrible crimes and the hatred of many victims. On Ungruwarkh we do not wish such justice upon anyone."

• • •

The Ungrukh would have liked to have the charges against Mercy withdrawn, but Man of Law did not believe she would suffer, and hinted that Authority, after all its high-risk work, should not be cheated, even as they themselves should not. Her trial was swift, the testimony of Bren and Etrem could do nothing to indict her; the jury, in reasonable doubt, found her not guilty.

"Indeed," said Bren, "she is free, right enough, but where is there a future for one like her?"

Enbhor said, "I am sure she is intelligent enough to train and educate for employment in GalFed Civil Service. There is always space—"

"Think of the ever-expanding mass," said the Lyhhrt dryly.

"—and I have already hired Anton Borisov to guard my modest self. Probably he has already thought of a score of ridiculous xenophobic terms for me—but he has promised to serve me as well as he did the Senator, a man he did not notably like."

"That is certainly very kind of you," Bren said.

"Tell me, Enbhor," said Man of Law, "can there possibly be any flaw in the character of the Durbha people?"

"Surely. We are cursed with one great flaw."

"And what might that be?"

"Don't tell me it is not obvious to you, Lyhhrt! It is our pride in our own morality."

Embrin, a smoky-red fuzz-ball, crawled all over his mother and father. Moon's Woman watched contentedly. "He ought to get teeth soon. He's been gumming my fingers hard enough. Are you leaving soon or staying for a while?" A light touch of anxiety in the voice.

"First we must testify at the trials of various Rasputins and Minotaurs. Then we see . . ."

Bren and Etrem, Mundr and Orenda, Sukey and McNelly gave testimony when the trials came up. Then, for the Ungrukh, in various convictions and acquittals, the leaves shriveled and fell, the branches withered, on their particular limb of the Tree of Justice, to renew themselves for others. Mercy sent a short message of thanks before she and Boris left together with Enbhor and Man of Law for GalFed Headquarters. They seemed fairly content with each other, but whether they stayed together, or even in GalFed, they never told, and no one disturbed their privacy. Haynes and McNelly made their good-byes to the Ungrukh with mutual respect and no sentiment, then went off to deal with different hot spots on the Continent. Sukey wangled her way to Mexico City to help cut off the Devil's Thumbs, and found her way to Jha's and her old job, where she set about accommodating the new lounger to her considerable shape. She was surprised and pleased to discover that some lean dark men liked the company of fleshy blonde gringas, and occasionally regretted having to turn them in.

The Ungrukh lived out the length of their contract in the Canyon so that women who were pregnant could bear and bring up their children until they were old enough to travel. They were particularly circumspect. If any group snarled and grumbled at another it did so within implicit limits. No one wanted to become *UNGRUKH* again. That must remain a being for rare and special purposes, which it would be their great problem to determine in the future.

Bren no longer wanted to conquer the peaks and howl from their tops. She had used too much of her strength for other things. But, in respect to her younger, fiery self, she did once with great effort climb up to stand baying the moon like any dog, while most Ungrukh and Solthrees within earshot listened in perplexity, except for Moon's Woman, smiling, with the twins, and Etrem, Embrin on his back, coughing and hissing in amusement touched with vicarious pleasure.

While they prepared to leave, Kinnear and Narinder Singh in GalFed Central were winding down their affairs toward retirement with a series of painful farewells, because after fifty-five years of friendship they would never see each other again. Many waited to take their places.

The dawn stars were fading. Emerald, looking with clarity on Sol III, and the landcars waiting to take the Ungrukh to their shuttle, swept eyes over the great shadowed depths and precipices of the abyss, and wondered if Prandra, far away, was dreaming of the cramped and ancient village, her first vision of Sol III.

"My old woman," said Raanung, "let us hope that whatever she dreams is in peace."

Emerald dared give herself no answer. A skimmer dipped

and hovered down the rim. Sun Rising High debarked with Moon's Woman—and with Tugrik and Orenda. On Orenda's back a very young female clutched and slept. The twins had permission to stay. They were no threat and their line of descent would probably not be long. Emerald and Raanung sent what love they could. Bren, rubbing her mother's cheek with her own, had much deeper wishes for their happiness, because they had been her babies, whatever they were to their family and Tribe. For Moon's Woman she wanted something more. The twins would join their self-absorption to their absorption in the child and he would be alone. She wished him a comforting love of his own.

"Sunup coming," said Bill Gonzales. "They're getting antsy over there."

"Guess I'll miss you," said Tom Green Corn.

Bren grinned. "After all the trouble we give? You look in on the twins, Tom, and you get a taste of Ungrukh."

"Sure, but they won't be so snappy and lively."

"Like Rosa?" Laughing.

"Yeah, but I won't tell her that. She'll get airs."

"Well," said Bill. "It's—"

He stopped. The dawn came.

Sun Father was climbing the curve of the world, long hair powdered in yellow cornmeal, white blank-masked face with three slits pouring blinding light, white buckskins crosshatched in black at sleeve's edge, multicolored Corn Mother in left hand and in his right a lightning bolt with a cloud caught on the top. He shook it once and thunder rattled like peas in a gourd.

The vision lasted five seconds and dissolved into yellow dawn.

Menirrh growled softly, "That is not *UNGRUKH!*"

Bren found her voice. "Perhaps it is a vision of Moon's Woman."

:No. I am not capable.:

Emerald kept her opinion, or suspicion, to herself.

Sun Rising High said in the old Tewa, "Whatever it is, I am grateful to have seen it."

The Ungrukh looked once more on their friends, and while those landbound ones waited, hunched the harness shoulder in the oldest gesture of Ungruwarkh's courtesy before leaping into a dark entrance until all were gone, the landcars skimmed away in dust and the bright sun sculpted the Canyon into its dimensions.

Half a lightyear from that Sun, a ship the texture and shape of an old bell clapper hovered; its occupant sparked and crackled to itself in some private and perhaps rueful amusement before it began to drift away, to no particular time or place, in no particular hurry.

Author's Note

This is the last in the series of Ungrukh chronicles under the comprehensive title *The Kingdom of the Cats*. Though there will be no more histories of Ungrukh, more may be told about them: GalFed will probably call on them if it needs their services, and they will come if they feel like it. Should they wish to give other accounts of themselves they will do so whenever they come to Sol III.

In the meantime I would like to thank:

Shirley Magder, friend, scholar and next-door neighbor for thirty-three years; K. Corey Keeble, Associate Curator, European Department, Royal Ontario Museum; Dr. Lionel Goldstein, Veterinarian; Dr. David Strangway, Geologist, President, University of Toronto; Dr. Richard Winterbottom, Associate Curator, Ichthyology and Herpetology Department, ROM; Adam Smith, master knifesmith; Taral Wayne, artist;

and Dr. W. C. Sturtridge, Clinical Investigation Unit, Toronto General Hospital, who kindly works to keep the headbone connected to the handbone.